THE *Oleander* SISTERS

Also By Elaine Hussey:

THE SWEETEST HALLELUJAH

ELAINE HUSSEY

THE *Oleander* SISTERS

HARLEQUIN® MIRA®

Recycling programs
for this product may
not exist in your area.

ISBN-13: 978-0-7783-1643-5

THE OLEANDER SISTERS

Printed in U.S.A.

First printing: August 2014
10 9 8 7 6 5 4 3 2 1

To the IT Girls, with love, laughter and gratitude.

One

THE DAY NEIL ARMSTRONG walked on the moon marked a summer where anything at all could happen. The brother you'd given up for dead in a war everybody hated could suddenly turn up alive, and the sister you'd protected all her life could finally be getting married. Any other woman would have been happy with the sudden turn of good fortune, but not Sis Blake. She was scared of happiness. Let too much joy seep into your life and you'd soon find yourself hunkered beside twisted wreckage wondering what you did to make everything turn out so wrong.

As if Sis needed any more evidence than her own history to tell her something awful was heading her way, the Amen cobbler cooling in the kitchen at Sweet Mama's Café gave off the scent of secrets, a spicy smell so sharp it could cut away everything you held dear.

Still, Sis kept her troubled thoughts to herself. There was no sense spoiling things for her sister. Emily was humming as she sliced into the cobbler, serving up hope by the spoonful.

"Eat up, Sis." Emily's face was radiant with happiness and heat from the ovens. "It's the best I've ever made."

Sis forced herself to eat so she wouldn't be the one who

wiped the smile off her sister's face, and Emily went back to her baking and humming, every now and then glancing out the back café window.

What was she seeing besides a backyard lit up with red and blue Christmas lights, though it was July and so hot in Biloxi the seagulls abandoned the beaches along the Mississippi Sound and pecked at Sweet Mama's display windows trying to get inside where it was air-conditioned? Was Emily seeing a six-year-old son who needed a daddy? Was she seeing a little boy born out of wedlock and tagged with ugly rumors by a few vicious gossips Sweet Mama had run out of the café with a broom? Or was she seeing what Sis did, an endearing little boy in an outgrown Superman suit who was thriving in a family of women?

Even that worried Sis. Get too complacent and bad luck would hunt you down. The bite of Amen cobbler went down hard and sat in Sis's stomach like an accusation.

"I've gotta get going or I'll be late." Glad for an excuse to push aside the cobbler, she hugged her sister, then hurried out the door, climbed into her sturdy black Valiant and headed toward the bus station.

Sis whizzed along the beach road, replaying the evening two weeks earlier when Emily had walked into Sweet Mama's Café on the arm of a stranger and announced, "This is the man I'm going to marry." Then she'd gone to every table and booth to show off her engagement ring, a stone so big it was bound to be a cubic zirconia.

Many of the diners were regulars who had watched Emily grow up, mostly at the café, shielded by the wide skirts and fierce heart of Sweet Mama. They knew how Mark Jones had gotten her pregnant, then run off to join the army to get out of marrying her, and they were happy she'd finally found somebody who would love her back.

Sis tried to be, too, but she was not the kind of woman to be swept off her feet. Emily's fiancé was handsome in the too-slick way that made her skin crawl. Every time Sis glanced at him, he was checking his reflection in the Coca-Cola mirror behind Sweet Mama's soda fountain.

Still, Emily had obviously seen something in her fiancé that Sis missed, so she'd trotted over to her future brother-in-law, determined to learn more about him.

"Larry, I guess you already know I'm the watchdog of the family."

"You don't do yourself justice, Sis." His smile was wide and easy, this pharmaceutical salesman named Larry Chastain, who had swept Emily off her feet six weeks earlier when she'd gone to Walgreens to get some Pepto-Bismol for Andy's upset stomach. "I'd call you Emily's guardian angel."

He oozed sincerity, and in spite of her reservations, Sis found herself smiling back.

"Tell me about yourself, Larry."

"Ah, the dreaded inquisition."

His smile was still in place, but Sis thought she'd seen a flash of irritation. Or maybe she was just looking for reasons to keep her trusting sister from racing to the altar with the wrong man.

"I'm blunt, Larry. Maybe too blunt. But I need to know my baby sister is going to be in good hands."

"I love your sister and make more than enough money to give her and Andy everything they want and need. Emily tells me you're a worrier, but rest assured, you have nothing to worry about, Sis."

Emily had walked up then and whisked him off to the kitchen to meet Beulah. It wasn't until they'd gone that Sis realized Larry Chastain hadn't told her one single thing about himself. She stood there looking down at the floor as if she expected to see a greasy spot where he'd been standing.

What was it about Larry that set her on edge? Sis hadn't been able to put her finger on the cause during that meeting two weeks ago, but driving along the beach road to pick up a brother who had received a Purple Heart, she wondered how Larry had managed to avoid the draft. The very idea of a draft dodger in a patriotic family where the men had served and sacrificed for their country made her want to snatch Emily up and run.

By the time Sis parked her Valiant at the bus station, she had to deep breathe in order to collect herself. It wouldn't do for her brother to see her in this shape. She adjusted the rear-view mirror in the off chance her reflection would show some magical transformation. Unfortunately, there she was—plain and chubby with a perpetual worry line creasing her forehead, and hair so curly it always looked like it had been styled by an eggbeater. Still, she tried to pat it into place, and even dug around in her purse to see if she could find a tube of lipstick, as if a little slash of red could turn back the clock. It had been two long years since she'd seen her brother, and she liked to think the sight of her would remind him of catching fireflies on summer nights and fishing off the pier and playing base-ball in the backyard.

She turned up nothing in her purse but a wallet, a wad of tissue, two pieces of bubble gum and the stub of a pencil. Sighing, she pinched her cheeks, bit her lower lip to add some color and then put on a smile she hoped would make her look like a woman who had everything in the world she'd ever wanted.

As she stepped out of the car, Sis held out hope that her brother would be the one to turn her hornet's nest of worry into something manageable, a funny story they'd all laugh at a dozen years from now when Andy was graduating from high school and Emily was baking a celebration cake at Sweet Mama's. But Jim was leaning against the wall on his crutch, blowing smoke from a Lucky Strike into the humid evening air, his face as closed as a fist.

"Jim. Oh, my God, Jim!"

"Sis," was all he said, and when she wrapped her arms around him, she understood that's all he could manage. His flesh had vanished from his bones, and with it the buoyant spirit that used to radiate from him in waves that made him almost hot to the touch.

Without another word, she led him to her car and headed back to the café. He stared at the Gulf as they barreled down Highway 90, the breeze from his rolled-down window blowing his yellow hair straight back from eyes turned as glassy and unseeing as the blue china plate Sweet Mama had picked to serve his welcome-home cake. Sis's hope flew right out the window. She imagined it sailing across the water like the favorite kite she'd loved and lost when she was six years old, before Emily and Jim were born, before their pink Victorian house across from the seawall became a place where a little girl had to grow up too fast.

"Jim, I know it must have been awful for you over there."

He didn't say a word, and who could blame him? *Awful* could hardly begin to describe it. The prosthetic leg he'd tossed into the car along with his duffel bag was a testament to the horrors he'd endured.

"If you want to talk about it, I'm a good listener."

"Give it a rest, Sis. I don't want to talk about it."

"That's okay. Maybe some other time."

That didn't seem likely. As she turned her attention to the radio, Sis tried to keep her despair from showing. She found a station where Elvis Presley was crooning "If I Can Dream."

Were there any dreams left in that car? Sis quickly switched to a station that wouldn't remind both of them of all they'd lost.

"You won't believe how Andy's grown. And Sweet Mama's still feisty as ever. She wanted to invite everybody in town to your homecoming, but I finally talked some sense into her. I thought it would be easier for you with just family."

Jim turned her way with a shut-down face full of sharp angles and shadows, then swiveled toward the window to stare at the water. Was he watching the whitecaps? Remembering Vietnam? Wishing on the moon?

"Do you want to hear about Emily's fiancé?"

"Not particularly."

"Well, you ought to. He's a jackass."

"They run the world."

"Not my world, not while I have breath."

Sis had been taking care of her family since she was fourteen and that awful accident took their parents. She didn't plan on stopping just because Emily was trying to outrun her past by racing toward the altar. And maybe that was Sis's fault. She'd always encouraged her baby sister to be the fairy princess in a fairy-tale world.

Sis took a sharp left in order to avoid Keesler Air Force Base. No sense giving Jim any reminders that the military had mowed the Blake family men down like ninepins, leaving only him behind to pick up the slack. Not that Sis held out any high hopes of that happening. A man who wouldn't even carry on a conversation about his family was as likely to see after their welfare as Sis was to have somebody stop her in the street and tell her she was beautiful.

Just look at the pair of them. She was an old sourpuss and Jim was still in the killing jungles somewhere on the other side of the world.

It was a pure relief to see the café, a fine, old building of moss-covered brick, reflecting the style of the Gulf Coast's Spanish history, shaded by a couple of hundred-year-old live oaks and lit up like a rocket ship on blast off. Christmas lights and silver tinsel circled the plate-glass windows where gold lettering proclaimed Sweet Mama's Café, and underneath in red was etched Home of the Famous Amen Cobbler!

Beyond the front window was Sweet Mama with her coronet of silver braids and a pearl brooch on her green linen dress, laughing at something Emily had said. That was a talent Emily had—making her grandmother laugh, making everybody around her smile. Everybody except Sis, who hadn't found much to smile about since she discovered she hated the idea of spending the rest of her life selling pies, Amen or otherwise.

The flush on Emily's cheeks could have been excitement or summer heat. With blond curls escaping from her ponytail, she looked sixteen. A strap of her yellow sundress had slid off one shoulder, and the blue apron she still wore was dusted with flour. Even disheveled, Emily was beautiful.

Sis would never be beautiful, with or without a dusting of flour. She would never look sixteen, even if she could get her frizzy brown bob into a ponytail. She would never be the kind of woman men wanted to sweep off her feet.

Envy ambushed her, so unexpected she almost crashed her car into a live oak.

"Watch out!" Jim grabbed for the steering wheel, but Sis slapped his hands away.

"I've got it. I'm just excited, is all."

How could you envy the sister you'd dressed and fed and soothed at night with silly, made-up stories so she'd sleep with the lights off?

Perhaps it wasn't envy but longing fueled by the perspective of age. How could Sis have known at fourteen that once you set out on a path, it can take you so far from your dreams you'll end up at the age of thirty-four not even remembering who you once wanted to be?

She'd given up everything for her family, even her name. Beth. Nobody called her that anymore. Everybody just called her Sis, as if she were nothing more than the role she played.

The sign on the door of Sweet Mama's read Closed for a Private Party. There was nothing private about it, of course. Tomorrow, word would be all over town. Sweet Mama would tell the breakfast regulars, and Emily was too gentle to refuse details to anybody who asked. By ten o'clock, everybody in Biloxi would know that Sweet Mama had made Jim's favorite red velvet cake, and Emily had forgotten to take off her apron and Jim had refused to wear his leg.

There it lay on the backseat of Sis's Valiant, another piece of sand in her craw. What do you say to a brother just returning from the hell of Vietnam? *Why don't you let me strap on your prosthetic leg so you'll look normal and Emily won't cry?* Or do you just stand there with sand drifting into your sandals while Emily races out the front door, already crying before she gets close enough to hug her twin, the Gulf breeze blowing both of them sideways?

Maybe the Gulf was blowing all of them sideways, and had been for so long Sis didn't know what normal was anymore. She thought about a brother coming home broken and a sister smiling as she raced toward disaster. She thought about a life gone so far off track she didn't even remember the direction she'd been going.

Best not to think too far into the future, to simply put one sandy sandal in front of the other until she was standing in Sweet Mama's, surrounded by the smells of cake and pie and fried chicken and freshly cut tomatoes from Sweet Mama's prize crop, just standing there silent, gnawing on a chicken leg and watching over her brother and sister as she always had;

watching as Emily laughed through her tears and Jim was engulfed by the ones who loved him best and would love him always, even if he never got his mind back from Vietnam and his leg out of Sis's car.

"Aunt Sis! Aunt Sis!"

The TV perched on the edge of the serving bar was blaring wide-open. Andy sat so close he was crossing his eyes to see.

"C'mon over! They gonna land on the moon!"

For two cents Sis would get on that rocket ship with the astronauts. And she wouldn't care whether she found the moon or not. All she wanted was to be as far away from her current life as she could get.

Sweet Mama was relieved when Sis quit glaring over her fried chicken leg at What's His Name and walked over to join Andy at the TV. Why, from the look on her face you'd think What's His Name was a fly set to land on Jim's celebration cake and Sis was a flyswatter.

Larry Chastain. That was the name of Emily's new fiancé. Sweet Mama would write it down this very minute if she thought she could do it without getting caught. But Emily might see her and start worrying all over again about her forgetfulness. And Sis was bound to notice. That girl didn't miss a thing. And she wouldn't stop at calling Sweet Mama forgetful, either. She'd use the scary words *senile* and *hardening of the arteries* and *dementia*.

"Larry Chastain." Sweet Mama mumbled his name, hoping it would make a lasting impression. If she forgot and called him Gary, everybody would look at her funny. And her older son Steve, the one who wasn't dead and wasn't Emily and Sis and Jim's father, would start that silly talk again about signing over power of attorney.

Sweet Mama would rather be six feet under than sign over

any damned thing. She'd built this place from scratch and had run it for nearly fifty years and she wasn't about to let somebody else take over now, especially her son Steve, who only came to the café when his bossy wife allowed. Besides that, he hated pie. What God-respecting man hated pie? No sirree, Bob. If anybody took over Sweet Mama's Café, it would be the Blake girls. Emily could make an Amen cobbler the customers couldn't tell from Sweet Mama's, and Sis knew more about running a business than any man Sweet Mama ever saw.

If her mind ever did go, God forbid, she'd have her granddaughters running the show and not somebody with a power of attorney, thank you very much.

Out of the corner of her eye, Sweet Mama saw Emily motioning to her fiancé to go on over and join Sis and Andy at the TV, trying to communicate with gesture and smile, as she always had, that everything was all right.

Lord God, Sweet Mama hoped so. The scent of sun-ripened peaches coming from the Amen cobbler was so sweet, if you squinted you could see bees buzzing around the crust. Sweet Mama couldn't recall what that was a sign of, but she knew it was a harbinger of something that made her bones feel heavy. She closed her eyes, just for a minute, and as clear as a summer day she saw a swarm of bees streaking down from the mimosa tree in the backyard, aiming straight for her head. She lifted her shovel to fight them back.

"Sweet Mama." Her granddaughter's voice drifted through the fog. "Sweet Mama. Wake up."

Emily was shaking her shoulder, and when she looked up at her granddaughter, it came as a great surprise that she was all grown-up instead of four years old. Momentarily panicked, Sweet Mama looked around for Sis, who was no longer fourteen, but a rather unstylish and pensive-looking woman past thirty.

"Are you all right, Sweet Mama?"

"Of course I am. Why wouldn't I be?"

"I thought you'd fallen asleep."

"In the middle of my own grandson's homecoming party?" Sweet Mama checked for the cake to be sure she was right. "I should say not!"

Emily sat down beside her and started patting her hand. Sweet Mama was torn between snatching it away, acting all huffy that her youngest granddaughter was treating her like an old woman and leaning into her to enjoy the petting. If you'd told her ten years ago she'd ever get to the age that she needed somebody treating her like a child, she'd have slapped you silly.

Before she could make up her mind which way to act, Gary came over and interrupted the whole thing.

"Larry, darling," Emily said, and Sweet Mama thought about her narrow escape. She'd come within a gnat's hair of calling him the wrong name. "I thought you were going to join Andy and Sis."

"Your sister doesn't seem to like me."

"Nonsense, darling. You have to know Sis. She's just protective, that's all." Emily patted him on the arm. "Go on over there now, and don't spare your charm."

He trotted off and Sweet Mama said, "Charm, my ass."

"Sweet Mama! What a thing to say!"

She knew it was a terrible thing to say, but she wasn't about to admit that it had just slipped out. To make up for the many ways she was now failing Emily, she was going to give her granddaughter the best wedding the Mississippi Gulf Coast had ever seen.

Sis was another thing—as tough and unbending as the live oaks that dripped with Spanish moss in front of the café. Sometimes Sweet Mama wished her oldest granddaughter would bend a little. She wished she wouldn't be so hard on people. And the way she dressed…Lord God, the more Sweet Mama tried to talk her out of wearing khaki slacks and black blouses all the time, short sleeves in the summer, long in the winter, the more Sis resisted.

Still, Sweet Mama knew Sis would make sure her sister got a wedding grand enough to make up for all those years wondering if Mark Jones would have changed his mind and married her if he'd made it back from Vietnam.

More and more, Sweet Mama depended on Sis to take care of the family. Any day now, she might retire and travel to some of the places she'd read about in *National Geographic*. She'd always wanted to, and now could be her big chance.

"I think I'll head to Pikes Peak first," she said.

"What?" The funny look Emily gave her said she'd done it again, gone off and said something that didn't have a thing to do with the conversation at hand.

She racked her brain trying to figure out what the latest subject had been. Emily was now looking alarmed.

She had to say something that made sense or Emily would tell Sis, and Sis would fetch Doctor…what was his name? He was an old fart. That's all she knew.

"You said you were going to Pikes Peak, Sweet Mama."

"Not this very minute, silly. But I'm getting so old, I'm liable to kick the bucket any day, and wouldn't it be nice to be up so high I could see Heaven?"

"I don't think you can see Heaven from Pikes Peak."

"I was just kidding."

Feeling backed into a corner, Sweet Mama looked around for a means of escape. And there was her poor grandson, leaning against the wall as if he could no longer see his place in the family.

"Help me up, Emily, and let's take your brother some of that Amen cobbler."

Food, that's all Sweet Mama could remember anymore. She watched as Emily scooped up a big helping and then put a smile on her face as she carried it to Jim.

Sweet Mama got that heaviness in her bones again, an uncomfortable feeling that could be anything from old age to angels whispering in her ear. If she could just ground herself in the café, she'd be all right.

She glanced around at the pictures on the wall. They told their own story—the history of a bakery that became a café and a woman too fierce to give up, the friendship against all odds with Beulah, who had been with her every step of the way, the ever-increasing number of patrons who carried on meandering conversations spun out like a roll of silk ribbon, linking the past to the present and binding people together as surely as tree-ripened peaches blended with fresh cherries in Sweet Mama's Amen cobbler.

"Amen cobbler, Jim," Emily was saying. "I made it."

Fear stung Sweet Mama as unexpectedly as a red wasp. Lord, she could have sworn she made that cobbler. Hadn't she stood in the kitchen not more than two hours ago adding peaches to the batter? Or had that been last week?

"I'm not hungry, Em," Jim said.

"Take a little bite, anyway. It's your party," Emily said. "Tell me if it's as good as Sweet Mama's."

The way Jim was looking at his plate, you'd think it was filled with mud pies. What do you say to a grandson who's standing close enough to touch but is so far away he's no more substantial than the moonlight laying a path over the water?

Beulah's shadow fell over Sweet Mama, a huge umbrella to shield her from a downpour of sudden sorrow.

"Honey, if you don't eat that cobbler, old Beulah's gonna think you don't appreciate none of this cooking we nearly killed ourselfs over."

"You're still a con artist, Beulah," Jim said. "And you don't look a day older than when I left."

"If you keep up that sweet talk, you're gonna have a girl before we know it."

"Don't hold your breath."

"I ain't holding my breath. I'm gonna put out the word to the reg'lars to be looking. Now, eat that cobbler pie."

Sweet Mama puffed up with pride as she watched Jim pick up his fork and dig in. The war might have taken his leg, but it hadn't stolen one iota of the Blake honor. She glanced at her granddaughter's fiancé over there with all his body parts intact, sleek as a tomcat.

"Emily, did What's His Name serve his country?"

"Please, Sweet Mama. This is a party. Let's not talk about that now."

"It's a legitimate question, Em," Jim said. "Did he?"

Suddenly, Andy shouted, "Com'ere, quick! That's him. There's a man on the moon!"

Emily raced off like somebody saved from the guillotine.

"Oh, it is, sweetheart!" She sat on the bar stool beside her son, her color suddenly so high she looked as if she might be the one standing on the moon.

Even Jim moved toward the RCA TV, and suddenly the whole family was riveted by the pictures being beamed back to them all the way from the moon. Relieved that she was no longer under scrutiny, Sweet Mama poured herself a glass of sweet tea and sat at a table close enough so she could see what was going on. It didn't look like much to her, just a bunch of blurry black-and-white images. For all she knew, this man on the moon stuff could be a big hoax.

"He looks like a monster, Mommy."

"That's the astronaut Neil Armstrong in his space suit," Emily said. "Listen, Andy. You're watching history."

"That's one small step for man, one giant leap for mankind," Neil Armstrong said.

An impossibly huge moon shone through the plate-glass windows. That a mere mortal—somebody not so different from her, except younger—was up there this very minute walking around in the moondust filled Sweet Mama with such hope the café could hardly contain it. Her grandson was home safe, one granddaughter was at the beginning of a new life and the other granddaughter had the grit and the brains to turn this café into the finest restaurant in the Deep South.

Sweet Mama looked around the room till she found the picture she sought, hanging on the wall beside the clock and dated April 1, 1921. There she was, posing behind the cash register in the bakery she'd opened herself, with Beulah as her only help.

If anybody happened to ask Sweet Mama what she thought about the lunar landing, she'd say she'd already been to the moon and was planning to go again.

Two

EMILY DIDN'T NEED AN alarm clock to wake up. She loved sunrises and rituals and the small, everyday miracles of family. When dawn pinked her lace curtains she hurried to the window to admire the sky, and then she raced back to the bedside phone to call Sis.

"Sis, are you awake?"

"I am now, Em."

Emily grinned. Sis might try to act like an old grump, but she counted on their early morning phone calls as much as Emily did. When you love a sister, you know her songs as well as her secrets. You know what makes her shatter and what it takes to put the pieces back together. You understand her as if you were standing inside her skin, counting the beats of her heart.

"I've decided to have a summer garden wedding," Emily told her sister. "In Sweet Mama's backyard."

"It's a disaster area."

"It's beautiful. All we need are a few chairs and some white satin bows, and it will be gorgeous."

"Good Lord, Emily. Are we talking about the same back-yard? It'll take a ton of fertilizer, six weeks of rain and a flat-out miracle to get Sweet Mama's backyard even halfway decent."

"It might take all that if I didn't have you, Sis."

"Are you trying to flatter me?"

"Is it working?"

"A little bit."

Sis's sigh was audible, and Emily felt a prick of guilt.

"Listen, Sis, I don't want to cause too much trouble. You need to spend time with Jim instead of fretting over a garden wedding."

"If you want a garden wedding, that's what we'll have. Jim's going to be fine. I won't have it any other way."

"He didn't seem so fine to me, Sis. Bring him to the café today so we can feed him and fawn over him."

"I don't think he'll come."

"Why wouldn't he want to come down to the café so he can be with all of us?"

"Because..." Sis hesitated. "Because he's as stubborn as I am."

What had she been going to say? Emily was certain it was something frightening Sis had edited out in order to protect her.

"You're not stubborn, Sis, just *certain*. I wish I had more certainty."

"If you're not certain about Larry Chastain, don't marry him."

"I'm not talking about Larry." Or was she? Emily felt a vague sense of dissatisfaction, as if she'd gone to the store for a carton of ice cream only to get home and discover the container was empty. "Let's not be serious today, Sis. We have so much to celebrate!"

"That we do, Em. See you at the café."

Emily dressed quickly, then went down the hall to check on her son. He was out of bed, wearing his Superman suit. It was from last Halloween and too short, but he didn't care. A little boy planning big adventures with his favorite teddy bear, Henry, didn't worry about things like dressing to the nines and combing his hair.

Andy hadn't seen her yet, and Emily stood in the doorway, watching as he picked up the picture from his bedside table, Captain Mark Jones, smiling at his son from a silver frame.

"I love you right back, Daddy," Andy said, then planted a big kiss on the picture.

That was her fault. She'd told Andy that Mark Jones loved him best. Was it wrong of her to tell such a lie? Wrong to let her son believe his natural father had wanted him, had loved him more than anything in the world?

She hoped that having a real daddy in the house would cause Andy to let go of the phantom father.

Andy spotted her and raced to hug her around the legs. When she knelt to fold him close, she put her face in his hair and inhaled the scent of shampoo and summer and little boy dreams.

"You think my daddy heard me?" Andy wiggled out of her grasp.

"I don't know, Andy."

"Maybe Heaven's got big speakers like the ice cream truck."

"Maybe so." Emily picked up the pajamas Andy had dropped on the floor. "Did you comb your hair?"

"I forgot." Andy raced off to the bathroom and turned on the faucet, making so much racket he sounded like a Little League baseball team. "I got important things to do, Mommy," he called.

"Like what?" Emily shook out his sheets and tucked the corners into his bed.

"Build a rocket ship." He poked his head around the door frame, his freshly wet hair sticking out at such odd angles he looked as if he'd had a big surprise. "If Nell Arms Strong can go to the moon, I can, too."

"Why, yes, you can. You can do anything you set your mind to, Andy."

"I might see my daddy up there."

The weight of being a single mother descended so quickly Emily had to struggle against defeat. Where was that line between making sure your son felt loved by his natural father and letting him live in a fantasy world?

"Let's not talk about that right now, Andy." She caught her son's hand, and he grabbed his old teddy bear. "Pretty soon you'll have a real daddy in the house."

Andy balked in the doorway, digging his heels into the shag carpet and sticking his head around the door frame with the anxious posture of a child searching for monsters.

"Andy, what are you doing? We don't have time to lollygag."

"Looking for a Larry Alert."

Emily sighed. No matter how hard she tried, she couldn't get Andy to warm up to Larry. Heaven knows, Larry had tried, too. He'd promised to take Andy fishing and to get him a new baseball mitt. He'd even said they could build a fort together in the backyard.

"We've talked about this, Andy. Until the wedding Larry will always sleep at his house, and then after, he'll sleep here and we'll be a family."

Andy crossed his eyes, his way of saying *I don't want to listen to this.* Maybe she'd been wrong to let him spend so much time at the café. Sis and Sweet Mama and Beulah encouraged every little thing he did. But still, what was she to do? Day care cost too much, and in her opinion, if you didn't have family, you didn't have anything worth talking about.

She went downstairs to her kitchen, which was her favorite room in the house, and began to fix breakfast while Andy raced around with his arms spread and his red cape flying out behind him. In a minute she heard him digging around in the pantry.

"What are you doing, Andy?"

"There's a ginormous box in here. Big enough for me and you and Henry to go the moon."

He dragged out the box their new television set had come in. A gift from Larry. Just one more piece of evidence that Emily knew what she was doing by marrying a man who could not only provide for her family, but was generous besides.

Andy raced back into the pantry and came out with an empty Tide box.

"I'm gonna take Aunt Sis, too. She knows 'bout boats and baseball and putting worms on hooks." Andy heaved the Tide box into the TV box. "You got any more boxes? It's gonna take lots for a rocket ship."

"I'm sure there are some at the café. We can bring them home this evening."

"I'm gonna build my rocket ship at the café. Aunt Sis can help. She knows lots of stuff."

"Yes, she does. Andy, you need to eat your breakfast so we can leave for the café. I don't know how the biscuits will turn out if I'm not there to make them."

"You reckon Aunt Sis and me and Henry can finish the rocket ship today?"

"Good heavens, Andy. Why don't you let it be a summer project?"

"'Cause I might need to make a quick getaway."

The words settled into Emily's heart like stones. What if the innocent recognized truths hidden from grown-ups?

Morning came softly to the Gulf Coast, tipping the waves with gold, rousing the terns from their nests along the beach and sending seagulls soaring across the water, looking for unsuspecting fish. After she'd hung up from talking to Emily, Sis threw back her sheet, slipped into sweat shorts, black T-shirt and gardening gloves, then tiptoed down the stairs.

Her sister had been wrong about Jim. He just wasn't ready for public appearances, especially at the café where everybody knew him and would expect to hear a blow-by-blow account of his experiences in Vietnam. Sis decided to stick to the one thing she could control, fixing up the garden, bedraggled from a brutal summer of heat and bugs. The wedding was only weeks away.

Still, Sis didn't mind the extra work. This was the part of the day she loved best, early morning when the dew was still on and she had the gardens to herself. Nature expected nothing of her. If she showed up to pull a few weeds and drench the beds with the water during dry spells, she was rewarded with prize-winning blossoms and tomatoes so big you could slice one and have plenty for five bacon and tomatoes sandwiches. If she didn't show up, the resulting weeds became homes for the geckos and frogs Andy liked to catch and carry to the little frog houses he built all over the backyard with sticks and dirt.

It always amazed Sis that he expected the frog to be grateful, to set up housekeeping and be waiting when Andy stopped by later to ask how to catch flies with your tongue. Failing to get advice from a frog, he always turned to Sis.

Even if she didn't have children of her own, Andy was the next best thing.

She eased the back door shut. Sweet Mama and Beulah were still asleep on the first floor, Sweet Mama in a big bedroom filled with mahogany furniture hauled from New Orleans in a wagon, and Beulah in a sunny room that had once belonged to Sis's mother and daddy.

There had been no sounds coming from Jim's room, either. Whether he was sleeping or lying on top of his covers with his eyes wide-open, Sis couldn't say. All she could do was remember how he'd taken his duffel bag straight to his old room on the second floor last night, then shut the door.

Carrying the prosthetic leg he'd left in the umbrella stand downstairs, Sis had gone right in behind him.

"Don't you ever knock?"

"You might as well not try your stinger on me, Jim Blake. I can still whip your butt." She laid the prosthetic leg on the end of his bed. "I'm not going to let you shut yourself up here and have a pity party."

"This is not pity, it's a fact. If you want somebody to wear that leg, wear it yourself."

"All right. Forget the leg for now. But don't think I'm done. We lost Daddy and Mark to war, and I'm not going to lose you, too."

"We lost Daddy in a car wreck."

As if she didn't know. Sis had turned and walked out of the room, the sound of crunching metal and the screams of her parents echoing through her mind. She'd been in that car, a teenager happy she didn't have to stay home with the twins and Sweet Mama while her mother picked up Major Bill Blake at the bus station and brought him home for the holidays.

The driver who hit them was so drunk he didn't see the red light, didn't notice the car or the three people inside who were singing "White Christmas." He never knew the look of surprise on Bill Blake's face or the way Margaret Blake reached for her husband's hand or the thoughts that tumbled through the head of a teenage girl flung clear of the wreckage. Sitting on the side of Highway 90 with her head hurting, Sis had checked her new red sweater set for damage.

What she should have been doing was checking her parents for a pulse, checking her future to see how she'd ever live with the guilt that she'd survived and they hadn't.

Remembering, Sis jerked weeds out of the flower beds so hard she rocked back on her heels. She was not going to get mired down in the past and she most certainly wasn't going to let her brother be one of those vets who returned from war but never really came home. The military had taken too much from her, and she was determined it would not take another single thing.

The back screen door popped, and Sweet Mama called, "Sis, can you help me with this?"

Her gardening gloves were on, her bonnet was askew and she was wrestling with a huge basket full of flowers. Plastic, for God's sake. Sweet Mama wouldn't be caught dead with a plastic flower in her house.

If Sis were Emily, she'd send up a petition to God, but she'd discovered if you wanted something, you'd best do it yourself.

"What in the world are you doing with plastic roses?"

"Shh, not so loud, Sis. I don't want to wake that heifer."

That heifer was Stella Mae Clifford. Sweet Mama marched to the edge of the yard and peered through the rose hedge toward the two-story Victorian house next door, a twin of theirs except it was painted yellow instead of pink.

Satisfied that her archenemy wasn't about, she came back across the yard, chuckling, then plucked a pink plastic rose from the basket and secured it to the hedge with green gardening tape.

"Imagine that silly cow's surprise when she wakes up and sees these on my rosebushes."

Emily would die when she saw them. Still, Sis started taping plastic roses onto the nearly naked bushes.

"She'll never believe you still have roses, Sweet Mama."

"Yes, she will. She can't half see."

Black spot blight and aphids, enjoying the long stretch of intense heat and dry weather, had stripped every rosebush in Biloxi, including the hedge Sweet Mama was now decorating with plastic blossoms.

"Hurry up, Sis, before it gets daylight. We've got to get down to the café so I can put the coffee on for the regulars."

"Emily can do that. Why don't you and Beulah stay here and enjoy Jim's first morning home? I think he could use the company."

"Beulah's in there now petting him like he's three years old. Jim's going to be all right. He's like me. Made of strong stuff." Sweet Mama plucked the last rose out of the basket and taped it to the disease-ravaged hedge. "Thank God he didn't take after that jackass I married."

There was a picture of their granddaddy on the walls at Sweet Mama's, captioned simply *The Jackass*. Everybody knew it was Peter Blake, and everybody knew the story.

Sweet Mama had the misfortune to marry a man who was already married—to the bottle. Hardly an evening passed that he didn't come home full of alcohol and bad attitude and smelling of another woman's perfume.

After she had two boys, she made up her mind they'd not have Peter Blake as an example. One full moon when he came home sloshed and fell dead asleep into his bed, Sweet Mama went into the garden and pulled up two stout, dry cornstalks. Then she proceeded to tie her husband to the bed with the sheets and beat the devil out of him. When she'd whipped him sober, she packed his bags, threw them out the door and told him she didn't want to ever see his sorry skinny self again.

Through the years he'd been spotted everywhere from Maine to California. The last they heard, he was up in Anchorage, Alaska. Wherever he was, that day he hightailed it was the last of Peter Blake in Biloxi and the beginning of Sweet Mama's transformation from wife and mother to independent businesswoman, an unusual thing for a woman in 1921.

Some said Stella Mae Clifford was Peter Blake's mistress, that he was the one who'd built her house next door. Once, Sis had asked Sweet Mama if the rumor was true.

"I like to keep people guessing, Sis. A juicy rumor is good for business. Better than a full-page ad in the newspaper."

With the last plastic rose in place, Sweet Mama settled her bonnet on her head and shot a bird to the house next door.

"Take that, you silly old cow."

What if Sweet Mama's escapade with the plastic roses was not a sign of senility but a sign that the sassy, unsinkable Lucy Long Blake of years gone by was still shining through? What if she were made of such strong stuff she could defeat all the alarming signs of a mind and a body roaring toward old age?

"Let's go inside so you can eat, Sweet Mama. Then I'll drive you to the café. We've got a wedding to plan."

"I don't want to ride with you."

"Why not?"

"You drive like a bat out of hell."

It was true. Was it because Sis was in love with speed or was she thumbing her nose at fate, saying *I cheated you once, see if you can catch me now?*

"All right. We'll go in separate cars. But you be careful, you hear?"

"Pshaw" was all Sweet Mama said.

Sis took her arm and led her up the back steps that might be a grandmother trap. Beulah was in the kitchen waiting for them.

"It's about time ya'll come in from the garden," she said. "Breakfast is getting cold."

"You and Sweet Mama go ahead and eat. I've got a few more things to do in the garden."

"Not without something in your stomach, you don't." Beulah slapped two pieces of bacon between a biscuit and handed them to Sis as she headed back to the garden.

Sis decided to leave the plastic roses for a while. By tomorrow, Sweet Mama would have forgotten all about them, and Sis could remove them without causing a fuss. The rose hedge itself was another matter. She could fertilize and water a few of the bushes and hope for a little bit of greenery in time for the wedding, but most of them had to be dug up. She'd plant new ones tomorrow.

She went into the double garage where Jim's baby-blue Thunderbird was parked, and the fishing boat Sis hadn't used all summer. Thinking that fishing might be just the thing for her brother, she found her spade, then went back to the rose hedge and started to dig.

In spite of spindly growth with only a few blighted leaves,

the rosebush had roots that seemed to go all the way to China. Sweat darkened her shirt and poured down her face as the mound of earth piled up.

Suddenly, her spade struck something hard. It was probably part of a brick or an old Mason jar. These old houses had yards full of junk tossed out and buried under years of accumulated dirt. Dropping to her knees, Sis leaned close to investigate, using her hands to carefully rake away the earth.

The bleached bones came suddenly into view, and Sis felt her breath leave her body. She bent closer to inspect her find. The bones didn't look like much at first, maybe the carcass of a dead squirrel. Or something larger. A dog, perhaps. A family pet.

That was the answer, of course. On a day when the sky looked as if angels had polished it with lemon wax, what could possibly be awry in Sweet Mama's garden?

Sis continued to dig, but as the mound of dirt collected at her feet and her discovery under the rosebushes revealed its true nature, she sank back on her heels, her heart hammering so loud it was a wonder they didn't hear it clear in the kitchen. That was no family pet under the roses. It was a skeletal foot, pointing straight toward disaster. She felt as if everything tethering her to earth had been cut away and she was tumbling headlong into that dark hole with the bleached bones. Questions spun through her mind with the dizzying speed of a comet. Who? Why? And how?

But the one that burned a hole through her was *What do these bones have to do with my family?*

The sun had already climbed into a hot blue sky and beat unmercifully on her and her eerie find, the toe bones attached to the foot, the foot attached to the ankle. And what else? If she kept digging would she find the entire body?

She poked gingerly with her spade, each thrust meeting a sickening resistance that told its own story. The weight of sudden fear dropped her to her knees, but no matter how hard she stared at the awful thing in the hole, no matter how hard she wished she'd never taken her shovel to the roses, the bones wouldn't go away. Bleached whiter than the wings of angels, they grew so big in Sis's mind they took up all her oxygen, deprived her of breath and speech and hope. They grew so big she felt as if they were splitting the earth beneath her feet. Any minute now it would open up and swallow her whole, and along with her, everything she loved.

Slowly, Sis pushed herself upright. The woman who had come blithely into the garden expecting to tidy up for her sister's wedding had suddenly become a woman whose awful discovery could destroy her family. Nothing would ever be the same. From this day on she would divide her life into two parts: before she found the bones and after.

The proper thing would be to tell the authorities, but then they'd have yellow crime scene tape all over the backyard during the wedding, reporters hounding their steps, gossips leaning on every fence post in Biloxi, speculating on the gruesome discovery in the Blake's backyard. The scandal would be worse than when Emily got pregnant in high school and then was ditched by a boy who'd rather risk getting shot than marry her.

Frantic, Sis spaded the dirt back into the hole, telling herself after the wedding was soon enough to report this. Besides, she'd more than likely uncovered a relic, one of those Civil War casualties whose body had never been found.

She tamped the dirt carefully back into place, and then with one last glance to make sure the bones didn't show, she stowed her spade, pulled off her gloves and went into the house.

"Lord God," Beulah said. "You're pale as a bar of Ivory

soap. If you ain't careful you're gonna work you'self into a heatstroke."

Beulah handed her a glass of water, but the lump of despair in her throat was so big Sis couldn't swallow a single drop.

"Beaulah, do you know what's buried under the roses?"

Setting her mouth in a straight line, Beulah turned her back on Sis and began washing dishes.

"More than likely a stray cat. I hope you covered it back up. Ain't no sense ruining Emily's wedding."

"It's not a cat. It's a body."

Beulah headed toward the table, a freight train gaining steam.

"You hear me good now, chile. Let it alone."

Sis nodded or maybe she said *yes* through a throat so parched words got caught and couldn't find their way out. A whole set of possibilities swirled through her mind, all of them tragic. If she could ever break free of Biloxi, she was going somewhere so frozen it wouldn't grow a single rosebush. She'd find a place with snow so deep she'd need an Alaskan husky to find buried bones.

"I want you to go on down to the café and forget about them rosesbushes. You hear me now, Sis?"

"Loud and clear."

"No use upsetting Emily and Jim, either. Just tell her to hold off on them German chocolate cakes. I aim to stay home and show Jim what he's got instead of what he's lost."

Sis understood the things Beulah left unsaid, her comprehension so perfect she wondered if she'd ever had a normal life in the little pink Victorian house by the sea or if she'd only imagined it.

Beulah leaned down and folded her into a voluminous hug.

"Don't you worry none. Everything's gonna be all right, sugar pie."

For a moment the thought of bones vanished, and Sis allowed herself to sink so deep into Beulah's endearment she became a little girl again with her whole life in front of her, a shining path she could follow to the stars.

Three

WHEN SIS LEFT THE KITCHEN she could hear Sweet Mama down the hall, singing some rollicking old song from the Jazz Age. Did she know about the bones in the garden? The last thing Sis wanted to do was ask her and completely undo a mind already coming unraveled. Instead, she hurried up the stairs and tapped on Jim's door.

"Come in." He was standing on his crutch at the window with his back to the door, his shoulders hunched in a too-big pajama top and his sleep-ruffled hair sticking up like Andy's.

The brother she'd sent to Vietnam was one she'd have confided in about the skeleton in the garden. This brother she wanted to fold into her arms and croon to the way she had when he was a child crying over a skinned knee.

"Jim, I'll be heading to the café soon. Would you like to come with me?"

"Not today, Sis."

He didn't even turn around, just kept staring out the window as if he couldn't believe the blue Gulf spread out before him, the white sand dotted with umbrellas and tourists, the seagulls wheeling through a sky the color of a robin's egg. Sis didn't even want to think what hell he'd seen *over there*, a vague euphemism she'd hated until she discovered there's only so much horror a person can stand in one day.

"That's okay, Jim. Take your time. Beulah's going to be here today, cooking up all your favorites." That turned her brother from the window, brought the ghost of a smile. "And I imagine Em's make you something special at the café."

"Tell Em not to worry about me."

"I will." Not that it would change a thing. Emily had always shared everything with Jim, the heartache, the joy, even the measles. Sis watched her brother standing there, sagging, a posture so foreign to him she wanted to cry. "It's a beautiful day, Jim. Why don't you get out your convertible and take Beulah for a spin?"

"Some other time, maybe."

What would he do all day? Hole up in the room staring out the window? Sis stood in the doorway torn between the urge to stay and take care of her brother and the need to go to the café to help Emily and Sweet Mama take care of business. In the end, her practical side won. If the café failed, they'd all go under.

She hurried to her room to dress, and then got into her Valiant and followed along behind Sweet Mama in her ancient, oversize Buick. Thank God her grandmother wrecked nothing but a hydrangea bush backing out of the driveway. And miracle of miracles, she stayed on her side of the road all the way to the café.

Still, by the time Sis got there, she was a nervous wreck. She made herself stand still in the center of the room, just breathing, grounding herself in the familiar smells of bacon and coffee and sugar and sweet, ripe peaches. Emily had already baked six Amen cobblers that were cooling on the countertop, and Sweet Mama was standing safe and sound at the coffee urns making a special pot for her customers who always asked for chicory—Burt Larson, the mailman, Tom and James Wilson, the brothers who had a barbershop next door and Miss Opal Clemson, the music teacher who claimed she'd once played the piano for a concert by Leontyne Price, Mississippi's famed opera singer.

It seemed so much like an ordinary day that Sis could almost forget her grisly find in the garden. But the Amen cobblers were sending up thick steam you could get lost in and never find your way out of, a sure sign of a disaster so huge even Sis wouldn't be able to contain it. The bones in the garden were just the beginning.

She pulled herself together and found her sister in the kitchen wearing a pink shirt with long sleeves, for Pete's sake, and it was already hot enough to fry an egg in the parking lot. Still, the sight of Emily covered with a dusting of flour and elbow deep in German chocolate cakes gave Sis a momentary respite from thinking about portentous cobblers and backyard bones.

"Hey, Sis!" Emily said, smiling as she poured batter into cake pans. "Where's Jim?"

"He's not up to socializing yet, Em."

"I should have known that." Emily scraped batter off the bottom of the bowl and held out a wooden stirring spoon. "Do you want to lick the spoon?"

She took up a spot by her sister and opened her mouth for the taste of raw batter, rich with sugar and butter. It brought back memories of childhood, with Jim and Emily perched on stools at Sweet Mama's side and Sis standing at her elbow, listening to stories of the café in its infancy, waiting their turns to lick the batter from the latest confection in progress—a German chocolate cake, a lemon icebox pie, a Coca-Cola cake or Emily's favorite, Sweet Mama's Amen cobbler.

"Beulah said for you to wait on these cakes," Sis said.

"If I had waited, there wouldn't be any spoons to lick." Emily bumped Sis's hip, teasing her, and then crammed the huge stirring spoon into her mouth. It left a smear of cake batter on her cheek that made her look like a little girl.

"How do you know, Em? Someday I might make a cake."

Emily whooped. "I want a picture of that. It would be one for the walls."

Sis stuck her finger in the bowl and dabbed batter on her sister's nose. Emily paid her back with a smear on the chin, and soon they were doubled over with laughter.

"Oh, my goodness." Emily put the bowl and spoons into the sink. "If I don't get this mess cleaned up, I'll never be ready to open."

"I'll rinse." Sis wiped cake batter off her face and moved to the sink. "You load the dishwasher."

"Good," Emily said. "That gives us time to talk about the wedding. I was thinking of putting flower baskets in the garden instead of depending on the roses."

Pricked with sudden alarm, Sis just stood there with the water running unheeded over the dishes.

"I don't think you ought to have it in the garden."

"Since when? Just this morning you said it would be fine."

"I checked it after we talked. It looks awful out there."

"I know it's not at its best this time of year, Sis, but I've always wanted a garden wedding."

Sis had an awful vision of Emily standing atop the bones saying *I do.*

"It's too hot, Em. Everybody will parch."

"We can put the chairs under the shade."

"I have a better idea. Wait till November when things have cooled off."

Could she report the bones and get the mess cleared out of her garden by November?

"I will not have Andy start school without two parents. Okay?"

Was Emily remembering walking the halls of Biloxi High to whispers of *easy* and *slut,* her baby bump showing and Mark Jones already enlisted and gone? Was she thinking about how she'd had to sit on the sidelines while the rest of her classmates walked onstage to get their diplomas?

"Nobody's going to call him names, Em. Not while I draw breath."

"What are you going to do, Sis? Go to school with him every day?"

"I'm not above it."

"You're not going to get me to change my mind, and you might as well quit trying. I will not have my son called *bastard*."

"All right. I understand. But at least think about getting married in Sweet Mama's living room. We could buy some of those pink roses you love so much and put them in wicker baskets on either side of the mantel."

"Forget it, Sis."

"You could walk down the staircase and not have to trail your wedding dress in the dirt."

"Good grief! Just let it alone. It's my wedding and I'm getting married in the garden."

Sis imagined Uncle Steve's nosy wife, Ethel, poking around the pitiful rosebushes and finding the bony foot sticking out of the ground, imagined cops and pandemonium and scandal.

"But, Em, think what a hissy fit Aunt Ethel will pitch if she gets too hot out there. Or what if it starts to rain?"

"I've had my say, Sis, and that's my final word."

Emily huffed over to the stove and turned her back.

Sis wished she could start the day over. She'd sleep late and never see Sweet Mama tying plastic roses on the bush, never drive along behind her at twenty miles an hour in case she ran over another hydrangea bush. But most of all, she'd never dig up a rosebush and find bones.

Sis turned to the window and saw her nephew in the backyard, surrounded by boxes.

"Is Andy building a fort out there?"

"No. A rocket ship. He's planning to fly me to the moon."

"Maybe he'll take me, too." She looked back at her baby sister standing there oblivious in her long-sleeved shirt, expecting every downpour to yield a rainbow. "I'm sorry, Em. I'm such a grump."

"You're not totally grumpy. Just a little."

"I'm going outside to cool off and visit with Andy, and when I come back inside, we'll plan a wedding that will turn your enemies green with envy."

"I don't have enemies," Emily said without a single hint of irony.

Lord, Sis hoped that was true. She raced through the door, the scent of Amen cobbler following her all the way, so strong it felt like somebody squeezing her heart. Outside, she leaned against the wall, trying to catch a deep breath. What would become of her family if she worried herself into a heart attack? It could happen. Last year a woman not three years older than Sis had keeled over on the front pew of the Biloxi Baptist Church, and her with three children to look after and a husband, besides.

"Hey, Aunt Sis," Andy called. "How many batteries you got?"

He was standing on top of a TV box in his Superman suit, his blond cowlick sticking up in front like the crest of a baby bird, his sturdy legs beneath the too-short pants turned dark gold from a summer in the sun, the big red *S* on his shirt faded from too many washings. His feet were bare and his face was filled with excitement.

"I don't have any batteries in my pockets, but I'll bet I can find some. What are they for?"

"My rocket ship. It's gonna take lots to get to the moon."

Hope is such a fragile thing, a butterfly wing you could crush with one finger. Walking a thin line, terrified of leaning too far to the left or the right, Sis squatted beside her nephew at the pile of boxes.

"Let me help you with that rocket ship."

"Me and you's gonna build the bestest one!" Andy scrambled among the pile and came up with a box still smelling of laundry detergent. "Mommy won't let me use a knife. Can you cut the window, Aunt Sis?"

"I can."

As she pulled out a pocketknife and cut a window right over the *T* on the Tide box, Sis missed the family she might have had as if they were real, as if she had a husband who kept her picture on his desk, a daughter named Susan who had inherited her aunt Emily's beautiful blond hair and a sturdy son named Bill after her own father, a son who loved baseball and digging for worms and sitting on the banks of the Tchoutacabouffa River with a fishing pole.

When Andy raced inside to peer out through the hole, her phantom family vanished, leaving her in the backyard of the café with a nephew whose grin lit a candle in her heart.

"Oh, boy. When I fly to the moon, I can see my daddy up there in the stars."

If Sis were in her sister's shoes, she'd never have painted Mark Jones as a hero. In her book, there was nothing heroic about leaving a pregnant girlfriend to face the fallout in a Bible Belt society. But what did she know about love and children? She'd never had either.

"Do you think I'll see my daddy, Aunt Sis?"

"Maybe."

Andy got that little boy skeptical look that said *I know you're going to break my heart with the truth but I love you enough to stand here and smile while you do it.*

"If you look with your heart, and maybe wear a special pair of glasses."

"What kinda glasses?"

"The kind I've got back home in my dresser drawer." It was an old pair of sunglasses, red with white polka dots and cat-eye frames. "Every astronaut ought to have a pair. I'll give them to you."

Andy clambered out of the box, then raced to the base of a live oak and dug a while in the dirt. When he came back, he handed Sis a white rock the size of a hen egg, along with a good-size chunk of soil.

"You the bestest, Aunt Sis. This is for you."

"Thank you, Andy."

"It's a magic rock."

"What does it do?"

"Wish real hard and rub it. See? Like this." He put his grubby little hand on the rock and rubbed with all his might. "Then your wish'll come true."

Sis kissed the top of his head, which smelled like sunshine and salty sea air and optimism.

"I've got to get back inside, but you keep up the good work, Andy."

Grinning, he made a fist and bumped it against hers.

"Later, 'gator," he said.

"After a while, crocodile."

Before she got to the back door, she rubbed the rock in her pocket. Just in case it might still contain a little boy's belief in magic.

That afternoon Sis left the café early, and if you looked close enough you'd see a cloud of anxiety over her head as dark as a flock of blackbirds. You'd see a woman who has lost her moral compass, one who stopped seeing in black-and-white the minute she dug under the rosebushes.

Driving by the seawall as familiar as the peaches in Sweet Mama's Amen cobbler, Sis glanced at the beach, hoping for distraction, longing to see a little boy in a baseball cap hitting a fly ball into a blue surf pounding the white sand. But all she saw were shades of gray. No color. No right. No wrong. Just a vast shadowy land where the truth was hidden under a rosebush and anything at all was possible.

Finally, the Victorian house came into view, but it no longer put Sis in mind of a tall glass of sweet tea on the front porch swing. She parked and hurried straight to the kitchen, but there was no sign of Beulah or Jim.

Perhaps it was movement in the backyard that caught her eye, or it could have been instinct, sharpened by years of trouble and perfected to art by constant vigilance.

Beulah wore a red hat with a brim wide enough to shade two people, and in her hand was a shovel.

Sis barreled through the back door and took the steps two at a time.

"Beulah! What on earth are you doing?"

"What does it look like, Sis? I'm planting roses."

There they were, new rosebushes all in a row, standing like sentinels over the bones. Even the bush that had sheltered the foot had vanished, and in its place was a Don Juan climber, its petals dripping to the ground red as blood. Closer inspection revealed that these end-of-summer bushes were hardly better than the disease-ravaged ones they'd replaced. Instead of rich, green branches full of life, the new bushes were mere skeletons, their limbs holding a puny offering of sparse leaves and small blossoms.

"Good Lord. Where did you find these?"

"Closeout sale at the corner market."

"They won't live in this heat."

"Yes, they will. I aim to water 'em every day." Beulah stripped off her gloves and handed Sis the shovel, as matter-of-factly as if she'd just planted prizewinning roses in a spring garden. "Stow this, will you, Sis? I'm gonna get some sweet tea before I melt."

Sis held on to the shovel and stared at the Don Juan, paralyzed. Were the bones still under there? Or had Beulah moved them?

Sis had an insane urge to ram the sharp edge of the shovel under the bush and see for herself, but it was broad daylight and there was no telling who might be looking out a window or passing along the street. What would they see? Would they see a decisive woman who never even blinked when she chose family over college, who ate the same thing every morning without once wondering if corn flakes would be better for her than biscuits and bacon, who got out of bed every day at the same time and did her job in precisely the same way without ever stopping to cry over what she might be missing? Or would they see a divided woman split by the need to protect her family at all costs and the urge to discover the truth behind the awful secret in her garden?

It seemed to Sis that the bones under her feet were calling out to her, trying to tell her of something she'd missed, some little clue from her past that might reveal why they were there.

She thought back over the years. Once there had been a mimosa tree where the rose hedge stood. Its twin was still on the other side of the yard, its branches sturdy enough to hold a tree swing for Andy. She tried to remember when the first mimosa tree had come down, but the red petals drifting over her shoes from the newly planted Don Juan brought her mind back from the past and into the awful present.

The back door popped open and Beulah called, "Everything all right out here, Sis?"

"Everything's fine."

As she hurried off to the garage to stow the shovel, she tasted the bitterness of her lie. Everything she'd held true about herself and her history was suddenly in question.

She heard the sound of Sweet Mama's powerful old Buick engine, followed by the slamming of a car door and Emily's voice. "Andy, be careful and don't drop the pie."

She'd followed Sweet Mama to make sure she got home all right, just as she'd promised Sis she would. The pie would be the coconut cream she'd made at the café especially for Jim. Soon Emily would be driving to her own house where she would stand in her little blue-and-white kitchen making cookies for Andy and dreaming of having a family complete with a husband.

Sis tried not to even think about that, about dreams that turned out wrong and dreams that got left in the dust.

"Watch your step, Sweet Mama!" Emily's voice echoed

through the stillness of a clear afternoon. She'd be taking Sweet Mama's elbow now as they climbed the front porch steps, something neither sister would have imagined the need for five years earlier.

The front screen door popped, and Beulah called out, "Ya'll set that pie in the kitchen, then come back here on the porch under the ceiling fan. I got sweet tea made."

Their voices receded and Sis stood in the doorway of the garage, half in shadow, half in sun, which seemed to her a metaphor for her life. Soon she would join her family, smiling while she sipped iced tea and discussed her sister's wedding. Looking at her, nobody would know she was the keeper of a nightmare, one so dark that if she made a false move her world would crumble. And with it the family she loved.

Four

SWEET MAMA'S KITCHEN SMELLED of fried chicken and field peas cooked with fatback, sweet corn seasoned with butter and sweet potato casserole cooked with chunks of pineapple, each scent as distinctive to Emily as if she'd personally stood at Beulah's elbow watching her cook for Jim. While Andy began a reconnaissance of the area that included looking in every cabinet and peering out the window, Emily set the coconut cream pie on the table beside a platter piled high with Beulah's biscuits.

The kitchen was Emily's favorite room in Sweet Mama's house, or any house, for that matter. Her best memories were here. She ran her hands over the scarred surface of the table. She'd sat at that same table while Sis struggled to explain the mystery of numbers and her twin brother breezed through the multiplication table as if he'd been born knowing it. She pictured her own little maple table and how Larry would soon bend patiently over Andy, helping him add and subtract and listening to him as he read about Dick and Jane from the first grade reader. Did they still teach Dick and Jane? She could hardly wait to find out.

"Mommy!" Andy tugged at her skirt. "Sis is out in the backyard! Can I go out and make frog houses with her?"

"That's a wonderful idea. But first go out to the front porch and tell Beulah and Sweet Mama I'm going upstairs to see Uncle Jim."

"'K!" He raced off, his sneakers skidding in the polished hallway.

"Andy," she called. "Don't run in the house."

"I won't."

Emily grinned. Of course he would. What little boy ever walked when it was so much more fun to run?

She got a dessert plate from the cabinet and cut a generous slice of pie, then headed upstairs to find her brother. Beulah said he hadn't come out of his room all day. When Emily got upstairs and pushed open his door, she saw evidence of his hermitlike day—his bed still unmade, the plate of half-eaten chicken and the glass with ice melting in leftover tea. Jim was sitting in a straight chair at his desk, an open book in front of him, his beard stubble so blond it was barely visible.

"Em!" His smile reminded her of Andy's, except for the vacant eyes.

"What are you reading?"

She walked over and put her arm around his shoulder, and he gestured toward the page, Constellations and Constitution in Volume C of the Encyclopedia Britannica. He could have been reading about either one with equal curiosity.

"I hope Andy inherited your brain," she said.

"I hope he's *nothing* like me." The force of his passion catapulted him from his chair, while Emily stood by, helpless. "Look at me, Em! I can't even stand the sight of my own face."

"It's a dear face. I love your face." She cupped her brother's cheeks. "Look at me, Jim."

"Don't, Em." He jerked away. "Everywhere I turn I see the eyes of the dead staring back at me. Even when I look at my own sisters."

He grabbed his crutch and clomped to the window while she stood in the middle of the room wondering what to do. When Andy was hurting she could pull him onto her lap and smooth his hair and sing-song his favorite nursery rhyme. *Humpty Dumpty sat on the wall. Humpty Dumpty had a great fall. All the King's horses and the King's men couldn't put Humpty Dumpty together again.*

Who would put her brother back together?

She joined him at the window and linked her arm through his, then just stood there, not saying a word, scarcely daring to breathe in case he pulled away. She tried to think of something wise to say, but in the end nothing came to her. In the end she said a silent prayer, not even knowing whether God would listen to something as simple as *Help my brother. Help me help my brother.*

A breeze came through the open window, welcome after a day of intense heat, and voices drifted through—the indecipherable, meandering conversation of Sweet Mama and Beulah on the front porch and the clear, high voice of Andy in the backyard, peppering Sis with questions.

"Do holes have bottoms?"

"Can I dig to China?"

"Do frogs get married?"

"Is first grade scary?"

"Can I come home if I don't like it?"

The sun was lowering toward the western horizon, reminding Emily she'd promised to cook dinner for Larry. An anxiousness rose inside her, the kind of wishy-washy feeling she hated. How could she leave her brother and yet how could she disappoint her fiancé? A mosquito buzzed through the window, and she balanced on one foot to scratch the back of her leg. She got red welts every time one bit her.

"Jim?" He turned toward her with a look of surprise, as if he were just returning from a faraway country and couldn't believe she was there waiting for him. "If I invite Larry over for dinner here, will you come down and eat with us?"

"I'm not good company."

"You don't have to be good company. In fact, you don't even have to make conversation. I'd just like for you to spend some time with the man who is going to be your brother-in-law."

His long silence was bound to be *no*. She scratched her mosquito bite again, waiting.

When her brother finally shrugged and said, "Okay," Emily felt as if she'd successfully led an expedition to the North Pole.

She left him heading toward the bathroom to shave, and went downstairs to call Larry. When she got to the telephone in the kitchen, she lost some of her resolve. Should she discuss the revised dinner plans with Beulah and Sis first? But what if Larry said no, and then she'd have to tell them he wasn't coming?

"Emily?" Sis was suddenly standing in the doorway, holding the hand of a dirty little urchin after an enthusiastic excavation of the backyard.

"Good Lord, Sis, you startled me."

"What's up, Em? You look like a scared rabbit."

"Mommy, what's a scared rabbit?"

"Go wash your hands and face, Andy," she told her son. "I'll explain later."

As he marched off, she told Sis about her plans to invite

Larry over for dinner and how it might turn out to be a wonderful ploy to get their brother out of his bedroom.

"That's great, Em!"

"I thought I could find something in the pantry to fix."

"Good Lord, Emily. Beulah always cooks enough to feed an invasion of Martians. And don't you worry about Sweet Mama."

"Are the Martians coming?" Andy was back, standing in the doorway bouncing up on his toes in his excitement.

"No, the Martians are not coming." Emily studied the level of dirt still on her son. "You forgot to wash behind your ears. I could build a frog house with that leftover dirt."

"'K."

As her son raced off once more and her sister puttered around the kitchen—washing her hands, pouring herself a glass of iced tea—Emily felt herself settle down. Apart from her family and Sweet Mama's café, she sometimes felt a bit out of her element, as if she'd taken a wrong turn on the road and ended up in an unfamiliar place.

"Okay, then." She smiled as Sis settled into a kitchen chair with her tea. "That settles everything."

"It's a good idea, Em. Larry needs to learn more about the family he's marrying into."

The way her sister's eyes gleamed, it seemed to Emily the shoe was on the other foot: Sis was the one who wanted to find out about the man Emily would soon be calling her own. Still, as she picked up the kitchen phone and dialed Larry's work number, she even felt a small sense of accomplishment.

When she said, "Hello, Larry," and he called her *darling,* she saw her future unfold as a series of Hallmark cards, each scene a perfect depiction of a happy family.

Words spilled out of her so fast, she got tangled up and had to start over. By the time she'd finished telling him about the change of plans, she was flushed as if she'd been running.

There was a deep silence at the other end of the line.

"Larry? Are you there?"

"I'm here."

"Oh, thank goodness. For a minute, I thought we'd been cut off."

"No, I was thinking…how could you just change plans without even discussing it with me?"

"Well, of course I should have. I know that." She bit her lip, feeling somehow inadequate and wondering what she'd done that was so wrong. "Still, my brother is just home from the war, and he's feeling so alone right now, I thought it would be nice if you could come over and cheer him up."

Why didn't Larry say something?

"You know, a little man-to-man talk in a house full of women?" She waited, nervous, and still Larry said nothing. "Of course, there's Andy, but I'm afraid his conversation runs to frog houses and rocket ships."

Emily twisted the phone cord around her fingers, and a little pulse started pounding in her temple.

"Larry? Are you still there?" She put a hand to her forehead and silently counted to three. "Say something. *Please.*"

Sis set down her glass in that slow, deliberate manner she had when she was getting ready to wade into the middle of a situation gone bad. Even worse, she pushed back her chair. Emily frantically signaled her sister to sit back down.

When Larry finally decided to talk to her again, she was so flustered she nearly dropped the receiver.

"You said you'd make spaghetti and meatballs, Emily." He was breathing hard, like somebody having a heart attack.

"Larry? Are you all right?"

"Of course I'm all right. Just disappointed, that's all."

"I'm sorry, Larry." She looked down at her engagement ring and twisted it on her finger. "I was just... I don't know what I was doing." She squinted at her ring. "I was just trying to be helpful, that's all."

Sis was scowling so hard it seemed to Emily the whole room had gone dark.

"I was looking forward to your spaghetti, Emily," Larry told her.

"I promise you I'll make spaghetti and meatballs the next time. And listen, Beulah is one of the best cooks on the Gulf Coast. I know you're going to enjoy having dinner with my family."

"I even told my boss I was eating spaghetti my fiancée made."

"I'm sorry, Larry. I really, really am."

She couldn't even look at Sis. She knew what she'd see: a sister getting ready to explode.

Emily frantically searched for a way to salvage the situation. It was too late to fix spaghetti from scratch and still have dinner at her house at a decent hour. But she could pick up some spaghetti sauce on her way home and doctor it up so Larry wouldn't be able to tell it from the real thing.

"Listen, Larry. Just forget I even mentioned dinner at Sweet Mama's. I'll hurry on home to cook and see you in a little while. Okay?"

His sigh was as dramatic as Andy's when he'd been told he had to take a bath before going to bed.

"I forgive you, sweetheart. And I'll come to Sweet Mama's for dinner. But next time, discuss plans with me first, okay?"

"Of course. I will."

Sis was out of her chair before Emily had even hung up the phone.

"That rat! What did he say to you?"

"He was disappointed about the spaghetti, Sis, that's all."

"Disappointed, my hind foot. It looks like he put you through the wringer." Sis stomped over to the sink and dumped the rest of her iced tea so hard ice cubes bounced over the lip of the sink and rattled to the floor. "I'd like to slap some sense into him. And if he gives me half a chance, I will."

"We have to all get along."

"If he wants to get along with me, he'd better start treating my sister right."

"He treats me just fine. Really, he does."

"Do you call that *fine,* being reduced to a nervous wreck just because you invited him to dinner?" Sis snatched up a dish towel and attacked the ice cubes on the floor. "*Apologizing* for Pete's sake, as if you'd done something *wrong!*"

"Please, Sis! He's going to be my husband!"

Sis went very still, collecting her rage the way the air collects turbulence right before a tornado rips through. If you didn't know Sis, you'd tremble in your shoes; you'd expect her to tear into you any minute and try to straighten you out. But Emily saw with a sister's heart. She watched Sis rein in her feelings and bury them so deep not a glimmer was left behind.

Sis dumped the ice cubes back into the sink, easy now in her movements and her posture.

"All right. I'll behave."

"Oh, Sis! I *knew* you would."

"But that doesn't mean I like it, Em."

"I know."

"I don't like this man and I don't like the idea of you marrying him. But we'll get through the evening. Now I'm going to clean up and then warn Sweet Mama and Beulah."

"Warn?"

"*Tell*. Is that better?"

"Much."

"Em, I want you to think about the way Larry acted over something as simple as coming here for dinner. If he's this controlling now, what will he be like after the wedding?"

"Sis, don't start on Larry again."

"I'm not starting on Larry. Just promise me you'll think about it. That's all I'm asking."

"I promise."

"Okay, then. I'll see you in a little bit."

Sis left the kitchen while the conversation with Larry burned through Emily. Not even the endearment he'd used to say goodbye could erase the sense that she'd headed out to pick a basketful of ripe strawberries and ended up in a tangle of briars. She bent over the sink to splash cool water on her hot face, then stood with water dripping down her chin, simply stood there staring into space.

Sis's footsteps echoed on the wooden floors upstairs. She'd be going about her business, getting cleaned up for dinner. From the direction of the hall closet came sounds of Andy's rambunctious search, probably for one of Sis's old balls and her baseball bat. Out on the porch, her grandmother and Beulah would be drinking sweet tea from tall, cool glasses, blissfully unaware of the little storm that had swept through the kitchen.

After a little while, Emily shook herself like a woman coming out of a bad dream, then searched the pantry till she found an apron. She wasn't going to let this little setback spoil the evening. It was going to be great, maybe even wonderful, that's all. She wouldn't have it any other way. Her brother needed *wonderful,* and right this minute, so did she.

Upstairs Sis washed the dirt off and changed into fresh slacks and a clean black T-shirt, but there was nothing she could do to erase the awful way Emily had looked during her phone conversation with Larry. He'd crushed her with the ease and carelessness of someone smashing a butterfly.

She thought about knocking on Jim's door and relating the incident to him, but he might be getting dressed, and besides, he was too hurt from his own wounds to be burdened with Sis's dark opinions.

She headed back downstairs to warn Sweet Mama and Beulah. They were both in rocking chairs on the porch, swaying gently to the ebb and flow of their conversation. Sis stood in the doorway a moment, the rhythm of their words running through her like a beloved song. No matter what was going on in the world around her, Sis could hear their voices and feel herself being tethered to this place she called home. She allowed herself the luxury of soaking up that comfort a moment longer, and then she pushed away and marched across the wooden porch.

"Guess who's coming to dinner?" she said.

"If you fixing to tell me you bringing Sidney Poitier, I'm gonna get all gussied up." Beulah chuckled, and after a heartbreaking lag, Sweet Mama joined her.

They both loved *Guess Who's Coming to Dinner.* When it had first come out two years ago, they'd planned the theater outing as if they were going on an overnight trip to the Peabody Hotel in Memphis.

"I hate to disappoint you, Beulah. It's not Sidney. It's Larry Chastain."

"Who?" Sweet Mama said, and Sis leaned down to put a hand on her shoulder.

"Emily's fiancé. Remember?"

"Of course I do. What do you think I am? Senile?" Sweet Mama eased out of her rocker, one blue-veined hand clutching the armrest to steady herself. "Come on, Beulah. If company's coming, we're eating in the dining room and using the good silver."

"I ain't sure that man's worth no good silver, Lucy."

"I'll be the judge of that."

"Ain't you always the judge?" Beulah winked at Sis, then took a hold of Sweet Mama's arm and led her back into the house. Sis would have followed them, but she knew they'd shoo her out of the way. She was useless around crockery and cutlery. She always ended up breaking or spilling something, and in general making a big mess that had to be cleaned up. She knew her place, and it certainly wasn't in the kitchen.

She leaned against a porch column and shaded her eyes, looking for signs of her future brother-in-law. She wanted to be the first to see him, to talk to him before Emily came out all flushed, trying to act as if Larry hadn't already spoiled her evening.

Sis flicked a speck of dust off the front of her shirt, harder than necessary, so hard in fact, that she ended up feeling the sting of her own slap.

His car came upon her suddenly, turning into the driveway before she had decided what she was going to say to him. Let him off the hook completely? Pretend she didn't know he'd acted an ass about dinner? Emily would be pleased if she kept quiet, but Sis might just choke on her own bile.

"Sis! Don't you look a vision?" Larry strode up the front steps with the confidence of a smooth-talking, handsome man used to turning heads. Before she knew what was happening, he was bent over her hand, kissing it, and she found herself staring at the too-straight part slicing through his black hair.

"A nightmare is more like it," she said.

Larry didn't respond to her self-deprecating comment. Instead, he let go of her hand, thank God, and looked out over the Gulf.

"You have a beautiful view. No wonder Emily loves this place."

"She does, but then Emily loves almost everything and everybody."

"Lucky me. I finally found a woman who could look beyond my flaws and see a hero."

"Emily's a sweet, trusting woman, Larry. And easily hurt."

"She's the woman of every man's dreams."

"Yes, she is. I'm glad you know how lucky you are to have her."

"Luck had nothing to do with it." Suddenly, Larry puffed up with such self-importance Sis thought he'd levitate right off the front porch. "A salesman learns to read people. When I saw your sister, I read her like a book."

"And what did that *book* say?" If he noticed her sarcasm, he didn't show a sign.

"'I'm a woman you can keep barefoot, pregnant and in the kitchen.'"

He laughed at his own Dark Ages attitude, and Sis wanted to slap him off the porch. Emily saved him, rushing out pink-faced and smiling, the only sign of her nervousness showing in the way she wadded a corner of her blue gingham apron into a tight fist.

"Larry! I'm so glad you're here." She rushed over to hug him, and he winked over her shoulder at Sis.

Did that jackass dare to think they were coconspirators? Or was he so certain of his hold over her sister that he didn't care how he flaunted his power?

Still steaming, she watched Larry lead her sister into the house. She had to stand on the porch deep breathing before she could follow. The evening couldn't be over fast enough to suit Sis.

Five

THE DINING ROOM TABLE looked elegant with Sweet Mama's china and silver gleaming in the candlelight. The candles had been Emily's idea, a last-minute addition to make Larry feel special. She couldn't help but take pride that dinner was turning out to be a great success.

Sis was playing hostess with such grace, Emily would never have guessed she'd pitched a hissy fit in the kitchen earlier. Sweet Mama and Beulah wore rhinestone brooches for the occasion, and Andy looked darling with his face scrubbed clean and his flyaway hair slicked back. It looked suspiciously shiny to Emily. Later, she'd have to find out what he used. Usually it was water, but his cowlick was too tame for that.

Even Jim had joined them. Emily was glad, though he hadn't said a single word except *hello*.

Fortunately, Larry didn't seem to notice. He was too busy fielding questions from Sweet Mama and Beulah.

"What brought you down here?" Sweet Mama said, and Larry acted as if she hadn't already asked him the same question three times. Emily hoped Sis noticed.

"I applied for a transfer to this area because I love fishing."

"It's his favorite pastime," Emily added, hoping Sweet

Mama would remember a granddaughter better than she did a virtual stranger.

"Before I met our girl here, I spent all my time with a fishing pole in my hands."

"Jim has a fishing boat and a convertible." Emily glanced at her brother, hopeful, but he was moving his mashed potatoes around on his plate. "It would be great if the two of you would let the top down and go fishing together."

When Jim's hand tightened over his fork, Emily had the awful feeling that she was pushing her brother back instead of drawing him close. To make matters worse, Beulah scowled at her and Andy started kicking the table leg.

"Fish ain't biting now or me and Jim would'a gone today." Beulah closed her hand around Jim's arm, and there it stayed, dark as sorghum molasses against his white shirt. "Ain't no telling when they gonna bite again."

Sis shot Emily a warning glance, but it was already too late to stop a conversation rolling toward disaster.

"Fish always bite for me." Larry turned his attention to Jim, looking pointedly at the crutch leaning against his chair. "How about it, Jim? Go fishing with me and I'll do all the driving. Thank God I avoided this senseless war and stayed in one piece."

"Our boy drives just fine." Beulah looked like a thundercloud that didn't care who she rained on.

"Jim's a hero." Sweet Mama peered at Larry. "All the men in our family are heroes."

"How come you didn't go to war?" Beulah asked.

"I didn't pass the draft. I was 4F."

Larry's face tightened and Emily wadded her napkin into a little ball. Did her future husband have some dire medical condition she didn't know about?

"Why were you 4F, darling?"

"Flat feet," he said.

Emily wanted to crawl under the table. Her daddy's World War II medals were on prominent display in a shadow box in the entry hall and Jim's Purple Heart would soon be there, as well.

Sweet Mama laid down her fork in that big, clattering way she had when she meant business.

"There's nothing but patriotic men in this family," she said, "and we're proud of it."

"Ain't that the truth?" Beulah patted Jim's arm. "In my day, we called them 4F-ers slackers."

Larry's face blazed and Emily's felt hot. She'd explain to Larry later that Sweet Mama was slowly losing touch with reality, that Beulah would say just about anything if she thought one of her *babies* was under fire, but how would she explain to her family that she was going to marry a man they considered a coward?

And still, there was the rest of this awful evening to get through. She shot a desperate glance at Sis.

"We're going to take dessert on the front porch," Sis announced.

"Make sure it's the good china." Sweet Mama picked up her fork and smiled at Larry as if the conversation about heroes and slackers had never taken place. "I always serve company on china plates."

Emily didn't know what to do except sit there with her hand on Larry's arm in the desperate hope that one small touch from the woman he loved would calm him down while Sis helped Sweet Mama from the table. Andy was already racing toward the front porch and, from the looks of things, Beulah and Jim were heading upstairs. She hoped so. She didn't know how she could get through the rest of the evening if Beulah kept acting like a bear protecting her cub.

And poor Jim. She couldn't endure thinking about him right now. If an intimate family dinner could render him speechless and wrecked, what would a public outing do?

When the dining room was clear of everybody except the two of them, she turned to Larry.

"I'm sorry, darling."

"Let's just eat dessert and get out of here," he said. "I knew it would turn out this way."

"Beulah and Sweet Mama didn't mean any harm. Really. They're just getting on in years and set in their ways."

"Thank God I don't have to contend with my family."

Why not? Emily didn't dare ask, not after Larry's humiliation at the hands of her family.

"I'll make it up to you later, Larry. I promise."

She led him onto the front porch where Sweet Mama smiled up from her rocking chair, Andy looked like an angel and Sis served up Amen cobbler on china plates. The moon hung low over the water, casting silvery patches on the porch floor. It was the kind of clear summer night that made you think there was nothing bad in this world that couldn't be fixed.

Late that night, Sis sat on the front porch in the dark alone, heavy with the feeling that something awful was happening to someone she loved. It couldn't be Jim. He'd been in his room ever since he left the table tonight without dessert. But Sis doubted he was sleeping, and even if he were, his slumber was unlikely to be peaceful.

And it couldn't be Sweet Mama or Beulah. She'd checked before she came onto the porch. If they were bothered about goading Larry because he'd shirked his military duty, you couldn't tell by the way they rested on their backs with their snores rattling the windowpanes. Had their bluntness been deliberate or was it old age? Didn't they know if you prodded a coiled snake it would strike back?

Sis jumped up from the swing, her sister suddenly so strongly on her mind she wanted to race inside and call her. Sis walked to a patch of moonlight on the porch and peered at her watch. It was after midnight, far too late to call Emily and say, *Are you okay? Did Larry punish you for what happened at dinner?* Sis had no doubt he would. A man who would reduce his fiancée to tears over a dinner invitation would use any excuse to exert his power over her.

Or would he do worse?

Sis paced the porch until she was so tired she thought she'd fall over. Easing through the front door, she tiptoed upstairs, got into pajamas and fell into bed. But her sleep was restless, broken by nightmares and the helpless feeling of being chased and unable to run.

When the morning light pinked her windowpanes, she sat up in bed with a headache so fierce she didn't know how she'd begin her daily routine, much less get through it with a shred of compassion. Just this once she wished she could wake up in bed with a good man who would say, *Honey, you rest. I'll take care of everything.*

She eased out of bed, tiptoed to the bathroom, then downed two aspirins and waited. When the jackhammers in her head subsided, she went back into her bedroom and picked up the phone. Emily answered on the first ring.

"Em, you sound funny. Are you all right?"

"Just a little tired is all, Sis. Too much excitement."

"I'm sorry about the way dinner turned out. Was Larry mad?"

"He was a little upset, that's all. What man wouldn't be? But after I talked to him, he was fine."

"You're sure?"

"Oh, for Pete's sake, Sis. Let it alone. Andy's downstairs dragging out more boxes and I've got to get to the café to put together an order list. I'm going to need more supplies for the wedding petit fours."

Sis hung up, still hoping there wouldn't be a wedding. But she had the sinking feeling that she was riding on a train that had already left the station. It didn't matter how hard she yelled, *Stop! Let's all get off.* They were going to end up listening to Emily pledge *Till death do us part* to a man they all considered a coward.

The aroma of coffee and bacon coming from the kitchen told Sis she'd better get moving. She dressed quickly, then went to Jim's room and knocked.

"Come in." He was sitting at his window wearing the white dress shirt she didn't know if he'd slept in or worn during an all-night vigil with the moon or put on again this morning.

An unbearable tenderness came over Sis, and she sank into the only other chair in the room, the one at his desk where the encyclopedia was open at *C* for *compass*. Or was it *compassion?* Did the encyclopedia tell you that compassion was not something you searched for, but a feeling you carried in your heart whether you knew it or not, one so powerful it could render you speechless?

Sis studied the slump of her brother's shoulders, the blond hair grown too long and straggling down the back of his neck, the hollow in his cheek as he tilted his head toward the view beyond the window.

"I thought you might want to go down to breakfast with me."

"Yeah, Sis. The family dinner went so well."

The flash of sarcasm gave Sis hope that the Jim of old was somewhere inside those baggy clothes.

"Did you see the look on his face when Beulah talked about 4F-ers?" she said.

"It would have been funny if Em weren't fixing to marry him."

"Well, she is, and there's not a thing either of us can do about it except carry on."

"You carry on, Sis." He turned his back to her and stared out the window.

Sis sat there awhile, undecided, and then she went downstairs to brace herself with a cup of coffee. A day that had started off so badly was bound to get worse.

The scene in the kitchen stopped her cold. Sweet Mama was sitting at the kitchen table with her hat on. It wasn't a garden hat, which might have made sense if she'd been working outside and just forgot to take it off. It was a wide-brimmed white Panama with a virtual flower garden on the brim, red and pink peonies the size of saucers with a big blue feather spouting out from the bouquet.

Beulah looked up from the coffeepot and lowered a look at Sis that said *Don't you say a word*.

Sis hurried to the cabinet and turned her back to hide her dismay. She took her time selecting a mug from the array that had collected over the years. She selected one with *Alabama the Beautiful* from a long-ago trip to Natural Bridge. Then she stood there just holding on, wishing the grandmother wearing the flower garden hat was still the same strong woman who had loaded Beulah and her grandchildren into the car for a three-hundred-mile trip in spite of the fact that she'd had to fight for Beulah every step of the way.

When Sis had regained composure, she went to the pot and poured her coffee.

"We having a garden party in here." Beulah smiled at her. "Where's your hat?"

Sis grabbed her garden hat off the peg by the back door and sat down to have breakfast. Carrying on.

Still, wearing a hat at a battered old table for a nonexistent garden party would be mild compared to the facade she'd have to wear once she got to the café. How she would ever get through the petit fours and the cheese balls, not to mention the wedding madness that had overtaken the regulars, Sis didn't know.

Sometimes she wished she could hole up in her room like her brother while Beulah trekked up the stairs with sweet tea and sympathy.

Six

EMILY DIDN'T KNOW WHAT was wrong with Sis. Ever since their talk about having her wedding in the garden, she'd been snappish and forgetful. It had gotten worse since that awful dinner with Larry, and that was more than a week ago.

Yesterday Sis forgot to order coffee with chicory, and she still hadn't brought those polka-dot sunglasses she'd promised Andy last week.

Still, nothing could mar Emily's happiness. The cheese balls for her reception were in the refrigerator, the petit fours decorated with pink icing were rapidly piling up in the chest freezer in the pantry and she was going to do one last campout with her son before the wedding.

Standing in the backyard of Sweet Mama's Café, enjoying a cup of coffee before the breakfast crowd started getting too big for Sweet Mama to handle, Emily kicked off her shoes and smiled as Andy raced around the ship, his untamable hair flying every which way. She made a note to add a trip to the barber to her list of things to do before the wedding.

"Can we camp out here tonight?"

"No. We're going to camp out at Sweet Mama's house."

"Can we take the rocket ship?"

"We're going to sleep in a tent."

"Why can't we sleep in the rocket?"

"Because then there wouldn't be enough room for Aunt Sis. You want her to join the campout, don't you?"

"I can sleep on the roof. See?" Andy clambered on top and stretched out. When his feet hung over the side, he curled up in a little ball. "Just right," he yelled.

"That's not a good idea, Andy."

"How come?"

Ordinarily, Emily reveled in these meandering conversations with Andy, but lately he'd been trying her patience. Deliberately, it seemed. Was it because he didn't want to share her with Larry or was there some deeper motive?

It was a relief when her neighbors Tom and James Wilson came through the back door of the café. Still bachelors at fifty and some said set in their ways, they were nonetheless two of the sweetest guys Emily had ever met. Tom was carrying a toolbox and James was wagging a little stack of lumber.

"We've been seeing you and Andy toting stuff out of your house for his little project out here," Tom said. "Hope you don't mind some help."

"Of course not!" Emily hugged them both and they got pink in the face.

Soon the sound of hammering blended with Andy's laughter as they shored up the cardboard boxes with scrap lumber. Tom looked like a rumpled, friendly elf with his shirtsleeves rolled up and his white hair sticking out from an old fishing hat with the lures still attached to the band. James was just the opposite. Tall, reserved and elegant, even with a hammer in his hand, he was dressed in a summer suit of blue pin-striped seersucker.

"That ought to do it," Tom said, pushing back his fishing

hat and reaching over to ruffle Andy's hair. "Now that little rocket ship is sound as a dollar, even if it rains."

Emily hoped the little ship didn't have to be put to the test. She was still planning on a garden wedding, in spite of Sis's long lip. As much as the new rose hedge would benefit from a shower, she didn't want anything to ruin her wedding.

"It just needs this one last thing." James bent over his toolbox and pulled out a wooden box with a little red steering wheel attached. It was covered with dials that looked as if they'd come from old car parts. Inside he'd rigged a set of hair clippers that buzzed when Andy turned one of the dials.

Being part of her little boy's quest for the moon might be the biggest event in their lives. Neither Tom nor James had ever been married, and they both still lived with an ancient cat and their even more ancient mother, who had taken to her bed when she was fifty for reasons nobody knew or would tell.

Emily teared up, but she didn't know if she was crying because Andy didn't like Larry, or because the Wilson brothers had to find joy in a little rocket ship made from cardboard boxes, or because her own sister could end up exactly like them, with nothing to show for her years except gray hair and an old cat.

As they loaded up their tools, Emily said, "I'm going to give you an Amen cobbler to take home. Your mother might enjoy it."

"Mother eats like a bird," Tom said, "but she's still partial to Sweet Mama's cooking."

"Good, then. That's settled."

They trudged back to the café, turning in the doorway to wave just as Burt Larson came out.

"I had some old sheets of plastic up at the house," Burt

said. "I thought I'd help out with that little rocket ship, if you don't mind."

Andy squealed and hugged the postman around the legs. Emily wished he'd show half that much enthusiasm with the man who was going to be his daddy.

She thanked Burt and then left him in the backyard, helping Andy with the rocket ship while she hurried back to the café. A cloud of sugar and spice rose from the cobblers Sweet Mama had lined up on the counter.

Wouldn't it be wonderful if a big bowl of cobbler for dessert worked its magic on Andy? Wouldn't it be great if the steam that rose around him softened her son so that viewing Larry as his daddy would be as simple as a hug?

They'd eat it tonight in Sweet Mama's backyard, while the moon was high and the stars looked like a blanket of lights thrown across the sky. She was smiling as she got a big bowl to serve up Andy's surprise cobbler, and a length of tinfoil to cover it.

Emily dug through the flaky crust and into a mixture of peaches and cherries so deep she could see her future. The sweetness of love long denied wafted around her, and the joy of having a real family of her own.

But as she dipped toward the bottom, she felt an overwhelming sadness, as if something waited for her in the dark with fangs bared.

"Oh, I'm just being silly." She quickly covered Andy's bowl, then wrapped cobbler for Tom and James.

"What was that, dear?"

Miss Opal Clemson was standing behind Emily, a little blue hat perched on her gray hair, a black patent-leather purse tucked over her arm and a wide smile on her face. Emily made a mental note to pay her a visit. Miss Opal lived just around the corner from her, and she thought how lonely it must be to rattle around in a house all by yourself.

"My goodness. Miss Opal." She smiled at the petite piano teacher who had tried her best to teach Emily the mysteries of the keyboard. It hadn't worked. Emily didn't have a musical bone in her body.

"I was thinking about your wedding music, dear. Have you thought about using a recording of 'Clair de Lune'?"

Burt Larson, just coming from the backyard, chimed in with, "Seems to me like Emily's Big Event ought to have music plain folks can understand."

The regulars at the next table joined in, and soon the entire café was abuzz with plans for Emily's Big Event, spoken as if each word were capitalized and ought to be posted out by the Gulf on the huge billboard that advertised Baricev's Seafood Harbor.

As the customers continued to offer unsolicited advice about the wedding, Emily saw Sis materialize in the doorway of her office, then turn and walk back inside.

Excusing herself from Miss Opal, Emily handed Tom an Amen cobbler then stowed Andy's in the kitchen and hurried after her sister.

She found her seated at a battered oak desk glancing at the clock as if she could cling to the march of time and soothe herself with the thought that two o'clock would eventually come and she could close up Sweet Mama's.

As Emily sat in the other chair, an uncomfortable old thing with a slatted back and a cane bottom losing some of its canes, she was certain Sis chose it deliberately to discourage visits.

"How was Jim this morning?" Emily asked.

"The same. Hunkered down in the house like he's in a foxhole."

"Maybe my wedding will be just the thing to bring him around."

"I wouldn't hold out any high hopes, Em."

Sis always looked on the gloomy side of life. Emily refused to let it sag her spirit.

"Did you bring those special astronaut glasses for Andy?"

"I forgot. Sorry, Em."

Good grief! Forgetting was so unlike her sister, Emily wondered if Sis was getting a brain tumor.

"Just give them to him tonight at the campout, will you? He's worrying me to death over those glasses."

"I don't know that camping out in the backyard is such a good idea."

"Why not? We always camp out in Sweet Mama's backyard."

"It's too hot to camp out."

"It's *never* too hot for a six-year-old. Besides, it'll be fun. We can pitch the tent by the new hedge so we can smell the roses."

"Not the rose hedge!"

"Good grief, Sis. What's the matter with you?"

Sis just clamped her mouth shut and refused to say another word, which was fine with Emily. She had too much on her mind to continue this silly argument with her sister. If she didn't hurry back to that growing café crowd, there was no telling what kind of mess Sweet Mama would make. She seemed to be having one of her good days, thank goodness, because Beulah had stayed home again to be with Jim, who seemed to be going backward instead of forward.

Still, something had to be done to help Sweet Mama, but Emily didn't know what. After the wedding she'd ask Sis. But not until her sister got in a better mood.

"I've got to get back in there," Emily said. "You didn't forget that we're looking at dresses for the wedding this afternoon, did you?"

Sis rolled her eyes and looked as if she'd been asked to stand before a firing squad. But Emily refused to be daunted, even when her sister glanced at the clock again as if it had suddenly become her enemy.

"How could I forget, Emily?"

"Good, then. We'll leave at two."

Emily could hardly contain her excitement. They'd drop Andy off to stay with Beulah, and then Emily could enter that sacred territory she'd fantasized about ever since she met Mark Jones—the bridal shop.

As she stepped back through the office door, she drew the sound of laughter and lazy chatter around her like a beloved shawl. But the Amen cobblers gave off such a scent of sorrow she wanted to weep.

Quickly she skirted around them, wishing it was already two o'clock.

The clock on the wall had become Sweet Mama's enemy. Every loud ticktock meant she was roaring closer to the edge of a looming precipice. Sis was saying, "Sweet Mama, are you sure you can lock up?" and she didn't have the faintest idea what this fierce granddaughter of hers wanted her to put under lock and key.

"Of course," she said. "Go on and have fun. But don't pick out a blue dress for me. If you do, I won't wear it."

She'd been wearing blue on the four worst days of her life— the day in 1920 that jackass came home drunk and all hell broke loose, the day horrible Ethel Williams sank her claws into Sweet Mama's son Steve and dragged him to the altar, the Christmas her son Bill and his wife, Margaret, had died in a car crash and the day one year later when she'd stood in the doorway of her café and faced down the KKK with her double-barreled shotgun.

She was standing now in the café on a hot July day in 1969, waving cheerfully at her two departing granddaughters and her great-grandson, but she had the eerie sense of standing smack-dab in the middle of a brisk winter day in the forties with the double barrels of her shotgun pointed at a ragtag group of cowards. She could almost hear their voices, almost see the white hoods.

Through the echo of time, she heard the bell over the café door ringing. Sweet Mama came back to herself in time to see her granddaughters departing. Now, what was it they'd told her to do?

She sifted through a mind that felt like a sieve. Her memories were leaking through the holes so fast sometimes Sweet Mama felt as if she'd wake up one morning and see her past scattered around her on the floor.

Something kept nagging at her, something she ought to remember. Suddenly, it came to her, and she hurried to the kitchen to get the notepad she kept in her voluminous purse.

Sinking into a cane-bottomed chair that Beulah used when she was peeling potatoes, Sweet Mama thumbed through the pages. One was titled "Customers." Tom and James Wilson were there along with Opal Clemson, the music teacher and Burt Larson, the mailman—every one of them described right down to the roots of their hair.

Sweet Mama found herself shaking again, an old woman with a rapidly fading memory depending on a notebook to keep her straight and wondering how much longer she'd be able to hang on to her secret and fool her granddaughters.

Beulah was another story. Nobody could fool her. When

Sweet Mama had first started forgetting things she'd said, *Beulah, my mind's going and you've got to help me.*

Beulah didn't ask any questions. That was her way. She just folded Sweet Mama in one of her wide hugs and whispered, *I ain't about to let Mr. Steve and that uppity Miss Ethel put you in a nursing home.*

That's when the Remembering Book had been born. The only trouble was, she often couldn't get to it in time to bail herself out of public embarrassments. More and more, she had to throw up smoke screens or pretend she was just kidding.

The clock in the café chimed three, and Sweet Mama knew she was already an hour late leaving. If she didn't get a move on, she wouldn't make it home before Sis and Emily got back from their shopping trip. Emily would worry and Sis was liable to call for a search party.

She scanned through her book till she found a page titled "Locking Up." It told how to turn the open sign to Closed, how to find the key to the café on a peg in the pantry, and how to put it in the top zippered pocket of her purse after she'd gone out and locked the front door behind her.

Sweet Mama read the entry twice before she got up enough courage to execute it. Then she gathered her hat and her purse and stood awhile, trying to think if she was forgetting something.

Finally, she ended up at the front door where the key seemed to have outgrown the lock. It took her five minutes to discover she was holding it upside down.

By the time she got to her Buick, she had sweat patches under her arms and a bead of perspiration lining her upper lip. Thank God the key she put in the ignition caused the car to roar to life. Sweet Mama drove out of the parking lot as smooth as if it were 1921 and she was driving her Tin Lizzie, heading to her brand-new bakery with Beulah at her side.

With the windows down, the Gulf breeze got under the brim of her black straw hat, making her feel twenty-seven again and ready to show the Jazz Age that a young divorcée with two little boys could start a business the same as a man, only ten times better if it's a bakery.

She started to sing, but was shocked at the thin, reedy voice she heard. She and Beulah used to ride along in that Tin Lizzie, singing in harmony as good as the Boswell Sisters, Sweet Mama belting out the alto and Beulah adding her soaring soprano.

Determined not to be depressed on such a beautiful day, Sweet Mama glanced toward the beach. Terns called from sandy knolls and seagulls wheeled over the Gulf and everything was exactly where it ought to be. Sweet Mama didn't know why Sis worried so much about her driving. She'd lived in Biloxi all her life and knew it from one side to the other.

The usual souvenir shops lined the highway, eventually giving way to a row of waterfront houses. Her own pink Victorian house would be coming up any minute now.

The bridge loomed in front of her, and she eased off the accelerator. Sweet Mama didn't believe in crossing bridges at full speed. It was a sure way to cause an accident. As much as she enjoyed looking out over the water, she kept her eyes straight ahead till she was over the bridge and cruising down the highway where long-legged storks lifted toward the tops of cypress trees sprouting out of the shallows.

Always a lover of nature, she admired the sight while the Buick hummed along the highway.

Was that the sun already sinking over the water? Where was her street? Where was her house?

Panicked, Sweet Mama eased her Buick into a side road that looked like it didn't lead anywhere, let alone her house where Beulah would be waiting with a glass of sweet tea. She stumbled out of her car and held on to her hat, searching her surroundings.

It seemed to her the sun was sinking in the east.

Then it occurred to her that she'd been driving along in exactly the opposite and wrong direction.

Frantically, she grabbed her purse out of the car and dug out the Remembering Book. But it was already too dark to read driving directions from the café to her house, and there was nothing written about a bridge to the unknown.

She was lost. And no matter how hard she searched the little notebook in her hand, it wouldn't tell her how to find the way home.

Seven

Driving to the bridal shop Sis felt as if she were in two places at once, behind the wheel of the car where she was borne along in a rushing torrent of Emily's chatter and on the beach with the crowd of little boys playing a game of baseball.

"There's no use counting on flowers from that new rose hedge," Emily said.

Sis refused to think about the rose hedge till after the wedding. Even when she was in the garden, she skirted around the roses.

"Nothing's surviving the heat except the oleander and the day lilies," Emily added. "White oleander will be fine, but maybe I can use some baskets of pink roses to camouflage all that orange."

His baseball cap was orange, that little boy on the beach who lobbed the ball toward center field and then spewed up a fine storm of sand as he slid into first base. He looked about ten, the age Sis's son might be…if she had one. If she had a house and a husband and a dog in the backyard. She'd have a large breed, a golden retriever, maybe, or even a Border collie. Her son would call him Boy and play fetch with him in the backyard using a small baseball mitt to match the one she'd used when she was a child.

Her fantasy became part of Emily's enthusiastic monologue.

"I thought for the music, we'd just move Sweet Mama's turntable to the back porch and put on a record."

The little boy in the orange cap was stealing into home. If she'd had a son, he would have done exactly that. He might even have grown up to be a professional baseball player.

"Sis, are you listening to me?"

"I'm listening."

"I was going to use Judy Garland singing 'Somewhere Over the Rainbow,' but Larry doesn't like that song."

Just the mention of that fool's name had Sis tightening her grip on the wheel.

"Emily, if you want to use that song, use it."

"After what happened to her, I don't know if that's such a good idea."

"Good grief!"

Judy Garland had died last month of a drug overdose. The famous singer's death had made no impact at all on Sis. Music was just something to fill the days that seemed to go on forever. When had she realized she'd never marry, never have children of her own? When had the door slammed shut to a future that included a man with dark eyes and gentle hands who would hold her close and whisper her real name?

She could almost hear his voice. *Beth, Beth, Beth.*

"Sis!" Emily grabbed ahold of the dashboard. "Slow down."

"Why? I'm not five miles over the speed limit."

"You're going to whiz right past the bridal shop."

If Sis had her way, she'd fly past. She'd sprout wings so strong they would carry her and her sister far above the shop with pink-striped awnings where fairy tales were wrapped in pearls and lace and sold to gullible women who expected life to be one big happily ever after.

Wondering if she was being cantankerous or practical or just plain jealous, she parked under the spreading branches of an ancient magnolia tree so huge it shaded three spaces. The only good thing she could say about this shopping trip was that she didn't have to lock the car. Thank God Biloxi was still that kind of town.

Sis followed her sister into a shop that smelled like ripe pears. Little sachets of the potpourri were piled high in crystal bowls along the glass countertop.

A set of full-length mirrors along the east wall showed her sister, multiplied, surrounded by wedding dresses in an endless sea of white.

When the heart breaks it makes a sound so small there is nothing to show for it except a hand clutched over the chest and a sudden smothering sensation. Was it breaking for Emily or herself, a homely woman who would never catch a husband, let alone have a little boy stealing into home plate?

Feeling guilty and remorseful for her unbecoming jealousy of a sister she loved more than all the would-be suitors in Biloxi, Sis followed Emily into an area of curtained dressing rooms where her sister insisted she try on a bridesmaid's dress. Pink, for God's sake. Even worse, it had ruffles.

The mirror confirmed that Sis looked as bad as she'd imagined.

"I look like a linebacker dipped in Pepto-Bismol."

"Hush up. It brings out some color in your face." Emily walked around her, admiring the awful dress from every angle. "With some pearls and a touch of lipstick, you'll be sensational."

Sis had never been sensational in her life. She didn't know

how she was going to start now, with or without lipstick. She didn't ask what color. She didn't even want to know.

"Fine." She couldn't get out of the dress fast enough. What did it matter how she looked as long as her sister was finally going to get the wedding of her dreams? "You're the one who ought to be trying on dresses."

Emily rifled through the rack and held up a floor-length satin dress.

"I like this one. It's the perfect dress for the perfect wedding."

Sis wished she could believe that. But since she'd gotten a glimpse of Larry's true nature, she felt like they were all in the middle of one of the hurricanes that sometimes swept through the Gulf Coast, blowing away everything in its path.

"The dress is lovely, Em. I'll help get you zipped in."

"No, no. I can do it by myself."

Emily clutched the dress to her chest, and for an instant, she wouldn't even look at Sis. Emily had ocean eyes, a blue so deep it could hold the endless moods of the sea, every one of them reflected in a glance. What was she trying to hide?

"I'm fine, Sis. You wait out here."

She sank into an overstuffed chair covered in hideous-looking pink chintz wondering what that skunk had said or done to her sister now. Since that awful dinner, Emily hadn't brought him back to Sweet Mama's, and he certainly hadn't shown his slick face in the café. Even worse, Emily, who told her everything, had told her nothing of any importance since that night.

By the time her sister reappeared, Sis was biting her nails down to the quick.

"What do you think, Sis?"

"It's beautiful."

"I think it has too many sequins on the bodice." Emily twisted this way and that in front of the mirror, viewing the dress from all angles.

"Okay. I'll help you get out of it and you can try on another one."

"No. You wait here. I want to surprise you."

Emily selected three more dresses off the racks and disappeared once more into the dressing room while Sis sat there wondering what was taking so long and what in the world was wrong with sequins.

"What about this one?" Emily was in a getup with long, satin sleeves and a tight bodice.

"Can you breathe in that thing?"

"You think it's too tight?"

"No, I just think you ought to be comfortable at your own wedding." Emily's face fell. Had Sis hit a nerve? "But what do I know?"

"I have two more I want to try."

If the dresses had those silly little buttons in the back like the one she was wearing they'd be there till Judgment Day. And maybe that wasn't such a bad idea, considering who would be waiting for her sister at the altar.

"Hey, Em," she called. "Before the wedding, why don't I take you and Andy somewhere?" Maybe if Emily had some time away from Larry, she'd come to her senses. "Maybe up the Peabody in Memphis so Andy can see the ducks?"

"We're going camping in the backyard tonight. That's enough."

Sis sighed. It was bad enough to keep fighting a battle she couldn't win. Sitting still for so long in a shop filled with things as breakable as her sister made the situation even worse.

"Need any help in there, Em?"

"No. I'm not even going to zip this one. It's too pink."

"I thought you wanted pink."

"Not this pink. I just don't want white, that's all. It doesn't seem appropriate."

Emily's sensitivity to her so-called scarlet past made Sis want to smack somebody. Just about anybody would do.

In a whisper of blush-colored silk that looked like the underside of a camellia, Emily emerged from the dressing room and stood in front of Sis with her yellow hair glowing under the lights and her mouth turned into a shy smile.

"How do I look?"

Beautiful and *breathtaking*—even *happy*—were the words that would come to mind if you didn't know Emily. But Sis had seen how Emily beamed every time she glanced in the direction of her son. There was something amiss here, something as subtle as an undertow in the Gulf you wouldn't notice until it had swept you out to sea.

Sis looked beyond the swirling skirts, beyond the bodice beaded with seed pearls, beyond the tiny, long-sleeved lace bolero that covered Emily's arms and shoulders. And that's when she saw it, the darkening skin of her upper arm.

She leaped up and grabbed her sister's arm, leaned close for a better look. It was definitely a bruise. Sis had the sensation of looking into a chasm, one so deep and wide it would swallow them all.

"Em, what is this?"

"It's nothing." Emily pulled her arm away, but Sis pushed her sister's sleeve back until she had uncovered the mottled discoloration of a fading bruise.

"How'd you get this?"

When Emily didn't want to answer a hard question, she got

so still you could pass right by and hardly notice her standing there.

"You know I won't stop till I find out, Em."

"It was an accident, Sis. Really. For Pete's sake." Emily pulled away and pushed her sleeve over the bruise. "I was going down the stairs too fast and fell against the banister. You know how easily I bruise."

Emily was lying. Sis could tell by the way her sister wouldn't look into her eyes.

If rage were a country, Sis would be China. This was her baby sister, the one Sis had loved and fought for, even to the point of cornering the Bible school teacher at Biloxi Baptist Church and threatening to beat the snot out of her if she didn't put a star on Emily's chart.

Looking at her now, Sis wished she'd taught Emily to cuss and fight and stick up for herself. She wished she'd never let her baby sister believe the world was a wonderful place where there would always be a big sister to make somebody give her a star.

"Let's get out of here, Emily." Sis jerked her car keys out of her purse, still so upset they clattered to the hardwood floor.

"I've got to pay for the dresses, and we haven't even found anything for Sweet Mama and Beulah."

"You can't marry this man, Emily. Don't you see that?"

"I'm going to, Sis, and you're wasting your breath if you try to stop me."

Emily swept past her and began going through a rack of dresses underneath a sign that said Mother of the Bride. While Sis was marshaling her next argument, a salesgirl in a designer dress and pearl earrings approached Emily.

"May I help you?"

"Yes. I'd like something for my grandmother in rose."

Feeling helpless, Sis sat back in the ridiculously frilly chair and watched as her sister continued to barrel toward disaster. Even worse, she felt like an outsider looking in as Emily selected dresses for Beulah and Sweet Mama without even turning to ask Sis's opinion.

At what point should a big sister let go of the little sister she's cared for all her life?

Emily glanced at Sis waiting in that lovely pink chintz chair with her brow furrowed and her face stormy. Suddenly, she had the strangest sensation that she was standing in the bridal shop alone. The salesgirl faded until she was nothing more than a shadow, the rack of dresses vanished and even the chair Sis was sitting on disappeared behind a cloud of panic that descended over Emily.

Still clutching the dress she'd picked out for Beulah, she replayed that scene with Larry. It had been awful and unexpected, the kind of shock you'd get if you walked into your bank to withdraw money for a vacation and found yourself facing a robber with a gun.

If Emily were more like Sis, smart and savvy, she'd have seen the argument coming. She'd have taken notice that Larry's silence in the car coming home from the dinner at Sweet Mama's was a signal of a tumultuous inner landscape.

But, no, she marched into her house and straight up the stairs to put Andy to bed. Happy because her fiancé was waiting patiently in the new recliner he'd bought for them. She was even singing, for goodness' sake, totally unaware of the tornado brewing in her own family room.

Andy had wanted a bedtime story, and she read from *The House at Pooh Corner*, a tale about Heffalumps and Woozles and Jagulars that satisfied her son's craving for adventures of every sort. She smiled as she read, thinking that soon Andy would have a new daddy to read these stories with him.

After the story, Andy said his prayers, blessing everybody he could think of, including the astronaut he called Nell Arms Strong and the teddy bear he called Henry, whose fur was almost completely loved off. As always, she gave her full attention to Andy's bedtime ritual. The great thing about Larry was that he understood she would always put Andy's needs before her own, that she would never shirk being a mother just because she was getting married.

She tucked Andy in, snapped off the light and went back down the stairs. Larry was waiting for her, standing beside the fireplace, holding a silver-framed picture in his hand.

"What is this?" he asked.

It was a picture of Mark in his high school football uniform, his smile so like Andy's her heart broke a little.

"Goodness, you've seen that before. It's just Mark."

"I know who it is. What I don't know is why it's on your mantel."

"Because of Andy."

After she got engaged, she'd tried moving all the pictures to his room, but Andy got so upset over the change, she put them all back.

"You keep pictures of the coward who wouldn't even marry you and give his son a name?"

"That was my fault. Not Andy's." Her face flamed and her voice got squeaky the way it always did when she felt ambushed. Emily hated that about herself. Why couldn't she be more like Sis? She reminded Emily of those sturdy, indestructible tugboats that could plow through all kind of water to guide ships safely into port. "I want my son to know his daddy."

"Worship, you mean." Larry banged the picture down so

hard it rattled the brass candlestick on the mantel. "Just look at all this. Your whole house looks like a damned shrine."

He stalked around the room, snatching her treasures off end tables and shelves, the snapshot of Mark and Emily on the beach that night she'd finally lost her virginity to him, the one they'd taken in Sweet Mama's backyard in front of the rose hedge before he found out he was going to be a father and Emily found out he'd rather join the army than marry her.

Had it been because he was young and scared? Or had it been because she was a girl who couldn't hang on to her morals because the moon was full and the temptation too great?

"Larry, stop it!"

She tried to take her pictures and he grabbed her arm.

She'd never meant for Sis to see the bruise, never meant to be the cause of the little vertical lines that now made a deep groove in her forehead. If her sister weren't careful, that line would become permanent, and then all the Pond's cold cream in the world wouldn't be enough to remove it.

Emily hated that most of all, that she was the cause of Sis's distress. There was no need for her to fret. Larry had been so sincere in his regret, so humble and sweet that Emily had kissed him on top of the head the way she did Andy. Besides, he had a point. What man would want to sit down in his den and stare at pictures of the man who had so easily taken what Emily ought to have saved for her marriage bed? What man in his right mind would want reminders that his wife was tarnished?

She'd move the pictures to Andy's room. That was all. Problem solved. Andy would pout for a while, but he'd get over it.

How could she get Sis to see that everything was going to be all right? It really was. As soon as she was Mrs. Larry Chastain, her son would have a father and she could hold her head high. And this fall, when Andy started school, nobody would dare call him names. Not that they had, at least not in her hearing. But she'd rather be swallowed up by the Gulf than be the cause of somebody calling her son *illegitimate*.

Emily gathered up the skirt of the wedding dress she still wore and headed toward the dressing room. The gown was buttery soft, the blushed color of the sky just as the sun peeks over the horizon. Emily had always loved that time of morning, a new day where birds sang in the gardens, the air smelled fresh and anything at all might happen, something so wonderful you'd find yourself stopped in your tracks, no matter what you were doing, just standing there smiling because it felt so good to be alive.

Her optimism restored, Emily got back into her clothes and paid for her purchases. Sis was still sitting in that pink chair, morose as ever.

"Are you coming, Sis?"

When she didn't reply, Emily marched to the car, her arms full of purchases and her back stiff. She had her pride.

By the time she'd stowed her packages in the trunk, Sis had come out of the shop and climbed behind the wheel. Through the rear window, Emily watched her reach into the car pocket for a cinnamon candy. Sis always did that when she was upset.

Wishing she could think of something to lift her sister's mood, Emily crawled into the passenger seat. The sun was setting, turning everything in its path a rosy hue. Still, the dead quiet as Sis drove along stole Emily's satisfaction with the view. When she and Sis were together, talk flowed continuously between them, as effortless as waves lapping against the shore.

Finally, her sister sighed, and an overwhelming tenderness rose in Emily.

"Emily, do you love him?"

"Oh, Sis…" Emily turned to face the Gulf. How could she explain to her sister that sometimes you don't get what you want; you learn to want what you can have?

"You don't have to marry him, you know."

"Yes, I do."

"Just because the dresses are in the trunk doesn't mean you can't back out."

The sun dipped lower, shading the inside of the car purple, but even the shadows couldn't hide Emily's determination as she turned back to face her sister.

"Larry's willing to overlook my past, Sis."

"But you've survived all that, Em. The worst part is over."

It was true that the whispers and a reputation in tatters no longer clung to her as thick as pollen from the mimosa tree near Sweet Mama's rose hedge, but what of Emily's dream? As long as she could remember, she'd always wanted a home where the family room rang with children's laughter, and the kitchen smelled so fragrant with yeast-rising bread her husband would nuzzle her neck.

"Sis, I won't have Andy go through what I did."

"Things are different now. Besides, that's no reason to marry the first man who comes along."

"Larry's not perfect, but neither am I."

"You're as close as they get."

"Good grief, Sis. You *know* I'm not. I'm just a woman who is lucky enough to have found somebody to marry me."

"There are plenty of really wonderful men out there who would worship the ground you walk on."

"Then why haven't you found one?"

Sis set her mouth in a straight, hard line, a sure sign she wasn't going to get into a discussion about her future.

Emily remembered the first boy her sister had ever dated,

a pimply faced redhead named Glen Woods. Watching her sister dress for the date, Emily's six-year-old heart longed to be all grown-up so she could wear stockings and high heels and paint her lips pink. She remembered Sis's prom date, too, a boy so tall he almost had to stoop to get through the doorway. Sis had worn a green taffeta dress that made her look like a movie star. Emily used to sneak into her sister's room and sit on the floor of her closet just so she could feel the cool taffeta between her fingers.

One day Sis caught her, but she hadn't been mad.

"What are you doing in my closet, sweet pea?" she asked.

"It smells like you."

Emily still loved to be near her sister. It was not the scent of green taffeta that drew her now, but something more potent, more substantial. If courage and loyalty had a name, it would be Sis.

Watching her sister drive along tight-lipped, Emily couldn't remember the last time Sis had dated, let alone worn a pretty dress. Thank goodness her wedding would remedy that. For one day, at least, Sis would be feminine and frilly. And maybe, just maybe, that might set her to thinking about making a few changes in her life. Why, Emily would bet if Sis started wearing pretty clothes and letting her true heart shine through, she'd attract a really nice man like Larry.

Emily's question still hung in the air between her and her sister.

"See! You can't even answer that," Emily said. "Now that Jim's home and I'm getting married, you can start taking care of yourself for a change."

"Good God, Emily. Is that why you're getting married? So I'll be free?"

"I just want to be happy, that's all." Emily reached over and squeezed her hand. "Be happy, Sis. For all of us."

The list of things that bothered Sis was so long, Emily wondered if her sister had been born with a defective gene, one that would forever cause her to look on the gloomy side of life. She could hardly wait until the wedding. That was going to change everything.

She settled back into her seat, and watched for the first glimpse of the pink house. She couldn't wait to show Sweet Mama and Beulah their dresses. Beyond the avenue of stately live oak trees, the house suddenly came into view.

Beulah was waiting for them on the front porch. Picturing a welcoming smile and a cool pitcher of sweet tea, Emily leaned forward as Sis parked. But it was not a smiling Beulah that lumbered down the steps toward them.

Both sisters barreled out of the car.

"Lord God. I'm glad y'all are here! Jim's done disappeared and Lucy never made it home."

Eight

STILL STANDING ON THE SIDE of the road, Sweet Mama gave the Remembering Book an accusatory glance as it might be the source of all her problems. It was useless in her current situation. She stuffed it back into her purse.

What was she going to do now? If she turned her car around, she would be going in the right direction, but she was so far from her reference point she still didn't know the way home. Even if she accidentally blundered upon the right house, she would be so late getting there everybody would know she'd been lost. And then Sis would never let her drive again.

Her independence would be gone. She'd be just another old woman losing her mind and dreading the day her son Steve and his hissy-fit-prone wife declared it was time to put her in a nursing home.

"Nursing home, my foot."

The sound of her own voice bucked up her courage. Sis was probably looking for her by now. Sweet Mama wasn't about to be caught sitting on the side of the road waiting to be hauled off like garbage.

Humming a little song to keep her spirits high, she climbed

back into her Buick and adjusted her hat. All she had to do was back up a bit and she'd be on the highway heading east once more.

The backing wasn't as smooth as she'd planned. A hateful loblolly pine got in the way. Fortunately, the tree was so small her car bent it double. It would make hardly a dent.

On the road again, she hastened along driving faster than she ordinarily did. The sun was rapidly sinking, and her last-ditch plan would be useless if she couldn't see what was along the side of the road.

For a while, she saw nothing except a formation of pelicans sailing along the coastline. The Gulf was already losing its sunset glow. Soon it would be dark and everything around her would blend into a forbidding blur.

Just when she was about to lose heart, she saw a row of squat buildings, pink stucco with a flashing neon sign. Sand Dunes Motel it said, and underneath Lodging and Food. She just hoped the café wasn't on the back side of the motel.

Sweet Mama pulled into the parking lot, mindful to stay far away from the pole that held up the sign. She didn't fancy bashing in the front of her Buick.

Getting out of the car, she surveyed her surroundings. The motel was right on the side of the highway and the parking lot was well lit. It would be easy for Sis to see the big Buick parked in plain view.

Sweet Mama gave a little nod of satisfaction, then went into the motel lobby, a dreary place with brown walls and plenty of room, but not a chair in sight. Where did they expect folks to sit down and rest?

A tired-looking woman who had ruined her face with too much sun said, "May I help you?"

"I'm looking for the café."

"Just past the newspaper rack."

Exactly where was that newspaper rack? Standing in the middle of the Mexican tile floors, Sweet Mama searched in every direction. Panic was about to set in when she spotted it by an arched opening. It was the same dark color of the tiles, and it blended in.

Much to her relief, the café was right beyond the arched opening where it ought to be and she soon found herself seated in a booth overlooking the parking lot. There was her Buick, sturdy as a land barge, and there was the highway, a dark ribbon glowing with headlights. Sweet Mama's heart sank. In the dark, she couldn't see whether the headlights belonged to Sis's car or a Peterbilt rig. She couldn't tell whether she was looking out at a highway that would take her home or a backyard where the thunderstorm cracked the mimosa tree in half. Terror overcame Sweet Mama and she covered her mouth lest the bitter taste of fear escape and poison them all.

Lost in memories, she saw the twins asleep in their little beds and Sis with her stubborn hair held back by bobby pins and her face bent into an algebra book. She saw the lightning that tore the sky in half and the backyard lit with a glow that looked like the pits of hell.

"It's coming down," Beulah had yelled, and the tearing of tree limbs sounded like somebody screaming in the dark, somebody crying out to Sweet Mama.

"Ma'am? Ma'am?"

Sweet Mama jerked and found herself sitting at the Sand Dunes Motel with a brown-haired girl standing beside her. What was Sis doing calling her *ma'am*?

"Are you ready to order now, ma'am?"

The name tag on the girl's mustard-colored uniform said

Abagail, and she was not Sis at all, but a waitress who had caught Sweet Mama lost in time.

She hadn't even looked at the menu, hadn't even thought about what she might order. Her hands shook and the words blurred. Was that *catfish* or *crawfish?*

"I'll have the catfish?" She hated that she sounded hesitant, an old woman losing her eyesight as well as her grip. It was a great relief when the girl who reminded her too much of Sis as a teenager wrote down the order and left.

Catfish was the first thing she and Beulah had added to the menu after they decided to turn their bakery into a café. The Great Depression was on and nobody had the money to buy cakes and pies.

"What are you gonna do now?" Beulah had asked.

"We're going to expand."

"Expand? Lucy Blake, are you out of your mind?"

"Think about it, Beulah. Nobody's giving parties anymore, but everybody has to eat."

"After we buy the food and fix it, how they gonna afford it?"

"Who said anything about buying food?"

Every Saturday they'd loaded up their fishing poles and Sweet Mama's two boys and went to the Tchoutacabouffa River. Wild and untamed, the river fed into Biloxi's back bay and was filled with shaded spots where saltwater catfish waited to snap up the bait they cast into the deep green water. Their catch was enough to supply the café for a week at a time.

They'd kept it iced down and then cooked it the simple way, dredged in cornmeal seasoned with salt and pepper and deep-fried in a cast-iron pot.

The catfish the waitress brought to Sweet Mama's table

didn't compare to the dish she served. Still, she had more to think about than paying too much for a supper she didn't like.

She glanced anxiously out the window, but the endless stream of headlights along the highway only depressed her. What if Sis didn't find her?

Sweet Mama refused to give in to fear. She'd kept her business going through the Great Depression and three wars, four, counting the one still going on. She wasn't about to let something as simple as being lost defeat her.

If Sis didn't come, she'd check in to the Motel and spend the night. In the morning she'd call the police. And she'd have a good story handy, too. Not some woeful tale of an old woman lost in the dark.

Still, as the patrons in the restaurant began to drift out, Sweet Mama became more and more anxious. The clock on the wall relentlessly marked off minutes. Soon it would be closing time, and she'd be left sitting there without a single option except checking in to a motel where the sheets wouldn't even be starched. She and Beulah always put Faultless Starch in their sheets.

She wished she were home right now, sitting on the front porch with Beulah, drinking a glass of sweet tea and watching the stars. Once Sweet Mama could have named every star in the sky and now the only one she could remember was Venus.

With fresh alarm, she realized she couldn't even name the President of the United States.

"Sweet Mama!"

Thank God. It was Sis, barreling through the archway. Sweet Mama fumbled about, trying to smooth her skirt and pat her hair in place so she'd look like somebody on an innocent outing. By the time Sis was standing over her, she felt flushed and uncertain, even a bit foggy.

"Good Lord, Sweet Mama. What are you doing all the way across the bay?"

"What does it look like? I'm eating supper."

"Without telling anybody?" Sis slid into the opposite side of the booth.

"I'm free, white and twenty-one. I don't reckon I have to tell anybody when I take a notion to drive somewhere for a good plate of fish."

Sis studied Sweet Mama as if she were a frog she planned to dissect.

"You passed right by Baricev's."

Baricev's Seafood Harbor had the reputation of being the best fish house on the Gulf. When the Blakes wanted to eat somewhere besides home or their own café, they usually went there.

"Who wants to go there all the time?" Sweet Mama forked a bite of catfish and started chewing. It was cold and the grease was already congealing in the crust. "If I'd known you were coming, I'd have ordered for two."

Sis didn't reply, which wasn't a good sign. To make matters worse, she reached over and put two fingers on Sweet Mama's wrist.

"Your pulse is high and so is your color."

"Don't even think of calling my doctor."

His name was lost somewhere in the fog. Or maybe, it was written down somewhere in the Remembering Book.

"You got lost, didn't you?" Her granddaughter's face gentled and she held on to Sweet Mama's hand.

"I don't know why you'd say that. I'm clearly enjoying a night out by myself. I get tired of everybody hovering."

"We were all worried about you, Sweet Mama. Why didn't you at least call and let us know you were here?"

The plain fact was that Sweet Mama never once thought of calling home.

"When you've finished eating, I'll take you home, Sweet Mama."

After the big hullabaloo she'd been through, Sweet Mama was scared to drive home. Even if she followed Sis's taillights, it would be all too easy to get lost again in the dark. Worse, what if she mistook the railing on the bridge for a line in the highway and drove straight into the bay?

Still, pride compelled her to pretend otherwise.

"I have my car. I'll drive myself home."

She glanced slyly at Sis, judging her reaction. Thank God, her granddaughter puffed up like a blowfish.

"I've spent all evening driving around looking for you. If you think I'm going to let you get in the Buick and drive off again, you're fooling yourself." Sis chewed at the end of a nail she'd already gnawed down to the nub. "Don't even think about putting up a fuss, Sweet Mama."

"You must have me mixed up with that heifer next door." Sweet Mama hid her relief by bustling around, gathering her purse and signaling her waitress for the check.

"Emily and I will come back and get your car."

"Good. I'll need it tomorrow to drive to work."

"I don't think that's a good idea."

"Sis, if you're going to tell me you're taking my car keys so I can't drive again, I'll not set foot in your car. I'll stand here till Gabriel toots his horn."

She would, too. Letting Sis take her home was one thing, but letting her granddaughter take her independence was entirely another. She knew a dark cloud was just over the horizon waiting to overtake her, but as long as she had the least bit of clarity, she was going to continue living as if she had her whole mind.

"Please, just get in the car," Sis said. "We'll talk about this after we get home."

Not if Sweet Mama could help it. Still, she heaved a sigh of relief as she sank into the passenger seat. Everything was familiar in her granddaughter's car, the blue upholstery, the air that smelled like the cinnamon drops Sis always kept in the car pocket, the way Sis hummed under her breath when she was mulling over a problem.

"There's really no reason for you to keep driving, Sweet Mama. Emily or Beulah or I can take you wherever you want to go."

She closed her eyes and pretended to be asleep. She was too tired to put up an argument. Besides, the bay bridge was coming up and she never had liked crossing a wide body of water in the dark. What if the brakes gave out and the car went over the edge? Would the car sink right away or would it float till they could clamber to safety?

A floating sensation overtook her, and the next thing she knew Sis was saying, "We're home, Sweet Mama."

Her house was standing right where it had been all along, and now she had to add falling asleep when she hadn't intended to the many ways old age was stealing her capacities.

The front porch light was on, and Beulah came rushing out, followed by Emily and Andy. Beyond the doorway she could see Jim leaning on his crutch, staring into the night like he was the one lost. Then he vanished like smoke, as if this smiling family reunion had nothing to do with him.

Sis came around the side of the car and opened her door.

"Let me take your arm, Sweet Mama. I don't want you stumbling in the dark."

It seemed to Sweet Mama that her whole family was stumbling along in the dark. Jim would eventually come around, and Sweet Mama would hang on to her mind long enough to make sure Emily's wedding went off without a hitch.

But what of Sis? You couldn't cut out worry and transform a granddaughter the way you could cut the bones out of a fish and turn it into a fillet.

Even worse, Sweet Mama knew she was part of the problem. As they walked the pathway in the dark, she kept a tight hold on her granddaughter's arm, this role reversal suddenly so stark and painful it felt like knives in her chest.

Nine

As HER SISTER DROVE BACK across the bay to get Sweet Mama's car, Emily sat in the passenger side, wondering how an otherwise perfect day could go so far awry. The way Sweet Mama had looked coming up the steps, hanging on to Sis's arm like a party balloon with the air slowly leaking out, made her want to cry.

If Sis was the lighthouse beacon that steered the family away from sandbars and rocky shoals, Sweet Mama was the anchor that kept them all firmly attached to the magnolia and mint julep land Emily loved. Until today, she thought she'd still be hanging on to that anchor when she was seeing Andy off to college and sitting on the front row of Biloxi Baptist Church watching him marry a lovely girl who would be like a daughter to her.

"Sis, what are we going to do about Sweet Mama?"

"Keep her out of Uncle Steve's clutches, for starters. If he gets wind she drove off across the bay trying to find her way her home, he'll try to put her in a nursing home."

"She'd die."

Emily had seen how the old folks wandered the halls at Seaside Rest, their faces blank, their feet shuffling along in felt slippers, their only hope framed in a question they asked everybody who came through the door. *Can I go home with you?*

She'd been only ten at the time, one of a little group from her Sunday school class who had gone to sing "Jesus Loves You" to the residents there.

Later that evening when Sis was brushing her hair one hundred strokes, she'd asked, "If Jesus loves them, how come they look so sad?"

"They're not sad, Emily. They're just floating along in a little God cloud till they can join their family in a happy reunion in Heaven."

"Like we'll join Mama and Daddy?"

"Exactly like that."

It was only after Emily was grown that she realized Sis believed in happy reunions for everybody except herself.

Outside the car, wind stirred the water into whitecaps and moaned across the seawall, the sound so mournful Emily felt like weeping. Only the sight of Sis, barely visible in the faint lights from the dashboard, kept her from breaking down.

"Sis, did you hear what I said?"

"I heard you. I just get so mad thinking about Uncle Steve I could spit."

Emily's most vivid memory of her daddy's older brother was at the reception in the pink Victorian house right after her mama and daddy's funeral. She'd had little understanding of why her parents were in boxes, and even less of why they had to be buried under the ground. Filled with fear and sorrow and covered with cookie crumbs and mucus, she'd raced toward Uncle Steve, who was sitting in a rocking chair on the front porch. With her arms wide-open, she'd expected to be lifted into a hug that felt like starched shirts and smelled like tobacco and sunshine.

"Good God," he'd said, holding her at arm's length. "Ethel, take this child in the bathroom and clean her up before she ruins my suit."

She'd been marched off with Aunt Ethel, who was starch from head to toe and had a face like a hatchet. Nobody would want to sit on her lap.

Now Emily told Sis, "So could I," though she was rarely angry, and could think of no other people in Biloxi she'd like to spit on.

"Sweet Mama's not going to a nursing home, Em. I can promise you that. She took care of us and we're going to take care of her."

"Maybe we can find ways to help her remember."

Flash cards came to mind, and little signs Emily could tape to the furniture. Chair they would read, and Table, giving Sweet Mama clues to the surroundings that were slowly becoming as strange to her as if she'd entered a foreign land.

Now that she had a plan, Emily was so relieved she didn't even get depressed again when Sis asked her about Jim. The telling brought her search vividly to mind, the desperation she'd felt, the way it seemed all the air had gone out of her car and she might never be able to breathe again.

Still, Emily had known just where to look. This twin brother, this other half of her, would go to their childhood haunt, their thinking place, their secret hideaway under the pier near the lighthouse.

She'd found him there, hunkered down in the sand, staring out over the water as if he could see all the way to Ship Island, one of the barrier islands that had always been part of their childhood escape plan.

In case we ever need to run away, Jim used to tell her, and Emily loved her brother too much to say that she could think of no reason they'd ever need to flee. *I can steal a little skiff, and you can help me row, Em.*

What was he thinking as he sat there so still that the seagulls flew in close and the terns paid him no mind? Was he still thinking of escaping to an island, one not merely ten miles away but so remote it would take years of searching to find him?

Emily removed her sandals and walked toward her brother, leaving her footprints in the sand beside his, a trail they could follow home, a path they could navigate together back to safety. She sat down beside him, her silence a perfect match to his, and leaned against his shoulder. His arm stole around her and they sat that way, without explanations and accusations, until the first stars popped out.

Finally, Jim said, "I lost track of time."

"I know," she said, then stood up and held out her hand. "Let's go home, Jim."

By the time Emily had finished telling about Jim, the Sand Dunes Motel was in sight with Sweet Mama's sturdy Buick still sitting under the light pole where she'd left it.

They got out of Sis's car to stretch their legs, and finally Sis handed her the Buick's keys.

"I'll see you back at the house, Em. Drive carefully."

"I was planning to run into the ditch just to add a little excitement to the day."

They both started giggling, and their giggles soon became great heaves of laughter that had them hanging on to each other, limp with release and relief.

Sis was the first to recover. She got into her car and pulled out of the motel parking lot, and Emily was close behind. Though she knew the way home and would never in a million years get lost, she kept her sister's taillights always in sight.

It seemed to Emily that she'd been following Sis all her life, that as long as she could keep the light of her sister in view, she could always find her way home.

If you'd told Sis this awful day would end with her sitting in a tent in the backyard while Emily and Andy raced around the yard trying to catch starlight on their tongues, she'd have said you were crazy. And yet, here she was, sitting cross-legged on the lumpy tent floor, finishing off the last of the Amen cobbler Emily had brought.

In addition to everything else, Emily had insisted on putting the tent by the rose hedge. If Sis hadn't been equally insistent on the opposite side of the yard under the mimosa tree, her sister would probably have driven a tent stake right through the bones.

Sis couldn't think of a single thing that was good about this day except the sight of her too-big sunglasses perched on Andy's little face.

"Come join us, Sis." Emily leaned over and smiled at her through the tent flap. With the moon lighting up her face and hair, she looked like a star that had fallen from the sky and landed right at Sis's feet.

She'd as soon drop face-first into a cauldron of boiling soup as romp around the yard pretending that everything was all right when she could see the mound of dirt under the rosebush, raw as an open wound. Still, she caught her sister's hand and let herself be dragged around the yard with her tongue stuck out.

Andy raced toward them, laughing and yawning at the same time, and Emily finally led him into the tent. The minute he grabbed that beat-up little teddy bear and shut his eyes, he was fast asleep, one arm thrown back and his face decorated with cookie crumbs.

If you didn't know what lay under the rosebush, you'd be content to sit on the quilt and make lazy conversation. But if you were Sis, you'd look anxiously at the Don Juan to make sure the moonlight didn't show a bone sticking out of the ground, stark as fear.

"Em, do you remember what happened to that other mimosa tree? The one that used to be where the rose hedge is?"

"It's been gone so long the only thing I remember is that I had a tree swing there."

"No, your swing was always on this tree."

"Oh, I remember now. I wanted it on the other tree, but Beulah said no."

Regret sharp as cinnamon wafted off the remains of the Amen cobbler, and Sis wrapped her arms around herself to hold back a shiver. Who was regretful and why?

"Did she say why?"

"Good Lord, Sis, I don't know. I was just a kid."

Emily stretched out on the quilt, a beautiful patchwork Beulah and Sweet Mama had made years ago with scraps left-over from the Blake girls' homemade school dresses. Rolling onto her stomach, she propped herself on elbows and gazed through the tent flap.

"Look at that moon, Sis. If astronauts can walk around up there, can you imagine what other wonderful things are in store for us?"

"The space program will take off now."

"No, I mean us. All the Blakes." Emily smiled up at her. "Though I guess after Sunday I'd better start thinking of myself as a Chastain."

"Why? You'll always be a Blake."

"You're right." Emily took off her ponytail band and shook out her hair. "Besides, Larry is so nice he won't care if I call myself Emily Sue Ledbetter. Do you remember her, Sis?"

"Do I remember her! Good Lord, you got so mad when your second grade teacher mixed the two of you up and kept calling you Emily Sue, I had to go to school and straighten her out."

"You did, too. I never knew how you managed that."

Sis couldn't recall the details. All she knew was that she'd learned fierceness sitting on the side of the highway, watching her parents die in twisted wreckage, fierceness and a stubborn determination that she would never again be a bystander while one of her family vanished before her eyes.

"I'm too stubborn to take no for an answer, I guess," Sis said.

"You're not stubborn. You're a kind of wonderful I can never hope to achieve." Emily rolled onto her back and closed her eyes. "'Night, Sis."

Her sister's generous opinion bloomed through Sis like the moonflowers growing along the side of the garage. Too full to settle down, Sis sat beside Emily until her sister's breathing signaled the change from light sleep to deep. The slight upward curve of her lips told of dreams that made her smile.

Beyond the tent flap the backyard took on an ethereal look, a moonscape filled with light and shadow and the secret of bones. Suddenly, a moving shadow appeared in the yard, an apparition who knew the value of stealth. Her heart pounding, Sis squinted through the night until she could make out the details, a lanky body, blond hair glinting in the moonlight, the unmistakable silhouette of a crutch.

Careful not to wake Emily, Sis crawled from the tent and started toward her brother just as he disappeared around the oleander bush at the side of the garage. The clang of metal against metal echoed through the darkness, and she picked up her pace.

"Jim?" she called out. "What are you doing out here?"

What if he was leaving again, this time for good?

"Go back to the tent, Sis," he called. "This is none of your concern."

She smelled the smoke before she rounded the corner and saw the glow of his cigarette. Jim was balanced on one leg against the side of the garage, his crutch propped up beside him.

Sweet Mama would have a conniption if she saw him smoking. She'd banned cigarettes from the house when they were growing up, and she'd have plenty to say now. What she didn't understand was how a teenage boy would find small ways of rebellion, and how a big sister who only wanted her brother to be happy would sometimes join him in a forbidden smoke.

"Hand me one, too," she told Jim.

She hated the bitter taste of tobacco and the idea of what inhaled smoke might do to her lungs, but even more she hated the thought of this broken-to-pieces brother smoking in the dark alone. As she leaned against the garage beside him she wondered if it were possible for silence to convey what her brother refused to hear in words. *I will always be beside you. I will hold you when you cry and pick you up when you fall. I will never let you carry your burden alone.*

They stayed that way, side by side in perfect stillness, until the cigarettes were reduced to a glowing nub you could barely hold without burning yourself. Jim tossed his stub and ground it out with the tip of his crutch, then hobbled back to the house.

Sis ground hers under the toe of her sandal, then bent to

pick up both stubs and toss them into the garbage can. But something was catching the lid. She prowled around in the dark till she found a stick to pry it up. It came off with a loud pop, and there among the tomato peelings lay Jim's prosthetic leg. Moonlight glinted on the metal, and tomato juice stained the straps.

There are a thousand ways to break a heart. As Sis picked the leg out of the garbage can and headed back to the house, she told herself over and over, *I will not cry.*

Passing by the tent to check on her sister and Andy, she found Emily still smiling in her dreams and Andy hanging on to that old teddy bear. Sis glided on by, her shadow ghostly on the sides of the canvas. Maybe that's what she was, the mere shell of a woman who had died by the side of the road along with her parents, a ghost whose name nobody bothered to remember.

She went quietly through the back door and into the kitchen. Placing the prosthetic leg on the draining board, she began to clean off the tomato peelings.

She didn't know how long the process took, didn't want to know, didn't even glance at the hall clock as she stowed the leg in the downstairs coat closet. She'd think of a way to deal with it later.

By the time she went back outside, clouds had gathered over the stars. In the dark Sis slid back into the tent, never even looking toward the raw earth underneath the rosebush. Then she lay down on the quilt beside her sister and closed her eyes.

But her dreams didn't make her smile.

Ten

A RED BIRD FLYING against the window woke Sweet Mama up. She'd heard that a bird trying to get into the house was bad luck. Or had she just made that up? Was it the sight of wings the color of blood beating against the glass that made her hold on to her heart as if any minute it might fly out of her chest and leave her behind on the bed, an old woman in a billowy white nightgown, struggling to catch her breath?

She threw back her sheet and heaved herself upward, then walked to the window. It was still partially dark outside with just a few pale fingers of light beginning to show, but that was enough to see a figure under the mimosa tree. What was Peter Blake doing coming home at this hour? If he'd been with that bunch of gambling fools and lost the money needed for the house payment, she was going to teach him a lesson he wouldn't forget.

Her gun was in the hall closet. If she could just get to it before he saw she was awake, she'd put a scare into him that would make him think twice about frittering their money away on cards. Beulah would help her. She always helped.

Her gown flew out behind her as she hurried toward the front hall.

Without snapping on a light that might alert her husband, she went straight to the front hallway and eased open the coat closet. But it was not her shotgun she found among the folds of the coats, it was a leg. Feeling disoriented, she sank onto the velvet-covered bench beside the umbrella stand. What was a leg doing in her closet?

And where was her gun?

She hung her head and stared down at her gown. It had white lace on the sleeves and two tiny pearl buttons on the bodice. She'd bought it at J. C. Penney during the lingerie sale in January. With a growing sense of alarm she realized the figure on her lawn couldn't be her husband. That had been in 1920.

And the shotgun she was looking for was long gone. Sis took it when Sweet Mama thought poachers were in the back-yard stealing chickens.

We don't have chickens, Sweet Mama, Sis told her, then she hid the shotgun somewhere under lock and key.

Sweet Mama wiped sweat off her face. Until she could fig-ure this thing out, the best she could do was keep the leg safe. Somebody was bound to come looking for it.

She carried it back to her room and set it on her dresser where it would be in plain sight. It was hard to forget some-thing in plain sight.

Sounds drew her back to the window, and she watched while a little boy came streaking across the yard. At first she thought he was her son Bill, but that would mean she was young and skinny, not some fat, old woman standing at the window with a long, gray braid hanging over one shoulder and memories that gave her nightmares.

There was a woman right behind him. Thank God it was

Sis, the strong-willed granddaughter nobody could forget, even a woman whose mind was rapidly becoming a sieve.

Emily followed behind, calling for Andy, and the three of them headed toward the house, laughing.

Sweet Mama wanted to cry. Instead, she got her Remembering Book and opened it to a blank page.

"I am Lucy Long Blake," she wrote. "It is 1969." July or August? She couldn't recall. All she knew is that it was the hottest summer she remembered.

I live in a pink Victorian house facing the sea. My address is 1629 Highway 90, Biloxi, Mississippi. I own a café called Sweet Mama's. I was born January 8th, 1894. I am 75.

My granddaughters are Sis and Emily. My great-grandson is Andy. The girls are...

How old were they? Surely she would remember the day they were born, first Sis and then ten years later, Emily. She recalled the smile on Bill's face and the way Margaret looked on their big four-poster bed, pale but happy. She rubbed her hand across her face, but the dates still eluded her.

"They are grown," she finally wrote, "but Andy's just a little boy."

My best friend is Beulah. She is the greatest woman I know, black or white. She cut the mimosa tree down.

The lightning had been fierce that night. Sweet Mama thought they'd be struck.

Her last sentence leaped out at her, and she read it with alarm. She marked through it till not a single word showed, her hands shaking so hard she could barely hold the pen. Then she wrote another sentence.

"I drive the Tin Lizzie." No, that wasn't right. She crossed it out and wrote, "I drive a black Buick."

"My telephone number is…" Sweet Mama racked her brain for the numbers but nothing came of it except a headache and a sick feeling in the pit of her stomach.

"Lucy?" It was Beulah, calling from outside the bedroom door. "Are you up?"

"I'm up."

"Do you need me to come in and help you with anything before I go down to start breakfast?"

"No, thank you, Beulah. Everything's fine."

"Well, you hurry on down now, you hear? Emily's gonna show us them dresses you was too tired to look at last night."

It would help her to be amongst her family, listening to them talk about everyday things, watching them go about the business of living. Lately, she'd found herself watching Sis to see whether she ought to pick up the fork or the spoon to eat her pie.

She hurried with her bath and put on a yellow seersucker dress. Lightweight and short-sleeved, it was made for the hot weather. How soon would the day come when she needed Beulah to help her dress for the season? Would she walk into the middle of a hundred-degree day wearing wool? Is that how it would happen? Or would she let something slip, something so terrible it would ruin them all? *I'm just teasing* wouldn't cover that kind of awful downward spiral of the mind.

Still, as she faced the mirror so she could see to wind her braid into a coronet, she was proud that she still knew how to choose a summer dress.

There was a leg on her dresser. Good Lord, when had Jim put it there? He must have come in with the leg while she was in the bathroom. She wondered whether she ought to take it to him, then decided that if he wanted to stow it there a while, she'd just leave it. If the sight got to bothering her, she could always hang a hat over it.

She grabbed her purse and walked out, closing the door behind her. She was halfway to the kitchen before it occurred to her that she'd forgotten to add her grandson's name to the Remembering Book. If she went back to do it now, she'd be late and everybody would start fretting over her.

Putting a little extra pep into her step, she hurried into the kitchen. Beulah and Sis were already having coffee. Andy was stuffing cookies into a paper sack while Emily smiled over the tops of two pink-and-white-striped dress boxes. Jim was nowhere to be seen.

"Sweet Mama, you look so nice," Emily said, hugging her. "Wait till you see what I got for you and Beulah!"

When Emily whisked the dresses out of the boxes, Sweet Mama was reminded of Christmas mornings gone by. This lovely granddaughter who shared her love of cooking had always been the one to add a high note of excitement to the holiday.

Today, everybody in the kitchen caught Emily's excitement, everybody except Sis. She just looked on over the rim of her coffee cup.

Emily held up a dress the color of roses, the real thing, not the plastic ones Sweet Mama had attached to the bushes to make the heifer next door envious. What had happened to those roses?

"Don't you just love it, Sweet Mama? And look…" Emily pulled another dress from the box, the same color in a darker shade. "Beulah, you'll be gorgeous in this."

"That would take an act of God, but this comes close." Beulah held her dress in front of her and pranced around the kitchen. "First one that says I ain't pretty in this outfit is gonna get his block knocked off."

Beulah folded the two dresses and put them back into the boxes. "Now, y'all come on and let's eat before everything gets cold."

They gathered around a table piled with sausage and eggs and biscuits and the sawmill gravy Beulah always made with lots of milk and plenty of black pepper.

"Andy," Emily said, "do you want to say grace?"

He blessed everybody at the table and even a few people Sweet Mama didn't know, but she noticed he didn't bless Gary.

"Honey, you forgot about Larry. Don't you want to add him since he's going to be your new daddy?"

Good Lord. *Larry.* Sweet Mama still hadn't added him to the Remembering Book. Now that he was going to be a member of the family, she might as well. But that didn't mean she had to like him.

Picking up her fork without even having to check which utensil Sis was using, Sweet Mama felt her day taking an upward turn. She could recall every ingredient of every recipe she'd created, right down to the eighth of a teaspoon. As soon as she got to the café, she was going to write them all down while her thinking was still clear as a bell.

After breakfast, Emily and Andy hurried off to the café, a reminder that Sweet Mama ought to get her purse.

"I'll be right there," she called after them.

"Sweet Mama," Sis said. "I don't think you ought to go to the café today."

"I don't know why not. It's my café."

"I know that. I just don't think you ought to be driving today."

"I can drive as good as anybody. I'm going."

Determination screamed from every pore as Sweet Mama scrambled in her purse and came up with car keys.

Sis rubbed her temples. "Beulah, I'm going to stay here a bit and check on Jim. Since Sweet Mama's so all-fired determined to go, can you drive?"

"I can drive as good as you," Beulah said, then held out her hand to Sweet Mama. "Lucy, if you'll hand over them keys I'll do the hard work and you can enjoy the scenery."

Sweet Mama wasn't about to admit to Sis or anybody else how relieved she was to hand over the keys, especially after that little episode of going the wrong way on the bridge.

She held her head high as she went outside and climbed into the car. Then she watched with a bit of envy as Beulah backed out of the driveway without hitting a single bush or tree. Soon they were on Highway 90, going along a modest pace, which made both of them comfortable and conversation possible.

"You got lost yesterday, didn't you, Lucy?"

"Yes, but don't tell Sis."

"Don't you think that girl knows? Nothing escapes her sharp self. She's just going along with your pretense because she's got so much else on her plate."

"Beulah, I'd be scared if I didn't have you."

"Well, you got me, Lucy Blake, and don't you be forgetting it."

Beulah had come into her life when she married Peter Blake in 1911.

"Here's your maid," Peter had told her.

But Sweet Mama had never thought of her as anything except a friend. She and Beulah had been hardly more than children, seventeen, and both newlyweds who depended on each other to learn the mysteries of becoming a woman.

She and Beulah had been together through the births and weddings of both Sweet Mama's boys. They laughed together over the births of Sweet Mama's grandchildren, and cried over the deaths of her son Bill and his wife, Margaret. They mourned Beulah's inability to have children and the death of her beloved husband, Eustace, who had dropped dead of a heart attack behind the plow at the young age of thirty-four.

That's when Beulah moved into the house with Sweet Mama, and there she had stayed, more sister than friend, bound by shared history and love so strong nothing could break them apart.

"Beulah, do you like Emily's fiancé?"

"He's got the evil eye."

"He could use a big helping of Amen cobbler," Sweet Mama said, and they both laughed.

"Lord, Lucy, if Amen cobbler had the magic folks said, me and you'd be rich."

"I reckon it's got enough magic for us, Beulah."

Remembering all they'd been through together, Sweet Mama turned to enjoy the sea coast. She never tired of the view—the seabirds sailing over the water, the pristine white sand dotted with umbrellas as colorful as snow cones and the tourists who flocked to the longest man-made beach in the world. The summer heat bore down on them today, and though Sweet Mama remembered with a certain nostalgia the sweet summer days at the beach with her own children, she was happy to be cool inside her car and even happier to arrive at the old brick café guarded over by ancient live oaks dripping with Spanish moss.

As she got out of the Buick, Sweet Mama felt herself filling up from the inside, strength and memories flowing through her like an untamed river. Through the window she saw Emily at the coffee urns getting ready for the breakfast crowd.

As long as Sweet Mama had the café, she would be all right.

★ ★ ★

The kitchen was empty now, with only a lingering scent of fried bacon overlaid with the White Shoulders eau de toilette Emily loved to use. Sis tried to suck in air, but the idea of Emily's wedding to a slick manipulator made it impossible to breathe.

She raced outside where the air was already so hot it shimmered. Not even the breeze coming off the Gulf could lift the blanket of heat that had Biloxi in its grip. Sis found herself wishing for snowflakes and icicles and rivers so cold your fingers would turn blue the minute you dipped them into the water. She longed for parkas and snowshoes and a remote log cabin high in the mountains where you'd have to have sled dogs to find her and her family.

Her stride was determined as she crossed the yard, her grip fierce as she snatched canvas off poles and jerked tent anchors out of the ground. By the time she'd dismantled the tent and stowed it in the garage on a shelf beside Jim's convertible, she was sweating so much she figured she'd need another bath.

She glanced at the darkened second-story windows, a stark reminder that she didn't even know how to bathe with Jim in the house, whether to tiptoe around her own bathroom or run the shower full blast and hope it gave him a reason to get out of bed.

Fueled by determination so deep you couldn't see the bottom with a telescope big enough to find the man in the moon, Sis marched back into the house. She thought about veering by the hallway to retrieve the prosthetic leg she'd left in the coat closet, but decided, instead, to continue her march up the stairs.

When she was standing outside Jim's door, she knocked twice, sharp raps that showed she meant business. Receiving no answer, she barged inside and snapped on the light.

Jim cowered against the headboard, his hands and arms in a defensive position, his eyes staring at a horror only he could see.

"Oh, my God." Sis covered her mouth with her hands.

He came to himself slowly then lowered his arms. Affecting a slouch against the headboard, he reached for his cigarettes.

"I'm sorry, Jim." She silently berated herself for not having realized how years of jungle warfare had trained him to expect the enemy at every sound. "I should have known better."

Uncertain now, she lingered by the door, watching Jim fill the distance between them with blue smoke. Finally, she opened the window so Sweet Mama would never know about the cigarettes, though that was probably just wishful thinking, considering the way her mind was drifting off.

Sis went back to Jim's bed and perched on the edge, hoping her nearness would wipe away the sounds of gunfire and screams.

"If you've come to talk about yesterday, just don't, Sis."

"I'm not. I thought we might load up the boat and go fishing today."

"Deep sea?"

"We can. Or I was thinking we'd go to the Tchoutacabouffa. It's a beautiful day. We could ride in your convertible with the top down."

While he stared into space, she tried to remain positive, but her imitation of Emily's optimism probably didn't fool her brother.

"The trailer hitch is still on the Thunderbird," she added, "and I can fix a picnic in the kitchen."

What would he do if she folded him in her arms and soothed him the way she had that night when he was four and crying because he'd dropped his ice cream on the sidewalk or when he was scared of a storm?

"I don't want to fish, Sis."

"Okay, then. Why don't you come down to the café with me? I know all the regulars would love to see you."

"I'm not ready to talk to people. And if I sat in the kitchen moping around, I would just cause Emily to worry." He stubbed out his cigarette. "Go on to the café, Sis. Em needs you to help get ready for her wedding."

The secret of their sister's bruise suddenly felt too heavy to bear. Still, Sis rose from the bed and headed toward the door.

"Breakfast is in the kitchen, Jim. Promise you'll be here when we get back, or at least call the café and tell us where you'll be."

"Maybe I ought to just get my own place. It would be easier for everybody."

"Don't you even think about that until you get your feet on the ground."

"What feet?"

Irony tinged with bitterness played across his face as he lifted his stump of a leg then quickly hid it back under the sheet. Sis wanted to go to Washington and shake everybody involved in sending America's young men to a place that was more torture field than war zone.

"Jim, I found your leg and put it in the hall closet. I do hope you'll wear it for Emily's wedding."

"I'm not going to watch my sister marry that 4F piece of shit."

"I don't like it, either, but I'm going to that wedding."

"Fine. Just don't expect me to stand by and watch Em walk into a land mine."

"What do you know that I don't?"

Jim stared at the wall beyond her, and though Sis could still see him on the bed, it seemed to her that he was walking past, trailing a wake of fear so unbearable it left her chilled.

"Tell me, Jim. What have you seen?"

The heavy silence lasted awhile longer, and then he grabbed the crutch leaning against his nightstand and hobbled to the window where he stood with his back to her.

"Do you want to know how I lost my leg?"

Oh, God. "Tell me."

"It was early morning, beautiful if we didn't know what waited in the jungle. My patrol headed out. Though I'd done it a hundred times before, something was different about that day."

He went very still, but Sis didn't dare say anything. Even breathing felt like an invasion of her brother's private hell.

"I could *smell* the evil, *feel* it. Though I couldn't see it, I knew it was there—the land mine that blew my leg off and would have done worse if I'd hit it dead center."

He lit a cigarette, inhaling and exhaling until he was almost hidden behind a curtain of blue smoke.

"That's what it's like with Em's fiancé. I smell the evil."

Sis lingered in his doorway, staring through a haze of blue smoke and through the window to what lay beyond. The world was a dangerous place, one where a single event could change everything.

She closed her eyes and breathed, simply breathed. Tomorrow her sister was getting married, and she'd rather be anywhere in the world except watching her tie the knot with Larry Chastain.

Eleven

THE MORNING CAME WHETHER Sis wanted it to or not. She rolled over and tried to glare the clock into submission, but it just kept on ticking off the minutes till her sister's wedding. Sis didn't want to call Emily or check on Jim or hurry down to the kitchen, even though the aroma of coffee drifting up the stairs told her Beulah had added chicory.

She pulled the sheet over her face and wallowed around in something resembling self-pity until she finally drifted back to sleep. When she woke up to the sounds of Beulah banging and hollering through her door, it came as something of a surprise to Sis that the world had gone on without her.

"Are you sick in there? Lord Jesus, Sis, if you sick I ain't gonna be able to handle this wedding by myself."

"Coming!" She bolted to the door and opened it to find Beulah in her yellow housecoat with her hair twisted into a dozen pink plastic curlers and a breakfast tray in her hands.

"Thank you, Lord Jesus!" Beulah barged in with the tray and set it on Sis's dressing table.

"What's wrong?"

"Nothing. I just wanted to make sure you wadn't dead in there and a house full a company heading this way." Beulah whisked the cloth off the tray. "Eat everything on it. If you don't keep your strength up, you ain't gonna be able to stand watching Emily marry that coward and slacker."

"I don't know if biscuits will do the trick."

"Add some butter and jelly. That'll help."

"If I thought it would, I'd eat a ton."

"If you eat a ton, you ain't gonna never get into that fancy dress." Beulah marched to the closet and pulled out the god-awful bridesmaid dress, then stood there admiring it from all angles. "Ummm, hmmm. Ain't that pretty?"

"I'm going to look like a pink barge."

"You ain't gonna look like nothing if you don't hurry up and quit your grouching. You gonna be standing here in your gown tail when Emily comes." Beulah took the dress off the hanger, shook it out then laid it across the bed. "Last time you acted like this, I made you stand in the corner."

"I'm too old to stand in the corner."

"You ain't ever too old for nothing."

Beulah marched out without another word, and Sis was left feeling the way she had when she was twelve and Beulah caught her pouting because she couldn't be on the boys' base-ball team. She'd received the same kind of pep talk, one she still remembered as she slathered a biscuit with butter, then washed it down with good, strong coffee.

There's one thing ain't nobody can take away from you, Sis, and that's who you are. And who you are is a smart girl gonna grow up to be a woman who won't let nothing stop her.

She shoved aside her breakfast tray, then grabbed her robe and marched to Jim's room, only this time she tapped lightly. When Jim called, "Come in," she found him standing in the middle of the room with his crutch tucked under his elbow, trying to knot his tie. Sometimes it's not the big surprises that take our breath away, it's the small, everyday miracles that leave us standing in the middle of the room, blinking back tears. Filled with unutterable gratitude, she moved to her brother and reached for his tie.

"What changed your mind?" she said.

"Em."

"Did she call you?"

"No. I just did some thinking, that's all."

"About what?"

"It's like this, Sis. When your best buddy is going into battle, you go with him. Then when the mortar heads your way, you can grab hold and pull him into a foxhole."

"I'm glad you'll be there, Jim. Emily would have died without you at her wedding."

How she could talk around the lump in her throat, she couldn't say. Nor could she tell you where she found the strength to pat his arm and leave to help Beulah set up for Emily's garden wedding without crying. The tears didn't start till she was back in her own room behind a closed door. And then she put her fist in her mouth so her brother wouldn't hear.

She stripped, then went into her bathroom and turned the shower on full blast. With water pouring over her like a baptism, she turned to loose control and stood shaking while heartbreak and fear washed down the drain with her bathwater. But if she expected to climb out of the shower cleansed inside as well as out, she was in for another surprise. All she saw in the bathroom mirror was the same burdened woman, only this time she was dripping wet and wearing a towel that wouldn't fit around her hips.

Good Lord, she'd never be able to get into a horrible bridesmaid dress. She toweled herself off and tried to blow-dry her hair into submission. Then she stepped into her dress and sucked in her stomach enough to get the dratted zipper closed. The mirror confirmed her worst fear: she looked like a pink hippo.

"You look gorgeous!" Emily burst through Sis's bedroom door, hanging on to a fingertip wedding veil and a tiny beaded purse, glowing as if somebody had lit candles under her skin.

"Where's Andy?" Sis asked.

"In the kitchen with Beulah. He looks so cute in his little suit and tie."

"How'd you get him out of the Superman suit?"

"By reminding him he's going to stay with you while I'm on my honeymoon, and you'll probably let him wear it every day."

"I probably will."

Once Sis had asked Andy why he wanted to wear it all the time and he said, *'Cause it makes me feel good*. If she thought a Superman suit would do that for her, she'd buy one. If she could find one big enough.

Emily tossed her veil and purse onto the bed. "Here, let me fix you up."

Her sister grabbed a brush and tackled Sis's hay-bale hair. Finally, she managed to subdue a few strands and pin them to the top of Sis's head where they sat like fat brown sausages. Smiling with satisfaction, Emily whipped a tube of lipstick out of her purse, some hideous rosy color she slathered onto Sis so that now she looked like she'd kissed a baboon. Thank goodness nobody would be looking at her, though she prided herself on not caring what others thought about her. Really, she didn't.

"Sis, you look beautiful!"

"That would be a miracle right up there with turning the water into wine."

But as she turned toward the mirror, Sis was astonished at her own transformation. The woman with a touch of color on her high cheekbones and mascara making her dark eyes look even bigger was attractive, some might even say beautiful in an offbeat sort of way.

"See?" Emily said. "You're gorgeous!"

"I wouldn't go that far." Still, Sis was smiling as she smoothed a dress that had turned out to be flattering.

The sounds of chatter drifted up the stairs as family gathered for Emily's wedding. Sunday mornings, the pink house by the sea was usually quiet, with Beulah and Sis in the kitchen, enjoying a second cup of coffee and Sweet Mama out in the garden talking to the tomatoes. She said that made them perk up and grow because they were alive, just like people.

If you asked Sis, tomatoes were more alive than some people.

Emily grabbed her veil off the bed and put it on. As Sis adjusted it, she noticed the bruise on her sister's arm, yellowing now and barely visible—unless you knew where to look. She wished she were the kind of person who believed in the tender mercy and invisible grace of a God who would lift her sister up so high nothing bad could ever touch her. She wished she believed in prayer that would enclose Emily in a circle of white light so the bruising hands of Larry Chastain could never get through.

Downstairs the front door banged open and the deep voice of Larry Chastain floated up the stairs.

Suddenly, more than anything, Sis wished she had the power to march down the stairs and give her future brother-in-law such a rip-roaring pep talk he would turn into the perfect husband for her sister.

"Sis," Emily said, bringing her back from wishful thinking to the awful reality that she was about to witness her sister moving into the care of a man Sis didn't trust. "Wish me luck?"

"Oh, Em." She wrapped her sister close and held on for a long time, held on as if her own fierceness might magically transfer to this soft sister who still wished on stars.

"Sis?" Emily's voice was muffled against her shoulder.

"Yes?"

"Jim's not wearing his leg." Emily turned out of the embrace and walked to the mirror to adjust her veil. "I hope nobody stares. He's going to hate that."

"If anybody stares, I'll slap them silly. Better yet, why don't I take the leg to him. He just might decide today is the day to wear it." Sis headed toward the door.

"Wait, Sis. You forgot your shoes."

Pumps, for God's sake. With three-inch heels. If it weren't for Emily, Sis would wear her tennis shoes to the wedding. She crammed her feet inside, saying, "Wait right here, Em."

"Of course I'll stay here, silly. It's bad luck for the groom to see the bride before the wedding."

The only luck Sis believed in was the timing that sent her racing down the stairs to retrieve a leg from the hall closet when nobody was looking. At the end of the stairs, she surveyed the area as if she were on a reconnaissance mission with national security at stake.

"What're you doing skulking around here like a thief?" Beulah said.

Standing in the doorway of the kitchen, she barely looked like her old comfortable self. Her gray-streaked hair was in corkscrew curls all over her head and when she moved, her rose-colored skirts gave off the scent of lilac talcum powder.

"Lord, Beulah. You scared me half to death, but you're just the person I need."

"Ain't I always? What do you need, sweet pea?"

One small endearment, just that one little reminder that Sis had needs, too, and she almost came undone. Pulling herself together, she caught Beulah's arm and leaned over to whisper.

"Stand guard and don't let anybody come into the hall."

"How come?"

"I've got to get Jim's leg out of the closet. If somebody stares at him with that pant leg tucked under, Emily's going to cry at her own wedding."

"*I'm* gonna cry at her wedding. One of us is enough." Beulah stationed herself where she could see all entrances to the hall and planted her feet apart. "Go ahead and grab that leg, Sis. Ain't nobody getting past this double-wide trailer."

Sis eased open the closet door, but the leg was nowhere to be seen. Suddenly, remembering that she'd put it farther back, she pushed aside coat hangers and peered into the corner behind Sweet Mama's black winter coat.

"Sis, somebody's coming."

Good grief. Where was her brother's leg? Sis made one last frantic search of the closet before she gave up. One of the bobby pins Emily had put in her hair caught the sleeve of a sweater, and she was still fighting to free herself as Beulah said, "Hurry up, Sis. Here she comes."

Thank God it was only Sweet Mama. With her hair in a silver coronet and a big rhinestone brooch on the shoulder of her dress, she looked like the queen of some small country.

"Thank God I've found you, Sis."

Even better, she seemed to be fully in charge of all her faculties, today of all days when Sis needed her most. Maybe there was invisible grace, after all.

"What's wrong, Sweet Mama?"

"My shoes are missing."

"What kind of shoes?"

"My black patent-leather pumps."

Sis and Beulah glanced down at Sweet Mama's feet. There were the patent-leather pumps, big as you please.

"If I get my hands on who took them, I'm going to wring somebody's neck." Sweet Mama passed a shaking hand across her face, looking so confused Sis didn't dare tell her the shoes were on her feet.

"Don't worry, Sweet Mama. I'll find them."

"I bet that heifer next door took them."

"Lord, Lucy," Beulah said, taking her arm. "Let's get you in the kitchen and have a little snort of that wedding wine. We don't want our baby seeing us puffed up like setting hens."

Sis would have a snort herself if she thought it would do one bit of good. She pushed everything back into the closet and shut the door. For all she knew Andy had found it first and the leg was now a vital part of his rocket ship.

The thought of going back upstairs where her sister was waiting in a wedding dress held Sis in the hallway with her heart hammering so hard she could barely catch her breath. Sounds drifted from the kitchen, Beulah and Sweet Mama laughing over something one of them had said. By now, Sweet Mama would have forgotten about her shoes. Thinking how everyday blessings often come with small heartbreaks, Sis marched up the stairs to face her sister.

"Is everything all right, Sis?" Emily said.

"Everything is just fine, Em."

The thing about little white lies is that you can suddenly find yourself so entangled you forget why you told one in the first place. Sis's head hurt, her feet hurt and her heart hurt.

The sound of music drifting up the stairs was the only thing that saved her—Judy Garland singing "Somewhere Over the Rainbow."

If there was one hopeful thing about the day, it was the fact that her sister had defied Larry in choosing her wedding music.

Emily reached up to pin Sis's awful sausage curls back into place, but as the sisters walked down the staircase, arms linked, one of the curls slipped its pins and bobbed over her ear. At the bottom, they were joined by Andy with his cowlick slicked down and Jim with the leg of his suit folded under. Sweet Mama and Beulah waited for them in the garden, their hats settled rakishly and a telltale spot of red wine on Sweet Mama's bodice. Somebody had moved the brooch in an attempt to cover up the stain. Probably Beulah.

If you were on the outside looking in, you'd see a motley group of people coming unraveled. But if you were Sis, standing at the heart of things, you'd see a sturdy fortress surrounding the bride, the walls so strong they could hold back both heartache and disaster. You'd see a family.

Sis had been right about a garden wedding. The rose hedge looked scraggly, and the heat was awful. Still, as Emily walked toward Larry, his expression told her exactly how he felt, that this was the most important day of his life and she was the most important woman. Emily glanced anxiously toward her son. Andy had made it perfectly clear he didn't want her to marry Larry, and yet there he was, smiling at her. His shirt was untucked and his face bore a smudge that looked suspiciously like chocolate. Emily felt a little tug at her heart. How her son could go from perfectly groomed to scruffy in the time it took to walk from the staircase to the garden was one of those remarkable things a mother treasures about her child.

She smiled wider at her future husband, thrilled with the new life opening up for her.

"That's my granddaughter." Sweet Mama made her announcement from her front row seat in a voice so loud it could be heard above Judy Garland, and then she jumped up and waved.

Beulah stood up, too. "Looking good, sweet pea!" she said, and then she grabbed Sweet Mama's arm and they both sat back down.

Larry looked momentarily taken aback, but oh, Sweet Mama and Beulah had made Jim smile, a sight so welcome Emily felt as if the universe had turned upside down and she was walking toward her future through blue skies.

"Dearly beloved," the little Baptist preacher said, "we are gathered here today to unite this man and this woman in holy matrimony." He was so short Emily could see over the top of his head, and he was sweating so profusely she wondered if somebody ought to get one of the fans Beulah had borrowed from the black establishment, Raymond & Johnson, whose motto was We Provide the Best Funerals in Town.

Though Larry had sweat running down the side of his face, he squeezed her hand and mouthed *I love you,* right in the middle of the preacher's vows. Emily wished she'd thought to write her own. But she wasn't sure how Larry would feel about that, so all in all, it was best just to be traditional.

Somebody had forgotten to turn off the music, and the record was stuck on the line "skies are blue." The preacher was having to shout over Judy Garland, and Andy was tugging at his little tie and eyeing a frog that had hopped over and decided to join the wedding party. If her son started building a frog house, Emily was going to die laughing at her own wedding.

Right in the middle of *I now pronounce you man and wife,*
Sweet Mama said, "What's he saying?"

Beulah said, "He's tying the knot."

Emily felt something expand inside her chest, and she was
certain it was hope. Beulah's pronouncement was better than
anything this little borrowed preacher could have said. As
Larry leaned in for the wedding kiss, she felt like a woman
now bound to her husband with a knot that was well and truly
tied. She turned her cheek for a discreet peck. After all, Larry
didn't like public displays, and wasn't that tacky, anyhow?

You could have knocked her over with one puff when Larry
gave her a kiss that would rival Rhett Butler in *Gone with the
Wind.* Then he dipped her low and treated the audience to
his movie-star smile.

When Larry straightened them up, laughing, Emily turned
to her sister, who stood there with her curls wilting and her
mouth stretched into a fake smile. That was Sis, being brave,
seeing her family through, no matter what toll it took on her.

Emily squeezed her hand. "It's all going to be wonderful,
Sis. Just you wait and see."

"I'm going to be watching to make sure it is." Sis cast a
dark glance at Larry, but fortunately he was looking at Andy
with a new father's consternation.

"You need to get cleaned up, son. It's your mother's most
important day."

Andy crossed his eyes, then trotted over to Beulah who
grabbed a hold and took charge.

"Come here, sweet pea. We're all going down to the café
to eat cake at the reception."

"What's a deception?"

Something rippled through Emily in the way of a dream

that startles you from deep sleep and leaves your heart beating too fast.

"Wedding jitters," she said, and Larry immediately bent close to her.

"What was that, my love?"

"Nothing, darling," she said.

Her family was leaving now, with Sis in the middle of them trying to decide who would ride together and who would drive. Suddenly, she was alone with her new husband, embarking on a new life, while a host of friends waited at the restaurant to send her off with their blessings.

"Let's get out of this heat." Larry grabbed her hand and raced into the kitchen where he backed her against the wall and kissed her till she lost her breath.

"Well, my goodness."

"Welcome to my world, Mrs. Larry Chastain."

She waited for him to say something else, something so reassuring and wise she'd tuck it into her memory so she could take it out through the years and marvel.

Instead, he took her elbow and said, "We'd better get going, Em. We don't want to keep your family waiting."

Before she could get used to being Mrs. Larry Chastain, Emily was standing in front of Sweet Mama's Café reading the sign that said Closed for Emily's Wedding Reception. The gathering inside the café was so heartwarming she stood outside with her wedding veil pushed back and her left hand with the new ring pressed against the window, soaking it all in.

There were the dear old Wilson brothers and Burt Larson over by the punch bowl, all three of them sweating in their summer suits. Near the wedding cake, Sweet Mama and Beulah stood side by side in their pretty new dresses, unmistakably in charge of things.

Larry shifted from one foot to the other. "Let's get inside. The sooner we can leave the reception, the sooner we can get started with the honeymoon."

She felt the exact opposite. Instead of hurrying through her own reception, she wanted to linger over every moment, memorize every face. Still, why shouldn't he be anxious? He'd planned their honeymoon trip as a big surprise. Emily could only imagine how eager he was to load her blue Samsonite suitcase into the trunk of his Bel Air and drive her off to their secret destination.

Her suitcase was waiting in the foyer of the little house that would soon become theirs, stuffed with enough clothes to last a month, though she knew they'd only be gone a week. She didn't know how the café would do without her that long.

And leaving Andy behind was another little heartbreak. She'd wanted him to come with them, and not just for her own selfish reasons. She thought being on the honeymoon might make him feel better about this new family. But that wouldn't be fair to Larry, so she hadn't even asked.

Sweat was running down his face and pooling beside his mouth in deep grooves she'd never even noticed. The poor dear was about to melt in the Biloxi heat. She guessed it was a little cooler where he was from, up there in Kentucky. She hoped she'd get to find out, though she didn't have any fixed notion of whether she would.

"Emily," he said. "I'm about to melt out here."

"Oh, I'm sorry."

She grabbed his hand and hurried inside. Though she tried to keep a hold on Larry, she was soon swept away by the crowd of well-wishers. She winked at her husband over the top of dear, sweet Opal Clemson's head, but she didn't know if Larry saw. If he did, he didn't give a sign.

Miss Opal looked like a little canary, her bright brown eyes peeking out from under a yellow hat and her blue-veined hands curved into tiny claws from years of stretching over the keyboard in the big octaves required by Rachmaninoff and Tchaikovsky.

"My dear, what a lovely reception." Miss Opal's voice moved up and down the treble scale like the music she'd taught since Emily was old enough to remember. She motioned to somebody behind Emily's back. "Come on over here, Michael. There's somebody special I want you to meet."

A big man with a square jaw, dark eyes and black hair moved toward them, not handsome in the traditional way but appealing in the way of a favorite oak tree where you knew you could have a picnic and be safe under the spreading branches, even from sudden showers.

"My great-nephew, Michael," Miss Opal said. "You remember him, don't you?"

"Oh, my goodness! You're the one who used to come every summer and play ball with Sis!"

Emily had been too young to remember, but through the years Sis had told her stories that turned the summer ball games with Michael into legend. She still kept a snapshot of the two of them standing on the beach with their baseball caps on backward, squinting into the sun.

His smile was shy and his handshake hearty. She was still smiling at something he'd said about being in the National Guard when she glanced up to see Larry heading in their direction with his jaw tight. Emily paled, imagining everything from a heart attack to a phone call that had brought bad news

Miss Opal was going on and on about Michael's divorce and his cute little house when Sis moved toward Larry and caught a hold of his arm. Relief flooded Emily. Whatever was wrong, Sis would take care of it.

She tried to follow Miss Opal's chatter about her nephew being an engineering consultant, but Jim was now headed in the direction of Larry and Sis, and her brother didn't look any too happy. Emily didn't know whether to be polite and remain captive to the sweet little old lady, or to race across the room and find out why her siblings were now ushering Larry off to the kitchen.

Were they going to wet a dishcloth in the sink and hold it to his head? Give him a few minutes to sit down out of sight and cool off? The garden had been awfully hot and Emily had the sinking feeling she should never have insisted on keeping everybody out there in the heat for a wedding.

She was just getting ready to excuse herself from Miss Opal when she saw Sis emerge from the kitchen, followed by Jim and Larry. Everybody looked calm, and when Sis headed out the back door and Jim led Larry over to the punch bowl and started chatting, Emily felt such relief at how well the two of them were getting on, she started to enjoy talking with Michael Clemson.

She guessed her relief showed in the way she smiled at him, because when he smiled back she had an amazing epiphany.

"We've got to find Sis," she said. "Do you remember her?"

"How could I forget? She used to beat my socks off at baseball."

Endless possibilities ran through Emily's mind, all of them wonderful. Sis finally finding a good man who would be her match. Sis falling in love. Sis having a wonderful family all her own. They would get together every Friday night, Emily and Larry and Andy with Sis and her new husband. Larry and Michael would grill hamburgers in the backyard while Sis and

Emily laughed over the same thing, domestic choices such as choosing curtains to match the sofa and finding just the right cut of meat for the Sunday pot roast.

She was so excited she grabbed Michael's hand and practically dragged him toward the back door. Sis was in the backyard with Andy, just standing there in the grass with her pretty high heels kicked off and the curls Emily had so carefully fashioned falling down around her ears. Emily wanted to say to Michael, *Wait right here,* and then rush out to tidy up her sister. But that would be embarrassing for everybody, and so she forged forward, counting on this comforting oak tree of a man seeing beyond Sis's dishevelment straight to her good heart.

"Hey, Sis!" Emily called as soon as she was out the door, giving Sis time to pin up her hair and step into her shoes. Instead, she just stood there, her face turning as rosy as her pretty pink lipstick.

"Look who I've found!" Emily expected excitement or at the very least a smile.

"Hello again," Michael said, flashing a smile that was not too forward but still showed his pleasure.

When all Sis said was "Hello," all formal and stiff-necked, Emily's hopes fell.

She wanted to pinch her sister. She wanted to lean over and whisper, *Tell him you're glad to see him.* Instead, she prattled on about Michael's move and his house near Miss Opal and the National Guard.

"He's in my neighborhood, Sis!" she said, hoping for some reaction.

But they stood there like carvings, this sister she loved and this nice, shy man from her childhood who had so much potential.

"I bet they teach you to shoot a gun in the National Garb,"

Andy said, and Michael squatted beside Emily's son, relieved, it seemed to her.

So was Sis. Emily could tell by the way her sister stepped back, her stiff posture relaxing. Still, she rolled her eyes heavenward. Not a good sign. The vision of backyard cookouts faded while Andy grabbed Michael's hand and showed him the rocket ship.

"You want'a see inside?" he said, then without waiting for an answer he opened the little door and Michael squeezed inside. Mostly. His long legs and big feet were left sticking out.

"Relax," Emily whispered, but Sis didn't seem to notice. She just stood there, looking as uncomfortable as Michael Clemson when he finally untangled his long legs and emerged from the rocket ship.

She wanted to tell both of them that being friends with somebody was as easy as grabbing his hand and showing him your rocket ship. Emily had learned a lot from Andy, how you can be upset about something one minute and laughing the next because you saw a mockingbird in the tree chasing a squirrel, or how you can say your prayers with absolute confidence that God is listening, or how you can take a Tide box and build a rocket ship that you fully expect will fly you to the moon.

"I guess I'd better get inside and see about Aunt Opal." Michael had a nice smile and he aimed it straight at Sis. Or so Emily hoped. "It was good to see you again, Beth."

"You, too," Sis said, but she looked like she meant just the opposite. As soon as Michael was out of hearing, she added, "I can't believe you did that, Emily."

"What's the matter with you, Sis? He's your friend."

"For God's sake, Emily, we were twelve years old."

"He's a really nice man, Sis. You ought to invite him over."

"Good Lord! I don't even know him anymore."

"Well, why don't you get reacquainted? He's divorced."

"Available, you mean."

"For Pete's sake, Sis! You once thought he was the best thing to happen to your summer."

"A lot can happen in twenty-two years."

Sis looked like she might be planning to launch into a long list of reasons why she wouldn't invite Michael over or even give him one of her smiles that was so dazzling Emily used to call it Sis Shine. Sometimes she still did.

Instead, her sister reached for her hand. "I know you were only thinking of me, Em, but this is your day. Go find that new husband of yours and have a wonderful honeymoon. I'll take good care of Andy."

Through the café window Emily could see Larry talking with Sweet Mama but peering anxiously over her head, probably searching for his bride. He was extremely handsome in that dark brooding way that always made you wonder what he was thinking.

She caught hold of Sis's hand, and suddenly she didn't want to let go. She didn't want to leave her son and her family and the kitchen in the café where sugar spun magic and spice made you dream of the future.

Emily hugged her sister close and whispered, "Oh, I know you'll take care of my son, Sis."

Finally, Emily let go of Sis and bent to hug Andy.

"You be sweet, you hear? And mind your aunt Sis."

He nodded vigorously, the cowlick she'd tamed for the wedding already loose and standing up like the crest of a curious baby bird. She wanted to hold on longer, but he squirmed away.

"Later, 'gator," he said, bumping his fist against hers.

"After a while, crocodile," she said, but he was already climbing to the top of his rocket ship, his bow tie askew, his shirt a wrinkled mess and his grimy little hand held against his eyes as he peered toward the sky.

"It's almost blast-off time, Aunt Sis," he yelled.

"Almost," Sis said and winked at Emily.

Emily winked back, then went into the café to say good-bye to her twin brother and to find her husband. It was time to blast off toward her new life. She thought it might be as exciting as landing on the shining surface of the moon.

Twelve

THE TIRES OF THE BEL AIR hummed along Highway 10 and Emily smiled as she watched an osprey spread its wings and lift from a cypress tree. The bayous were exactly as she remembered them, a wide sweep of water filled with wildlife and cypress knees.

She knew they were almost to New Orleans, the city where she and Sis had once come to hear a concert by Pete Fountain, though Larry still hadn't said a word about their destination. In fact, he'd hardly said a word since leaving Sweet Mama's Café. Emily figured that was because she'd talked nonstop the entire trip, partly about her own excitement but mostly about her sister and possibilities of Miss Opal's great-nephew.

"He's very shy, Larry, but really nice. I think you'd like him."

She glanced at her husband's profile, but he kept his eyes on the road.

"You should have seen him trying to get into Andy's little rocket ship. Those long legs. Longer than yours, even."

She laughed, thinking about it, but Larry was totally preoccupied with navigating the traffic that suddenly appeared out of nowhere, cars whizzing past on a network of roads and bridges that would have scared Emily to death if she'd been behind the wheel.

Cooking, that's what she did best. Just put her in a kitchen, and she could make any kind of dish you wanted, bake any kind of cake or pie, no matter how fancy.

She had decided that tonight she'd discuss the café with Larry. She had some ideas she'd like to try. Catering children's parties, for one. The backyard in the café was plenty big enough, and Andy's little rocket ship gave it a look of grand adventure that would appeal to children. Wouldn't it be great if they could add a swing set and a jungle gym? They could get kid-size picnic tables with rainbow-colored umbrellas in the center so that even on the hottest days, even in the blistering heat such as they'd had this summer, the children would still not get sunburned.

The sun suddenly dropped out of the sky, and Larry leaned over the wheel, his face in a tight mask as he wound through the congested streets in the French Quarter.

"If you'll tell me the hotel, I can be on the lookout," she said, but he just clamped his jaws tighter and continued his single-minded search.

What was wrong with him? She settled back into her seat and tried to make herself small. Finally, her husband pulled into a parking lot reserved for the Hotel St. Helene. It was a quaint, small hotel in the heart of the French Quarter with a courtyard that had a real parrot, according to the brochure Emily scanned while Larry registered. She pictured them sitting in the courtyard, drinking juice from freshly squeezed oranges while the parrot looked on from his perch. She'd have to get someone to make a picture of them with the bird. Andy would love that.

"Will there be anything else, sir?" the desk clerk said. She was a beautiful silver-haired woman wearing rings on every finger and a name tag that said Madeline. She had a wide smile and spoke with a soft accent that blended the Deep South with echoes of Arcadia.

"That's all." Larry sounded curt.

To make up for it, Emily said, "We're on our honeymoon."

"It shows, darling," the woman said, elongating her vowels and dropping her *g*'s in a way that made Emily smile.

She felt as if the two of them had been friends forever, which was the Southern way. She met no strangers, only people whose history she hadn't learned. Of course, Sis was just the opposite. She didn't let anybody close, not even a returning childhood friend. She wished she could call Sis right now and tell her about the hotel with the parrot in the courtyard and the lovely woman behind the front desk who would fit right in with the café crowd. She wished she could check on Andy, though she knew perfectly well he was in good hands.

So was she, and calling home might make Larry think he was second best, that his own wife couldn't even let go of her family enough to concentrate on having a good time with her husband on their honeymoon.

Fortunately, he was gathering suitcases and didn't notice her sudden longing for home. He even picked up the little travel case she used for her makeup, so all she had to do was follow along behind.

Their suite was as charming as the rest of the hotel. As Larry set the suitcases on the luggage racks, Emily inspected her surroundings. The bedroom and sitting room were tucked into L-shaped spaces filled with polished antiques and pictures that made you think of the Old South where women wore hoop skirts and bonnets with pink ribbons.

The pink silk blouse Emily had packed for her wedding

dinner would be perfect. Smiling up at her new husband, she took out her white linen skirt and laid it on the bed.

"This is a beautiful room, Larry."

"Reckon he would approve?"

The chill in his voice wiped the smile right off her face.

"He?"

"The man you talked about all the way from Biloxi."

"Oh, my goodness. *That* man." Relief flooded through her, but still she couldn't stop her hands from shaking. So he wouldn't notice, she leaned over her suitcase. "For a minute, I thought you were serious."

Larry went into the bathroom and she stayed bent over her suitcase, smoothing and resmoothing her pink silk blouse, chattering nonstop to disguise the way her heart hammered.

"It was really so nice to see him again. Because of Sis, I mean, and I guess I'm being a hopeless romantic but it seems to me he's perfect..."

Something made her turn, a sound, instinct, a feeling of walking over a grave. With the blouse clutched in her hand, she stood there staring at a husband transformed, her mouth still open in the shape of words that would no longer come. The blow caught her in the solar plexus and knocked her flat on her back. The second knocked her breath right out of her, and along with it, little fragments of her dreams.

"That will teach you to go off with another man," Larry said.

Emily was so horrified she couldn't even cry. The skirt she'd laid out on the bed was bunched underneath her, and instead of wondering how she could not have seen this coming, an admission that would have made her feel foolish and inadequate, she wondered how she'd ever get the wrinkles out.

"Larry, what in the world is..." His fist slammed the words

shut and her breath whistled out behind the blow that landed on her cheek.

In the kind of grace that is offered to the wounded, Emily didn't think of a future suddenly turned dangerous. She didn't question her judgment and pity herself.

She didn't even cringe or cry out. She simply lay there, deadened, enduring.

"He's perfect, is he? Did you think I didn't see the way you flirted with him? The way you went off together when you thought I wasn't looking?"

His voice had turned soft as a lover's, but his face was that of a stranger. Her honeymoon suite suddenly became as forbidding as a desert filled with rattlesnakes.

Slut and *whore* and *white trash,* he called her, and she spun through time, back to that awful spring when there was no place in her high school to escape. Neither the bathroom stall nor the space under the stairwell nor the janitor's broom closet could protect her from those same words, aimed at her like arrows.

Her family had stood up for her, Beulah and Sweet Mama and Sis and Jim, glaring at her detractors, daring them to say a word, even when she got so big there was no way to camouflage her belly. Still, she had broken the rules, defied a Southern society that revered the pure and damned the fallen. She deserved every slur, every slight.

And now she was getting her punishment. Emily made herself so small a puff of wind could carry her away.

Slowly Larry's fists unclenched. He stood over her a while, his fingers curling and uncurling, then suddenly he bent over and buried his face in her stomach. Sobs wrenched through him so hard, his shoulders shook.

"Larry?" Numb, Emily put a hand on his shoulder, a mother's instinct to comfort.

"I'm sorry," he said. "I'm so sorry, baby." He lifted a face as contrite and tear-streaked as Andy's after some misbehavior that got him into big trouble. "I don't know what came over me. I don't want to lose you. Tell me I won't lose you."

"You won't." Her mouth trembled so she could hardly get the words out.

"Promise!"

"I promise." Oh, Lord, did she? How could she ever keep a promise like that?

"That's my girl." He straightened up, smiling as he wiped his face, and then leaned down and planted a light kiss on her cheek.

"I'm going to leave you alone so you can fix yourself up pretty for dinner. I want to show off my girl."

When he walked out, the door clicked behind him, releasing a tidal wave of shock and pain. She heard the whimper of something lost, a stray kitten or a small child. Her eyes darted about for danger as she put her hand over her mouth to stifle the sound. What if Larry were waiting outside the door? What if he burst inside again with his fists like hammers and his mind unhinged?

Emily sat up slowly, her stomach heaving and every part of her body burning. If she retched, she'd have to clean it up. And what if he came in before she could? Biting her lips against the pain, longing for home, longing for her sister, Emily inched toward the bathroom, holding on to the backs of chairs and the surfaces of marble tables that were cool to the touch. Sis's touch would be cool on her forehead, her words a stream of comfort that poured over Emily like healing waters.

The mirror showed a woman with a flat expression and

dead eyes, a woman empty of every dream, drained of every hope except one—that she could somehow get through this till she could decide what to do. And if she happened to hear Judy Garland singing "Somewhere Over the Rainbow," she'd refuse to remember her fantasies. If she happened to see a full moon shining over the Gulf, she'd fail to recall another time, another place when the sand was soft beneath her hips and the man she'd thought would be hers forever said he loved her.

Emily's hands shook as she cleaned herself up with a washcloth. Larry had been careful to land most of the blows on her torso. In skirt and blouse and with a little extra blush on her face she'd look perfectly normal. Even in short sleeves.

She unwrapped a plastic cup and filled it with water. Feeling parched inside and out, she drank five cups before she could make her way back to the bedroom to dress. The pink blouse that had looked so hopeful now lay on top of her suitcase where she'd dropped it, just another frivolous piece of clothing. The skirt on the bed was hopelessly wrinkled.

She buttoned her blouse and smoothed her skirt, then viewed herself in the pier mirror. Looking back at her was a woman shattered like glass, a woman whose blissful week ahead had suddenly turned as forbidding as a pit full of vipers.

Defeated, she sank into a chair to wait for her husband.

Emily had been gone only a few days, and Sis could not have told you what made her more anxious—the bones she still hadn't reported because she didn't want cops all over the place while Andy was there, the idea of Emily being off with a man neither she nor Jim trusted or the man who'd just walked into the café. Of course, he was escorting his aunt, but that didn't lessen her anxiety one bit. Watching the way Michael held on to Miss Opal's elbow as he seated her in the corner booth, seeing how he smiled when he spotted her, Sis suddenly wished she were tucked out of sight in her office instead of standing at the coffeepots.

She could wish on a million shooting stars, but that wouldn't change the fact that her black shirt made her look like a crow and her hair stood out from her head as if she'd had a bad fright. The only good thing she could say was that she no longer had sausage curls.

Miss Opal waved her over.

"Sis, I was telling Michael about the Amen cobbler and he said he had to have some."

"How have you been, Beth?"

Sis stood there, breathing in the sound of her name. It made her feel like a woman who had a closet full of pretty clothes, a bottle of gardenia perfume on her table and a future filled with possibilities.

"Busy helping Sweet Mama and Beulah with the café and helping Emily watch after Andy." She sounded as boring as she looked, and for the first time she could remember, Sis wished she could report a different, more exciting lifestyle, one that included baseball games in Wrigley Field, sailing in the Gulf and weekend trips to New Orleans.

"Sometimes I fish," she added, hopeful for reasons she couldn't begin to imagine.

"I enjoy fishing." He smiled at her while Miss Opal beamed. "Do you still play ball on the beach?"

"With Andy."

"I haven't played ball in a long time."

He sounded nostalgic. But most of all, he sounded like the little boy she'd found one summer on the beach, the skinny kid with a baseball in one hand and a bat in the other, playing ball all by himself because he didn't know anybody in Biloxi.

Something inside her settled down. Remembering the peanut butter sandwiches they'd shared and the cherry Cokes and the way the wind used to catch their laughter and send it spiraling over the water like a yellow kite, she scooted into the booth beside an old friend.

"Do you still have your bat?" she asked.

"Same bat, different hat, and a bigger glove."

"If you'll come over sometime this week while I'm still keeping Andy, we'll all play ball on the beach."

"Do you still live in the same house?"

"Same one, and it's still pink."

"I used to call it the birthday cake house. Remember?"

"I do, but not where Sweet Mama could hear you."

As if she'd been called up by the sound of her name, Sweet Mama came over and sat down in their booth. She brought an Amen cobbler, four bowls and the unmistakable scent of peaches, a peculiar sweetness mixed with spices that spoke of faraway places and secrets both dark and delicious.

Sis felt split in two. Part of her yearned toward the delicious unknown and part of her braced for something so awful it sent a shiver down her spine. Still, she savored the ripe juice of peaches and the tartness of cherries, not knowing until the evening news that while the sun was shining through the window of Sweet Mama's Café glinting in the silver strands in Michael's hair, hot air drifted off the Sahara Desert, west toward the Atlantic, where it collided with the cooler coastal air over the Gulf of Guinea.

The upper atmospheric disturbance created tropical waves so big that when satellite photographs were beamed into the Blake living room on the ten o'clock news, Sis shut off the TV and rushed to make sure the windows were closed and the doors were locked. As if the waves had already turned into a monster. As if she could hold it back with the strength of her stubborn will.

Afterward, she raced into Emily's old room to check on Andy, sound asleep in his polka-dot astronaut glasses, his arms wrapped around his teddy bear and his mouth curved into a smile as he dreamed of flying to the moon.

Outside his window the moon laid a path across water still as glass and along a sturdy seawall said to be indestructible. It illuminated the tops of live oak trees where nothing stirred, neither leaf nor Spanish moss. On the moonlight marched, over the mimosa tree and across a backyard so serene you'd never guess what lay beneath the roses.

She tucked the sheet under Andy's chin then tiptoed to the window and pressed her face against the glass. Any other woman might have been fooled by the perfection of her view, but not Sis. She'd grown up with Beulah's wisdom, Sweet Mama's instinct and the magic of a cobbler called Amen. Something was waiting out there, something huge and dark and dangerous. Something so horrible she didn't dare give it a name.

Thirteen

IN THE STILL HOURS of dawn, Sis bolted suddenly awake. Something was not right. Hot and sticky, even with all the window units going full blast, she kicked back the sheets and lay in bed, listening. What she was listening for, she couldn't have said. A sign, maybe. Some small clue that the heartbeat of her family held steady, that they would move forward as they always had, safe under the roof of the high-ceilinged Victorian house by the sea.

She heard the slow drip of her bathroom faucet that needed a new washer, the sound of snoring from Jim's room and the clattering across the hall from the air-conditioner unit that needed replacing. But there was something else, a pulsing in the skies, as if a thousand seagulls were on the wing.

Sis went to her window but the slice of sea and sky in her view showed nothing extraordinary, only a band of pink over the horizon, announcing that the sun would soon be up. If she hurried she'd have time to search for Jim's missing leg before anybody else got up and she was plunged headlong into another day at the café.

She dressed quickly in shorts and an old white T-shirt she found in the bottom drawer of her dresser. Buoyed up by her change from black clothing, she tiptoed down the stairs and opened the door to the hall closet. Jim's leg had to be in there somewhere. It certainly didn't walk off by itself.

In the hope that it had fallen behind the boots, she piled them onto the hall floor. Looking at the empty floor where the prosthetic leg should have been, she felt anxious sweat collecting in the roots of her hair and across her forehead. She removed all the coats and rain slickers, and the pile on the floor grew until there was not a single thing left in the closet. Certainly not Jim's leg.

"Aunt Sis." The sound of her nephew's voice made her jump. Andy was standing behind her, holding on to his teddy bear with one hand and a little red plastic bucket and shovel with the other. "Can me and Henry go outside and make frog houses?"

"You can, sweetheart. But don't be long. We'll have to eat breakfast and clean up for the café."

"Can I wear my Superman suit?"

She really ought to say no. He hadn't had it off since they got home from the wedding. But he looked so excited and his mother was off with that jackass and what would it hurt?

"All right, but when we get home this afternoon, you need to take it off so I can wash it. Okay?"

"'K."

As he skipped off, Sis felt another twinge of inadequacy. Wouldn't somebody suited for motherhood have insisted he change into clothes that weren't rumpled? She sank back on her heels. The day had barely started and already she felt a vague dissatisfaction, as if she'd meant to go somewhere wonderful and found herself, instead, mired in a muddy rut.

There was nothing to do now but put the boots and coats back. A door slammed and Sis heard footsteps.

"Lord, Sis, what's all this mess?" Coming down the hall in a voluminous yellow robe and a yellow hairnet over the clips she was using to hold her wedding curls in place, Beulah looked like a school bus.

"I'm looking for Jim's leg. Have you seen it?"

"I ain't seen hide nor hair of it."

"Well, be on the lookout."

"What'd it do? Run away all by itself?"

"No. It had a little help from Jim."

Sis told her about finding the leg in the garbage can and Beulah went off to the kitchen shaking her head. Soon, the sound of humming drifted from that direction. Beulah would be making biscuits, the way she did every morning.

Sis wondered where to search next for Jim's leg. He was too smart to throw the prosthesis into the garbage can again. He'd figure that's the first place Sis would look. Had he put it in the garage? It would be easy to tuck it out of sight behind the hoes and rakes and shovels, or stick it behind the bicycles, rusting and forgotten now, forlorn as they leaned against the wall and waited for the children who had once pedaled them down the beach as fast as they could, scaring up nesting terns and startling the seagulls who had dropped down to scavenge in the shallows.

Suddenly, there was a loud screech from the kitchen followed by Beulah yelling, "Lord Jesus!"

Imagining Beulah stretched out on the kitchen floor with her lips turning blue or Andy racing out of the yard and into the path of oncoming traffic, Sis flew into the kitchen. Beulah was standing at the window with her hand over her heart.

"What is it?" Sis shouted, but Beulah just stood at the window pointing, her face ashen and her finger shaking like a leaf in a bad wind.

Andy was out there in a grimy Superman costume happily building frog houses. But Sis saw what Beulah did—Andy squatted beside the Don Juan, scooping up the mounded dirt that covered the bones.

Sis burst through the door and bounded down the back steps two at a time.

"Andy!" He flashed a smile that melted her heart every time and kept on digging. "Stop!"

He looked up once more from the earth he'd excavated, the sandy soil filled with black loam that would make it hold together exactly right for frog houses. Suddenly, his smile faded and his plastic shovel fell to the ground.

Still, Sis couldn't see what he'd found, didn't know if his pile of dirt held the tip of a little toe or the more distinctive ankle bone. Fear drove her to extremes. Still racing toward her nephew, she yelled, "You can't dig there."

His face crumpled, and in the way of a child whose heart is broken at the sight of a crushed butterfly wing, he wailed so loud it sent Beulah rushing out of the kitchen. Sis got to him first, but even as she wrapped Andy in a tight hug, she scanned the soil he'd spaded up with his plastic shovel. Short of sifting through it, she could see nothing except the raw materials for a child's engineering project.

Andy clung to her, inconsolable it seemed, while Beulah cut her eyes to the dirt he'd moved from the terrible rosebush.

"Are they still there?" Sis asked.

Ignoring her, Beulah caught a hold of Andy and folded him close, making soothing sounds and promising him everything from chocolate milk and cookies to the moon.

"Are they, Beulah?"

"Ain't nothing under there but trouble, Sis. If you go looking for it, you gonna wish you hadn't."

"We can't just ignore it. Look what happened here this morning."

Andy was sniffling now, his face still hidden against Beulah's shoulder.

"You keep on, Sis, and you'll upset this child so bad he ain't ever gonna get over it."

"All right, then. But after Emily gets home, you and I are going to have a long talk."

"We'll see."

Andy peered over his shoulder and gave Sis a tremulous smile.

"That means no," he said.

"It does?" Relief made Sis feel foolish and awkward and inadequate. She decided there must be some kind of cosmic order, after all, some kind of Superior Being jotting her name down beside a note that said "Must never be turned loose to raise her own child."

"Yeah. Mommy says it all the time and it always means no." Andy squirmed out of Beulah's embrace and picked up his little bucket and shovel as if nothing had happened. "Do you want me to put the dirt back?"

"No, honey, I'll do it. Don't worry about this old dirt." Sis held her breath as she flicked at the pile of dirt, but nothing flew up except sand. "I was afraid you'd cut yourself on a thorn. Let's not dig any more frog houses by the roses. Okay?"

"'K."

"Good." She kissed him on the top of the head. "You go in and let Beulah clean you up and get you some breakfast. And maybe we'll paint your rocket ship."

"Oh, boy! Today?"

"Not today. We have to buy the paint first. Okay?"

Andy headed toward the house with Beulah, trotting to

keep up, and Sis was left in the yard with her heart pounding too hard. She used to love being in the garden alone this time of morning when the air was still and smelled faintly of the salt breezes that sent the Spanish moss in the live oak trees along the avenue swaying. She closed her eyes, trying to recapture some of that long-ago peace, but the ground beneath her feet held a secret too horrible to imagine and the air was charged with restless static.

Shading her eyes, Sis looked at the sky. It was alive with planes roaring into the Gulf from the direction of Kessler, their contrails crisscrossing as they lifted over the water, then vanished. Though she was too far away to identify the planes, her guess was hurricane hunters. Jim's best friend, Gordon, flew one of the sophisticated planes that tracked storms. He'd told about flying into the eye of Hurricane Betsy in 1965 before she hit the Gulf coast.

You drop out of the howling fury of wind and rain and into a lull so unnatural it steals your courage. A wall of black clouds closes in on you, and you feel alone in the world. Then the heat ratchets up, and as you fly straight into the eye of the hurricane you feel as if you've just plunged into the bowels of hell.

Betsy had been a Category 3 and so had the storm Sis remembered only because it was the year her parents' car crashed, 1949. They'd boarded up the windows and hunkered down behind a mattress in the hall, then ridden both storms out in the same way all seasoned residents along the Mississippi Gulf Coast had dealt with nature's fury through the years.

Though Sis anxiously scanned the sky, there was nothing left of the jets except a long white trail that looked like the tail of a dragon. If you didn't know better, you might think it was nature putting on a cloud show for the entertainment of little kids.

In the house, Sweet Mama's bedroom light came on and from the street Burt Larson called out as he delivered the morning mail. Next door, Stella Mae Clifford yelled at her dog to stop peeing on her petunias. It was business as usual in the neighborhood.

Turning her attention back to the little hole Andy had dug beside the rosebush, Sis raked the dirt back over the bones. Still anxious, she glanced toward the house. Where was Andy now?

She found him in the kitchen, hanging on to his scruffy teddy bear and chattering away with Sweet Mama, his cowlick bouncing as he swung his legs against the chair. Though Sis searched for signs she'd damaged his spirit and ruined their relationship besides, it wasn't Andy who broke her heart; it was Sweet Mama. She was wearing her dress inside out.

Sis slipped her arm around her nephew. "You okay, pumpkin?" He nodded vigorously. "I'm sorry I yelled. Grown-ups get upset sometimes, too. Okay?"

"'K." He scrambled out of his chair. "Can I paint my rocket ship red, Aunt Sis?"

"You can paint it any color you want."

"Blood is red." Sweet Mama clapped her hand over her mouth as if she could hold back the awful, irretrievable thing she'd said.

Sis glanced at her nephew to see if Sweet Mama's uncensored talk scared him, but he was already racing toward the stairs yelling, "Hey, Uncle Jim. You want'a play jacks with me and Henry?"

Sis sank into the kitchen chair.

"Have you seen Beulah this morning, Sweet Mama?"

"No. I wonder where she is."

That would explain why Sweet Mama's dress was on wrong. Beulah watched over her like some dark, avenging angel.

Any other day Beulah would have come straight from the garden, back to the kitchen. But nothing was the way it used to be. It seemed to Sis that Neil Armstrong's walk on the moon had stirred up a cosmic storm where truth was obscured by smoke screens and secrets were hidden in plain view.

"I heard the children playing outside," Sweet Mama said. "She must be with them."

"That was Andy. You remember? Emily's little boy."

"Of course I remember," Sweet Mama said, but alarm crossed her face, and Sis understood with heartbreaking clarity how her own great-grandson had slipped from her memory. Soon all the family would fade away, leaving Sweet Mama with the terrible feeling that she was alone in the house, surrounded by strangers.

There must be something Sis could do. Put signs all over the house. Go through the photograph album with her every evening. Label the pictures in her billfold. But would any of it help?

Sweet Mama's hands trembled as she picked up a biscuit and handed it to Sis. "I made the biscuits this morning. Eat up."

Sis slit the biscuit she knew full well Beulah had made and put a piece of bacon inside because that's what she always did. She thrived on routine, and if she didn't miss her guess, it was becoming Sweet Mama's map to the unfamiliar territory of her life.

"Sweet Mama, there's a little stain on your dress, but I think if you just turn it inside out, nobody will ever notice."

"I already knew that."

"Well, of course you did. Why don't you go fix it while I look for Beulah?"

Sometimes the world gets to be too much and all you can do is try to find something to hold on to. Too heavy to move,

Sis sat in her chair, searching. There was the Maxwell House coffee can on the counter, the cast-iron skillet Beulah had used to bake her biscuits for as long as Sis could remember, the canisters with yellow tops that held the staples in the Blake kitchen—sugar and flour and cornmeal and leftover bacon grease to season black-eyed peas and mustard greens. Familiar things, ordinary things.

Beulah had given the canisters to Sweet Mama for her sixtieth birthday. They'd celebrated with Amen cobbler because Sweet Mama said a birthday cake would have so many candles it would burn the house down. Sis wondered if this year she'd even remember how many candles her birthday cake needed.

"Ain't no need looking for me," Beulah said, and suddenly there she was, sweeping into the kitchen like an enormous dark thundercloud. "Lucy, fix that dress and grab your purse. That cooking down at the café ain't gonna do itself."

While Sweet Mama left the kitchen, Beulah lumbered over to the coffeepot and poured herself a cup.

"You might as well quit trying to ignore me," Sis said, but Beulah just sat down and started drinking her coffee. "I'm right here, and I'm not going away till we talk."

"My head feels like the devil's got a hold of it with a pitchfork. If anybody says one word to me, I'm liable to bite their head off."

"You've never taken off anybody's head in your life, Beulah."

"That don't mean I'm not fixing to start. You hear me now, Sis?"

"I hear you, but you know we can't go on pretending nothing's out there."

"Ain't no buts about it. Go on now, Sis."

Sis searched Beulah for little clues. She'd always been easy to read, openhearted with those she loved, which included everybody in the Blake family, especially Sweet Mama. She'd saved barriers for the few people she didn't like—Stella Mae Clifford and a couple of the town's bigots who had a fondness for Amen cobbler and a high opinion of their own ignorance.

The fact that she was shutting Sis out meant she not only knew who those bones belonged to, but she was intimately linked to them. But who? Sis understood her own history better than she did her future. She'd heard the family's stories so many times they were woven through her like silk threads.

Everybody in her family had been accounted for, even the grandfather she'd never met and the great-grandparents who had all died before she was born. Could it be a drifter out there under the rosebushes, somebody who had wandered in for a handout, then met an accidental death that scared Beulah so much she'd buried the body? It could have happened during the Great Depression.

"Sis, you'd best get ready for the café now, sweet pea." This softer Beulah was the one Sis knew and loved, the one she had come to depend on. "And don't you worry about Lucy. I'll drive her car."

"Maybe you ought to keep her keys, Beulah. I think it's time."

"I ain't gonna break her heart like that, Sis, but from now on I can make sure she ain't the one behind the wheel of that big old car she's so fond of."

"Can you do that without upsetting her?"

"She won't ever know what I'm up to. I'm good at distractions."

"That's the understatement of the year, Beulah."

Leaving her sitting at the table calmly sipping her coffee,

Sis went back to her room where she'd started a day that already seemed a hundred years long.

She longed to climb into bed and start the day over. Barring that, she sank onto the mattress and tried to think of something that would take her mind off family problems. His smile came to mind first, and then the lock of dark hair that wouldn't stay out of his eyes. Michael. The one good and ordinary thing that had happened to Sis the entire summer.

She felt a sudden lightness of being, as if years had melted away and she was once more a young girl on the beach with a friend at her side, a glove in her hand and her baseball cap on backward.

What if she wore bell-bottoms today instead of hiding behind dark baggy clothes? What if she could tame her hair with a barrette or a ponytail holder? If Emily were there, she'd suggest a pink ribbon but Sis drew the line at both pink and ribbons.

She found the bell-bottoms at the back of her closet. By sucking her stomach in and tugging really hard on the zipper, she got into them. A little shiver of hope went through her, but as she turned to view herself in the mirror, the air around her vibrated like the sustained buzz from a hive of angry bees.

Her zipper and her hope popped at the same time. As Sis peeled off the bell-bottoms, another wave of hurricane hunters soared into the long blue horizon.

Fourteen

ABANDONING THE IDEA OF bell-bottoms and trying to be something she was not, Sis dressed in her usual black garb. In the front yard, the Buick engine fired up as Beulah and Sweet Mama headed toward the café, and down the hall, Jim hobbled out of his room.

Sis left Andy gathering his teddy bear and his astronaut glasses, and intercepted her brother at the top of the stairs.

"Jim, I'm glad you're up. I thought it would be nice if Andy stayed with you today." He didn't say anything, and she rushed ahead, hopeful. "He was looking for you earlier to play jacks."

"I don't play jacks anymore."

"You don't have to play jacks. You can take him out to the beach for a game of baseball."

"Do I look like a man who could play baseball?"

"For God's sake. You don't have to run the bases. Just throw the ball."

Jim stared at her as if she'd proposed he blow up Biloxi's lighthouse, and Sis batted her frizzy hair away from her hot face.

"Andy could use a man's touch, Jim."

Without a word, he started downstairs, deliberately striking his crutch harder against the wooden steps, she decided.

"Jim! You can't run away forever."

He never even turned his head. She barged after him, formulating her arguments. *For Pete's sake, what do you do all day? Sit in your room and brood? Go to the beach and stare at the water? Read the encyclopedia?*

When she arrived at the center of the staircase, she stopped, suddenly out of steam. Then she took a deep breath and hurried back up the stairs to collect Andy for the drive to the café.

By the time she got there, a bigger than usual crowd had already gathered. Tragedy, and even the threat of it, brought out the herd instinct in Biloxi's populace. People flocked to Sweet Mama's as if they might take solace from one another. They filled every booth and table, their faces turned to the TV on the serving counter as Sweet Mama and Beulah poured coffee and the local news reporter gave the latest storm update.

Sis poured herself a cup of coffee, then lingered by the urn and listened to the latest weather report.

Even if a storm was picking up speed in Cuba, there was not a sign of it in the flat blue Gulf and the seagulls that wheeled toward a sun so hot it made white spots dance before your eyes. Still, as Sis stared through the plate-glass window, she felt a gnawing sense of fear.

"It's nothing to worry about," Tom Wilson announced to the café crowd.

His brother James said, "Remember Galveston."

"That's right," Burt Larson chimed in. "They talked about that hurricane for years. It was the worst natural disaster in U.S. history."

Stella Mae Clifford and half the customers nodded in agree-

ment, while Miss Opal led the optimistic group who agreed
with Tom that there was nothing to worry about.

The Amen cobblers told a different story. An outsider seeing them lined on the cooling rack might have mistaken them
for just another of Sweet Mama's desserts. But Sis saw how
the wisps of steam that escaped and swirled upward in little
eddies took on the shape of sea serpents.

Coming back to the coffeepot, Beulah rolled her eyes toward the ceiling.

"You see that, Sis?" she whispered. "It's a sure sign the sea
is going to rise up and swallow us all."

"It's no such thing," Sweet Mama said as she joined them.
"See how that steam's headed straight for Stella Mae Clifford.
It means she has a forked tongue."

But Sis, seeing how the steam drifted over the empty seat
beside Miss Opal, thought of the Garden of Eden and temptation. She thought about dashed dreams and foolish hope.
Only yesterday Michael had sat in that very same seat and
talked about baseball on the beach. Just one small conversation, and yet Sis had spun an entire fantasy around it. She'd
fully expected to walk into the café today and see him smiling at her over the rim of his coffee cup.

She carried her own cup into her office, telling herself that
she was being ridiculous. But that didn't keep her from glancing through her doorway at odd moments during the day, just
in case Michael came in.

And that afternoon, as she and Andy shopped for paint, no
amount of reasoning kept her from veering into a dress shop
where she purchased a green dress that made her think of the
promise of spring and a T-shirt in an outrageously gaudy shade
of yellow just because it reminded her of those long days of

sunshine and baseball she'd spent with her childhood friend during the best summers of her youth.

She added bell-bottoms for good measure, the size so shocking she decided to go on a diet.

As Sis headed home with Andy, her history and her good common sense caught up with her. She'd never been on a diet and probably never would. She'd never attracted a man, and it seemed unlikely she was going to start now. If Michael wanted to sit in the café and talk about playing baseball with her on the beach, he'd have to accept her just the way she was, an independent woman who knew her own mind and didn't hesitate to speak it.

Sis decided she was not going to waste another minute thinking about him. But as she parked her car and saw Sweet Mama and Beulah on the front porch sipping tea, the first thing she thought was how nice it would be to come home and sit on the swing with a glass of sweet tea and a man with eyes so deep you could see his soul.

"Any calls for me while I was gone?"

"Ain't nobody called," Beulah said.

Andy raced into the house calling Jim's name, and Sis tried not to let her disappointment show as she sank into a white wicker chair beside Sweet Mama and Beulah. Their purses, sitting on the wicker table beside the tea pitcher, told their own story. The two women always put their purses on the table when they got back from the café, then one of them sat down while the other went inside to brew tea in Sweet Mama's antique teapot for their afternoon ritual.

As Beulah poured a glass of tea and handed it to her, Sis couldn't help but smile. There was something comforting about routine, about knowing these two strong women would be waiting on the front porch, their purses at hand in case they needed to race off on a moment's notice to handle a family crisis.

"It's got plenty of sugar, Sis," Beulah said. "You look like you need it."

"Thanks." She lifted the glass to her face and ran its icy side against her hot cheeks. It was hot, too hot, the kind of August that stirred up tempers and discontent and storms. She glanced at the Gulf again, but nothing had changed. Charter boats heading toward Ship Island and fishing boats setting out for deeper waters dotted the smooth blue expanse. Tourists who loved the white sand but hated the sun raised red and yellow umbrellas over their beach chairs while sun-browned children romped in the shallows.

Turning from the view, Sis said, "Do you know if Jim's been outside today?"

"He passed through the kitchen for some tea, but he didn't look like he'd been in the sun," Beulah said. "Maybe he'll feel more like himself tomorrow."

Sis didn't hold out any high hopes, but she didn't see any point dwelling on it.

"Sweet Mama, can I see the photographs in your purse?"

"What for?"

"Lord, Lucy," Beulah said. "You're pricklish as an old cactus. What's got into you?"

"This heat." Sweet Mama pulled a little pack of photographs out of her purse and handed them to Sis. "Nothing good can come from heat like this, Beulah."

"Are you talking about the storm?" Sis asked.

"It was huge," her grandmother said, and then got a far-away look that signaled the past was pulling her backward.

Sis grabbed Sweet Mama's hand, trying to anchor her to the present.

"It's still out in the Atlantic, Sweet Mama. We don't know how big it will get."

Quick alarm played across Sweet Mama's face, followed by the sly look she got when she was trying hard to cover up the awful truth that she was slipping out of touch.

"I think it's going to peter out," she said. "Get that, *Peter.*" Then she and Beulah cracked up.

Feeling bittersweet that her grandmother could still make jokes, Sis took Sweet Mama's billfold out of her purse, spread her pictures on the table and began writing on the backs. "Your favorite son, Bill, and his wife, Margaret, 1947." Looking at them leaning against their car, would Sweet Mama remember that they were dead? As much as it still hurt to think about how her parents had died and why, Sis wrote, "They died in a car wreck."

She picked up the next picture and then the next, continuing to write the story of Sweet Mama's life on the backs of the photographs she carried, trying to ensure that her grandmother would never be without memories of her family.

The evening shadows lengthened and the three women went into the house. Jim and Andy joined them, and they had supper around the kitchen table as they had for years. Surrounded by her family, Sis wondered if they would be doing the same thing twenty years from now, gathered around the same oak table, Andy all grown and Jim perhaps with a wife and a child of his own.

The idea both comforted and distressed her.

Even after she went to bed, she still felt a vague unrest.

"It's the heat," she said.

Lately, she had a frightful habit of talking to herself. Maybe she ought to get a cat. At least she'd have the excuse that she was making conversation with a pet.

A shower did nothing to relieve her discontent. Nor did the few chapters she read in *Gone with the Wind* before she turned off her bedside lamp. Was reading the same book over and over another habit that signaled she was slipping away? Not like Sweet Mama, into a world where the familiar became mysterious, but into the kind of life Sis had never imagined herself having. With nothing to show for her years except an album of fading pictures.

Hoping sleep would bring some peace, Sis closed her eyes. But it was not oblivion that came to her; it was nightmares filled with thunder and lightning and the women around her gone mad.

The storm was one of the worst Sis had ever seen. Thunder cracked and something in the backyard gave off a horrible groaning, as if the earth beneath had split away.

"It's coming down!" Beulah yelled, her voice ricocheting up the stairs where Sis was bent over her algebra book, studying for a test.

What was coming down? The house?

Suddenly, all the lights went out. Sis slammed her book shut and put her hands over her head, expecting at any moment to feel the roof caving in. Panic clawed at her. Were the twins all right? Sweet Mama and Beulah? Cowering in the pitch-black of her room, Sis couldn't see anything.

Another roll of thunder reverberated through the house and lightning turned everything in her room a ghostly blue. She raced to the window and saw one of the huge mimosa trees split in two, its roots sticking straight out of the ground.

"We've got to get out there, Beulah," Sweet Mama yelled. "Quick, before something awful happens."

The door downstairs slammed, and Sis saw Sweet Mama and Beulah streaking across the backyard in their nightgowns. Another crack of lightning tore branches off the already downed tree and sent them flying over the garage.

Sis banged her fists on the window and yelled at the top of her lungs, "Come back!" but Sweet Mama and Beulah kept racing through the storm. Sis yelled at them again, but they disappeared into the garage.

Were they taking shelter? Trying to rescue somebody foolish enough to be out there risking death?

Sis pressed her face to the window, her tears blending with the savage rain that slashed the glass. The storm was so horrific now she could barely see Sweet Mama and Beulah as they emerged from the garage. When another flash of lightning illuminated the sky, Sis saw something that chilled her blood: Sweet Mama had an ax and Beulah had a saw.

Horrified, Sis watched them attack the tree, hacking at the branches and sawing at the trunk. Thunder rattled the windows of the house and lightning shot jagged streaks across the backyard, but Sweet Mama and Beulah worked on, undeterred.

Sis tried calling out to them again, but they didn't hear. They hacked and sawed, their arms rising and falling in the blue lightning like a freak show Sis had seen at the county fair. She slid down the wall, leaned her forehead against the windowpane and continued to watch. But it didn't feel as if she were watching her own backyard; it felt as if she were in the middle of a horrible collision between her past and her future.

Sis jarred awake, sweating, the covers twisted around her legs. Untangling herself from the sheets, she went into the bathroom to get a drink. As she lifted the glass to her lips, it dawned on Sis that she had not been in the midst of a nightmare but a recollection so disturbing it had finally pushed its way through.

It was Sweet Mama and Beulah who had taken the mimosa tree down in the middle of a storm. The next day when Sis returned from school, they'd planted a row of roses where the tree once stood.

An act that had made no sense when Sis was fourteen was now perfectly clear. More than roots had come up the night the storm overturned the mimosa tree. Sweet Mama and Beulah couldn't risk leaving bones exposed in broad daylight.

But who did the bones belong to and why were they there? Did Sweet Mama know who was buried under the roses? Had one of those awful KKK cowards she'd faced down with her shotgun in the café sneaked to the Victorian house in the dead of night and met his fate? Maybe it had been an awful accident. Maybe Sweet Mama had been shaking so hard the gun had simply gone off.

If Sweet Mama was involved, all Sis's earlier theories were now turned upside down. It would also lend more weight to Beulah's caution to leave the bones a mystery.

Sis felt the beginning of a fierce headache. Reaching into her medicine cabinet, she took two aspirin and crawled back into bed. But sleep was a long time coming.

Fifteen

THE BREWING STORM CHANGED nothing in the glittering city on the banks of the Mississippi. The river continued dumping its waters into the Gulf and tourists continued arriving in droves. New Orleans was bright with lights and jazz and Southern women who floated down the streets in floral-printed bell-bottoms and halter tops in neon colors.

Emily stood out from them, not only because of her lady-like silk blouse and linen skirt, but also the corsage of garde-nias on her shoulder, another floral gift from Larry, one of the many he'd showered on her since the night of what he referred to as *that little incident*.

The first time he'd brought roses, returning to their room with the exquisite pink corsage and an equally exquisite promise that he would *never* raise a hand against her again.

"I don't know what came over me," he said. "I'll make it up to you. I promise."

He'd leaned over to kiss her throughout that first dinner, whispering, "I'm insanely in love with you, Mrs. Chastain. And I will *never* hurt you again."

She'd believed him—she'd been desperate for his words to be true.

Now, as they headed into Antoine's for lunch and Larry leaned down to nuzzle her cheek and say, "You look beautiful, Mrs. Chastain," Emily imagined how each day would make *that little incident* fade until it was nothing more than a vague memory. The dreams she'd had when she packed her pink nightgown and imagined the two of them together while Jay and the Americans played "This Magic Moment" were all going to come true. She wouldn't have it any other way.

Still, as Larry slid his arm around her waist and led her toward their table, she glanced around for time bombs, a too-handsome man who might stare at her, a chatty waiter who might linger too long over her order like that poor unfortunate young man at the Café du Monde. All he'd said was, "That's a really pretty dress you're wearing."

Larry had shoved out of his chair so fast it toppled. "Do you *mind?* That's my wife!"

The waiter was so upset he knocked a beignet off Emily's plate and got powdered sugar all over her dress. When he tried to wipe it off with a napkin, Emily thought Larry was going to hit him.

"It's okay, it's okay." She pushed the waiter's hand away, and finally Larry sank into his chair like a ship torpedoed.

"I'm sorry, baby." He squeezed her hand, then leaned across the little bistro table to wipe her tears that had sprung up, unawares. "Don't cry, darling. I'm just being a big daddy bear. I want everything to be perfect for you."

Just thinking about it made her shiver. Larry pulled her so close she felt the scratchy fabric of the dinner jacket he was wearing.

"Cold, darling?"

"No, I'm fine. Just perfect." She glanced around Antoine's

as if somebody was going to leap out of the corner and rescue her. "And you've chosen a fabulous restaurant!"

"Nothing's too good for my girl." He pulled out her chair, then leaned down to whisper, "Happy, Mrs. Chastain?"

"I couldn't be happier." Emily wanted desperately to mean it. Still, there was something overly possessive about the way he insisted on calling her *Mrs. Chastain,* the way he lifted her hair and spent such a long time kissing the back of her neck that diners from the other tables turned to stare.

The waiter headed their way, zeroing in on Emily with an overly solicitous manner that made her jerk the dinner napkin into her lap and tighten it into a little ball.

"Will you order for me, Larry? Anything you choose will be great."

"Now, that's what a man likes to hear."

He ordered steak when she'd much rather have eaten seafood, but it was a small price to pay for peace. By the time Larry paid for the meal, and hurried her back to the honeymoon suite, she was congratulating herself on a successful outing with her husband where not a single thing had gone wrong.

She supposed each marriage had a unique rhythm, and she was going to have to get used to hers, that was all. There was Larry, drawing the curtains shut and flipping on the TV set to catch the latest update on the storm, a rhythm that was now as familiar to her as the mixing bowl she used to make biscuits at the café. He was stripping off his clothes, a signal for Emily to hurry and climb under the sheet, already naked. Larry didn't like to bother removing clothing that was simply in his way.

Mark had been just the opposite, tender and sweet in ways that made Emily feel as if she were the heroine in one of the

romance novels she loved and Sis read when she thought nobody was looking.

Maybe when they'd settled into this marriage, Emily would
ask Larry to take a little more time to set the mood.

Larry didn't seem to notice that his wife's attention was on
the TV, that she equated him with a storm taking his howling courage from something other than himself. She was the
fuse to Larry's dynamite. From minute to minute, she never
knew whether she'd ignite her husband to passion or jealousy.
Maybe she was trying too hard to be attractive to him. Maybe
if she stopped wearing perfume except on special occasions,
he'd stop paying such close attention to every little thing she
did. Maybe if she stopped faking it in bed, he'd tone his own
libido down a bit.

Still, she was respectable now, and hadn't that been what
she was after all along?

Suddenly, Larry levered himself onto his elbows and stared
down at her with his brow furrowed.

"Am I not pleasing you, Mrs. Chastain?"

"Yes." Emily bit the inside of her mouth to keep the quiver
out of her voice. "Oh, yes."

"If I'm not, you just tell daddy bear what you need. I aim
to please."

"If I were any more pleased, I might just levitate off this
bed."

"That's my girl."

Emily could endure or she could end it with a performance,
something she'd become very good at during the past week.
She couldn't wait to laugh about it with Sis. They'd drink
sweet tea and make up outrageous Oscar categories for per-
formances such as hers. But the telling would bring questions
she couldn't answer, and so Emily would just have to content

herself with the knowledge that every new trick she learned would keep her husband happy.

"That's one for the road," Larry said, then got off the bed and went into the bathroom.

When Emily heard the water running, she put her hand over her mouth to hide the desperate laughter she'd been holding back. *One for the road,* and she was going home, home where she could disappear in the kitchen at Sweet Mama's Café for glorious hours, lost in her world of confections and laughter and the glowing opinions of the people who loved her. In one of those mercurial mood changes that she'd come to expect since Larry sent her sprawling on her honeymoon night, Emily fought back tears.

Was Andy missing her? She knew he was safe with Sis, and happy. He loved being in the Victorian house where Beulah would pet him extravagantly and Sweet Mama would make him giggle with her stories and Sis would let him get by with just about anything.

But what if something happened to her? What if Larry got mad and went too far? Would Andy remember his fourth birthday when she'd made a cake that looked like a carousel complete with miniature animals she'd found at a craft store, tiny zebras and horses and unicorns. She'd wrapped narrow gold ribbon around matchsticks to make the carousel poles. Would he remember what she looked like? That she smelled of sugar and spice and sometimes let him have sweet treats in bed?

She eased off the bed she'd never have to see again and started packing. When they got home, things would be better. Emily always took strength from the familiar—the wallpaper in her bedroom that featured apple blossoms and tiny songbirds, her blue-and-white kitchen, Andy with his cowlick standing up, the regulars like the sweet old Wilson bachelors waiting at the café.

When she got back, she'd make an Amen cobbler with extra peaches and sugar and plump, ripe cherries that squished when you bit into them, the juice so sweet it made you think of honeysuckle and sunshine and summer picnics on a quilt underneath a live oak tree. She'd serve it to Larry on their first night home, and then perhaps Emily would get some of the magic she'd imagined as she hummed and dreamed and planned her wedding.

"Bathroom's all yours." Larry came out with a towel wrapped around his waist and water dripping off his chest. "Don't take long. I want to get back in time to go to the office."

"I won't."

Emily hurried through her bath, then applied some heavy makeup she'd bought at Walgreens on Canal Street, guaranteed to cover the bruise and put the color back in her cheeks. When had she lost it? The night of *that little incident,* or had it been the next night when they'd listened to jazz on Bourbon Street? Just remembering made her stomach hurt.

The jazz was great, the corsage of violets Larry had bought made her feel special and she'd been particularly happy that her seat was next to a nice young man whose blond cowlick reminded her of Andy.

Larry's unusual quiet during the performance should have tipped her off—and the way his fingers pinched into her arm as he hustled her back to their room and kicked the door shut behind them.

"Is something wrong with me, Mrs. Chastain?" There was something tight and ugly in his voice, something that made Emily's insides quiver.

"No. Of course not."

"Of course not," he mimicked, a muscle going tight in his jaw. "Then why were you flirting?"

"Flirting?" His silence, worse than any accusation, made sweat collect in Emily's hair and roll down her cheek. She stumbled through the events of that night in her mind, trying to make sense of this accusation. "Oh, you mean that young man sitting on the other side of me? He reminded me of Andy. All I did was say hello."

"How long does it take to say hello?"

"Well, maybe I did more than that."

"How much more? Did you let him touch you when the lights went down?"

"What? No, Larry."

"Did you lean over to whisper in his ear when he ran his hand up your skirt?"

"No! He never did that."

"Then what were you whispering? Something you couldn't tell your husband, Mrs. Chastain?"

When she'd been pregnant and her classmates savaged her with gossip, she'd learned to vanish inside herself where there was nothing except the quiet beat of her heart and the rush of her own blood. She did that now, burrowing into her deep cocoon while Larry and the bed and the curtains and the awful accusations faded to nothing.

"Tell me." Larry's deadly soft voice was more threatening than a scream.

"I was just..."

"Just what?" Again, he spoke in that quiet voice that held the distant rattling of sabers. "Speak up, Mrs. Chastain. I can't hear you."

"I was just telling him about the little horn I got for Andy's rocket ship, and I know it was rude to not include you in the conversation." She hadn't meant to cry, but there was nothing she could do about it now. "I'm sorry, Larry. I didn't mean to hurt you. I don't want to ever hurt you."

His grip loosened and his face got softer.

"You're my husband, Larry," she whispered. "I love you."

"Oh, my God. I know you do." He dropped to his knees in front of her and pressed his face into her thighs. "I didn't mean to make you cry, baby."

He kissed her through her clothes, then grabbed her hands and kissed the palms, one at a time.

"You're just so damned beautiful I can't stand the idea of some other man snatching you away."

They'd ended up together on the floor, with him saying, "I'm sorry," over and over again and her faking love for all she was worth.

Emily stared at herself in the mirror and added another layer of blush. She hadn't meant to flirt with that young man. But had she? Was it in her nature? Was she the kind of woman born to seduce and destroy? Thinking of Mark, dead in a jungle because of her, she started crying and then saw with dismay that her tears were making tracks through the heavy makeup she'd so carefully applied.

A loud rap on the door made her jump.

"Emily! I'm not waiting out here all day."

"Coming." She pasted a smile on her face and pushed through the door.

"You look gorgeous, babe." His eyes were hot looking and his face was flushed. "If we had time we'd have another little romp."

Thank God they didn't have time. Thank God he picked up her suitcase and hurried off to the lobby where Madeline waited behind the checkout counter. Her eyes narrowed as she studied Emily.

"Is everything all right, hon?"

"Oh, everything is just wonderful!" Emily made herself sparkle like a debutante at her coming-out ball. "We've had a *wonderful* time. I'm just worried about the storm, is all."

"That's nothing to worry about," Madeline said, her focus still narrowed on Emily's face. "We get these scares every summer. They never amount to anything."

Emily wanted to agree. She wanted to stand in the cool lobby and exchange addresses with Madeline and promise to send Christmas cards. She wanted this one small good thing to come out of her honeymoon horror.

But Larry took a firm hold on her elbow, paid the bill and hustled her out. Emily didn't even have time to say goodbye. Still, she was so grateful to be back in the car heading home she felt herself choking up. That was another failing of hers, crying when she was happy, her emotional landscape obscured by tears.

Fortunately, Larry was too busy with traffic to notice. Even after he got on the long stretch toward home, he still concentrated on his driving. The one useful thing Emily had learned about her new husband was that his needs were simple. Once his basic cravings for food and sex were satisfied, Larry cared nothing for conversation. Maybe Emily bored him. She'd never been to college and didn't keep up with world events the way Sis and Jim did. The only things she really knew about were cooking and taking care of Andy. Add her limitations to her unfortunate history, and was it any wonder she had attracted somebody who knew how to punish?

She turned her face to the window, and the sign announcing the Biloxi city limits blurred from a fresh threat of tears.

"Emily? Do you want me to drop you off at the house?"

"The café's still open. Can you take me there?"

He reached across the seat to caress the back of her neck and she thought of spiders that crawled out of dark places to bite you when you least expected. But wasn't that being a bit hard on him? After all, he'd never hit her except that one time, and then he'd gone out of his way to show his love for her. All those flowers and expensive dinners. And really, what wife in her right mind wouldn't be happy with a husband who couldn't keep his hands off her?

"It's great to be home, babe. Don't you think?"

"Yes."

"Now that we're here, we can be a real family. Just you and me and Andy. I'm going to show you what a good father I can be."

Emily felt a tug of hope. Could they erase the honeymoon and start over?

"That's what I want more than anything, Larry. A real family and a father for Andy."

"Well, you've got it, babe." He winked at her. "I'm glad we feel the same way. You know I'd do anything for you, don't you, Emily?"

"Of course." Did she? All she knew was how you could look at Larry and think you were seeing a big handsome man with dark hair and a wide smile and never once think that the smile reminded you of a shark.

"That's good to hear. A man needs to know he can count on the loyalty of the woman he loves. He needs to know that what happens behind closed doors is private. Can I count on you, Em?"

She didn't have the heart to tell Sis what had happened in New Orleans. Besides, now that they were home, it might never happen again. And then she'd feel bad for having betrayed him.

"You can count on me, Larry. I'm your wife."

"That's my girl."

When he made the turn into Sweet Mama's Café, her heart lifted. He came around to open her door, then bent over and kissed her in plain view of Sweet Mama and Beulah, who were watching out the window.

"Emily, I want you to do something for me." He cupped the bruised side of her face. "Can you, sweetheart?"

"I'll try."

"Tell your family you won't be at the café for the next few days."

"But why? I do most of the cooking, Larry. They need me."

"*I* need you. Is it too much to ask that we have a few days to get settled into our home?"

"Well, no. Of course not."

Emily tried to keep from bursting into tears. He'd said a few days, but would he be content with that? Would he want her to quit work so she'd be at his beck and call?

She swallowed her protest and kept smiling at her husband.

"All right," he said. "That's settled, then."

He was whistling when he got back into his car and drove off. Emily smiled and waved, like a good wife should, and then she pulled a compact out of her purse and powdered her face. The small mirror reflected back a woman wearing too much makeup, but even with the sun slanting through the Spanish moss, Emily couldn't see the bruise.

Satisfied, she pushed open the café door, smiling.

Sis guessed she looked foolish standing in the backyard of the café dressed in a ridiculous yellow T-shirt and floral bell-bottoms as she helped Andy paint his rocket ship, but she didn't care. With her nephew she didn't have to put up any pretense at all.

The same was true of café regulars like Tom Wilson. There he stood, still in his barber's apron, watching Andy and Sis paint as if he were the one planning to launch into a new life somewhere far away from his shop and his cat and a mother in love with hypochondria.

Andy danced around them, smearing more red paint on his T-shirt and shorts than he did on the cobbled-together ship. He chattered with every breath, his dreams spinning around him like fireflies. It was easy to fall into his fantasies, to pretend the little makeshift rocket was going to take off to the moon with Andy at the wheel and Emily and Sis as the passengers.

"Maybe we ought to add a caboose for me," Tom said, then chuckled at his own joke. He'd left his brother in charge of the barbershop, telling James and anybody else who would listen that he had to "supervise this job."

"Rockets don't have cabooses," Andy said. "Just trains."

Tom slapped his knee. "You're a smart one, young 'un."

"I'm like my daddy," Andy said. "My *real* daddy." Then he stuck out his chin and dared anybody to contradict him.

"Sure enough." Tom winked at Sis. "But I bet if I scraped some of that paint off your nose I'd find a little boy who was mighty like his amazing Sweet Mama."

Andy tilted his head to think about this for a while, then he nodded his solemn agreement.

"Beulah, too," he added.

"I sure can see that." Tom squatted so he would be eye level with Andy. "Why, I can see her big old spirit shining right through your eyes."

Andy crossed his eyes, which tickled Tom so much he had to wipe tears of mirth.

Suddenly, the back door popped open and Beulah called out, "Sis! Emily's home!"

Dropping his paintbrush, Andy flew toward the door. Sis didn't have the heart to collar him and clean him up first. What was a little paint between a mother and son who hadn't seen each other for a week?

"I'll take care of that paintbrush," Tom said. "You go on inside and see your sister."

"Thanks, Tom. That will help a lot."

"While I'm out here, do you mind if I paint a bit? The faster this little boy's ship gets done, the faster he's going to get to the moon."

"That would be great, Tom."

Hurrying into the café, Sis had the eerie sensation of being pulled out of Andy's world where every journey led to the moon, and into the real world where somebody had stolen her sister. It didn't matter that Emily was right before her, smiling as always, clinging to her son as if she might never let go, not caring that Andy had smeared paint all over her pink silk blouse. This was not Emily with eyes like oceans and skin like peaches. This was not the sparkling sister who made everybody around her feel better. This was a woman who had aged twenty years in one week, a stranger with dead eyes and heavy makeup who couldn't have sparkled if you'd lit a fuse under her.

Sweet Mama and Beulah flanked her, and Miss Opal Clemson, who was still at the café though it was minutes from closing time. They were all laughing and talking at once. Didn't they see this was not Emily? Didn't they notice how her eyes darted about as if danger lurked in every corner, as if any minute she might be set upon by hooligans?

Emily bent over her son and held out a little yellow horn with a big red bulb attached.

"This is for your rocket ship, Andy."

"Oh, boy! Wait till Mr. Wilson sees this!" Andy honked the horn then raced back outside to his rocket ship.

Suddenly, Emily spotted Sis, and for a moment she was her shining self, her face alight as she raced toward her sister and wrapped her in a tight hug.

"Oh, Sis. I've missed you."

Emily's voice was a breakable thing, shattering against the words and falling into a thousand pieces onto the side of Sis's neck.

"I missed you, too, Em." Sis tried to lean back to get a closer look at Emily's face, but her sister wouldn't let her go, wouldn't budge from her viselike grip.

"Em?" she whispered. "What's wrong?"

"Nothing."

Across the room, Miss Opal was saying goodbye to Sweet Mama and Beulah. The bell over the shop tinkled as she left, the last customer of the day except for Tom Wilson, still in the backyard painting Andy's rocket ship.

Beulah turned the sign on the door to Closed, then she and Sweet Mama headed toward the kitchen, hopefully to get their purses and head on home. Sweet Mama looked unusually tired, and Sis was glad she'd promised to lock up.

She waited till they were out of earshot before she forced Emily to look at her. Up close her appearance was even more shocking.

"What happened on that honeymoon, Em?"

"I'm just tired, that's all. Larry carried me to New Orleans, and you know how nobody in the city ever sleeps."

The awful, heavy makeup, the lifeless eyes and the listless voice told another story, but Sis decided to let it go. At least for now. Her sister looked as if she'd crumble over any little thing.

"I know," she said, making herself as gentle as it was possible for a dedicated curmudgeon to be. "You need some rest. Why don't you take a few days off?"

"Oh, that would be wonderful! It will give me time to help Larry get settled into the house."

Emily's extraordinary relief was as puzzling as her appearance. Considering that she loved cooking more than Sweet Mama and Beulah combined, Sis had expected her to put up a fuss.

"Can you take Andy and me home, Sis?"

"Yes, but you've got to see Andy's rocket ship before you go home. It's a pure wonder."

"I could use some wonder," Emily said, and Sis thought it might be the only true thing she'd heard coming from her sister's lips since she got home.

They stepped outside and into a cloudless day so glorious you'd never know there were two storms brewing, one out in the Atlantic and the other inside Sis. She didn't know what had happened to turn her sister into the tragic woman who stood placidly while her son and dear old Tom Wilson both greeted her with hugs. But she was certain it was Larry's fault, and she would not rest until she got to the bottom of it.

As if she needed more evidence that the jackass was behind Emily's dramatic change, she heard an engine revving across the street. The car was a big Bel Air with none other than her brother-in-law at the wheel. Sis glared in his direction and he peeled off, tires squealing.

Emily jerked as if she'd been shot, but thank God the Bel Air was gone before she saw it. She looked so frail standing there in her spattered blouse and awful makeup that Sis thought she might not be able to endure one more bad thing.

Anybody looking at Sis would have seen a sturdy woman in a yellow T-shirt, shading her eyes against the sun and biding her time while Tom Wilson said goodbye. They would never have known the tornadic thoughts that whirled through her, the desperate plans hatched and then discarded as the silver-haired man made his way out of the backyard. They would never have seen the iron control that kept her from tearing off after Larry Chastain and persuading him to tell the truth, even if she had to use her baseball bat.

She waited, though what she was waiting for, she couldn't have said. Maybe it was the sound of the car engine on the other side of the chain-link fence. Maybe it was the sight of Sweet Mama's big Buick pulling out of the parking lot with Beulah at the wheel. *Thank God.*

"Emily, I think it might be a good idea if I ask Beulah to come stay with you a while."

"No!"

Emily's overreaction confirmed Sis's fears. Larry had done something so awful to her sister that he could wield control even when he wasn't there.

"Just to help you and Larry get settled, Em."

"Sweet Mama and Jim need her."

"I can take care of them, and I think Beulah would love to come over. She dotes on you and Andy. And it will give her a little relief from constant vigilance with Sweet Mama."

For a moment, a little spark showed in Emily's eyes, and then she sagged.

"I couldn't possibly ask her to do that, Sis."

"Why not? She's been taking care of you since you were in diapers."

"I'm not in diapers anymore, Sis."

Let me come, Sis wanted to say. *Let me move in with you. I'll see that nobody ever does anything again to take the light out of your eyes.*

But knowing her sister would say *no,* knowing how it might humiliate her, knowing it might make her situation even worse, Sis held her silence.

"Besides," Emily added. "I have a husband to take care of me."

The only sound in the yard was the tiny pop as Sis's heart broke.

Sixteen

THE STORM HADN'T EVEN come close to Biloxi, and yet after she'd dropped Andy and Emily off and then headed home, Sis felt as if she were already drowning, pulled beneath the waves by the dark undertow of her sister's secrets.

She and Emily were not only sisters but best friends, keepers of each other's dreams and deepest desires. Since Larry had come into the picture, they'd been dancing around the truth, throwing up smoke screens, creating a chasm that Sis might soon be unable to cross.

As she parked her Valiant she noticed Sweet Mama's Buick was not there. Where in the world could they be? The only comfort Sis took was that when she'd last seen them, Beulah had been at the wheel.

She grabbed her purse and hurried into the house. Jim was on the staircase, hobbling along on his crutch. When he saw her, he stopped midway, his jaw dropped open.

"Good God, Sis. You look like you're on the warpath."

"We've got to talk."

As Sis steamed toward the kitchen and waited for Jim to hobble in on his crutch, she felt as if she'd shifted a bale of cotton off her shoulders.

"Jim, Emily's back. They got in this afternoon."

"I'm glad. With that storm brewing, she needs to be home."

"Do you know something I don't?" Considering his connections, it was highly likely.

"I talked to Gordon this afternoon. He says the storm is picking up strength and it's going to be big."

"How big?"

"A monster. It could get so huge it carries the energy equivalent of five hundred thousand atomic bombs."

"Oh, my God. Is that true?"

"Yes. An ordinary summer storm carries the equivalent of thirteen thousand atomic bombs."

"I could have lived the rest of my life without knowing that, Jim."

Now, every time it thundered she was probably going to board the windows and prepare for disaster.

"Did Gordon say it was headed this way?"

"Not yet. But if it turns, I'll start boarding the windows."

He couldn't balance on a crutch and wield a hammer. Feeling beleaguered from every direction, Sis hardly knew which way to turn.

"That storm may or may not become a hurricane, Jim, and we certainly don't know if it's heading this way. The most pressing matter is Em. She looked as if she'd been whipped like a dog. I think Larry's abusing her."

"Where is he?" Jim jumped out of his chair, his fists balled, his body perfectly balanced on one leg.

"It won't do Emily any good if you go flying off the handle, Jim. This is exactly why I didn't say anything before the wedding."

"You knew about this before she married that jackass and didn't tell me?"

"I couldn't be certain. I saw a small bruise on her arm when she tried on her wedding dress. But it was nothing compared to the way she was in the café." Sis drank a long swig of tea, trying to collect herself.

"You saw bruises?" Jim asked.

"I couldn't under all that makeup."

"Emily hardly ever wears makeup."

"Exactly." With her heart pounding too fast and sweat soaking the underarms of the T-shirt she'd foolishly bought in a failed attempt at giving herself some fashion flair, Sis had the awful feeling that something was clawing at the house trying to get in, something beyond imaging. "I don't know what to do anymore, Jim."

"I can beat the shit out of Em's husband." Jim's grin was reminiscent of the carefree brother he'd once been, the one who found humor in every situation.

"Let's call that plan B."

The phone on the kitchen wall started ringing, but Sis didn't want to answer it. It was bound to be bad news.

"Sis, how about if plan A is you answering the phone, and me calling in a few favors from old friends to see what I can find out about Larry Chastain?"

"Do I have to answer it?"

They both regarded the jangling phone as if it were a knife-wielding enemy in the kitchen, set to launch an attack. Finally Sis dragged herself over to answer it.

"Hello?"

"Beth?"

It was Michael. Sis leaned against the counter, hip-slung, letting the miracle of his apology wrap around her. He was still caught up with an out-of-town client, he said, but would be free later in the week and wanted to take her to the Fiesta Club.

For a moment, Sis panicked at the idea of going to the most-talked-about hot spot for singles on the strip. That was for popular girls, women like Emily who knew how to make small talk and dance to the Rolling Stones' "Honky Tonk Women" and cuddle up at the Moonlite Drive-In over in Pass Christian while *Midnight Cowboy* and *Easy Rider* played on the outdoor screen.

She almost said no, except that he was saying her name again, *Beth,* in a way that made her breathless.

"Yes," she said, and when she hung up she stared into space, smiling.

"Who was it, Sis?"

"Just an old friend," she said, but it felt like more.

Sweet Mama was in her own car with Beulah going someplace, but she'd forgotten where. There was a picnic basket on the floorboard that probably contained some clues if she could remember what was in it.

Was that food she smelled? It was something deep fried overlaid with a scent so sweet she thought she was sixteen again and falling in love with Peter Blake.

Alarmed, Sweet Mama glanced over at Beulah. That's how she remembered her own age now. Nobody would mistake that largish black woman with the belly pooching out around her belt and all that gray hair for somebody sixteen. Which meant she was old and Peter Blake was gone, but where was he? She vaguely recalled something about him being in Alaska. Or was that Africa?

"Lucy, you remember what we're gonna say, now, don't you?"

Nothing came to mind except the thought that maybe the basket held fried chicken and Amen cobbler. She didn't know why.

"Certainly, but I'll bet you don't. See if you can tell it."

"We'll say, 'Hello!' all innocent and happy like we just accidentally dropped by Emily's house. Don't forget that part, Lucy. Act innocent."

As Beulah recounted how they would drag out the hamper full of food and might as well stay for supper, whether that jackass wanted them to or not, Sweet Mama wished she had diabetes or tuberculosis or a broken hip. Something that could be treated, something she'd know how to fight. Anything except this awful deterioration of the mind that made her feel as if she were setting out to sea in a leaky boat without a compass while her family stood on the dock waving goodbye.

The long goodbye, her doctor called it, but how long? When would the time come that she didn't know to put on her stockings or wear her hat or find her purse? Already she was struggling with what to put in it. Car keys. That she knew. A billfold. But why?

"That man ain't got no business mistreating our Emily. I aim to set with my feet under his table as long as it takes to see that she won't come to harm this evening."

Suddenly, her granddaughter came to mind as clearly as if she were standing right before Sweet Mama. In the café this afternoon Emily had put on a brave front, but she'd looked like the one drifting away in a worthless boat.

"Beulah, I lied to you. About knowing why we were going to see Emily."

"I know you did, Lucy."

"Something awful happened to her on that honeymoon, didn't it?"

"From the looks of her, it did. If I'd ever dreamed that snake would hit her, I'd a spoke up before the wedding."

"She wouldn't have listened. Both my granddaughters are stubborn."

"Like somebody else I know."

"I've got to take care of her. Bill and Margaret will be mad if I don't."

"Bill and Margaret are not here. Remember?"

"Oh."

She sat crestfallen until she remembered why she kept the billfold. Sis had labeled all of her pictures on the back with names and significant dates and little reminders such as *grand-daughter, son, daughter-in-law, grandson* and *great-grandson*.

She drew the billfold out of her purse and flipped the small cellophane album to one of her favorites, Bill and Margaret leaning against the side of their Ford automobile, smiling into the camera without a clue that the car they were so proud of would become their death trap.

Sweet Mama moved her hand over the photographs, desperate to capture the past through her fingertips. But no matter how hard she tried, it didn't work.

Beulah reached for her hand.

"Don't you worry none, Lucy. As long as you got me, you got a memory and you got a friend."

"Does that mean I can drive the car home?"

"I ain't letting you drive and you might as well quit asking me about it." Beulah's face softened as she parked the car in Emily's driveway. "But you can keep the keys, Lucy. You always get to keep the keys."

A beautiful woman opened the front door and Sweet Mama had the awful certainty that she knew her. But she couldn't think of her name.

"Hello!" she said, innocent and perky, like Beulah had told her.

"Sweet Mama! What a wonderful surprise."

This beautiful granddaughter whose name was on the tip of Sweet Mama's tongue hugged her close while she looked around for Beulah.

Emily, Beulah mouthed, and suddenly it all came back. The wedding, the fiancé whose name Sweet Mama could never remember, the fried chicken in the picnic basket, the storm.

Panic crept over her again. Was it a storm heading this way, or was it the storm she could never forget?

What's His Name appeared in the doorway, and Sweet Mama's instincts kicked in. The stench of beer and lies wafted off him, and it didn't bother her one whit that she could never remember his name.

Beulah elbowed her way forward, the picnic hamper over one arm and her purse over the other.

"We brought fried chicken with all the trimmings, and we aim to stay for supper. Ain't that nice?"

Emily said, "Yes," and her husband didn't say anything, which caused Sweet Mama to chuckle. It didn't matter what situation she got herself into, she could count on Beulah.

As they traipsed inside, Sweet Mama hoped she'd remember everything in Emily's house, including the direction of the bathroom. But what was that big TV doing in the corner and where did those god-awful huge chairs come from? It seemed to her that she'd ended up someplace foreign where she didn't know the language and she couldn't find anything because the landscape around her kept changing.

Still, when everybody sat down as if they belonged, Sweet Mama did, too. And then Andy came flying down the stairs to lean against his mother's knee. Emily kissed the top of his head, a gesture that was as familiar to Sweet Mama as the movement of her own hands. For a blessed moment, she felt fully anchored to the present.

"Emily?" What's His Name's voice was soft, like a caress.

She startled, her whole body going stiff. "Yes, Larry?"

"Why don't you go into the kitchen and make us some coffee, darling?"

The *darling* part made Sweet Mama's skin crawl. Beulah cast a dark look in Larry's direction and then reached over and pulled Andy into her lap.

"What you been up to, sweet pea?"

"I been in my room, playing." He glanced sideways at Larry, then back at Beulah. "Can I have some coffee?"

"It'll make you big and black and ugly like me," Beulah said, but Larry was quick to contradict.

"That's just an old tale, Andy. You'll drink milk so you can grow up to be a man, like your new daddy."

Andy turned his back on his new daddy and crossed his eyes, then jumped out of Beulah's lap and leaned on Sweet Mama's knee to whisper, "Can you come play in my room? I got checkers."

Relieved to be leaving this room where the air felt too thick to breathe, Sweet Mama stood up and announced, "I'm going to play checkers with Andy."

"I don't think that's a good idea," Larry said. "Andy, the stairs are too steep for Sweet Mama. Go on upstairs and bring the checkerboard down here."

Sweet Mama didn't like the idea of climbing all those steps, but she wasn't about to bend to the will of this unpleasant man.

"The day I can't climb stairs, I'll be at the funeral home waiting for my granddaughters to pick out my casket."

The way Larry cracked his knuckles and tightened his

mouth reminded her of that jackass Peter Blake when she used to get the best of him. Finally he said, "Andy, be a gentleman and hang on to Sweet Mama's arm. And don't go saying anything that will upset her." His sudden smile flashed to everybody in the room. "We're a close-knit family here."

It took longer than Sweet Mama thought it would to get up the stairs, but she was glad when Andy shut the door and she could flop into a chair to catch her breath.

Andy raced over to the bed and grabbed his old teddy bear, then brought it over and set into her lap.

"Henry's scared," he whispered.

"What's he scared of?"

"Larry's big ugly voice." Andy tiptoed to his door, cracked it open and peered down the hall. Satisfied, he came back and leaned on Sweet Mama's knee. "He talked real loud and mean to my mommy."

"Why?"

"'Cause of Mr. Michael."

It took a while to figure out who he was talking about, but it finally came to her that long-time customer Opal Clemson had lately come to the café with a handsome man she called Michael. She didn't recall when.

"What about Mr. Michael?"

"Me and Mommy was playing kites and mine got all tangled up in the tree and Aunt Sis was gone home and Mr. Michael comed and climbed up the tree."

"That was nice of him."

"Larry said it was flirting. What's flirting?"

"Never mind what that fool said. What else did he do?"

"He made Mommy cry."

If Sweet Mama were twenty years younger she'd march downstairs and threaten him with hellfire and damnation if he was ever mean to her granddaughter again. She might not remember where her shoes were, but she remembered how to take care of the ones she loved.

Feeling her infirmities like a tooth gone bad, she said, "Did he talk mean to you, too?"

"I runned inside and hid in my closet."

She had an image of a scared little boy trying to make himself invisible in a dark closet, and she got so upset she forgot why he was in the closet in the first place. Something awful had happened, that's all she knew.

"You have to tell Sis."

There were footsteps on the stairs, followed by Larry's calling, "Andy, come on down here for dinner now. A family always eats together."

"Can me and you have a secret?" Andy whispered.

She barely had time to tell him yes before Larry opened the door, all smiles. "Andy, have you been a good boy like I told you?"

"Yes."

"Yes, what?"

"Yes, sir."

"It pays to teach children manners," he told her, and she wanted to slap him down.

Her skin crawled when Larry helped her up and led her down the stairs. It seemed urgent to her that she remember a little boy's secret, but it had already vanished into the same cloud that made it impossible to know which piece of cutlery to use when she sat down at the dining room table.

"Use this one, Lucy," Beulah whispered, then placed a dinner fork in her hands.

The food smelled good and she was hungry. What did it

matter which fork she used or how long they spent in the dining room eating fried chicken on Emily's blue plates?

There was no kind of measurement you could put on keeping your granddaughter safe.

The only thing Sweet Mama knew about time anymore was the moon. When she and Beulah finally left Emily's it made a bright pathway to the car. That meant it was night and the time of dreams that carried her back to the days when other women wore flapper dresses while she wore an apron in her own kitchen. The darkness also brought memories of standing elbow to elbow with Beulah as they created the very first Amen cobbler.

That was either the most wonderful thing that had happened to Sweet Mama or the most horrible. She could no longer remember.

Seventeen

LARRY LAY ON HIS BACK, one arm thrown above his head and one across her thigh, the heavy weight of it a stark reminder that he viewed her as his possession. Wide-eyed and weary, Emily lay staring into the dark.

As if it weren't bad enough that Larry didn't want her to go back to work, he'd come home early and found Michael Clemson in her front yard. The way Larry had stood under the tree cracking his knuckles and holding his mouth in a tight little line, squeezing the stems of the red roses in his hand, she thought he was going to climb up that tree after the man and drag him down by the hair of his head.

Oh, he'd said, "Thank you for getting my son's kite," but his cool politeness and barely controlled rage wouldn't fool anybody. Then, the minute Michael left, he'd lit into Emily in her own front yard.

"What was he doing here, Emily?" A polite enough question, but delivered like a hurled dagger.

"He was on his way home and stopped to get Andy's kite out of the tree."

"*I* could get my son's kite, Emily. Didn't you ever think

about that? That a brand-new father wants to get his own son's kite?"

"I'm sorry, Larry. I didn't think."

"I *know* you didn't, sweetheart. But the next time he stops by to *help,* tell him *no.*"

"Larry, nothing happened. The kite was stuck and he was helping. That's all."

"That's all?" His voice went hard and high, and the roses fluttered to the ground. He cupped her chin, his thumb making tight little circles along her jaw. "Why are you blushing, Emily?"

Tears started rolling down her cheeks and she saw Andy race into the house.

"Please, Larry, not in the front yard."

He took hold of her elbow and marched her into the house, tromping over the fallen roses and slamming the front door behind them. She didn't know what would have happened if Sweet Mama and Beulah hadn't driven up with a basketful of fried chicken.

The scent of it was still in the house, causing such a longing in Emily she couldn't lie still. She eased out from under Larry's hold, praying every breath that he wouldn't wake up. What would he do? Insist on another bout of hard, punishing love, or would he take up the fight over Michael again?

It had been awful. More accusations of *whore* and *cheating* heaped on her head after everybody had gone and Andy was tucked into bed. Larry had backed her up against the bedroom wall, his fists clenching and unclenching.

"Please, Larry." She put her arm over her forehead to ward off the expected blow. "You promised!"

The rage had gone out of him as quickly as it had come.

"I don't know what I'd do if I ever lost you." He knelt and

started kissing her through her gown. "I can *never* lose you, Emily."

He'd picked her up and carried her to bed, but she didn't know which was worse, the fight, the makeup sex or the chilling idea that she was in a prison and Larry held the only key.

Now, Larry moved suddenly in his sleep, rolling toward her side of the bed, his arm stretched toward her pillow. She held her breath, waiting, and when he finally settled back into deep sleep, she tiptoed from the room and down the stairs.

She'd fix tea. Beulah and Sweet Mama said there was nothing that couldn't be figured out over a glass of sweet tea. Tonight, though, Emily would drink it hot with lots of cream and sugar, comfort in a cup.

She stopped in the kitchen doorway, alerted by a sound, a premonition, angels whispering in her ear. Emily didn't dare turn on the light, so she stood awhile, letting her eyes adjust to the dark. Suddenly, she saw him, her little boy crumpled in a pile in his pajamas, hugging his teddy bear to his chest. On the floor beside him was Larry's big black coffee mug with *The Boss* written in white lettering.

Something burst through Emily with the force of a train hurtling off the tracks, a mother's primitive urge to grab her son and run. She stood there with her hand over her mouth, holding back a howl of despair. When she collected herself, she scooped up the cup and set it in the sink, then sank beside her son and rolled him onto her lap.

"Shh, it's me. Don't make a sound."

"Mommy?"

"Be really quiet, Andy. We don't want to wake Larry."

"I got my brave bear. He's not scared of a thousand million monsters."

"Is that what you think of Larry?"

"He's donkey doo doo." He peered up at her. "Are you mad 'cause I said a ugly word?"

"No, I'm not mad." Her dismay at what she was doing to her son suddenly grew bigger than anything Larry could possibly do to her. "What are you doing down here, honey?"

"Drinking coffee. But I wiped the Larry germs off first."

"Why would you drink coffee?"

"Beulah said it would make me big and dark like her, and then I could scare Larry off." Andy held his hands out for her inspection. "Am I turning black?"

It was so quiet, you couldn't hear a thing, not even the sound of a sob. Emily swallowed her tears and hugged her child closer. Already he was nodding off. She struggled upright, then carried Andy upstairs to his room, praying with every breath that Larry wouldn't wake up and catch her on the stairs in the dark.

She tucked Andy into his bed, making sure the teddy bear was in his arms and the sheet was just right under his chin. Even when she got it exactly the way she wanted, she still didn't leave. She wanted to lie down beside him and wake up to his smile and then pull the covers over their heads where they would play one of their many games of pretend. They'd be elephants or pink flamingos or one of the many exotic animals Andy loved to read about in Sweet Mama's *National Geographic*.

She brushed a lock of his hair back from his forehead. "I'm not going to let a thousand million monsters scare you," she whispered, and she tiptoed back to her room.

It took her a while to ease back into bed without waking Larry, and then she lay under the covers, wide-eyed, till dawn. When she heard Larry stirring, she closed her eyes and

feigned sleep. He kissed her shoulder, waited awhile for a response then finally showered and dressed.

He left the room softly in perfect imitation of a man in
love respecting his wife's need for sleep. Even when the door
closed, she lay quietly until she heard him banging cabinet
doors in the kitchen.

It seemed forever before she heard the front door slam. Still,
she waited till there was not a sound in the house except her
own rushing blood.

Emily snapped on the light and there was a note on the
bedside table, scrawled on a pharmaceutical notepad in Larry's bold handwriting. "Darling, I love you more than life itself. Have a great day and be careful of the neighbors. Yours
forever, Larry."

Forever chilled her to the bone, and Emily shivered as she
tore the note into little bits, then marched into the bathroom
and threw it down the toilet. She was flushing when the phone
rang. Knowing before she answered that it would be her sister, she picked up the phone and said, "Hello."

"Em, are you all right?"

"Just breathless, that's all. I was in the bathroom when the
phone rang." She glanced at the clock. "Are you already at
the café?"

"Sweet Mama and Beulah are. I thought I'd come by and
see you and Andy on the way to work."

Emily thought about the way sisters can take one look at
each other and know a thing without being told. Her face
overheated as she imagined Sis gauging the consequences of
Emily's terrible choice, then marching to the closet to get the
suitcases. Humiliation and stubborn pride turned her red as
the roses still lying crushed in her front yard. Thank goodness
they'd been under the tree where Beulah hadn't seen them.

"No, don't, Sis. Everything's great here, and I have a ton of things to do today."

"I'll just stay a minute."

"That's really not a good idea, Sis." Emily pushed her hair away from her hot face. "I think I'm coming down with a virus."

Sis got really quiet in that way she had. Emily seized the silence.

"Enough about me. What's going on with you?"

"Well...I'm going out with Michael Clemson tonight."

"Oh, my gosh! That's so wonderful, Sis. Wear something really pretty."

Andy slipped into her room and then stood by the door, hanging on to that old bear and tucking one leg under in his best imitation of a flamingo.

"I thought I'd just wear my slacks and black T-shirt," Sis was saying. "It's not really a date."

"It most certainly is, and don't you dare wear that frumpy old black. You dress up and look pretty."

"Maybe I will. Bye, Em, gotta run."

Emily hung up and Andy said, "Can I make a peanut butter sam'wich for breakfast?"

"Yes." She didn't even say, *be careful*. What did it matter if he got peanut butter all over the kitchen? "And you can watch cartoons all day if you like."

"Like on vacation?"

"Just like that, Andy."

If Andy felt like he was on vacation, it didn't show in the way he slipped from the room.

Emily sank back against her covers, trying to marshal her thoughts into some kind of order. She was aware of only one truth: she had built a booby trap, and now her own son was tangled up in it.

Though it was the middle of August and so hot and still outside even the Spanish moss on the live oak tree beside her bedroom window looked listless, Emily reached for her old cozy pink robe that had most of the chenille rubbed off. Trying to steal comfort from the familiar. Then she went into the bathroom, hoping a nice, hot soak would make her feel less fuzzy-headed.

But the tub held no magical restorative powers. As she watched the water go down the drain, she thought she heard someone crying in the distance and wondered if it was the echo of tears she'd dammed up inside.

Suddenly, every inch of her body went on alert. The crying wasn't coming from a distance; it was her own son in her own home, a place she hardly knew anymore.

She found Andy sitting on the stairs, sobbing, a puddle of milk at his feet and a lopsided sandwich in the plate beside him.

Defeated, she sat down and put her arm around him. What do you say to a son who has suddenly discovered his house is enemy territory? What do you do if you've made the biggest mistake of your life and you don't know how to correct it? You don't know whether it would be worse to stand your ground and try to dodge the hand grenades the enemy lobbed in your direction, or to flee and chance getting blown up by the land mines he was sure to plant in your escape path.

Nothing the gossips had said when she was unwed and pregnant could compare to the nightmare of her life as Mrs. Larry Chastain. Too late she realized the price she'd paid for respectability was far, far too high. Too late she understood that her greatest threat was neither gossip nor the weight of public opinion, but the man she'd brought into her home to be a father to her son. A father should be someone like Major Bill Blake who fought for his country but treasured his wife and children.

"I spilled milk," Andy said, his voice as small as Emily felt.

"It was just an accident, Andy."

She smiled at him, hoping to cheer him up, and suddenly she saw an endless string of years stretching before her, laced with lies, camouflaged with pancake makeup and false smiles.

"Andy, if you'll run to the kitchen and get a dishcloth, we'll clean the milk right up. Okay?"

"'K!" He raced off, recharged with the exuberant energy that was as much a part of him as the cowlick in his blond hair.

How soon before the darkness in Larry spilled over to Andy? How soon before her child was no longer an innocent little boy who believed he could fly to the moon? How soon before he became as scared and secretive as she?

Andy was heading her way with the dishcloth, his step and his cowlick both bouncing, and she pasted a big smile back on her face.

"Boy, that was quick."

"I can fly like Nell Arms Strong."

"I can see that."

He attacked the puddle with the same enthusiasm he'd used to build his rocket ship.

"I made you a sam'wich, too, and it didn't even spill."

"This is mine?" Emily picked up the lopsided sandwich, cradling it in her hands with the same care she'd give to an exotic baby bird. "That's wonderful, Andy. I'm so proud of you."

"Can me and you eat together in front of the TV?"

Eating in front of the TV was an occasion reserved for birthdays and holidays. But she said yes, anyway, because she didn't want Andy to have any more disappointments that day, because she needed Andy as much as he needed her. "We'll have an indoor picnic."

"Wait till I get Henry!"

As he raced toward the kitchen, Emily carried her sandwich into the den, turned on the TV and curled up on her sofa. An image of the local weatherman filled the screen.

"In the latest weather advisory, the storm over the Atlantic is now officially a Category 1 hurricane," he said. "Winds are at ninety-five miles an hour but we expect the hurricane to upgrade rapidly as it gains strength from the warm currents and heads toward land."

Dear God! What land? Emily wrapped her arms around herself so her terror wouldn't escape and frighten Andy.

"The storm has been named Camille, and it's heading straight for Cuba. Residents of western Cuba can expect this hurricane to make landfall sometime Friday as a Category 3. But that's likely to be just the warm-up. We're keeping a close eye to see if Camille holds her track toward the Mississippi Gulf Coast."

Emily felt as if the world as she knew it had been obliterated. There was already a hurricane on the Mississippi Gulf Coast. Its name was Larry and it was right inside her house.

The very nature of a hurricane makes you feel helpless. No matter how many seawalls you build, no matter how many hurricane hunters you send into the eye, no matter how well trained your state's National Guard, you are still defenseless in the face of nature's most deadly fury.

The wise always evacuated. If Emily stayed in this house, Hurricane Larry would destroy her and Andy and everything in his path long before Camille had a chance. Suddenly, something strong rose up inside her, a She Bear with claws and fangs and fierce, hot blood that flowed through her like a river.

"Mommy?" Andy was standing in the doorway, his eyes wide and his arms clutching Henry. "Is that hurricane gonna get me?"

The river grew in her until it washed away every sign of weakness. If she were alone, she might stay in this awful farce of a marriage and give Larry a chance to change, but she would never hang around and give him a chance to turn his rage on her child. It was bad enough that he'd caused Andy to cower in the kitchen and cry on the staircase.

She went to the doorway and put her arms around her son. "No, Andy. I won't let that hurricane get you."

Eighteen

SIS HAD THAT DREAM again where she was pressing her face against the windowpane, crying out to Sweet Mama and Beulah in the storm. She fought her way out of the nightmare, kicked back the sheet and sat straight up in bed with her head buzzing and sweat drenching her shorty pajamas.

The buzzing increased, and she realized it wasn't her head at all, but the telephone beside her bed. How long had it been ringing? She grabbed the receiver and said a gruff hello.

"Sis?"

It was Emily, sounding nothing like the sister who had lied to her on the phone yesterday about having a virus. Sis didn't have to see her to know. She understood Emily better than she knew herself. Still, today there was a note in her voice that Sis couldn't decipher.

"What's wrong, Em?"

"Good grief, Sis, does anything have to be wrong for me to call?"

"I'm just jumpy, that's all. First, you lie to me about having a virus and then Beulah starts coming unraveled over Hurricane Camille."

"What's going on with Beulah?"

"She piled every bit of rain gear we own out in the front hall. The mattresses would be out there, too, if I hadn't talked her out of it."

"Do you think the storm is coming this way?"

"I don't have a crystal ball, Em, but I can tell you one thing. If it does and if it's as big as they're predicting, the Blake family won't be around to see it. I'm getting us out of here."

"Sis?" Emily's voice changed notes again. Where it had been a lighthearted piccolo, it was now the deep quiet of a cello. "I'm already packing."

"To evacuate?"

"To leave Larry."

Sis wanted to shout hallelujah. She wanted to weep. But most of all, she wanted to wrap her arms around her sister and simply hold her close.

"Did you say you're leaving that jerk? Em, say it again!"

"I'm leaving my husband. You were right about him all along."

"I didn't want to be right. I just wanted you and Andy to be safe and happy."

"We're coming over tomorrow. Don't tell anybody yet."

The stout fragrance of good, strong coffee with chicory drifted up the stairs, and the sounds of Beulah and Sweet Mama stirring around in the kitchen, little things, ordinary things that signaled a family going about the daily business of living. This was where Emily belonged, safe inside the home where she'd wished on stars and dreamed of sugar and spice and depended on her family to catch her if she fell.

"Don't wait, Em. Leave him today. After the café closes, I'll come over and help you pack."

"No! I don't want you to miss your date tonight."

Emily's sudden panic sliced Sis with such sharp regret she

actually looked at her hands to see if they were bleeding. What sort of hell had her sister endured, and why had Sis sat back and let it happen?

Never again, she vowed. *Never again.*

"You need help, Em. Besides, I don't think it's really a date, just a couple of old friends having drinks together. I'll call and cancel, that's all."

"Please, Sis! I don't know what Larry would do if he saw you here. He's capable of anything. And I don't want Andy to be involved in one more thing that scares him."

"I'll come and get Andy right now."

"I've thought this out, Sis. I'm going to spend the day packing just enough for Andy and me till we can get settled somewhere else, then I'll hide the suitcases before he gets home and be ready to leave right after he does in the morning."

"There's no reason I can't come over and help."

"No, Sis! The only way my plan will work is if I don't arouse Larry's suspicions. Please, say you'll stay away."

"All right, then. I will."

"Promise!"

"I promise." Her sister was crying now, each quiet little sob an ice pick that jabbed Sis's heart. "My God, Em, what did he do to you?"

As Emily cataloged the blows and the many ways Larry was scaring Andy, rage overflowed Sis and turned everything around her red. It tinted the air and the windowpanes so that even as she sought release from her view of the Gulf, she could see nothing except the color of her own fury.

"What's so awful is that Larry keeps saying he'll never let me go. I don't even know if he'll give me a divorce."

"Everything's going to be all right, Em. We'll get the best divorce lawyer in the state. Just stop worrying."

"It's hard not to. I just get this awful feeling that I'm running out of time."

"The storm won't be here for a while, Em. And it might veer off in another direction."

"It's not the storm, it's this feeling I have, like somebody walking on my grave."

"You sound like Beulah. Just stop that. Everything's going to be okay. I won't have it any other way."

"Okay, then."

"Better now?"

"All better. See you tomorrow, Sis."

When Sis hung up she had the strangest feeling she ought to call Emily right back. Things she'd left unsaid roared through her mind with the force of Camille storming toward landfall. *I'm coming right over,* she should have said, and then she wouldn't be sitting on the side of the bed, worrying about her sister as she listened to her brother pace his bedroom, his gait marked by the thump of his crutch. *I'll bring Sweet Mama and Beulah with me. We can handle Larry.* Oh, Lord, why hadn't she said that? Didn't Emily know that those two strong women would do anything to save the one they love?

Their voices drifted up the stairs, indecipherable as words and sentences, but recognizable as the kind of lazy, meandering conversation you only have with someone you feel as if you've known forever. Sis sat very still, letting their voices drift over her like smoke, letting herself fall into the beauty of their friendship until the air around her cleared and she could once more see the sea and the sky, not a cloud in sight. It was the kind of day made for picnics and easy confessions with best friends. The kind of day where Sis should have told her sister the truest thing of all.

I love you.

★ ★ ★

That evening could not be distinguished from any other they'd had in Biloxi all summer. It was cloudless with the stars and moon shining over a flat, calm Gulf.

A huge crowd flocked to the Fiesta Club and there was a carnival feel that spilled over to Sis as she went through the door on the arm of Michael Clemson. In her green summer dress with her hair caught back in a barrette, she felt young and frivolous and almost pretty. She felt like the sort of woman who waited every evening on her front porch swing for a good man with a big heart and a shy smile to take her arm and say, "You look nice tonight, Beth."

Sweet Mama and Beulah had been on the porch, too, sipping iced tea and waiting in rocking chairs for their chance to see Sis go *courting.* That was their terminology, as if the word itself could turn a simple evening into a romantic interlude with endless possibilities.

Still, as Michael led her to a small table for two near the back of the packed nightclub, she dared to believe this evening might lead to something more than an enduring friendship, the kind where she could call on a whim to say *Let's go fishing* or *Do you want to sit on the porch and drink sweet tea* or even *I just wanted to talk,* and he would say *yes.*

What he did say was, "Would you like a drink?"

"Yes, I'd like that."

"You'll have to tell me what kind. There's a lot I don't know about you anymore, Beth."

"White wine, any kind of Chablis but not Chardonnay."

He placed the order and then smiled at her as the waitress left.

"I see you're still partial to something sweet in the summer."

"I am," she said, and she didn't feel the least bit of compunction to refer to the evidence on her hips. She had no vanities and she certainly didn't intend to enter into a relationship being anything except who she was. This man already felt important to her, and had since he'd sought her out at the café after Emily's wedding. It was wonderful to think of what might happen after a long, brutal summer of utter chaos.

Sis found it easy to laugh with him, natural to reminisce about their summers of long ago when she'd invite him back to the pink Victorian house for lemonade after a game of beach baseball and then always add extra sugar to her glass.

"Beth, do you know the first thing I noticed about you at Emily's wedding reception?"

"Probably the sausage curls."

"It was that you hadn't changed. You're still that unusual combination of fierce and soft I saw so many years ago."

Elevated by his viewpoint to the woman she might have been but for fate, she fell into his words, savored them like one of Sweet Mama's finest confections. There was something unfathomable in the way he studied her, as if he were reaching from a faraway place to find what had been lost.

They seemed suspended there, alone in a crowded room where anything at all might happen, where time could march backward and dreams could bloom again, where Sis might forget that joy always comes with a price.

The waitress set their glasses on the table, and the slender thread tethering them to endless possibilities snapped with a sound as audible as a sigh. Sis shifted backward and Michael picked up his glass.

"I'll admit the curls took me aback," he said, and Sis was surprised at how disappointed she felt that he seemed to be deliberately steering them away from a deeper connection. "They were so unlike you."

"But very much like my sister."

When Michael leaned back from her, it occurred to Sis that every time he tried to get personal, she either didn't respond or veered the conversation in another direction. She didn't know if she was simply devoid of any flirtation or she was scared of reaching out for something she wanted but might not get. She wished she could call Emily for advice. Her sister could put men into a dither with nothing more than a smile.

Of course, look what that smile had brought to her doorstep. Had Emily managed to get all the packing done? Had she hidden the suitcases so Larry couldn't find them? Would she be able to act natural so he would never suspect that after tonight he'd never see her again except in a courtroom?

Sis hadn't dared call her again for fear Larry had come home unexpectedly for lunch or because he forgot his briefcase or simply because he had the sort of suspicious nature that had made him lurk around looking for reasons to be angry.

"Beth? Where did you go?"

Michael covered her hand with his, and it felt as natural as breathing. Sis felt herself letting go of her uncertainties and her awful sense of impending doom. With his skin warm against hers, she knew she wasn't going to lie to him. Deep down where the truth dwells, she understood that no matter what kind of relationship developed with Michael Clemson, it would not be built on pretense.

"Personal problems, Michael."

"Anything you'd care to discuss with me? I might be able to lend a hand or I can just listen."

"I'd like that, Michael. But not right now. Tonight, I'd like to shut out everything except the wine and the music and our friendship."

"It's a deal, then. No talk of problems."

His smile was carefree, but he kept his hand over hers in a way that felt protective, and so wonderful Sis would think about it later as she lay in her bed and watched the moon track across the sky.

Up front the band started playing Johnny Cash's big hit, "A Boy Named Sue," and a crowd rushed toward the small dance floor.

"Would you like to dance, Beth?"

"I'd hoped you wouldn't say that."

"What a relief. I'm not much of a dancer myself. More of an observer." He grinned. "But a keen one."

Sudden pandemonium broke out up front, interspersed with yells of "Hey, now" and "What do you think you're doing?" The spotlight on the musicians showed a bowlegged man wearing a bandanna tied around his balding head, leaning drunkenly into the microphone.

"Everybody listen up, now," he said. "There's gonna be a hurricane party."

"Sit down," a male voice from the other side of the room yelled. "Let the band play."

But somebody else yelled, "Where at?" while the rest of the crowd cheered and clapped. The band put down their instruments and lit up cigarettes.

"At the Richelieu Manor apartments over in Pass Christian. If Camille shows her ugly face, we aim to ride her out in style."

Whoops and cheers went up again, with only a few sane voices urging caution. The man who had issued the party invitation staggered back to his seat and the band started playing once more, but the specter of Camille was now in the room, sucking out all the air.

"Let's go outside," Michael said.

Without waiting for a reply, he put his arm around her and

led her to a huge live oak tree just beyond the perimeters of the parking lot. Though Spanish moss made a deep curtain around them, the Gulf reflected the light of millions of stars and a moon that looked as if it were close enough to touch.

"Thank you," she said. "I needed to get out of there."

His arm was still around her, and she let herself lean into him and breathe, simply breathe.

"Beth, I know you're too smart to subscribe to foolish talk like that."

"I'm too stubborn, Michael. I rarely listen to anybody about anything."

"How did I know you were going to say that?"

"Because your memory is long and you still recall telling me that I should pitch underhanded because girls always do."

"And you threw a fastball overhand that knocked me down."

"I can still throw a fastball."

"As long as you don't throw me a curve." He smiled down at her. "Beth, I couldn't believe my good fortune when I came back and found you here, the same as always."

"I *am* the same, Michael. Stubborn. Independent. Outspoken."

"You forgot loyal."

The way he looked at her turned so personal Sis marveled at how you could be traveling alone one minute and the next find yourself in the company of a man whose easy presence made it feel as if he'd never left in the first place.

"Beth, I'd very much like to explore what's happening between us."

"So would I."

"I'm glad." He toyed with her hair, letting it curl around his fingers and filter through so the strands caught the moonlight. "I know you're a woman who makes up her own mind, but you have to listen to me now. The National Guard's been put on standby."

"Do you think the hurricane's really going to hit Biloxi?"

"I'm not taking any chances. I'll have to stay, but I'm going to make sure Aunt Opal evacuates."

"How long do you think we have?"

"Two days maybe three, and then all hell's liable to break loose."

Emily would be home before then, and Sis would have time to storm proof the café as best she could and help Sweet Mama and Beulah pack a few things and maybe even find Jim's leg.

"Beth?" His arm was still around her, and he was leaning so close she could feel his warm breath brushing her cheek. "If they give the order to evacuate, tell me you'll leave," he said, but it felt as if he were saying something else, something as intimate as a promise.

She nodded, and opened her mouth to say yes, but his mouth got in the way. And yet, how could it be in the way when Michael was kissing her and holding her close and telling her without words that they were going to be more than friends?

It was the briefest of kisses, no more than his lips brushing against hers, and yet he held her hand on the walk to the car and the drive home. Sis swung between wild hope and the absolute certainty that the universe wasn't going to turn her loose from the past.

Finally, they stood in front of her door where the glare of the porch light stole the ease they'd had under the Spanish moss and every bit of glamour she might have enjoyed in the darkened corner of the Fiesta Club. As he stood slightly apart, looking down at her, did he see how her hair had flattened in the humidity and how she wore worry like a facial mask? Did he see a woman past her prime who now felt foolish because she'd sought youth by putting barrettes in her hair? Even her festive green dress was no longer right. It made her look like she was trying too hard.

More than anything, she wanted him to see her for what she was, a strong, independent woman, his equal in every way, a woman who might not bring beauty to the table, but who would certainly hold her own in intelligent discourse. Sis changed her posture, becoming that self-contained woman who had attracted him in the first place.

But the moment he might have bent down for a good-night kiss came and went, and with it the breath Sis had been holding to keep her stomach in. What did it matter anymore?

She stepped back and smiled brightly at him, letting him off the hook.

"Thank you for a lovely evening. It was nice to renew an old acquaintance."

"Not that old, I hope." He smiled and took her hand. "I'll call you, Beth. Tomorrow."

Did she nod? Did she say *yes?* Did she even breathe as he left the porch, got into his car and drove off?

She let herself through the front door, tiptoed upstairs and got into her pajamas quietly so she wouldn't wake anybody. Then she lay under the covers lost in thought and the aftermath of an unfamiliar ritual Sweet Mama and Beulah called courtship.

Sis finally drifted asleep, but in the dark of the night she jarred awake as if Camille had just sent a thirty-five-foot storm surge straight through her window. With her heart pounding too hard and sweat drenching her pajama top, she got out of bed and went to her window. But there were no boiling clouds and wind-whipped water, no comet burning through the sky

in a harbinger of doom. There was nothing to see except fading stars and a faint pink glow across the water as the sun rose.

Still, Sis sank to the floor and pressed her face against the
windowpanes so she could see what was coming.

Sometimes it's not the disaster you see coming that breaks
your heart but the one behind you, coiled like a snake, waiting to strike the minute you walk back across the room to
pick up the ringing telephone.

"Sis, it's Larry. Emily has fallen down the stairs."

Nineteen

Sis wanted to jerk the phone cord out of the wall. She wanted to cover up her head, close her eyes and wake up to discover Larry's call was a bad dream. But most of all she wanted time to spin backward to the day Neil Armstrong walked on the moon and Jim came home and hope was so high anything was possible, even that she could talk her sister out of marrying a dangerous stranger. Then Emily would still be safe in her house where her lost dream of love was scattered about in silver frames.

Sis threw on some clothes and went down the hall to break the awful news to Jim. Thank God he was stoic. Thank God he said, "I'll be downstairs as quick as I can."

Then she hurried downstairs to break the news to Sweet Mama and Beulah, which would be considerably harder. It took superhuman effort to keep from jumping into her car and leaving her molasses-slow family behind while she raced off to snatch Andy out of Larry's clutches.

Sis had to focus on the task at hand or she was going to tumble into dark despair and be useless to everybody. She tapped on Beulah's door first.

"It's Sis, Beulah. We've got to get to the hospital. It's Emily."

"Lord God Jesus!" Beulah said, but Sis didn't wait to hear more. There wasn't time. What if Emily died before she got to the hospital?

As she tapped on her grandmother's door, Sis shoved the thought out of her mind. There was no answer, and Sis knocked again. She was just getting ready to go inside anyhow when Sweet Mama called out, "Is that you, Beulah?"

"No. It's Sis."

Sis went inside and fumbled along the wall for the switch. Light flooded the bedroom and she was stopped in her tracks. There on her grandmother's dresser sat Jim's leg. Sweet Mama's gardening hat was perched on top of it, and one of her silk scarves was curved around the prosthetic foot. Sweet Mama had even tucked a pink plastic rose among the folds of the scarf.

Hysterical laughter bubbled up followed by equally hysterical tears. Sis reined it in.

"Sweet Mama, we need to get you dressed as fast as possible. It's Emily."

"What's wrong, Sis? Is Emily having her baby?"

Sis didn't know how many times a heart could break before the damage became irreparable. She sat on the edge of the bed and took her grandmother's hand.

"You remember, she got married in the garden to a man we didn't like."

"What's His Name."

"Larry Chastain."

"No, that's what I call him. He's too sorry to deserve a name."

"Amen," Beulah said from the doorway. She hurried into the bedroom and pulled a summer dress out of Sweet Mama's closet. "Jim's out in the hall. Y'all go on, Sis, and get that child out of the clutches of that devil from Hell before he does any more harm to this family."

"You and Sweet Mama be careful. And don't let on to Larry that we know anything. We don't want him running and taking Andy. We want him arrested and put in jail."

"Jail's too good for What's His Name," Sweet Mama said. "And if he tries to take Andy, I'll shoot him."

"Amen, again!" Beulah said.

Sis left the two pillars of the Blake family still casting aspersions on *that devil* and *What's His Name*. Then she and Jim got into her Valiant, and she drove like the road to the hospital was the speedway they were building over in Alabama.

Her brother didn't even notice.

"Aren't you going to say anything about my reckless driving, Jim?"

"Why should I? If you'd let me drive, we'd be going twice as fast."

"With one leg?"

"It's my driving leg, Sis."

"The other one is on Sweet Mama's dresser."

"How'd it get there?"

"God only knows. But she's decorated it with pink plastic roses."

"Great. It deserves a decent burial."

They looked at each other in the pink light of a new dawn and cracked up. Laughter through tears. It was the Southern way, and it might just be the only thing holding Sis together.

"Jim, when you get home, I want you to put the darned thing on and not take it off. With all that's happening, I need all the help I can get."

Thank God he didn't say no. He didn't say anything as she roared into the hospital parking lot and found a space on what

Sweet Mama would have called the back forty. If she had a handicapped sticker, she could have parked right next to the door, but Jim would hate being labeled. He'd hate being singled out for privilege.

They got out of the car and every slow step she took beside her brother on his crutch was a teeth-gritting moment.

"Sis, you go on. I'll catch up."

She didn't argue, but tore ahead until she found out where her sister was. Intensive Care. The very name sent chills through Sis.

Even more chilling was the sight of Andy in the intensive care waiting room, scrunched down in his chair, cringing against the arm Larry had around his shoulders.

"Sis, thank God you're here," Larry said.

Tears rolled down his cheeks, crocodile tears, Beulah would have said. Sis wanted to claw them off his face. Instead, she casually plucked Andy out of his grip and took him to the other side of the room.

"How is my sister?"

"In a coma, but she's hanging on. Our Emily is a fighter."

She wanted to slap *our Emily* out of his mouth. Forcing herself to calm down, she asked, "What happened?"

Andy hid his face against her side while Larry spun out his lies. The tremors that went through her nephew's narrow shoulders made Sis so mad it took an iron will to keep from spitting on the evil man across the room.

Larry rubbed a hand across his face as if he couldn't believe what had happened, and then he gave Sis a smile she supposed he meant as reassuring.

"Don't you worry, Sis. Thank God I know the compound of drugs. I've checked on every medication they're giving her, and we're on the right track here. I've made sure of it."

"I'm sure you have, Larry." Sis made herself smile sympathetically at the man she hated. "Andy can stay with me while she's here."

"Andy's mine now," Larry said, and ice water ran through Sis's veins.

"Perhaps I didn't make myself clear, Larry. What I meant to say was that I know you'll want to stay here until Emily is out of the woods, and I think it will be better if Andy doesn't have to hang around the hospital. He's just a little boy."

"He'll be better off with his own things, Sis. Besides, we're family now. We'll hang out together here, then go home and rest when he gets tired."

"Ain't that the biggest bunch of foolishness I ever heard?" Beulah steamed into the waiting room with Sweet Mama and Jim right behind her. "Ain't no little boy I ever heard of belongs in the hospital when he can be sitting on a stool in Sweet Mama's kitchen eating sugar cookies."

"We'll make some for you, too, Larry." Sweet Mama actually sat down beside him and patted the hand of the man whose name she purportedly could never remember. "There's no need for a nice man like you to starve to death here at the hospital when we've got plenty of good cooking at home."

"You family now," Beulah said. "It's gonna hurt my feelings something awful if you don't let us make you some fried chicken and Amen cobbler."

"That's right now, hon," Sweet Mama said. "Family sticks together. Emily would be so upset if she found out we didn't take good care of her son and her husband while she's recovering from her unfortunate accident."

Larry's jaw fell open, and Beulah stepped up to the plate.

"Lucy, you forgot to tell Sis we saw the doctor on the way in. He says the accident was bad but she's gonna pull outta that coma." Beulah beamed in Larry's direction. "Don't you worry none, sugar pie. Old Beulah and Sweet Mama's gonna take good care of you."

Sis felt as if she'd dropped into an alternate universe. She'd told Sweet Mama and Beulah to pretend nothing was amiss to Larry, but she'd never expected them to be such good actresses. To her amazement, their con job was actually working. She saw Larry's defenses slipping, saw how the hard shell he wore like armor melted.

Sis cut her eyes toward Jim, but he was staring at a spot on the wall. Whether he was holding back laughter or rage, she couldn't tell. All she knew was that she no longer had to worry about Sweet Mama crumbling in the face of Emily's tragedy. Even with a mind slowly coming unhinged, she was still capable of rising to any occasion.

A nurse, wearing rubber-soled shoes that made a swishing sound on the tiles, appeared in the doorway.

"The family of Emily Chastain can visit now," she said. They all stood up and she added, "One at a time. Except the little boy. He can come in with somebody."

Larry took Sweet Mama's elbow. "You go ahead, Sweet Mama. I know you want to see your granddaughter." He smiled in Andy's direction. "My son can go with you."

Beulah pursed her lips, Jim stared at the wall and Sis endured. Waiting in the same room with her enemy was one of the hardest things she'd ever done. She couldn't have done it for her outspoken, waspish-tongued self. But she did it for her sister.

Twenty

EMILY WAS WRAPPED IN a shroud of darkness, lost in deep, cool woods where tall oaks and spreading magnolias whispered around her. She could feel their branches dipping and swaying, brushing against her face, her hair and the hurting skin along her arms, singing to her in a low, sweet language she used to know.

She strained upward, trying to catch hold of the words and hang on, but they floated away, leaving her alone with nothing but the black of endless night and the fear that hovered over her like a shadow. She tried to call out *I am here. Don't leave. I am here,* but nothing came out of her mouth, not even a sigh.

Where am I? Why am I so cold? Why am I so far away?

In the same way she'd learned to vanish inside herself when Larry first hit her, she concentrated until she felt herself shrinking to the size of a pinhead. She made herself so small not even a shadow could find her.

Something whispered over her, soft as snow falling, and Emily felt the weight of warmth settle around her, the shape of comfort being tucked around her legs, her arms, even her neck that had twisted at an impossible angle on her headlong flight down the stairs.

It's a blanket. The words sifted into her mind like the sugar she used in the Amen cobbler at Sweet Mama's Café.

Emily drifted for a while. She wanted to keep going, just drift away entirely, leaving behind a puff of smoke and the scent of sugar. But the warm blanket pulled her back, reminded her of winter days around the hearth in the Victorian house by the sea, the smell of popcorn in the long-handled popper Beulah held over the fire, the sound of Andy's laughter.

Where is he? Where's my son? Oh, God, does Larry have him?

Emily fought her way out of the darkness that wanted to hold her. She tried to get her bearings, but she couldn't see. Panic rose in her, but she tamped it down, packed it into a box along with the questions that still raged through her mind. She might later take the box out and examine the questions, one by one, until she could decipher the answers.

But for now, she focused every inch of her broken-to-pieces body on hearing. She'd heard sounds earlier, hadn't she? Faint strains of a song as familiar to her as the sound of her own blood coursing through her veins.

At first there was nothing except a murmurlike water rushing over rock. Then words started coming through, disjointed but clear. *Em* and *Andy* and *okay.* The voice was strong and true, one that would not be ignored.

It was the voice of her sister.

Emily tethered herself to the words and held on. As long as she could hang on to Sis's voice, she could keep from being sucked so deep into the darkness she disappeared altogether.

"I don't know if you can hear me, Em, but you're going to be all right. I promise you that."

Sis. I'm here. I can hear you.

"You're in Intensive Care. In a coma. It's just us, Em. They won't let everybody in here at one time."

Sis's hands were strong as she adjusted the blanket, then grabbed Emily's hand and held on.

"I know he did this, Em."

Yes. Yes. He found the suitcases.

"He's out there in the waiting room carrying on like a dying calf in a hailstorm. I'd like to slap the shit out of him. And if he's not careful, Sweet Mama will. Even if she's losing her mind, she's nobody's fool."

Emily laughed, but the sound couldn't rise out of the darkness. Kaleidoscopic images ricocheted through the tunnel where she lay, suitcases hurling through the air, her hands clawing at the banister, the prayer that had died on her lips as she lost her grip and landed in the hallway downstairs. *Please don't let Andy see. Please keep Andy safe.*

"But don't you worry about anything, Em. You just rest and heal."

Sis's voice cracked a little, but it didn't break. Not Sis. Never the sister who had the courage of lions.

Andy? What about Andy?

"I'm taking Andy home with me, and I can guarantee you that monster will not get within shouting distance of him. If he so much as breathes in Andy's direction, it will be over my dead body."

Emily felt her sister's firm grip, felt her standing by the bedside solid as an oak, felt the love and courage and strength that poured off her like a heat wave in August. As long as she could hold on to Sis, she'd be all right.

Sis didn't want to leave Emily's bedside. Her time was up, but she selfishly wanted to stand there and hog the few minutes that had to be parceled out among the family. Still, Beulah was standing in the doorway to the intensive care unit waiting her turn while Sweet Mama was back in the waiting room holding on to Andy as if she'd stitched him to her side with indestructible cotton quilting thread. Jim and Larry were there, too. Sis had to get back to make sure their carefully constructed ruse didn't fall apart.

Sis leaned down to kiss the top of Emily's head, and then hurried out before she cried.

Keeping her head high and her face from showing a single thing, she strode down the antiseptic hallway and into the waiting room. On the wall-hung TV, Cuba was being pounded by Camille while a voice-over talked about hundred-mile-an-hour winds and a storm that could head their way. As if Sis needed any other disaster to think about.

Larry sat in a straight-back chair nearby with his head in his hands. He looked up expectantly. What did he think she was going to do? Break down and embrace him, hang on the way a normal sister-in-law would and console him in his deep grief? For two cents, she'd knock the smug out of him with a baseball bat.

"How do you think she's doing?" he said, trying for anxious, a loving husband inquiring about the clumsy wife who had little enough sense to throw herself down the stairs.

"No change," she said, curt, sharp. She'd leave the sweet lies to Beulah and Sweet Mama.

He opened his mouth as if he were going to start a conversation, but she wheeled out without even bothering to say *coffee*. He might ask her to bring him a cup. Sis would rather cut off her hand than bring him anything. She'd rather be in Cuba with a hurricane than in the waiting room with a man she'd like to see thrown into the bowels of hell.

When she rounded the corner where the coffee machine was, she was shaking. Thank God nobody was there to get coffee. People weren't standing around consoling each other over a family member who might not make it out of Intensive Care.

Sis leaned her head against the coffee machine, and a sob hitched up through her throat. *Oh, my God.* Why hadn't she insisted on going over yesterday to pack up Emily and Andy and bring them home? Why had she listened to her sister? Why had she not seen this disaster coming? All the signs were there, including those coming off the Amen cobbler.

Another sob bubbled up, but Sis bit her lip against it.

"Sis?" Jim put a hand on her shoulder.

She hadn't even heard his approach. She wiped her hands across her face and tried to get a grip on herself.

"Beulah and Sweet Mama want you to take them and Andy to open up the café," Jim said.

"For God's sake, Emily's in a coma!"

"You know how Sweet Mama is about that café, and I'll stay here with Em."

"I don't want to leave her."

"I know you don't. But Andy needs you."

The thought of how her helpless nephew had cringed before Larry shot Sis so full of adrenaline she could have flown to the moon without a rocket.

"You're right. It will do nothing but upset him to hang around here in the waiting room all day. Besides, I don't want him near that jackass."

"I feel the same way," Jim said. "It's all I can do to pretend I believe his sorry lies and not take a punch at him."

"We've got to make sure he pays, Jim. What did the doctor say about her injuries? Does he know what happened to Em?"

"He was very careful in his choice of words, Sis. But he did tell Sweet Mama and Beulah and me that Emily's injuries weren't consistent with an accident, that some of them happened earlier than last night."

"Beulah said Em was going to pull through." In spite of the evidence of her own eyes, Sis desperately wanted to believe her.

"That's not what he said, Sis. He said it would be a miracle."

Sis didn't believe in miracles. But if that's what it would take to make her sister well, she'd become a convert on the spot.

"How could he do this to my sister?"

Jim put money into the machine, then handed her a cup of hot coffee. "Just go on and get everybody out of here, Sis."

"You're right. But you'll call the café the minute you hear anything, Jim."

"I will. Don't worry."

"Promise you won't let that scumbag near her unless you're there."

"Are you kidding? Before this day's over, he'll think we're Siamese twins."

"Good. I'll see you after the café closes." She hugged her brother close.

Thanks to Sweet Mama's and Beulah's cooking, he now had some meat on his bones. Although the vitality and joy that used to pulse in him like a heartbeat were still lost in the deep jungles and dark tunnels of Vietnam, she could see a little spark, as if any minute now her brother might catch fire and once more become the dazzling comet of a man he'd once been.

"Take care of yourself, Jim," she whispered, pressing her car keys into his hands. "I'm leaving the Valiant for you."

Sis hurried off before he could see how she was starting to fall apart again.

Around the corner, she leaned her head against the wall.

What if she lost her sister? Sis thought of the author Virginia Woolf, who had put heavy stones in her pockets, then walked into the water and kept on going. She thought of Hemingway who had preferred a big game-hunting rifle.

Oh, my God. Sis rammed her fist into her mouth and bit back a scream. Fury roared through her. Rage at Hemingway and Woolf and Larry, but most of all anger at herself.

What in the world was she doing, standing there acting like a self-indulgent coward? Andy needed her. So did Jim and Sweet Mama and Beulah. But most of all, Em. Her sister was not dead yet, and by God, Em was not going to die, not if she had any say so in the matter. And she planned to have plenty.

She straightened herself up and steamed toward the waiting room to get her family. As soon as she got everybody settled she was going to find out of if this bunch of doctors knew what they were talking about. And if they didn't, she'd find some who did.

The Blake family plus Larry sat on their hard chairs, watching the TV where a reporter was issuing the latest warning.

"Somebody turn that thing off," Sis said, but nobody paid her any attention. Least of all the TV reporter who droned on about being prepared for a disaster.

Sis wondered if the reporter had ever suffered a disaster. She thought about her parents' death and the bones in the garden and her sister lying in a coma. How do you prepare for such disasters? Even if you close your windows and lock all your doors and say your prayers, you're still going to find yourself standing in a waiting room door with your head spinning.

She shook off her gloom and hoped she looked efficient and certain as she marched across the room and took her grand-mother's arm.

"Sweet Mama, are you ready to go to the café now?"

"I need to make the Amen cobbler," Sweet Mama said.

"That's a good idea. You and Beulah can make the cobblers while Andy and I wait the tables." She winked at her nephew. "How about it, buddy? You think you can wait tables?"

"Can I wear my Superman suit?"

"You sure can."

It would mean a trip back to the house before they went to the café. His Superman suit was still in the laundry room, clean, thank God, after that awful morning he'd almost dug up the bones.

With a curt, "See you later," to Larry, she hustled her family out of the waiting room and into Sweet Mama's big Buick.

The drive home was shocking to Sis. With Emily's life in the balance and Camille out there somewhere gathering fury, the city should look different. People should be screaming in the streets; boats should be putting into port; businesses should be closed; the sun should not be shining. Just the opposite was true. Charter boats and shrimp boats and sailboats dotted the water; children romped on the beach in the sunshine; locals and tourists alike plowed up and down the streets looking for good food, good company and tacky souvenirs—seashells turned into ashtrays, T-shirts featuring laughing gulls flying over the lighthouse, and faux silver collectors' spoons stamped BILOXI, MISSISSIPPI.

The next thing she knew, somebody would be planning a neighborhood hurricane party like that fool from the Richelieu apartments. Nothing felt real to Sis anymore, certainly not the eerie silence inside the car as she drove home.

Sweet Mama and Beulah had wedged Andy into the backseat between them as if Emily's *accident* had taken up all the space in the front. There it sat breathing down Sis's neck, the elephant in the car nobody would talk about. The four of them traveled along as if they were the ones comatose.

Sis felt her nerves unravel one by one. She imagined them streaming out behind her like the echo of a scream. Glancing in the rearview mirror, she saw how Sweet Mama and Beulah leaned toward one another, how their sturdy shoulders and linked arms tented over Andy like a wide shelter in the midst of a storm. Something inside her sighed, settled back into place, saying *yes, yes.* Anybody else would have seen two old women protecting a vulnerable little boy but Sis saw an indestructible force, a family forged out of hardship and bonded by such fierce loyalty they'd needed nothing more than a caution from Sis to spin their lies to Larry Chastain.

When she parked the car, Sweet Mama and Beulah heaved out of their seats and then leaned back in toward Andy.

"You coming, sweet pea?" Beulah asked, but he shook his head so hard his hair flew around him like thistles. Then he scrambled over the front seat and climbed into Sis's lap.

"Aunt Sis? Is my mommy gonna die?"

"Oh, sweet pea." She gathered him up and held him close. "Of course not. The doctors are going to make her all better. Why, before you know it, she'll be back at the café making Amen cobblers."

"I'm gonna put on my Superman suit and never, ever take it off again. 'K, Aunt Sis?"

"Okay, Andy."

"It's a magic suit." His little boy's belief was so fierce, she could feel the passion for wonders and miracles pulsing off him in hot waves. But most of all she could feel his unwavering hope. "Do you believe in magic, Aunt Sis?"

"Yes, I do, Andy."

Sis had already told her nephew three lies. But she would tell a thousand more to keep his childlike belief alive. He sighed as he leaned into her, unfolding in the way of a moonflower who has lost the sun but found the moon. Suddenly, it seemed to her that the greatest tragedy of growing up was not in losing innocence but in losing hope.

Twenty-One

IT TOOK LONGER THAN Sis wanted to find Andy's costume in the basket of clean laundry that hadn't yet been folded and put away. Another small eternity passed before she got Sweet Mama and Beulah out of the kitchen where they were whispering over two tall glasses of sweet tea.

"It's time to go," Sis said.

They startled as she walked into the kitchen, their color rising as they reached for their purses and trotted toward the car.

The drive to the café was so different from the one home, Sis had the sensation of being whisked back in time. Andy, sitting in the front seat beside her, chattered about seeing his rocket ship while talk of recipes flowed between Sweet Mama and Beulah as naturally as tides responding to the pull of the moon.

When Sis neared the café, she saw the regulars lined up outside. The minute she opened the door they streamed in and crowded around.

"I was vaguely aware of a siren this morning, but it was so early I thought I might be dreaming," Miss Opal said. "Then when I got here and found the café closed, I nearly died."

"She came running over to the barbershop all out of breath," Tom added.

"I thought for sure something had happened to Sweet Mama." Miss Opal put her hand over her own heart as if it were in imminent danger of failing. "You could have knocked me over with a feather when James and Tom said it was Emily."

It didn't surprise Sis that the Wilson brothers knew. Not only were they Emily's neighbors but the grapevine flourished in all the hometown businesses along the strip, including the barbershop and the café.

"That blaring siren woke us up before daylight," Tom explained, "but by the time we got outside, Emily was already being loaded into an ambulance."

An image of her sister being carried off on a gurney reignited the rage Sis had managed to tamp down after leaving the hospital. She tightened her grip on Andy's hand.

"How is she?" Tom added while James and Miss Opal chimed in with their concern.

Sis kept it simple, saying only that Emily had a bad fall and would be in the hospital a few days. She even forced a smile for them. Still, Emily was a favorite with the regulars, and if Sis thought to placate them with bare-bones information, she was mistaken.

"How did it happen?" Miss Opal wanted to know while James asked, "How much damage did it do?"

"Little pitchers have big ears," Beulah said, not even bothering to cover her scowl.

"Poor little guy." Tom squatted beside Andy and pulled an Indian head nickel out of his pocket. "Look what I've got for you, Andy."

"I'll put her on my church circle's prayer list." Miss Opal's face lit up as if she'd solved the problem. "You just wait and see. She'll be out in time for Sunday dinner at the café."

Suddenly, it seemed to Sis that she was viewing the café regulars through underwater goggles. Tragedy was sucking her under, and no matter which way she turned, she couldn't escape. She cast a desperate look at Beulah.

"Coffee's ready," she hollered. Of all the people in the room, it was Beulah who knew the full extent of the problems bearing on Sis.

Quick to pick up Beulah's lead, Sweet Mama announced, "It will be on the house today."

Her transformation from this morning's befuddled old woman to this afternoon's undisputed queen of the café was a small, everyday miracle. Another was the reaction of the regulars.

"I'll pitch in and help with the cooking till Emily's back," Miss Opal told Sweet Mama, but it was Beulah who had a quick answer.

"Ain't no need."

Undeterred, Miss Opal pressed forward, trailing along behind Beulah to the kitchen chattering, her voice rising with hope.

"Music is not all I know. I'm pretty handy in the kitchen, and I've always wanted to learn to make that Amen cobbler."

Beulah rolled her eyes, which told Sis loud and clear that she might let Miss Opal wear an apron in Sweet Mama's kitchen but she wouldn't let her within a mile of that secret recipe.

"I'll help, too. James can handle the shop." Tom glanced toward his brother for confirmation, then down at Andy. "Little buddy, what do you think we can do?"

"Me and Aunt Sis is gonna wait tables."

"How about if you teach me, then Aunt Sis can get her office work done?"

"'K!" He beamed. "Can I have a cookie first? We gonna need lots'a sweet power."

It didn't surprise Sis that the regulars acted more like family than customers. What took her aback was how they were all carrying on as if the Gulf Coast would always remain as it was that hot summer day in mid-August, with the seawall holding back the storm while everybody stood as firmly as the hundred-year-old live oaks.

God, let it be so. The thought that drifted through her mind was so like prayer Sis knew she was a fraud. Through the years she'd told herself she was the driving force behind the Blake family, that she didn't need anybody or anything. But all along, there was God, moving over the water and breathing in the wind, smiling down in starlight and weeping in the rain.

Somehow the idea made Sis feel better. With Andy safe under Tom's wing, she turned toward her office, which had suddenly become a haven.

Behind her, the bell over the café door tinkled.

"Beth." His voice was unmistakable.

Michael Clemson headed in her direction, smiling in the way of a man who is glad to see a woman, in the way of a man who had kissed her beneath a curtain of Spanish moss and who just might do it again if he got a chance.

Even more amazing, he reached for her hands right in front of everybody.

For once, she was taking a chance. She was slipping into the skin of a woman she wanted to know, a woman Michael Clemson called Beth.

She led him into her office and closed the door.

"I've been worried about you, Beth. How's Emily?"

He was asking about her sister, but what she heard was *I've been worried about you,* as if she were the kind of woman he would lead to a chair with soft cushions and bring a cup of tea and then put her feet into his lap for a massage. The tears she'd dammed up since morning threatened to break through and spill over.

"After I couldn't get you at home or the café, I called Aunt Opal to see if she knew why nobody was answering the phone."

"This day has been a nightmare, Michael." Sis told him what the doctor had said, and though she was careful to leave out any hint that Larry was at fault, she heard the black hatred that leaked through her voice every time she mentioned his name.

"I get the sense you're worried about more than your sister, Beth."

Sometimes you can carry your burden a hundred miles without getting winded, and suddenly you'll know you can't go another step. With a deep certainty you feel in your bones, you'll understand that if you don't let go, your troubles will drag you to the ground and crush you.

"I think Emily's husband did this to her, Michael."

Her voice cracked, not because she wasn't strong, but because he offered sympathy and a strong shoulder. Without a word he folded her into his arms. The invincible woman who could move mountains on a daily basis stole a few moments to become a woman with softened edges and rising needs and long-forgotten dreams. Finally, she shoved her wrecked hair off her hot face and stepped back from him.

"I didn't mean to do that," she said.

"You *should* do that, Beth. Everybody needs somebody."

"I can't afford to have needs." What was that look that

crossed his face? She hoped it wasn't *goodbye*. And then she was immediately ashamed for thinking of herself when her sister was the one in a coma. "At least not till my sister is okay."

"Have the authorities been called?"

"Not yet. Emily can't tell us what happened, and the doctors have been very cautious about making any accusations until they know the full extent of damage and try to determine the cause."

"Is there any way I can help you take care of Emily?"

"She's my sister. I've always taken care of her." Too late she realized her words sounded sharp as a slap. "But I thank you for offering. I really do."

Tears pushed against her hot eyelids, but she batted them back.

"Take this, Beth." He pulled a white handkerchief out of his pocket and gently closed her hand over it. "It's okay to cry."

"It is *not*. I don't have time for tears."

"Well, at least take the time to sit down." He led her to her desk and pulled out her office chair. "Besides, I want you sitting while I say what's on my mind."

"Good Lord, that sounds ominous. Can it get any worse?"

"It can and it will. I'm taking Aunt Opal to Hattiesburg this afternoon and I'll take your family if you want me to. Camille has already moved out of Cuba and is heading this way."

He was only confirming what she'd known all along. Her instincts and the Amen cobbler never lied. Still, the news left her too exhausted for speech.

"Conditions are just right for a perfect storm, Beth. She's likely to be Category 4 by morning. You really should get your family out."

"I can guarantee you, I will." Emily would die if she knew Andy was in the path of a hurricane.

Her sister might just die, anyhow. She'd looked like a wax carving. The image filled Sis's mind until she could see nothing except Emily's white skin, the only sign of life the blue veins that pulsed beneath it.

"Beth, keep this in case you need to get in touch with me." He put a card on her desk that read "Michael Clemson, Engineering Consultant," and then he squatted beside her and took hold of her hand once more. "If you change your mind about evacuating any of your family today, let me know. I'm heading back to board up the windows of my office and then I'll head out with Aunt Opal. But I'll be back."

"When?"

"Tonight. I'll come over here and board up the café for you."

"Nobody seems to be boarding up anything, Michael. Do you really think we ought to close tomorrow?"

"I've seen the data from the hurricane hunters, Beth. By Sunday evening, it's going to be too late to do anything. You should get out, too."

His concern for her suddenly tasted like sawdust, and she pulled her hands away.

"If you think I'd leave my sister, you don't know me at all, Michael."

"I *do* know you, Beth. In all these years, the thing I remember most about you is your unselfish devotion to your family."

"Then why did you even ask?"

"Don't you know, Beth?" He reached up to touch her face, just a small, simple touch that wouldn't even qualify as a caress. "I'm selfish, too. I want you safe."

In a perfect world, Sis would have been sitting on the porch swing while a sliver of moonlight made her look softer and younger and even a bit pretty. There would be no Larry, no bones in the backyard and no Camille.

But she was sitting in an office that boasted not one feminine touch, in broad daylight that allowed for no invention, still in rumpled khakis and black shirt she'd thrown on this morning before daylight.

Her telephone started ringing, a stark reminder of the world outside her office door.

"You should get that," he said, "and I should go."

Michael stood up and waved from the doorway while Sis picked up the phone and listened as Jim delivered more bad news.

"They're taking Emily for surgery in the morning, Sis. She broke one of her ribs in the fall and punctured a lung."

"Where's Larry? I'd like to stomp him."

"He's still here. I'm not letting him out of my sight."

"Why can't they do the surgery today, Jim? I'm terrified Emily's going to get trapped by Camille."

"They're hoping to stabilize her first. Besides, even if they did it today, she'd be in no shape to evacuate."

"Do you think she's getting worse, Jim?"

"She's still in a coma, that's all I can tell."

Sis didn't try to stop the tears that rolled down her face. Thank God Michael had closed the door behind him. Thank God Andy was in the café, chattering away with Tom Wilson. Thank God Beulah and Sweet Mama were so busy doing what they loved best they wouldn't notice her ravaged face.

"I should never have left her." She wiped her face with the back of her hand, then found a crumpled-up tissue in her desk drawer and blew her nose. "I'm coming back."

"No, you can't be everywhere at once, Sis. Take care of Andy. I'll spend the night."

"You need your rest."

"Do you think this will be the first night's sleep I've ever lost?"

"All right, Jim. Besides, I need to start boarding up the house."

"Good idea. See you tomorrow, Sis."

As she hung up echoes of her brother's *See you tomorrow* played through her mind. That's what her sister had said, and look what had happened to her.

Twenty-Two

SWEET MAMA'S ALARM CLOCK went off, but when she opened her eyes it was pitch-black dark, not even a sliver of light showing through the window. Thinking she'd been confused when she set the alarm, she lay back against her pillow. Today was a very important day but she didn't remember why. If she could get a bit more sleep, maybe the fog in her head would clear up.

"Lucy!" It was Beulah, knocking on her door. What was she doing up in the middle of the night? "Are you up?"

"I'm up." If Beulah said it was time to get up, it must be so.

"You need any help in there getting dressed?"

"No, I'm fine." Where were they going at this time of night?

"All right, then. We fixing to leave here as quick as I can get breakfast. We don't want to be late for our baby's surgery."

It all came back to Sweet Mama in a rush, her sweet granddaughter lying still as death on the hospital bed while that rat sat in his chair acting like he cared. Just to make sure she wouldn't forget, Sweet Mama had written it all down last night in her Remembering Book.

She snapped on the light and opened the Remembering Book lying on her bedside table. That's when she saw that her window was all boarded up. Good Lord! Who would do such a thing?

Panicked, she hurried over to the window, racking her brain to figure it all out. Maybe if she opened the window and pushed from the inside, the boards would come off and she could see out. Suddenly it was very important that she see what was outside her window. She felt smothered, as if she'd been stuffed into a cave and any minute now somebody was going to roll a rock against the opening to seal her inside.

There was a loud knock on her door, and she jumped back from the window.

"Sweet Mama! Beulah said you were getting dressed. Are you about ready to go?"

Good Lord, it was Sis. The next thing she knew her efficient granddaughter would be in her room discovering the Remembering Book and all Sweet Mama's plans would be swept away in a big wind. A hurricane. Camille. That was it. She'd stood in the yard yesterday, watching Sis and Beulah nail boards over all the first-story windows. Sis had wanted to climb on the roof and board up the second floor, but Beulah talked her out of it.

"We got one girl in the hospital," she'd said. "We don't need two."

The knock came again. "Sweet Mama? Can you hear me?"

"Go on, Sis. I'll be there in a minute."

Shoot! Now she didn't have time for anything except to splash water on her face and throw on her stockings and a green-striped seersucker dress. After she'd fastened the last button, she grabbed her Remembering Book and stuffed it into her purse. She'd have to find someplace safe in the hospital where she could read it without getting caught.

Time was running out. Was it because of Camille? She didn't remember why, she just knew it was.

She hurried off to the kitchen, which soothed her with its familiar smells of home cooking in spite of the boards over all the windows. Sis had left all the lights burning, and the TV off. With Andy sitting at the table, looking dejected in spite of the jelly Beulah slathered over his biscuits, Sweet Mama knew her warrior granddaughter would do everything in her power to keep news of a monster storm from him.

Was it still calm beyond the boarded-up windows, or had the wind picked up speed? Would it soon be howling so hard it rattled the windowpanes?

Sweet Mama sat down to breakfast with her family, and as she buttered her biscuit, she remembered how the wind had howled that fateful night, like a woman crying. It was the night Peter Blake walked through the door, carrying the stench of liquor and defeat.

Memories came to her so clearly she could still smell the whiskey.

It didn't take her long to figure out her husband had gambled every penny they'd saved to pay off the house. The force of the wind gathered inside her until it was a storm she could no longer contain. She hated public scenes, and although she was standing in the kitchen of her own pink house, she was not alone. Beulah stood nearby with her purse and her husband, Eustace, who had come to take her home from work. Still, Sweet Mama's rage spilled over, a hurricane of fury at Peter Blake for losing their money. And now they might lose their house.

Thank God the boys were already asleep. Thank God they didn't come flying down the stairs while she berated her husband.

He lifted his large hand with the evil-looking Knights of the Green Forest ring to strike her. She put her hands over her face, expecting a blow that would break bones and knock her to the floor. Instead, it was Peter Blake who hit the floor, felled by a big black fist whose blow was as lethal as it was unexpected.

"Lord God, Eustace. Look what you done!" Beulah screamed. "They'll string you up for sure."

But Sweet Mama's husband was out cold. He wouldn't be stringing anybody up that night.

A hand on her shoulder drew Sweet Mama back to the kitchen where Sis was saying, "Are you ready to go? Emily will be having surgery soon."

Emily. Her broken-to-pieces granddaughter who lay helpless in a hospital bed.

"It's time," Sis said, then took Sweet Mama's hand and helped her from the chair.

Yes. It was time.

When Sis stepped onto the porch, the humidity was so thick an instant sheen of sweat covered her skin. It hung in the hot air like wet mosquito netting. As she ushered Beulah and Sweet Mama and Andy into the Buick, storm trackers soared overhead, racing toward the hurricane gathering force over the Gulf.

This morning before anybody else was awake, Sis had hurried down the stairs to Beulah's bedroom. She answered the knock in her nightgown.

"The hurricane is heading straight for us, Beulah. As soon as Emily's surgery is over, you've got to help me get Sweet Mama and Andy and Jim out of here."

"I can tell you right now, Lucy ain't gonna leave this house. Besides, we've been through storms before."

"Not like this one. If it hits, it will be the first Category 5 ever to make landfall on the U.S. mainland."

"Lord Jesus God!"

"A few boards on the windows and mattresses in the hall won't be enough." Sis took hold of Beulah's shoulders. "You're the only one Sweet Mama will listen to, Beulah. Jim, too. He's not going to want to leave Emily."

Sis gripped Beulah so hard she feared she might leave marks on her shoulders.

"Listen to me, Beulah. As soon as the surgery's over, you've got to help me get them out."

"How do you think I'm gonna get Lucy to leave? She's stubborn as any old plow mule I ever saw."

"Tell her that she has to get Andy out and keep him safe till Emily's well again."

"What about you, Sis? Will you be leaving, too?"

Beulah eyed her with such tender compassion, Sis had to claw her way out of self-pity and hysteria.

"I'll stay with my sister," she said, and whatever Beulah saw—the thrust of her chin, the steely resolve in her eyes or a heart so full it sent a rush of blood that colored Sis's skin deep pink—it was enough to stop any argument she might have made.

"I didn't figure you would. You just like Lucy. Stubborn and then some." Beulah patted her face. "Get on out of here now. I gotta get dressed and make breakfast or we ain't gonna make it to the hospital in time."

Now as Sis drove toward the hospital, the near hysteria she'd felt about Camille seemed like the wild imaginings of a woman going mad. Nothing outside her window told of a

Saturday any different from the ones that had gone before it. Still, she was relieved she had Beulah in her corner. It was one thing for adults to decide they had nothing to fear, but it was another thing to risk the life of a little boy who wasn't old enough to make his own decision. Getting Andy to safety was the one thing left that Sis could do for Emily.

She thought of the sister so charming men crossed the street just to walk along behind her and watch her hips sway in the sunlight. She thought of a sister who wept at sad movies, rescued stray cats and bent over her son reading stories of the Hundred Acre Wood. She thought of a sister who had said, *See you tomorrow, Sis,* and then never had.

Her insides felt like glass. Any minute Sis might explode and slice everybody within a three-foot radius. She gripped the wheel and turned her mind toward something that might hold her together, anything except the horrible fear that her sister would not survive. Unexpectedly, Michael drifted across her mind with his gentle soul and his unswerving loyalty toward a woman full of sharp edges and uncertainties, a woman who believed that reaching toward happiness was equivalent to reaching toward a hot stove.

But what if she was wrong? Something inside her settled down, breathed a bit deeper, whispered *yes.*

By the time Sis had parked the car and guided her family to the waiting room, she felt capable of anything, even walking into the same room as Larry Chastain without kicking him sky-high. There he sat, an evil, insincere man turned even more handsome by tragedy, while poor Jim sat wrecked— haggard and colorless and despairing.

Jim hobbled across to Sis, wrapped his arms around her and whispered, "They're going to let all of us see her before surgery. In case she doesn't make it." His voice split apart and he collapsed against her shoulder, trying to hold back his sobs.

"Shhh." She soothed him as well as she could, considering how she was screaming inside. "We've got to be strong for her. And for Andy."

She looked over his shoulder at Beulah, who had snatched up Andy and retreated to a chair on the opposite side of the room from Larry, and to Sweet Mama, who amazingly had perched herself right next to the most despised man in the Blake family. Sweet Mama was even patting Larry's hand and calling him *my poor boy.*

"You've got to stay strong for our Emily," Sweet Mama told him. "I'll bet you haven't left this hospital."

"Not once." Larry oozed false sainthood.

"I knew it. A good man like you." Sweet Mama was still patting the cad's hand. Had she vanished through a tunnel in time or was she putting on a show?

Still, there was only so much pretense Sis could stand.

"Jim and I are going to get coffee," she announced, and then led her brother out of the room and out of sight.

She got two cups of coffee from the machine, handed one to Jim and then waited quietly while he drank and the color gradually returned to his face.

"Did you sleep at all last night, Jim?"

"I didn't take my eyes off that rattlesnake."

"After the surgery, you go home and get some sleep. I plan to stay the night."

"I don't like the idea of you here with him, Sis. There's no telling what he's capable of."

"Maybe he'll go home himself."

"I think he enjoys putting on a show. I ought to nail a sign to his forehead. The Concerned Husband Weeps."

"Everybody's going to get through the surgery, Jim, including Em."

Sis pictured the alternative, her sister gone and Sis spending the rest of her life asking the awful question *what-if*.

"Sis, this hurricane's looking bad."

"I know. I've boarded up the downstairs windows. You rest up and then help Beulah get Sweet Mama and Andy out of here. This evening if you can."

"We can't just leave Em."

"I'm not leaving her, Jim. But my mind's made up. I'm keeping Em safe and you're keeping her son safe till she's well again."

Sis didn't know how long they stood that way, brother and sister hanging on to fragile hope. Nothing she'd seen so far told her that Emily would ever be well again. But if she didn't believe that she might as well get on the gurney with her sister and tell the surgeon, *Go ahead and take out my heart. I don't need it anymore.*

Over Jim's shoulder, Sis saw Beulah shuffling down the hall, her slow pace an aching reminder that even this bulwark would not hold strong forever.

"They getting ready to take our baby to surgery. The doctor says we can all go in and see her."

To say goodbye. The thought took up so much room, Sis could hardly breathe. As she walked off with Beulah and her brother, she found herself reaching for something bigger than herself. She found her heart yearning toward the mercy of a God she could not see.

Twenty-Three

THE QUIET IN THE HOSPITAL room was matched by the stillness outside the window. Alone beside Emily's bed, Sis felt the hair along the back of her neck stand on end. The sun hung low in the sky and not a leaf stirred, not even the Spanish moss draped from the live oak tree at the edge of the parking lot. Something was out there waiting, something filled with such fury its malevolent intent seeped through the cracks in the windowpane, smoked along the ceiling and settled into the corners of the room.

Sis tucked the blanket around her sister and tiptoed to the window. A man and a woman walked across the parking lot, moving with defeat in every step. They wove in and out of the blue shadows with their heads tucked and their hands joined. Not a single breeze lifted the brim of his hat; not a whisper of wind tugged her skirt. So perfect were they, trotting along in the airless evening, they seemed to be made of cardboard, soulless and dispensable.

Sis finished the bag of chips and orange soda she'd gotten earlier from the machines, then left the window and returned to her sister's bed. Emily had not stirred since the surgery. She lay there still as a carving. Before they'd left, Sweet Mama had brushed her silky hair and Beulah had tucked some pink crocheted sleeping socks onto her feet.

"In case our baby gets cold," she said.

Andy had left his brave bear, Henry, behind, and Jim had kissed his twin on the forehead.

Sis drew a chair close to the bed and reached for Emily's hand.

"The doctor says you're stable now and you're going to be okay, Em. It might take a little while before you wake up, but that's all right. I know you will. You're strong. Stronger than you think. And I'm going to be here with you every step of the way."

Could Emily hear her? The doctors said she could, but not the slightest movement of her hand confirmed that, not even the flicker of an eyelid.

"Sweet Mama and Beulah and Jim took Andy home. But Henry's here."

Sis moved the stuffed bear so it was tucked under Emily's chin. Could she feel the fur? Did she believe in Henry's magic the way her son did? *Probably.* In spite of growing up without parents, Emily had managed to retain her sense of wonder, her childlike belief in fairy tales.

"Did you hear what Andy said about the bear? 'Henry's full of sweet power and fierce growls, Mommy. He'll keep you safe while I'm gone.'" Did Emily's eyelids move? "Larry had gone to the bathroom, thank God, or I doubt Andy would have said a word."

Sis jumped up to tuck the blanket around Emily's feet, not because it needed adjusting but because she needed something to do, something that might make her sister feel more comfortable. She glanced toward the window at the gathering dark.

Something else was gathering, too, a brooding wrath that was growing stronger with each passing hour.

Where were they now? Had Beulah and Jim already left with Sweet Mama and Andy? Had they all gone in the Buick or had Jim taken his convertible out of the garage, packed it with belongings, then put the top up in case rains came ahead of Camille?

And where was Larry?

As if Emily had read her mind, she twitched, and her eyelids fluttered. Sis raced to the head of the bed and leaned close.

"Can you wake up, Em? Can you open your eyes?"

There was no response. Whatever force had shaken Emily so she tried to rouse, had disappeared. She now lay in such deep sleep she seemed to have vanished down a well.

Sis stalked around the room, walking off energy and rage and fear. Finally, she pulled herself together and settled back into her bedside chair.

"Larry left about thirty minutes ago, Em. I don't know where he went, but I'm glad he's gone. I can't stand to be around him. I hope the cops get him before I do something awful like spit in his face.

"The way I feel, I could, too. You're going to laugh at this, but Sweet Mama and Beulah and even Jim are doing a better job of pretending around him than I am. We don't want to tip him off before he's arrested."

There was a small movement on the bed again. Was Sis agitating her sister with talk of revenge?

"Oh, Lord, Em, I don't even know the right thing to say to you." She reached for her sister's hand, not knowing whether to hang on tight or hold it as gently as she would a broken sparrow. "I should have been there. I should never have listened when you told me not to come."

Sorrow bent Sis over the bed where she touched her fore-head to their joined hands.

"I'll never forgive myself for leaving you and Andy in the house with that monster. I wish I could take that day back. If I had gone over and taken you and Andy out right then, you wouldn't be lying here now. You'd be down at the café covered in sugar and laughing..."

Suddenly, Sis cracked like a paper shell pecan. Flattening herself over her sister, she wet their hands with her tears, and when she didn't have any more, she straightened herself up.

"I will never let him hurt you again. I promise."

She squeezed Emily's hand, searching for some small sign of recognition, but there was nothing. Still, it seemed to Sis that Emily's sleep was more peaceful than when she'd been in Intensive Care. She had appeared to be drifting away then, but now she seemed to be drifting back toward home.

"I love you, Em." Sis gave her sister's hand another squeeze, then tucked it under the sheet and tiptoed across the room.

Beyond the window, everything remained the same. Sis pressed her face against the cool glass and stared into the clear night. If Jim got the family out, she hoped he'd drive as far north as he could.

"Sis?"

Every nerve in her body went on high alert.

"Beulah?"

She turned to find Beulah standing in the doorway, her skin faded the color of unbleached muslin. Andy hovered against her, half-hidden by her bulk and the voluminous flower-print skirt she wore. Sis hurried across the room and took the load she was carrying, a batch of blankets, a picnic basket and a paper sack full of Andy's books and toys they always kept at the pink house.

"What happened? I thought you'd be as far as Picayune by now."

"You couldn't budge Lucy with a crowbar, and Jim looked so tired he was falling down in his tracks. Lucy sent him to bed, and then that Larry showed up."

"Larry Chastain is at the house?"

"Big as sin and twice as ugly. You ask me, ain't nothing about that man is handsome. I don't care what folks say. Andy commenced falling apart and I snatched him outta there so fast it made that devil's head spin."

"What's he doing there?"

"Sweet Mama invited him for supper."

"Oh, my Lord."

"It ain't the Lord needs telling, it's you. And that's what I done." Beulah settled into a chair. "You'd better get over there, Sis. Sweet Mama's gonna need you."

Sis started to tear out the door, but there was Andy, standing by the side of his mother's bed with his chin propped on the covers. He looked as listless as the Superman cape hanging from his narrow shoulders. He'd lost too much for her to just roar off without a word, leaving him to wonder if she'd ever come back.

"Can Mommy hear me?" he whispered.

"She can, Andy." Sis moved to her nephew and put her arm around him.

He stood on tiptoe and leaned closer to Emily.

"Me and Henry's gonna take real good care of you," he whispered. "When you wake up, we gonna get in my rocket ship and go live on the moon. Beulah'll make sam'wiches."

In one of those small miracles that lately seemed to be popping everywhere, Sis saw Emily's eyes moving rapidly beneath her blue-tinted lids, as if she were searching in the dark for her child.

"Keep talking to her, Andy. I've got to go. But I'll be back soon, and Beulah will be with you every minute. Okay?"

"'K."

"Later, 'gator." She leaned down to kiss the top of his head.

"After a while, crocodile."

"Beulah? You okay with that?"

"Don't you worry none, Sis. You couldn't blast me away from my babies with a stick of dynamite. Now, you'd best go on."

Sis walked like a normal person till she was through the door, and then she raced through the hospital corridors and into the elevator like a woman on fire, like a woman who planned to leap into her Valiant and fly to the little pink Victorian house by the sea. Her mind was racing as fast as her feet.

I can still get my family out in time.

I can still get my family out in time.

If she could talk Sweet Mama into leaving.

"Please God," she whispered, and then stepped into a night so eerie in its silence it sent shivers through her.

Chilled in spite of the stifling heat, Sis slid behind the wheel of her car and tore off as if she were being chased by wild dogs.

The city seemed to be going about its business as usual until Sis approached the small-crafts harbor. White sails fluttered over the dark water as the distinctive thirty-four-foot racing sloop, *Bella Elaina,* made her way eastward. An army of small boats followed in her wake, all leaving the exposed Mississippi Sound and making toward safer mooring in Biloxi's back bay on the eastern side of the peninsula. She'd seen the same sort of armada sailing for safety prior to Betsy.

Sailors were often the first to heed storm warnings. That

they were doing so in a perfect summer evening with not a cloud in sight made Sis tromp down on the gas pedal. She didn't let up until she'd nearly reached home.

The sight of Larry's Bel Air parked in the space normally occupied by Sweet Mama's big Buick would have made Sis furious if she weren't so glad that her sister's abuser was not back at the hospital posing a menace to Emily and Andy and Beulah. Sis sat in the car, collecting herself. She wished she had a weapon. She wished she'd raced by the restaurant and grabbed her baseball bat.

But then how would that look, her walking in with a baseball bat while Larry and Sweet Mama sat calmly around the dining room table? Or maybe even the kitchen table? Sis would be willing to bet that's what Sweet Mama had been up to at the hospital with all her *poor boy* talk and her outrageous kindness to the enemy.

After Sis sent Larry packing, she'd have to tell Sweet Mama not to go overboard with being nice to him. Sis didn't want him for a best friend. She just wanted him arrested before he could get wise to their plan and run off, taking Andy with him.

She got out of her car. Something was wrong, something so horrible she looked over her shoulder and then stood there in the front yard, listening. What she was listening for, she couldn't have said. What she heard was a quiet so deep not a single cricket song marred the stillness. Neither the cry of a seagull nor the whisper of wind cut through the thick blanket of silence.

Sis hurried through the front yard. The naked bulb over the front door was burning, and lights made a patchwork pattern all over the house, a large square of light from Jim's room on the second floor and slivers coming through the boarded-up windows in Sweet Mama's bedroom and in the kitchen downstairs.

She hurried up the steps and into the house where she was met with another wall of silence. The front hall was lit with one lamp, but not a sound drifted from any direction. Setting her purse on the hall table, she called out, "Sweet Mama?"

There was no answer, only an echo of Sis's own voice ricocheting off the walls of what seemed to be a ghost house.

Tiptoeing now, Sis headed toward the path of light coming from the kitchen.

Suddenly, the quiet exploded.

"You bitch!" Larry screamed. "What have you done to me?"

"Please. Don't." It was Sweet Mama, begging.

Sis flew toward the kitchen so fast her feet slipped on the polished wooden floor. As she scrambled to get up, Larry started yelling again.

"You old hag! I'll kill you for this!"

Sis scrambled forward on all fours. Drawers slammed in the kitchen and cutlery rattled, blending with indecipherable pleas from Sweet Mama. Sis finally gained purchase, then shot off the floor and raced through the kitchen door.

Sweet Mama cowered in her chair at the kitchen table while Larry stood over her, sweating profusely, his eyes turning bloodshot and his face half crazed. In his hand was a butcher knife.

"Stop!" Sis yelled. "Oh, God! Stop!"

With the knife poised in midair, Larry made a slow, drunkenlike pivot toward Sis.

"You're next, you meddling..."

There was a blur of movement, Jim appearing out of nowhere, racing forward on two legs, one of them a stark reminder that he was a Vietnam vet who could snap a man's neck with the ease of Beulah separating the neck from the gizzards of a hen she intended for the stew pot. He put his hands around Larry's throat and with one twist stopped the hateful flow of words and the knife that had been set to plunge into Sweet Mama.

Larry crumpled to the floor and the butcher knife intended for her heart skittered underneath Sweet Mama's chair.

"Oh, my God," Sis said. "Jim, what have you done?"

Jim stared at his hands as if he didn't even recognize them, and then he lowered his head and cried without sound, his shoulders heaving.

Sis stood frozen. The table was loaded with food, platters of fried chicken and biscuits, bowls of mashed potatoes and gravy and English peas. Remnants of an Amen cobbler sat in the center of the table in a blue bowl. There were two empty plates on the table, two half-empty glasses of sweet tea. The coffeepot was in its usual spot, and the copper kettle Sweet Mama used to heat water for tea. There were the aprons on pegs and the striped dishcloths, and there, over by the sink, was a giant bouquet of white oleander.

With growing horror, Sis stared at the lethal bouquet.

She squatted beside her grandmother and caught both her hands. They were icy to the touch, but it was her eyes that scared Sis most. Glassy and unfocused, they seemed to be staring at something beyond the walls, beyond the window, even beyond time. Sis cupped Sweet Mama's face, trying to refocus her attention.

"Jim, I think she's going into shock." He lifted a ravaged face. "I've got to get her to bed. Are you going to be all right?"

"What?"

Sis raced to the sink and filled a glass with water, her hands shaking so badly she spilled it all over the kitchen floor. Sweet Mama looked like she was about to topple out of her chair.

"Here, Jim." She held the glass to his lips, dribbling more water on his shirt than into his mouth.

When he finally took hold, she was shaking so hard she was barely upright. Her stomach heaved, and she rammed her fist into her mouth.

"Go on, Sis," Jim said.

She didn't look at Larry. She didn't dare.

"Sweet Mama." Once more, she bent over her grandmother. "I'm going to take you to bed now. Can you stand?"

"Don't eat the cobbler, dear."

"Forget about the cobbler."

Sis took a firm hold under both arms and hauled Sweet Mama upward. *Hurry, hurry, hurry,* pounded through her head, but there was no way to speed up the process. Sweet Mama seemed to be made of both lead and glass as she inched down the hall, weighted down by the enormity of what had taken place in that kitchen and yet so fragile any small movement might shatter her.

Sounds came from the kitchen behind Sis, sounds she didn't even want to think about.

Finally, they reached the bedroom with its old-fashioned, four-poster bed and crocheted coverlet. Sis got Sweet Mama into bed, removed her belt and shoes, then ransacked the closet for extra blankets. A sudden banging outside sounded like somebody knocking at the door. The cops? Sis jumped, nearly dropping the blankets. When the banging came again, she saw one of the boards flapping over the window, torn loose from the nail by the wind that had suddenly roared upon them and was gaining speed like a freight train out of control.

She hurried over and piled the blankets on top of Sweet Mama, then sat on the edge of the bed and chafed her hands.

"Sweet Mama, this is Sis. Can you hear me?"

"Sis?" The voice was so soft, she had to lean down to catch it. "Don't eat the Amen cobbler."

"Don't talk, Sweet Mama. Don't think about anything."

As Sis tucked the covers tight, the scent of lilac talc drifted around her. Forever after, the fragrance of lilac would remind her of the night her family was swept up in a personal storm so horrible it couldn't even be categorized.

Still, she leaned down to kiss her grandmother's cheek, clinging to normalcy with the tenacity of the barnacles that attached themselves to fishing boats.

"Everything's going to be okay, Sweet Mama. You just close your eyes and rest now. I'm going to take care of everything."

When Sweet Mama closed her eyes, Sis raced to the kitchen that echoed with emptiness.

"Jim? Where are you?" Her only answer was the howl of winds so fierce they sounded as if they were in the house.

She called her brother again, then tried to burst through a back door that pushed back. As she shoved at the door, sweat poured down her face and into her eyes.

"Come on," she said, putting her shoulder into the door. "Come on!"

The wind snatched it back and Sis catapulted into a yard as dark as death. A few stars straggled across the sky, casting a feeble light that made the rosebushes look secretive. Her heart kicked in to double time.

"Jim? Are you out here?" she called, her question disappearing in the darkness as if it had dropped into a tomb.

She wiped the sweat out of her eyes, then stood at the edge

of the yard with her pants legs billowing and her hair lifting skyward.

"Jim? Where are you?" She was screaming now to be heard, but the wind grabbed her words and cast them away.

The garage door yawned open, and a path of yellow light spilled across the garden. There, slumped against the side of the garage, was the awful truth she couldn't bear to face in Sweet Mama's kitchen—Larry Chastain, his eyes staring vacantly and his neck snapped sideways.

There was no mistaking that he was dead, just as there was no denying that they had killed him. Sis leaned over and lost her chips and orange soda.

Twenty-Four

JIM HAD HIS MOUTH OPEN, screaming at her, but she couldn't hear what he was saying.

He shut off the light and closed the garage door, but not before she saw that he was carrying a tarpaulin. She felt rather than saw him coming. When he got even he leaned close to her ear.

"Come on, Sis," he yelled, catching hold of her arm. "We've got to get Larry out of here."

The thought of arguing with her brother never crossed her mind. It was that kind of night, the kind where nothing was as it should be and the life she'd once taken for granted seemed like a long-forgotten dream.

Sis stumbled along beside her brother in the darkness and the roaring wind. Her foot smacked into the side of Larry, and she felt the chips and orange soda coming back into her throat. Sis gurgled to hold it down.

"Don't you get sick on me, Sis," Jim yelled. "Grab his other side."

She felt around in the dark until she found the edge of the tarpaulin they used to cover Jim's boat. Then she shut her mind to everything except tugging and lifting, dragging and keeping her footing.

Larry's body sagged as Jim let go with one hand to lift the door, then he hustled inside, dragging Larry and Sis with him. Quickly he turned to shut the door, leaving all of them plunged into a darkened garage smelling of dust and mildew and death.

"You can let go now," Jim said.

The deadweight that was her former brother-in-law bumped against the side of her leg as her brother felt along the wall for the light switch. Light flooded over the fishing poles on the wall, the fishing boat on the other side of the garage and Jim's baby-blue convertible with the top up and the trunk already open. But it was the grisly sight at her feet that made her cram a hand over her mouth. Jim had attempted to cover Larry Chastain with the tarp, but it was a haphazard job that left his awful eyes and his hurting hands exposed, the fingers rapidly turning stiff with rigor mortis.

"My God, Jim. What have we done?"

"Don't, Sis. It's too late."

"We've got to call the police."

"And tell them what, Sis? *My grandmother tried to poison our sister's abusive husband and when that didn't do the job, my brother finished him off with one twist to the neck?*"

"Oh, my God! The oleander!"

"Yes, the oleander. She was trying to save Emily and he was going to kill her for it."

Sis's legs gave way, and she slid down the wall, then sat on the packed dirt floor trying to catch a deep breath. It seemed to her that time had spun away and she was trapped inside a bubble where nothing existed except her brother, a deep musty smell that signaled disaster and the body at her feet.

"I thought you were evacuating," she said.

Still sitting there, a desperate woman buying time with a futile statement, she studied her brother. What she was looking for, she couldn't have said. It was no surprise that a Vietnam vet trained to defend and protect had acted instinctively to save Sweet Mama. What surprised her was his calm, take-charge attitude in the aftermath. Was he still in shock or was she seeing a return of the efficient, brilliant brother who thrived on adversity and challenge?

"That's what I thought, too," he said. "When we got back from the hospital, I strapped on my prosthetic leg so I'd have both hands, and then I went downstairs to get everybody packed up. Sweet Mama said she wasn't leaving."

"I know. Beulah told me."

"Beulah?"

"She's at the hospital now with Andy."

"She must have left while I was asleep."

"Thank God they weren't here. Listen, Jim, we've got to figure this out."

"Sis, just listen to that wind. We can't sit here in the garage with a dead man and the hurricane nearly on us. We've got to get rid of the body."

"My God, Jim. Just like that? You want me to get rid of a body?"

"Or we can just sit here and all get blown away." Jim grabbed her hand and hauled her up. "Listen, Sis, he nearly killed Emily, and he tried to kill Sweet Mama. Now, let's get moving."

It all fit. The knife in Larry's hand, Sweet Mama's warning about the cobbler, the bouquet of oleander, a poison that was lethal but slow to act. Larry would not have taken a bite of Amen cobbler and instantly toppled from his chair. He'd have felt nauseated and increasingly sick. A pharmaceutical rep would have recognized the deadly bouquet in the kitchen and put two and two together. A man that violent would have grabbed the knife just for the satisfaction of feeling his own power as he plunged it into Sweet Mama.

If Larry weren't already dead, Sis might kill him herself. She got up and dusted the seat of her pants. Yesterday if you'd asked her how far she'd go to save somebody she loved, she wouldn't have had any idea. Tonight she was as clear on the subject as if she'd earned her Ph.D. And in a way, she supposed she had. There's no better way to discover who you really are than to be thrust into the midst of your own worst nightmare.

"What do you want me to do?" she asked her brother.

"Help me get him in the trunk. Larry's going fishing in the Tchoutacabouffa."

"What about his car? It's sitting out there in the front yard big as you please."

"You drive it," Jim said, then edged back the tarp, but she couldn't watch as he searched Larry's pockets for the keys, didn't open her eyes until her brother pressed the cool metal into her hand. "We need to hurry, Sis."

There in the glare of the naked bulb on the garage ceiling, they exchanged a look that told of storms and a broken sister and a grandmother whose mind might now be shattered beyond recovery. And then, without a word, they grabbed the tarpaulin and lifted the body in the trunk of the car Jim hadn't set foot in since he got back from the war. He slammed the trunk shut and then they threw a fishing pole and a tackle box into the backseat. As an afterthought, Sis threw in a cooler.

"Good thinking, Sis."

"Hitch the boat while I check on Sweet Mama. I'll be back with some stuff for the cooler."

"I'll meet you out front. Hurry."

"I know, I *know*."

As Sis raced across the yard to the house, she could feel the hot breath of the storm in the night air that coated her skin with a thick sheen of sweat. She could feel the evil intent in the dark, brooding water.

Turning her mind from everything except the task at hand, she hurried up the back steps.

What happened here tonight was defense of the helpless, a tragic but logical conclusion to a horrifying string of events beyond her control. She had to hang on to that belief.

By the time she arrived at her grandmother's bedroom door, Sis had composed herself enough to ease inside and stand quietly till her eyes adjusted to the dark. Sweet Mama was on her side with one hand cupped under her cheek and her lips flapping with each burbling snore.

Thank God. Thank God.

Sis wanted to race across the room, wrap her grandmother in her arms and hang on until Sweet Mama sat back with a sassy look and said, "Quit hovering!"

With one last glance to ensure she was sleeping peacefully, Sis hurried off to the kitchen and threw together the kind of man-size picnic a foolish man might take to the river if he were going fishing—fried chicken with plenty of biscuits and a quart Mason jar filled with sweet tea.

She was almost out the door when she spotted the knife under the chair. Backtracking, she scooped it up, washed it off and put it back in the butcher block.

Sis locked the back door and heard the Thunderbird's engine and the crunch of gravel, a signal that Jim was coming around the house. She raced to the hall, snatched her purse and then struggled to get out the front door. For a while it seemed she'd remain trapped in the house.

She kicked the door open and lurched through. But when she was finally on the front steps, she ground to a halt like an overwound clock. Would the course she and Jim had set destroy her family or save it?

It seemed to Sis that Larry's car, sitting in the driveway like a malevolent insect, gave off the taint of evil. Once she set foot inside, there would be no going back. No more acting like a good citizen and calling the law. No more chances for justice by your peers.

A car door slammed, and Jim clambered up the steps and grabbed her arm.

"Time's running out, Sis."

If she could turn the clock backward and stop time altogether, she would. She'd freeze it in that jubilant moment when Emily raced out the door of the café to greet her brother returning from the dead in Vietnam. Neil Armstrong would be landing on the moon and everybody would be filled with such hope their skins could hardly contain it.

"Sis? Are you okay?"

"Yes." The lie felt as sharp as persimmons, and she was glad for the excuse to scream, even if it was just to be heard. "Why don't you follow me to the river, Jim? Do you remember our favorite fishing spot by the stand of willows?"

"I remember."

Sis got behind the wheel of Larry's car and almost gagged on the overpowering scent of his aftershave. She rolled down the window and tried to ignore the empty bag of potato chips on the seat, the newspaper flung into the floorboard and resting carelessly on a pair of rain boots—all signs of a man who only hours before had been very much alive, who had hovered over Emily's bed calling her *darling*.

Was that why Emily was keeping her eyes shut tight? So she wouldn't have to look at the face of the man whose possessive, warped kind of love had almost killed her?

Instead of driving along Highwy 90 heading east, Sis wanted to race to the hospital, grab her sister's hand and say, *He's gone now. You'll never have to worry about him again.*

Sis fought to stay on the road. Finally, she was able to steal a glance in the rearview mirror to see if Jim was keeping up. The low-slung silhouette of the snazzy car showed clearly, and she breathed a sigh of relief. She checked her speedometer, and saw that she was going ten miles above the speed limit. If she got caught how would she and Jim explain fishing poles and a picnic hamper in the car, let alone a body?

Sis's mind was in such a whirl, she barely noticed that Michael had kept his promise to board up Sweet Mama's Café. She hardly saw how the souvenir shops squatting along the waterfront still displayed their kites and beach balls, their plastic seashells and colorful beach towels. She never even glimpsed the Gulf, where lines of whitecaps turned the water angry and dangerous.

She made the turn toward the river, glancing to see Jim making the same turn, the fishing boat swerving behind him. Praying the boat didn't come unhitched, she drove along the winding road under a canopy of trees turned savage, their branches bent and the Spanish moss whipping about like dark fingers reaching to snatch the car off the road and toss it into the river.

She was *not* going to be swept off into the river, especially not in Larry Chastain's car. She made herself think of something pleasant, childhood days of sitting on the banks of the

Tchoutacabouffa while Sweet Mama and Beulah stood nearby wearing sunhats, laughing as a saltwater catfish tugged on their lines. Somehow it seemed right that a spot which held her memories should also hold her secrets.

The thick copse of willow trees came into view, and beyond, a river running wild, the Tchoutacabouffa, its banks overgrown with tangled trees and its deep shaded spots perfect for what they had to do. She pulled off the gravel road and onto a rutted path, gritting her teeth as the car jarred over roots and thick undergrowth and branches being ripped off the trees and slung into her path. One of them thunked the top of the car so hard she thought it would come right through.

"Stop it," she yelled.

The glare of wavering headlights in her rearview mirror told her that Jim was bumping along behind her. She came so suddenly into the clearing she had to slam on her brakes to keep from passing it by. She managed to pull the car to the side so Jim could pass. The boat threatened to slam into the side of Larry's car as Jim struggled to back it toward the river. Sis stared through the window, straining to see her brother, making bargains with God.

She knew she was being foolish and naive and desperate. Still, believing that Somebody Else was in charge was the one thing that might get her through the night.

When Jim finally killed the engine, she fought her way out of the car, then bent her head and struggled toward him. The dark rustled with sound, and twigs snapped under her feet. She ought to be praying a rattler wouldn't bite, or one of the water moccasins that lurked around the river, waiting to take revenge on anybody foolish enough to disturb him in his habitat.

"Sis! We've got to get this boat off the hitch and into the river while we still can!"

She barely heard him, and didn't even bother to try for a reply.

Neither of them had brought a flashlight. They fumbled and sweated in the dark trying to get the boat off the trailer, fighting against time and a storm determined to unravel them. After a furious struggle that left them both panting and Sis's arms aching, they loaded the boat with fishing gear and the man who would never know whether he got a strike on his line. Sis made herself think of Emily and how she would never again have to fear the fists of Larry Chastain. Next, she turned her mind to Andy, an innocent little boy whose future was now free of domestic violence.

When the boat with its macabre cargo finally hit the water, Sis doubled over, heaving. She didn't know how long she stayed that way, nor when the wind bent the trees toward the river as if the entire forest were praying. She only knew how the sound that suddenly came from her brother broke her heart in two.

Grief shook his shoulders and the moss in the tree above and the very bones in Sis's body. Without a word, she folded her brother close. They clung to each other, finally giving vent to their fear and their sorrow, their relief and their regret. They stayed that way while the winds sharpened, howling through the trees like Rachel crying for her lost children.

Sis took hold of her brother's arm and tugged him toward the convertible. When they were inside, they collapsed against the seat.

"If only I hadn't gone to sleep," he said.

"Shhh. It's not your fault."

"When the screams downstairs woke me, I thought I was back in the jungle."

"You're home now, Jim. You're home."

"I snapped, Sis. It was over before I even knew what I was doing. If only I had subdued him and called the cops…"

"Don't, Jim. You did what you had to do."

He nodded, or perhaps it was the movement of the curtain of moss. Without another word, they drove off. As the winding road took them away from their secret on the river, neither of them looked back.

Twenty-Five

Sweet Mama jarred awake to the sound of a riot outside her bedroom window.

She lay under the covers awhile trying to sort things out. When nothing came to her, not even the day of the week, she hung her legs over the side of the bed and searched with her feet until she found her bedroom slippers, and then she went down the hall to Beulah's door.

"Beulah? Are you awake?"

The answering silence struck Sweet Mama as odd. Beulah was a light sleeper. It didn't take more than one little bit of noise to roust her out of bed and send her flying through the house, searching for a mop to clean up the mess or a skillet to defend everybody with.

Sweet Mama pushed open the door and snapped on the light. The bed sat in the middle of the room like an accusation, empty as you please.

"Are you in the bathroom, Beulah? There's a riot outside the house."

No answer. Just the loud tick of the cheap alarm clock on Beulah's dresser and a scurrying in the walls that told she'd been right when she said, "Lord, Lucy, nasty old mice are gonna take over house and home if we don't get some rat poison."

Sweet Mama stood there until it was clear Beulah had left at the crack of dawn and headed off somewhere without her. As she trotted back down the hall to find the rest of her family, she heard some man yelling, "Get out! Get out!"

"Sis! Jim!" she called up the stairs. "Somebody wants us to leave."

The warning came again, fainter and farther away, but still the same.

"Get out! Leave now!"

Awareness came to her slowly, creeping over her skin and worming into her consciousness until the whole horrible picture was right there in front of her, so clear it might as well have been emblazoned on the wall.

"Evacuate!" The man screamed through his loudspeaker.

The big grandfather clock bonged five, making Sweet Mama jump. She tried to push through the front door, but something was on the other side, pushing back. She finally got the door open a crack, but the wind snatched it away and flung it back against the porch walls. Standing there exposed, her braid blowing straight back and her dress ballooning around her legs, Sweet Mama remembered Hurricane Betsy, and how the winds had arrived long before the wall of water.

Beyond the seawall, boats were being flung about like toys. Two of them collided and splintered into pieces that flew all over the beach. Camille was out there somewhere howling at her pranks, just getting warmed up.

Suddenly, a baby-blue convertible roared into the driveway, and Jim and Sis barreled out before the engine even died.

"Sweet Mama!" Sis bounded up the steps two at a time and grabbed her arm. "Let's get you back in the house."

Jim raced along behind and grabbed the door, but it took both her grandchildren to force it shut against the wind.

Twigs and leaves were caught in Sis's hair and there was mud all over Jim's boot and that leg she'd kept on her dresser. Instinctively, Sweet Mama opened her arms, and they came to her without a single word and huddled against her shoulder, grown-ups suddenly turned young again, children who needed a hug. Warnings sounded once more from the street, winds rattled the rocking chairs on the porch and a siren sent its mournful cry across the little tableau in the hallway. But still, they clung to each other, taking comfort and courage.

It was Sis who pulled away first.

"Sweet Mama, you have to pack a few things. Jim's going to take you and Beulah and Andy out."

"I've been through storms before." Even as Sweet Mama said it, she knew she'd never been through a storm like the one brooding out there in the Gulf.

"There's no need to argue," Sis said. "It's bad enough that Emily has to stay behind. I won't risk the rest of my family getting blown away by Camille."

"Sis is right, Sweet Mama," Jim said. "Camille's going to make landfall by evening, and they say she's coming in as a Category 5."

"Y'all go on and evacuate, but I'm staying here. This house has weathered storms for seventy-five years."

"Nobody's leaving without you," Jim said.

"Sweet Mama, they're talking about the worst winds and storm surges we've ever seen! We're not leaving you, so you might as well let me help you pack."

Sweet Mama searched around for Beulah. She always knew what to do. And then she remembered that Beulah had left yesterday with Andy. Suddenly, she saw her own stubborn determination as a selfish act.

Still, Sweet Mama wasn't about to let on that she had only the foggiest notion of what to take on an evacuation. The only thing she could think of was her *National Geographic*. She'd studied the travel stories and pictures for so long she couldn't remember when she first started dreaming of visiting the Grand Canyon, the Washington Monument and Pikes Peak.

"All right, I'll go. But I'll do my own packing," she said.

"We can do it faster together." Sis took her arm. "Come on, Sweet Mama. We don't have much time. We need to get this done while Jim gets some supplies."

Her grandson was already out the door. It slapped the walls with such a bang the china tea set nearly jumped off the hall table.

Sweet Mama picked it up and cradled it like a child. It was the only thing she owned that had belonged to her mother. The idea that it might get smashed like the boats in the harbor made Sweet Mama want to cry.

"I don't think we'll have room for things like that," Sis said, and Sweet Mama saw how foolish she looked, an old woman in her dotage hanging on to the things that didn't matter.

"But if you really want to take it, I'll pack it up," Sis added, her face and voice softening in the way of a woman who has lost too much and can't bear the thought of giving up one more thing. "Just remember, there will be four of you in the car and not much room for possessions."

"It's just a teapot." Sweet Mama set it back on the hall table. "I'd rather take biscuits."

Her granddaughter's unexpected laughter buoyed Sweet Mama up with such hope, she had the notion that they were all setting out on a vacation, that they might travel west through red canyons and deep gorges until they drove clear to the Pacific Ocean. She might even get to see a whale.

"Come on, Sweet Mama. We have to get started."

Sis took hold of her arm, and as she trotted down the hall trying to keep up, she thought about the long life she'd lived and the few years that were still ahead—if Camille didn't carry her off. She didn't have any regrets, not one, not even Peter and the oleander.

As she remembered that awful night, it seemed like yesterday. She could almost hear her assurances to Beulah that Peter was so drunk he wouldn't even remember how Eustace knocked him cold. Still, Beulah had sent Eustace off into the night to hide in the woods, then she and Sweet Mama spent an anxious night taking turns sleeping and watching Peter's door.

The boys woke up first, and Beulah packed them off to spend the day with Sally Kemp, a childless widow who adored children and had unofficially become the neighborhood's babysitter.

It was nearly noon before Peter Blake came out of his bedroom. He was carrying a pistol and a buggy whip, and he was in a killing mood.

Sweet Mama's mind spun backward, Peter's voice as clear as if he were standing right in front of her.

"Where is he?" he roared. "When I get my hands on Eustace, he'll wish he'd never been born."

Sweet Mama shooed a terrified Beulah into the kitchen, and put on the performance of lifetime.

"Honey, why should you be deprived of the things you enjoy just because Eustace doesn't have a lick of sense?" She smoothed his hair and patted his face, and then pulled her trump card. "You go on back to bed, sugar, and I'll have Beulah fix you a nice hot bath while I cook you something good."

When he finally went back into his bedroom, Sweet Mama raced out the back door to retch over the porch railing. Beulah was right behind her.

"What's he fixing to do, Lucy?"

"He's not going to do anything, Beulah. You're going to fill the zinc tub with hot water for his bath and I'm going to fix him something to eat."

"You mean he's willing to forget about last night?"

In the dark of night leaning against the wall outside his bedroom door, Sweet Mama had prayed that would happen. But sometimes mercy doesn't come in what we wish for; it comes in what we find ourselves capable of doing.

"No, Beulah. But after he eats, he's not going to remember anything."

"Lord Jesus God," Beulah whispered.

"It's going to be all right, Beulah."

"How can you say that, Lucy? I can see what you got up your sleeve."

"He's going to kill Eustace, and your husband will be just another colored man who got what was coming to him. Is that what you want?"

Terror was so thick they just stood there staring at each other, trying to breathe.

Finally, Beulah whispered, "We'll go to hell a poppin'."

"It's not hell I'm afraid of—it's my husband."

Beulah left to prepare Peter's bath, and by the time she returned to the kitchen, Sweet Mama was standing over a blue bowl of ripe peaches and dark red cherries, mixing in a double handful of white oleander.

Beulah turned a café au lait shade of pale. "Lord Jesus."

"Do you think that's enough, Beulah?"

"How should I know? I ain't never killed nobody."

"We're not killing anybody, Beulah. We're saving Eustace."

Sweet Mama didn't dare let Beulah know she was about to fly apart any minute. Her doubt would be Eustace's undoing. She knew it would come later, in the dark of night while her sons slept and she remembered.

"What're we making, Lucy?"

"A cobbler so good that when Peter Blake takes a bite he's going to stand up and shout Amen."

"From the looks of all that oleander, he ain't gonna be standing long."

They went into gales of nervous laughter that threatened to become hysteria. Sweet Mama held her apron over her mouth while Beulah stuffed hers with a dishcloth.

Sweet Mama pulled herself together first, and eyed the cobbler.

"Beulah, do you think one cup of sugar is enough?"

"I ain't fixing to taste that batter to find out," Beulah said, then dumped in another cup of sugar along with spices, cinnamon and ginger and just a touch of nutmeg.

Satisfied, they stuck their Amen cobbler in the oven, then went out on the back porch with glasses of sweet tea.

Seeing the two of them sitting there sipping tea while seagulls wheeled over the water and Spanish moss made lazy circles in the breeze, you'd never have guessed they were baking a cobbler that would turn out to be lethal. You'd never have seen how they swung wildly between terror and determination. You'd never have imagined that two women so young could spend the next fifty years keeping their sanity as well as their secret.

Still, Sweet Mama didn't believe in living life backward, agonizing over the things that had already happened. Her philosophy was *Look forward*. She'd read that book, *Look Forward,*

Angel. She was no angel, but she was a woman who would stop at nothing to save her family. She'd put that in her Remembering Book. *I am a woman who protects the ones I love, no matter the cost.* When the day came that she didn't know her own name, let alone the names of Sis and Emily and Jim and Andy and dear, faithful Beulah, she would turn to page ten and read that about herself. And she would smile.

Sis and Jim finally got Sweet Mama and her belongings loaded into the Thunderbird, along with personal possessions for Beulah, Jim and Andy. The beachfront highway was clogged with traffic. Most of them were heading toward the exits north, but there were still cars filled with people in their Sunday best heading toward church.

Sis was behind the wheel of her brother's car, but she had the feeling of being in another world as the church bells pealed from the tower on Biloxi's Church of the Redeemer while the National Guard's amphibious vehicles and two-ton trucks dispersed to strategic points along the highway. She glanced in the rearview mirror at her brother.

"They're posting the guard in the places most likely to flood," Jim said.

The flat, matter-of-fact way he said it was chilling. Her instinct was to floorboard the gas pedal, but even if she did, there was nowhere to go. The convertible was caught in a traffic jam traveling at a snail's pace.

When she got to the Buena Vista, she saw why. People and cars poured out of Biloxi's resort motel, trying to escape. Horns blared and people rolled down their windows to scream at each other.

Even the birds were flocking north. The sky was dark with wings as they heeded nature's call to leave a land under siege.

Sis had the awful certainty that she was too late. That she'd spent too much time in the pink Victorian house packing up possessions when she should have just snatched Sweet Mama out of there and hauled her to the hospital where Jim could pick up Beulah and Andy. By now they would have been past the turnoff heading north.

Even before she voiced her concern, Jim told her, "I'll get everybody out," as if the awful night on the river had joined his mind with hers.

"I know you will," she said, believing no such thing. "Why don't you take a nap? It's going to be a long day and a long drive for you."

He shut his eyes, but she could see in the mirror that he wasn't napping. He kept popping up to study the chaos. Winds battered the palm trees, and beach umbrellas left behind by careless bathers flew through the air like lethal kites. Two cars stood abandoned where they had smashed into each other in their headlong dash toward the same exit, while their occupants hurried ahead with their thumbs stuck out, desperate to hitch a ride out of hell.

By the time Sis got to the hospital, she was limp with fear and relief. The parking lot was jammed. Vehicles were parked haphazardly and people rushed about, some trying to leave the hospital, some trying to enter.

"Jim, it'll be faster if I go in and bring Beulah and Andy out."

"I'll turn the car around and keep the motor running, Sis."

She bailed out and hit the ground running. On her left a balding man and a doughy-faced woman in white uniforms ushered a long, creaky line of seniors from two nursing home vans toward the hospital entrance. Taking shelter. The idea lifted her spirits as she raced inside. The hospital would have backup generators, and it was far enough off the water that Emily might be safe when Camille whipped the Gulf into a fury.

Long lines of people snaked out from every elevator. Sis headed toward the stairs and took them two at a time. By the time she got to Emily's room on the fourth floor, she was so winded, she leaned against the door frame, gasping. When she finally got her breath back, she eased open the door.

Emily was as still as a wax angel, while Andy stood beside her bed, holding her hand. Beulah sat upright in her chair, snoring.

"Aunt Sis." Andy launched himself at her and wrapped her in a tight hug. "I *knew* you'd come back."

Beulah snorted awake and wiped her hands across her eyes. "Of course she's back, sweet pea. I told you so."

"Any change?" Sis asked, and Beulah just shook her head. "Jim and Sweet Mama are in the car downstairs. We need to hurry."

"Ain't that the gospel!"

Beulah began gathering her belongings while Sis squatted beside her nephew.

"Andy, there's a big wind blowing and they say a storm is coming."

"It blowed a man's hat off."

"I'm sure it did, but I don't want you to be scared. Uncle Jim is going to take you and Sweet Mama and Beulah some-place safe."

"Can't I stay with my mommy? I'm a big boy and I got my brave bear."

"I know you're a big brave boy, Andy, but your mommy would want you to go with Uncle Jim."

"Why can't she go, too?"

"The doctor says she has to stay here awhile longer to rest. But I'll be here with her, and I'll make sure she's safe."

Andy cocked his head, considering. When he nodded so hard his cowlick bobbed, Sis almost wept with relief.

"'K, Aunt Sis. I'll leave Henry. He'll take care of you and Mommy."

"Great. See you later, 'gator."

"After a while, crocodile." He raced to the bed, stood on tiptoe and whispered, "Don't be scared, Mommy. Aunt Sis and Henry's gonna take good care of you."

Her wide face glistening with tears, Beulah handed off her bundle to Sis, then picked up Andy.

"We ready when you are."

They followed Sis out the door, with Andy looking back the whole way, even when he could no longer see his mother. Still, he set his little face into brave lines as they pushed their way through halls bustling with people and back toward the elevators. But it was impossible to get to them through the milling crowds.

"We'll have to take the stairs, Beulah. Do you want to swap and let me carry Andy?"

"The day I can't take care of this young 'un is the day they gonna be lowering me six feet under. Go on, Sis. And don't think I can't keep up."

Though Beulah huffed as if she were trying to draw her last breath, she stayed with Sis every step of the way. The parking lot was even more chaotic than before.

"Grab my arm, Beulah, and hang on to Andy!"

Linked, they stood at the edge of the parking lot, a determined, immovable team, searching for Jim's car. In that awful moment when Sis realized he might be boxed in with no way out, she closed her eyes and whispered, "Please."

Born of desperation, it was both promise and prayer. While it was still on Sis's lips, the blue car snaked around a long line and eased to a stop in front of the trio. Sweet Mama sat in the front seat with her *National Geographic* magazines on her lap, so calm you couldn't have told by looking that she was a woman on the run.

Beulah clambered inside with Andy, and Sis waved them off. They drove away smiling, Andy and Beulah swiveling so they could wave at Sis until the car finally disappeared. Suddenly, the adrenaline that had kept Sis going through the long night and into the early afternoon vanished. She felt every part of herself sag, even her mind.

Only one thing kept her upright: the thought of all those stairs she had to climb to get back to her sister.

Twenty-Six

EMILY WAS IN THE EXACT position Sis had left her, one hand over her heart, the other on the side of the bed propped over Andy's teddy bear. She was so still she looked like a painting of herself, something done by one of the Renaissance artists who knew how to capture the perfect expression, the bloom of peaches on cream-colored skin. But more than that, they knew how to paint a woman's face in a way that made her look as if she were holding secrets she might be coaxed to tell—but only if it suited her mood.

Her hair was brushed back from her face and fanned over the pillows like starlight. That was probably Beulah's doing. She'd always taken pride in Emily's hair. She used to bring home shampoo with lemon to keep it golden and shiny.

Sis sank into the chair by the bed and reached for her sister's hand.

"Em, I don't know how much you've heard about Hurricane Camille, but I want you to know, I got Andy out. Sweet Mama and Beulah, too. Jim's driving north now. By the time the storm gets here, they'll all be high and dry in a motel somewhere.

"You're safe, too. I'm staying right here, and I'm not going to let anything hurt you. Ever again."

A vision of Larry floating down the Tchoutacabouffa in Jim's boat came suddenly to mind, and Sis got dizzy. It was probably nerves. Or lack of sleep. Maybe even lack of food.

"Em, I'm going around the corner to get some coffee and snacks, but I'll be right back. Don't you worry one minute. You're going to be fine. Everybody's going to be fine."

The fourth floor hallways were relatively empty, but a din of noise drifted from the direction of the elevators and the stairwell around the corner. Patients on the lower floors screamed and cried, footsteps pounded up and down the stairwell, nurses and doctors shouted orders.

She was so grateful to be out of that panicked, directionless crowd she started crying. And then she couldn't stop. Leaning her head against the cool surface of the drink machine, she sobbed for her sister, who might never come out of her coma, for Andy, who might lose his mother, for Beulah, who might lose her life trying to save Andy's and for Sweet Mama and Jim, who had done the unthinkable in the name of love. But she cried for herself, too, a first for Sis. Last night she'd gone to the blackest part of her soul, and now she was carrying a secret she could never share with anyone except her brother.

Saddened almost beyond enduring, Sis thought of her burgeoning relationship with Michael, of how he'd kissed her under a curtain of Spanish moss and held her hand and boarded up Sweet Mama's café—small intimacies, simple kindnesses that now broke her heart. How could she dream of a future with him and hold back a secret that might destroy them both?

Where was he now? Was he hunkered down in the barracks on Kessler? Out in this raging wind trying to shore up the seawall in order to hold back the storm?

"Be safe, Michael," she whispered, and then she wiped her face with the back of her hand and started dropping change into the snack machine.

She bought potato chips and candy and the corn chips she could eat by the bushel. Then she put her money into the coffee machine, balanced the whole stash of food and headed back to Emily's room.

"Em, I'm back."

She dumped her food on the serving tray, sank into her chair and ripped into a bag of potato chips. The empty bag in the floorboard of Larry's car flashed through her mind. Where was the car now? Had the wind already pushed it into the river?

Another lump formed in her throat, and she forced it back with a handful of potato chips.

"I wish you would wake up and help me eat all this, Em. I bought enough for Cox's army."

Sis plowed through the bag of chips, two candy bars and a cup of coffee. In spite of the jolt of caffeine, she fell asleep sitting straight up.

Sometime later, a woman's screams woke her. She jerked upright, groggy and disoriented. The screams were coming from somewhere behind her. Sis swiveled around to see the windowpanes rattling, palm trees bent double and a crazy assortment of things flying across the hospital grounds— wheelchairs, treetops, sheet metal and even a Chihuahua still on its leash. Down the street, traffic lights on the corner were blowing straight out.

That was no woman screaming: it was Camille, taking out her rage on a city trying desperately to shore itself up.

Sis glanced at her watch. Six o'clock. Was this the brunt of

Camille or was there more to come? Thank God her family was safe.

She turned on the TV, scrolling through static and blank screens until she came to a station with a signal. It was weak, but the image of the reporter finally became clear. He was standing on the beach where the roar of wind tore at his yellow rain slicker and almost drowned out what he was saying.

"Winds now battering the Gulf Coast at 180 miles an hour are expected to increase to more than 200 miles an hour. If you are hearing this broadcast and have not already evacuated, get to the nearest shelter. The arterial highways are clogged and all but impassable.

"Camille is on a collision course with Pass Christian, Gulfport and Biloxi. She is now only hours from landfall. By our calculations, the hurricane will come ashore about nine this evening.

"She's coming in as a Category 5, bringing with her a twenty-four-foot storm surge on top of ten-foot waves. We've seen nothing like this in our lifetime, folks!"

The camera panned wide to show a view of the Gulf. If you didn't see how the wind battered him, you'd hardly believe a hurricane lurked just beyond the horizon. At first glance, you'd think you were in the middle of a movie, that a wind machine off camera made the actor on-screen look as if he were in danger of being blown out to sea.

But on closer inspection, you'd see the solid wall of black beyond the horizon. And you'd know this was no movie. This was all too real. Camille was roaring toward you like a hurricane from hell.

Would she blow the windows out? Send winds that would snatch Emily out of her bed and into a whirling holocaust?

Such a burst of adrenaline pumped through Sis, she could

have picked up her sister's bed and carried it into the hall.
There Emily might be safe from flying glass and tree limbs
turned to shrapnel. But Emily was tethered to life-saving machines. The best Sis could do was scoot the bed as far away
from the window as it would get without unhooking her sister. Then she stationed her own chair and the extra one between Emily and the window.

Outside, Camille screamed louder, a premature death keen
that ripped through Sis's soul.

The TV screen flickered as the reporter continued to blare
warnings. Sis turned it off. She and catastrophe were old ac-
quaintances. She didn't need minute-to-minute updates to
tell her she faced an adversary so powerful she'd be no more
than a grain of sand trying to hold firm on the beach against
a tidal wave.

Turning her back to the window, Sis caught Emily's hand.
"Don't be afraid. I'm here, Em."

She sank into the chair and held on to her sister's hand, just
held on. Sis didn't know how long she sat there, didn't know
how she could endure the banshee screeching outside her window without screaming herself.

Emily's nurse came in to check on her and assure Sis the
patients on the fourth floor would be safe.

"Did you hear that, Em? You're safe." She smoothed back
her sister's hair. "Do you remember how you used to cry during storms? The only way I could soothe you was by singing."

Sis had never had a pretty voice, and her repertoire consisted
of "Take Me Out to the Ball Game" and the nonsensical lullaby, "Rock-a-bye Baby," she'd sung to the twins when they
were four years old. She rejected the lullaby in favor of the
little ditty that might make Emily think of wonderful summers gone by. The song made Sis think of standing on the

beach with her cap on backward and her bat over her shoulder, yelling at Michael to send her a fastball.

The wind sharpened and the sky darkened, but Sis sang on, trying to hold back disaster with off-key music. She was in the middle of "Buy me some peanuts and Cracker Jack," when the door flew open. The song died as Beulah marched in, hanging on to Andy and her big bundle of possessions. She hurried to the bathroom as Jim came through the door, loaded with blankets and a picnic basket. Right behind him was Sweet Mama, holding on for dear life to her purse and her *National Geographic* magazines.

"Jim! What happened?"

"We didn't get two miles in this traffic jam."

"I've never seen anything like it," Sweet Mama said.

The story was bursting to get out of her, to get out of all of them.

"This is the closest shelter, so I turned around and headed back." Jim piled the blankets and picnic baskets on the floor while Beulah burst back through the bathroom door.

"I thought the wind was gonna blow us clear to kingdom come. I nearly 'bout wet my pants." Beulah was so scared she looked as if she'd personally traveled to the Pearly Gates and back. "Lord God, I never saw anybody fight back like that, Jim."

The praise flowed through Jim like balm. Sis could see it in the way his eyes turned a deeper shade of blue and in the way he turned talkative, even expansive.

"It's a war zone out there, but if there's anything I know, it's coming out safe on the other side of hell."

"He got us all the way to the top of the parking garage," Sweet Mama said, proud.

"And then we had to wait forty forevers to plow our way

up the stairs," Beulah added. "But here we are, thanks to Jim." She snatched one of the blankets and tenderly tucked it around Emily, patting her face and crooning. "There now, sweet pea. Old Beulah ain't gonna leave you. You just rest easy."

The lights began to flicker, and for a moment it was if they'd dropped off the earth and into a deep chasm where nothing existed except the roar of wind and the sound of splintering and crashing as boats and trees and houses broke apart under the storm's wrath. Sis felt rather than saw the hands reaching toward her, Andy's small one and the large flat hand with calloused fingertips, Beulah finding her in the dark.

"Hold on, Andy," Sis said. "Don't let go."

She inched forward in the flickering shadows until she could feel her knees touching the edge of her sister's bed. Behind her, Sweet Mama and Jim closed in, and together they all formed a protective wall around Emily.

The backup generators finally kicked in. With a buzzing that sounded like a roomful of bees, the lights came up again and held steady while the wind screamed around them without ceasing.

Sis glanced at her watch. Eight o'clock. And the worst was yet to come—a twenty-four-foot wall of water pushed in front of wind that could uproot and hurl hundred-year-old oak trees as easily as a child hurls a toy.

Andy clung to her hand without whimpering. Still, with his fearful eyes and too-pale face, he didn't even resemble the little boy who had spent the summer in the sun building a rocket ship to the moon.

"I have a great idea, Andy." She squatted beside him and smiled. "Why don't we see if there's some fried chicken and biscuits in that basket. We can have a picnic."

"Henry, too?"

"Of course. A brave bear has to have lots of food to be big and strong and protect your mommy."

As Beulah spread one of the blankets on the floor while Sweet Mama set her travel magazines on the tray table and unwrapped chicken and biscuits, the very act of preparing to eat a family meal seemed so ordinary, Sis felt transported out of the hellish nightmare and back home where they would all gather around the table, safe. Beulah and Sweet Mama settled into the only chairs, and the rest of the family completed the circle, Jim sitting on the edge of the blanket with his prosthetic leg stuck straight out and Sis sitting cross-legged with Andy leaning into her.

Shivers occasionally ran through him, and Sis cast about for ways to ease his terror. If she'd led an ordinary life with husband and children, she'd have a mother's heart to know whether to read his favorite book or pull him into her lap. The burst of anger that flashed through her was so unexpected she almost cried. If Emily had listened to her in the first place, none of them would be on the floor in a hospital room waiting for Camille to wash them out the window. They'd be holed up safe somewhere far north of the Mississippi Gulf Coast.

Shame and regret followed on the heels of her anger. If life had taught Sis one thing, it was that surprise and catastrophe lurked around every corner, sometimes in recognizable form, but more often in such a harmless disguise you'd never see their true colors until it's too late.

I'm sorry, Emily. I'm sorry. Just please wake up and tell me what to do about Andy.

Sometimes mercy comes so quietly you don't even know you've found it until you've already opened your mouth and are saying, "Why don't we all tell stories?"

Sis remembered now how Emily used to come into the café,

smiling about the stories she and her son shared. Though he loved having his favorite books read to him at bedtime, the thing he enjoyed most were the make-believe adventures they imagined aloud.

"You can go first, Andy!"

"Oh, boy!" He came alive in the way of the innocent who can be distracted from disaster by a small joy. "When this big wind goes away, me and Henry and Mommy's gonna fly off in my rocket ship."

"Where all you going, sweet pea?" Beulah asked.

"To the moon. But first we might fly to Africa."

"I want to go to Pikes Peak." Sweet Mama spoke with such longing, Sis felt ashamed. While she'd bemoaned her fate, her own grandmother had been yearning toward dreams she'd postponed for seventy-five years.

"I'll take you, Sweet Mama," Andy said as if granting dreams were that simple.

"What else are you going to do in Africa, Andy?" Sis asked, and he leaned back to smile up at her.

"Henry wants to see the tigers. The only one he knows is Tigger, and he's not a very fierce animal."

"Now my favorite is Eeyore." Beulah chucked. "The two of us have so much in common, sometimes it's downright scary."

The House at Pooh Corner had been a favorite in the Blake household as long as Sis could remember. Jim and Sweet Mama chimed in, and soon Andy became a carefree little boy talking about his favorite characters in the Hundred Acre Wood and the many adventures he was going to have in his rocket ship.

With make-believe adventures weaving a spell as sweet as spun sugar, Andy began to wind down, his eyes at half-mast and his head drooping against Sis's shoulder.

"I'm going to put him in the bed," Sis said.

While Beulah packed up remnants of the picnic, she picked her nephew up and held on while Jim carefully moved Emily to make room.

As Sis tucked Andy under the covers with his mother, Camille aimed her evil eye at the Gulf Coast and struck with full force. Rain sounded like hammer blows against the windowpane, and the screaming wind clawed at the building as if a thousand wild animals were trying to get in.

"Move the chairs close," Jim said. "Form ranks."

They pushed the two chairs close to the bed, leaving just enough room to sit.

"Thank you, Jesus." Beulah crashed into her chair with such force, Sis feared it would splinter, but Sweet Mama refused to sit down until she had her purse and her stack of *National Geographic* magazines.

Sis's nerves frayed another notch. When they were finally settled, she draped a blanket over their heads and across their shoulders.

Leaning close, she whispered, "Stay safe."

Jim came up behind her with two more blankets. Without a word, he handed one to Sis then draped another over his head and shoulders, imperfect shields against a perfect storm. Then with arms linked and the two blankets held wider than Andy's Superman cape in full flight, Sis and her brother formed a barricade behind their family.

Twenty-Seven

SWEET MAMA HEARD THE WALL of water coming. It sounded like a freight train slamming through the hospital entrance, roaring through the lower floors, sending furniture crashing as people screamed up the stairs. The intercom on the fourth floor blared.

"Get to the higher floors. The first is under water, the second is not safe. Move up! Move up!"

Sweet Mama had lost track of everything except the screeching winds and roaring water and the sound of her own heartbeat. It was holding steady because she didn't intend to have it any other way, not as long as Camille was outside acting like the worst-behaved hurricane she'd ever seen. Betsy had ripped up the Mississippi Gulf Coast a right smart and the storm of '47 had scared a few folks so bad they left Biloxi and never came back.

That was back when hurricanes didn't have names, back in saner days where manners counted and wars were fought for the greater good of America and *respect* was not a dirty word. Still, Sweet Mama wasn't back in the olden days; she was sitting in a chair wondering if the floors underneath her would collapse and send her flailing off into the sea. She couldn't swim worth a flitter. When she packed her belongings, most of which were still in a car that would be halfway to Cuba if the water kept rising, she'd been thinking of a teapot instead of a life jacket.

The way the wind was blowing, she imagined her tea set had been slung clear up to Kentucky. She'd read about pictures from people's photograph albums being scattered across three states in a tornado. Hurricane Camille was worse than any tornado she ever heard of, or any other natural disaster, for that matter.

If she lived through it, and she was bound and determined to, even if she had to lash herself to Emily's bed with that blanket Sis had draped over her and float all the way to China, she was going to give her frivolous belongings away and do something that mattered while she still had mind enough to know the difference. She'd always tried to do the things that mattered. Her café had kept more people from going hungry during the Great Depression than she could count, and she'd guarded the ones she loved with the courage of lions. Hadn't she kept Beulah safe all these years and raised three fine grandchildren without any help from a soul except her oldest and best friend?

The door to Emily's room burst open and Emily's nurse came in with her loose cap flapping and her clothes soaked up to her waist. She stood there a minute with her hand over her heart, catching her breath.

"Is everybody still all right in here?"

"Fine," Sweet Mama told her.

"Everybody who is able needs to move into the hall, away from the windows."

She had her job to do, but Sweet Mama had hers, too.

"This is my granddaughter and my great-grandson on the

bed. I wouldn't leave them and go into that hall if Camille was already halfway up my dress tail."

"Ain't that the truth?" Beulah said, nodding with such emphatic motion her wooly gray hair stood out from her head like the quills of a moody porcupine.

It wouldn't do to cross both of them at the same time. Plenty of people who'd tried it before this little scared bird of a nurse had gone away with their tails tucked. Not that Sweet Mama wanted to scare the nurse. What she really wanted to do was put her arms around her and call her sweet pea.

"We've got some leftover fried chicken in the basket," Sweet Mama said. "Do you want some, hon?"

"No, thank you, ma'am. I'm just trying to get everybody to safety."

"We appreciate the warning," Sis told her. "We're keeping a close eye on the storm, and if it gets any worse, I'll get everybody into the hall."

"Keep away from the window," the nurse said.

Sweet Mama didn't even fight her irresistible impulse to look. The sky was lit with flames from houses that had escaped Camille's wall of water but succumbed to the tornadoes she spawned, the gas lines blown wide-open and the jagged lightning that split the sky. In the eerie glow, rooftops floated by, and whole houses. Cats and dogs and horses, some still kicking but most of them dead, drifted out of sight while a river barge as big as a schoolhouse threatened to crash right through the window.

Sweet Mama wished she'd grabbed up the Bible instead of her *National Geographic* magazines.

"God keep you safe," the nurse said, and then fled toward the door and disappeared into the hallway where she was greeted by the cries of the sick and the terrified.

Sis got towels from the bathroom to stuff into the cracks of the door and muffle the sound, then she stood flexing her shoulders and rubbing the back of her neck. Sweet Mama felt the weight of age and her fading mind like an anvil to her heart.

The wind roared on, the breath of a furious storm determined to hold a wall of water over Mississippi's coastal towns until everything in them was destroyed.

Sweet Mama clutched her purse with one hand and Beulah with the other. If she ever got to write in her Remembering Book again, she'd describe this night of horror and heartbreak as hell on earth, not because of the destruction to her possessions, but because it threatened to take away everybody she loved.

She reached up to adjust the blanket over Andy, who mercifully was still asleep. In the brief time it took to lift her hands over the covers, it grew so quiet outside the window you could hear the rush of your own blood.

"The storm's over," she said.

She suddenly felt every part of her body collapse inward, a reaction to the battle to keep her wits and to sit upright in a chair long past her bedtime.

"That's just the first wall of the hurricane, Sweet Mama," Jim said. "Now we're in the middle of the still eye."

Sis put a hand on her shoulder, and it felt like a prayer, a blessing, a sweet release from the vigilance that had her muscles screaming and her bones aching.

"Rest now, Sweet Mama," her granddaughter said.

"I think I'll put my head down for just a minute." Sweet Mama sagged against the bed and put her head on the sheet next to Andy.

She didn't intend to go to sleep, not with another wall of

the hurricane heading her way. There was no telling what that witch Camille would try to throw through the window next. Still, the sheet was cool to her cheek and her great-grandson's sweet breath fanned across her temple. The last thing she heard were the voices of Sis and Beulah, talking about wind and waves and water in a low murmuring that sounded like the blues.

Voices drifted into the darkness where Emily hung suspended. Her body urged her to plunge deeper and vanish while her mind screamed at her, *Rise up, rise up toward the sound of your sister's voice and the wide embrace of Beulah.*

The murmur of their voices grew stronger, and Emily strained upward to hear.

"Here comes the other wall of that witch hurricane," Beulah said. "Lord God, Almighty, listen to that wind howl! I'm glad Lucy's sleeping."

The hurricane sounded like a woman screaming and for a panicked moment, Emily thought it was her own shrieks as she was pushed down the staircase. And then she remembered where she was and how the storm that was outside her window was the same storm that had propelled her to pack her suitcases and get her son away from Larry.

Where was he now? Was her son safe?

Emily struggled to ask, but the questions in her mind wouldn't go through the layers of darkness that bound her.

"Look! Her eyeballs are moving!" Beulah said. "Emily's waking up."

"Em." She felt her sister lean closer. "Open your eyes."

No matter how hard she tried, Emily couldn't do what her sister asked. The struggle exhausted her, and she found herself spiraling back toward the tunnel that wanted to suck her away.

Was there nothing she could hold on to, nothing to keep her from falling into the void?

Just when Emily thought she was lost, she felt her sister grab her hand and pull her back. For a moment, she had the peculiar sense of being tugged in two directions, of watching her legs disappear down a tunnel while she struggled toward the people she was leaving behind.

Sis's grasp was firm, but it wasn't enough. It was no match for the irresistible lure of peace and comfort Emily felt waiting for her somewhere beyond this room. Desperate to hang on, she forced herself to concentrate on the things she knew—the indentation in the pillow behind her head, the weight of the blanket over her legs, the grating sound of Sweet Mama's snores and the moan of a dying wind as the hurricane released Biloxi from its grip and turned its fury elsewhere. But there was something else, too, a small weight pressing against her side.

Emily concentrated so hard she felt her brow furrow and her heart speed up. Curving into her like a new moon, the weight smelled of summer and sweat and innocence, of fried chicken and orange soda and dreams. It was the same weight she'd carried in her heart since before he was born—her son, sleeping by her side while Hurricane Camille slipped away.

With a mother's fierce heart, Emily yearned toward her son until she became aware of his head against her shoulder, his soft cowlick tickling the skin along her upper arm, and his left foot moving under the covers as he ran through his little boy dreams. Was he chasing the dog she'd promised him but never had time to get? Was he running through the backyard catching moonlight on his tongue, sitting in the driver's seat of his makeshift rocket flying toward the moon?

Emily lay quietly, gathering strength while the voices of her family drifted around her.

"Hear that?" her brother said. "The winds are dying down."

"Is that devil Camille finally gonna leave us alone?" Beulah's voice was unmistakable. Emily imagined her glaring at the storm and even shaking a fist in Camille's direction.

There was a long, low whine, like a freight train leaving the station. The air in the room felt static, as if you might rub your hand across your arm and shoot sparks that would catch everything around you on fire.

"Listen," Beulah said. "That old she-witch out there is turning her evil eye north."

It felt as if all the energy were being sucked out and the sudden stillness echoed in a room quiet now except for the lapping of angry water beyond the hospital walls.

"I wonder what's left standing." That was Sis, always the practical one, always assessing the problem and planning how she could fix it.

Emily heard footsteps tapping across the room, too light to be Beulah and Jim. It had to be Sis, probably going to the window to see what was out there.

"It's too dark to see," Jim told her, but Sis kept on going.

"I ain't even gonna look," Beulah said. "I don't want to know."

The room got quiet again, and Emily strained to pick out the sounds—a low humming Beulah sometimes made under her breath, the anxious foot tapping Jim did when he was revved as high as the engine of a race car, the steady snoring Sweet Mama always settled into as the moon faded and the sun got ready to put in its appearance.

"It'll be a while before I can see anything," Sis said. "We might as well stretch out on blankets and try to get some rest."

"I'm sitting right where I'm at," Beulah announced. "If I got down on that floor, it'd take a tow truck to get me back up."

Sis and Jim both told her they'd help her up, but she refused to get out of her chair, even when Sis issued a dire warning that she might fall out in her sleep and break her leg.

"I'm too tough to break. Now y'all leave me alone and go on to bed. Ain't much left of this devil night, thank God!"

Sounds drifted over Emily, her family's whispered good-nights and the rustling of blankets as they settled in for the rest of the night. Their voices faded, and panic threatened to swamp her. Sis had always fought Emily's battles, but she was alone now, trying to find her way out of the dark.

Forcing herself to get very still, Emily waited. And then she heard movement, footsteps as light as moondust and the faint click of a button, Sis turning on the TV, the sound so muted Emily couldn't make out the words no matter how hard she tried. Finally, in the deep quiet that followed she made out a faint line of static, a thin blue pathway she could follow home.

Twenty-Eight

IN THE EARLY DAWN HOURS, something roused Sis from sleep. She lay in her nest of blankets on the floor, listening. The distinctive sound of helicopter blades beating the air drew her toward the window. She inched the curtain back to view what was left of her old life. Water stretched as far as she could see, not the sky-blue of the Gulf under a new day, but a boiling, dirty brew filled with the wreckage of homes and cars and boats. Entire trees floated by, and the huge cross that had once sat at the top of Episcopal Trinity Church. A cross on the water seemed appropriate in light of the helicopters thick as bees in the sky, searching for victims.

Looking out the window, Sis understood just how many ways a heart can break. Was Michael up there in the sky conducting a macabre search? Was the pink Victorian house by the sea still standing? What of Sweet Mama's Café and all the dear regulars who gathered there every morning? Were they safe, or had they been carried off by the killing breath of Camille? And what of all the people along the coast who had not made their way to safety?

Pressing her face against the glass, she tried to gather the pieces of her broken heart. The time for mourning would come later, while she lay on the floor of this hospital room trying to sleep with a blanket as her only bed.

She didn't know how long she stayed with her face pressed against the window, didn't know what made her turn. Andy was asleep on Emily's bed, Jim on the floor and Sweet Mama and Beulah slumped in their chairs. Her grandmother still rested her head on Emily's bed, but Beulah drooped at such a crazy angle, Sis feared she'd topple out of her chair.

Tiptoeing, she made her way to the bed and gently tugged Beulah upright. The poor old woman was so exhausted she never batted an eye; she just gave a big snort and then settled back into her train-rumble snoring.

Let her sleep. Let them all sleep. Maybe by the time her family woke up, the wall of water that had torn through Biloxi in the night would have vanished back out to sea. What would happen next? Her mind raced ahead, gathering tragedies the way some people collect souvenir spoons.

"Sis?"

The whisper was so hoarse, so soft, Sis thought her mind had finally come unhinged, that she was now hallucinating. It came again, clearer this time.

Sis whirled toward the bed to see her sister staring at her with eyes so blue they looked like the Mediterranean.

"Oh, my God, you're awake." She leaned across Andy's warm, little body and touched her sister's face. "I can't believe it. It's finally you."

They both started crying at the same time, silent tears streaking their faces and running into their mouths, making talk impossible. They stayed that way awhile, trapped in feelings too big to escape, loss and love and the trembling hope of survivors.

"How much do you know, Em? About where you are and what's happening?"

"Everything. I heard it all, the doctors, the storm, the voices of my family. It was your voice that brought me back, and the weight of my sleeping son."

"How? I didn't say anything extraordinary."

"It wasn't what you said, Sis, it was your strong conviction that came through. Do you remember?"

"I just kept telling you that you were safe, you were going to be all right."

"Hearing that was like having a towline thrown into a deep well. I grabbed hold and hung on. Finally, I got strong enough to climb."

"I knew you would."

"See! That's what I'm talking about." Emily reached to touch Andy's soft hair. "And how could I ever leave my son? Sis, how did he do through everything?"

"He sailed right through. Of course, he thinks his courage came from the Superman suit."

"I've got to get him one that fits." Emily lifted the edge of his faded red cape. "Poor little fellow. He's seen things no little boy ever should have to." She glanced anxiously around the room. "Where's Larry?"

"He's not here, Em."

Anxious sweat broke out on Sis's face and soaked her T-shirt. She longed to tell Emily he was gone for good, that he could never raise his fists to her again, but that would make her sister a party to the awful night of white oleander, the dark river and the even darker secret.

"Is he at home?"

"I don't know, Em. The last time I saw him, he was too tired to move. He probably went off somewhere to relax." The web of lies drew so tight around Sis, she could hardly breathe. "Let's not talk about him anymore, Em."

"I hope he evacuated and kept on going. I hope he went all the way back to Kentucky."

Emily stuck out her tongue, and Sis got tickled. Suddenly, they both found themselves guffawing so hard they had to cover their mouths to keep from waking the rest of the family. If anybody had seen them, they might have thought the Blake sisters had lost their minds in the storm, but Sis knew better. You could laugh through your tears or you could drown in them.

"How bad is it out there?" Emily finally asked.

"You don't want to know."

"But I do. When I get out of here, I plan to take care of my son and my house and the café. I'm going to do it standing on my own two feet and God help the man who gets in my way."

"Good grief, Em. What did they put in that IV?"

"Sweet power. I'm just full of it."

"Does this mean I won't get to boss you around?"

"Occasionally. When the mood suits me."

"Emily Blake, it sounds to me like you've been to the moon and back."

"That's another thing, Sis. After the divorce, I intend to get my old name back. Legally. I don't plan to go through this life dragging Chastain behind me."

Sis thought she might just keel over on top of her sister. Events of the summer played through her mind like a horror film she couldn't stop watching, secrets and lies topped by a storm so hellish nothing would ever be the same. And now she was standing at her sister's bedside up to her knees in more deception. *After the divorce.* At what point could Sis put this final lie behind her? At what point would the summer of 1969 fade into a memory softened by time?

"Mommy!" The sleeping bundle in the Superman cape

came suddenly awake, saving Sis from having to invent more false stories to tell her sister. "You're awake!"

And now so was the whole family. As they crowded around the bed and Andy caught his mother in a hug so tight it seemed he'd never let go, Sis moved unnoticed toward the window.

The water was already receding toward the Mississippi Sound, and along with it, Sis's Valiant. It looked like a battered black toy floating off toward the Barrier Islands. Sis was already in such a state of shock and dismay, she barely registered her loss. *It's just a car,* was what she thought. Looking out the same window, safe inside a building that held firm, she'd seen the things that were lost during the long night of grief and terror.

Soon they could wade through the wreckage to discover what Camille had left behind. But for now, she rested her cheek against the cool windowpane, a survivor wondering if everything she'd done would be enough to keep her family safe.

Suddenly, a voice blared through the intercom.

"Families of displaced patients and those injured in Camille, please proceed to the nurses' stations on the fourth floor for evacuation instructions. The most critical will go first."

A commotion erupted in the hallways, people stampeding toward the desk, some shouting, some praying. But it was her brother who held Sis's attention, the way his face came alive as he listened to the mounting rumble of disorder, the way he seemed to be hearing something no one else could.

Without a word he headed toward the door.

"Where are you going?" Beulah asked, but Sis didn't have to. She knew what Jim was hearing, a call to duty, an order to serve and protect.

"They need me out there," he said.

"I can help, too." Sis started after him, but he held up his hand.

"Stay here, Sis. Somebody's got to keep the family safe."

"We're safe as a bug in a rug." Beulah folded her arms across her chest, daring anybody to dispute her.

But there was Sweet Mama, sitting crooked in her chair as if the storm had bent her sideways, and Andy standing on his tiptoes bedside his mother's bed, his wide stance and innocent grin evidence that he believed in his own invincibility and the power of his Superman suit.

Last night while they'd slept, she sat in the dark, listening to the TV, trying to find out the bad news before it could blindside her. Governor John Bell Williams called Camille the worst disaster ever to strike the U.S. mainland and declared martial law with a 6:00 p.m. to 6:00 a.m. curfew, which meant looters would descend on Biloxi and try to make off with what was left of value after Camille finished with the Gulf Coast.

Then Richard Nixon sat in the Oval Office and declared the Mississippi Gulf Coast a federal disaster area. He was sending Spiro Agnew down with his condolences, he said, which made Sis want to throw something at the TV. She didn't want condolences; she wanted chicken and biscuits. Just when she was thinking of him as a jackass, he redeemed himself by announcing he was sending fifteen hundred U.S. 3rd Army soldiers and eight hundred engineers, who would be bringing tons of food as well as vehicles to help clear the wreckage. Additionally, he was sending more aircraft to search for survivors and victims.

That kind of manpower in addition to the Mississippi National Guard and the Coast Guard already on the job spoke of a tragedy of such scope it would take the survivors months to fully comprehend.

"Go on, Sis," Beulah added, never suspecting what was out there, waiting.

"You might need me," Sis said.

"I ain't so old I gotta be mollycoddled," Beulah said. "The day me and Lucy can't hold our own against anybody who walks through that door will be one for the history books. Get on outta here, Sis. And if anybody needs petting, you just bring them back here to old Beulah."

Jim was already out the door, his prosthetic leg sounding like the drum cadence of a military marching song.

Beulah dabbed her eyes with the edge of her sleeve. "That boy's just like his daddy."

While Sis stood there, torn, her heart yearning toward her family and her mind urging her toward civic duty, Andy gave her a cheerful wave.

"Aunt Sis, see you later, 'gator."

"After a while, crocodile."

Gathering resolve from the innocence and expectations of a child, Sis marched out the door and followed her brother into bedlam.

In the hallway, Sis and Jim got borne along in a wave of shell-shocked people and deposited in an alcove where an empty wheelchair sat underneath a window. Sis leaned against the wall.

"I've got to catch my breath," she said.

"We need to talk, anyhow."

"I know. They're going to be looking for survivors."

"Not just looking," he said. "Asking questions about the missing."

"There's only one thing to tell them, and that's the truth."

"The truth! Are you out of your mind?"

"Listen, Jim. We can't help it if that stubborn brother-in-law of ours decided to go fishing like any number of fools before him who ignored storm warnings and then got caught out in it."

"Leave off the 'got caught out in it' part. We don't know that."

"I think I'm going to be sick." She wrapped her arms around herself, shivering.

"Don't you fall apart, Sis."

"Why did he go, Jim? What man in his right mind would leave a wife in Emily's condition to go *fishing?*"

Sis stared at her brother with the dawning comprehension of a woman with twenty-twenty hindsight.

Footsteps pounded their way and Sis jumped as if she were hooked up to an electrical socket. Rubber wheels squeaked, and two orderlies raced on by, wheeling a gurney with an ancient woman whose blue-veined hands held on to the towel wrapped around her bleeding head.

"What were we thinking, Jim?"

"I don't know, but we'd better decide something fast." He nodded at two uniformed policemen heading their way.

Their footsteps slowed when they spotted Sis and Jim, and she was certain that she'd be sick all over their shoes.

"Are you two searching for somebody?" the older of the two policemen asked. He had graying hair and wore a badge that said Pickett.

"No," Jim said, and Sis shook her head.

"All your family accounted for?" The younger officer had clear blue eyes and carried a clipboard with a thick sheaf of papers attached.

"All except one," Jim said, and Sis felt herself go clammy. "My brother-in-law, Larry Chastain."

"Any idea where he might be?" The cop's sharp gaze turned in Sis's direction.

"Fishing," she said.

"Fishing?"

"My sister—his wife—is here in the hospital. She was in a coma and Larry was torn all to pieces. He said he had to get away."

"He used my boat," Jim added. "I tried to talk him out of it, but he said he'd be back before the storm hit."

"He say where he was going?" the older officer asked.

"I don't recall," Jim said. "Do you, Sis?"

"I was so torn up over Emily, I wasn't half listening. I'm sorry, Officers, I don't know." She took hold of Jim's arm to hide how her hands were shaking. "My brother and I are just heading out to volunteer in the search for victims. Maybe Larry's somewhere doing the same thing. I hope so."

"We need all the help we can get." The younger officer tipped his hat. "Good luck on finding your brother-in-law."

"Thank you." Watching till they were out of sight, Sis couldn't have told you whether it was Jim's arm that held her up or her own lies.

"You did great, Sis."

"So did you. But do you think they believed us?"

"Even *I* believed us."

Jim squeezed her hand. Tight. They stood that way awhile, taking strength from each other. Finally Jim said, "Let's get out there, Sis. They need us."

They headed out in the same direction, but soon got separated in the crowd. Sis looked for someone who might be in authority and give her instructions. Finally, she found a nurse who told her to find out who was alive, who was missing and who was dead. Though Sis had no training for this sort of work, she knew the importance of records. As she asked for names and ages she would store away in her memory till she found someone who was cataloging Camille's death toll, she searched inside herself for compassion and tenderness, for the right word, the right touch to ease a suffering body and mend a broken heart, qualities she might never have known she possessed but for Camille.

Saying a silent prayer, Sis headed to the place where victims were being laid in a stark row with their faces covered and name tags on their toes.

A young National Guardsman who looked as if he hadn't slept or eaten in two days seemed to be in charge.

"I'm Beth Blake," she told him. "I'm here to help any way I can."

"Glad to have you, Beth Blake."

"My friend Michael Clemson is in the Air National Guard."

"Yeah. I know Mike."

"Is he okay? Do you know where he is?"

"He's in one of the search choppers."

Sis had heard the blades beating the air, had watched out the window as searchers flew low over the dangerous swell of water searching for victims. She said a quick little prayer that Michael was safe, and then turned her attention to the task at hand. The National Guardsman, whose name tag said Turner, took her elbow and led her along the heartbreaking line to a spot near the end.

"I wonder if you might tell me who these women are."

There were three of them. For an awful moment, Sis thought the birdlike one with the gray hair was Miss Opal Clemson.

"No, I don't know any of them."

"We found them in a brand-new Oldsmobile Delta 88 outside the hospital this morning. Cars were washed off the parking lot like toys but that big old car was just sitting there. They must have been trying to get to shelter when the storm hit. Nobody seems to know who they are."

Had they ever come into the café? Emily was the one who could remember the names and faces of perfect strangers who'd only darkened the doors once. She had that way about her that made strangers spread their life's history and their deepest longings in front of her.

I was going to get a divorce until I stopped here and had a bite of this Amen cobbler.

Aunt Hilda died last week but she didn't leave me a cent. Left it all to my sister. I was going to sue until I ate some of this divine pie.

My husband had a stroke and I don't expect to ever enjoy another conjugal right as long as I live.

Thinking about the small dramas of ordinary life, the funny and sad stories that came out of the café on a daily basis, made it easier for Sis to say, "I'm really sorry. I can't help you." Easier for her not to cry as the young man wrote out three name tags for their toes.

"Until I can find out," he said, "I'm just going to call them Faith, Hope and Charity."

Those names stayed with Sis through a long day of taking names, fetching water and hot coffee and blankets, soothing a child with a broken arm and a mother with a broken heart, helping the sick, the infirm and the aged to a long line where they waited to be airlifted by helicopter to hospitals in Hattiesburg and Jackson or the Hancock County test facility of National Aeronautics and Space Administration, which had opened its doors as a storm refugee center.

Sis thought about Andy's little rocket and how the test facility that had helped launch the rocket that landed on the moon would be the perfect place for him and Emily if their house had blown away.

But she couldn't make plans for that now. Another ragged, desperate group of survivors waited in the hallways and the wreckage of the first two floors to find out what would happen to them next.

It had been dark for hours when the exhausted volunteers began to disperse, some to homes left standing, some to a cot in a nearby shelter, some to the upper-floor hospital rooms where they still had loved ones receiving medical care. Sis found Jim around the corner from Em's room where the empty snack machines were now standing abandoned. He was leaning against the coffee machine as if it were the only thing holding him up.

"Jim." She put a hand on his shoulder. "Are you all right?"

"I'll be okay in a minute." When he rubbed his face, she saw the scratches on his hands, the flecks of blood that told his day had been as devastating as hers, if not worse. "This takes me back."

Thinking of the years Jim had spent in the unforgiving jungles of Vietnam in a war as relentless as it was senseless, she kept her hand on her brother's shoulder, holding on, just holding on.

Finally, he said, "I checked on the Thunderbird. It's still up there where I parked it. Not a scratch."

"Thank God. I think I saw my car floating off to China this morning."

"Sweet Mama's Buick's gone, too. I saw it out there along the beach in a pile of wreckage as high as a two-story building."

"You've been out there?"

He nodded.

"Can we get back home?"

"Power lines are still down everywhere and trees are all across the roads. Maybe by tomorrow afternoon we can try it."

A sudden vision came to Sis, rosebushes uprooted and bones

scattered in plain view, stark, white bones so old they couldn't possibly be the victim of Camille.

"Jim, there's something I have to tell you."

In the hush of a night that seemed made for revealing secrets, she told her brother about her discovery under the roses, the telling of it so cathartic she found herself crying without sound. When she had finished, they stood there in the dark, brother and sister side by side, filled with the awful certainty Camille was not done with them yet.

Jim lifted his slumped shoulders, shrugged off her hand.

"There's nothing we can do about it tonight, Sis."

"I know. Even if we could, I'm so tired I'd fall into the hole with the bones." She scrubbed her hand across her face, wishing she could wipe fatigue and fear away as easily as tears. "We'll deal with it tomorrow."

"We need to get back to the room," Jim told her.

"We need to wash up first. We don't want to take any germs back to Emily."

Putting aside thoughts of what she might see tomorrow in her front yard, she led Jim toward bathrooms she'd seen when Emily was first at the hospital, when she'd had to sit in a hard chair and act as if Larry Chastain were part of the family.

Sis forced back the image of him floating down the river in the fishing boat. She even managed to put him out of her mind until she was lying on her pallet on the hard floor trying to sleep. Visions of Larry didn't leave her until sheer exhaustion finally wore her down.

And then she dreamed she was drowning in a thirty-four-foot wall of water.

Twenty-Nine

THE NEXT AFTERNOON, inching along the beach road toward home, Sis was glad to be behind the wheel of the Thunderbird instead of having a front-row seat like Beulah, who sat stoic, or a panoramic view from the back windows like Jim, who was equally silent. She'd tried to talk Beulah out of coming, but it had been as useless as trying to persuade Sweet Mama to give up her car keys.

The past began to play through Sis's mind like an old record, and she forced herself to think about what lay around her. The gazebos that had once dotted the white sands had vanished, and in their place was tons of debris, the splintered remains of what had once been the palatial homes along a scenic beach drive. A single wing chair sat on the beach with nobody to occupy it. A child's tire swing hung empty from a battered tree in front a lot swept clean of house and cars and people. The Colonel Rebel sign that had once sat atop the Confederate Inn Motel now stood forlornly in front a gutted building with nothing but bare rafters holding up a buckled roof while the pier that had once led to Baricev's Seafood Harbor now led to a pile of bricks and lumber at the edge of the water.

The wholesale wreckage of churches showed Camille's con-

tempt for religion. Trinity Episcopal Church had entirely disappeared, leaving behind two once-proud live oaks stripped
of leaves and a sidewalk to nowhere. The enormous fishing
boat the *Wayde Klein* rested on the rubble of the Church of
the Redeemer, and St. Thomas Catholic Church was a pile
of splinters.

And that was just the beginning. She didn't even try to
keep count of the carcasses of animals piled up, the buzzards
circling, the flies swarming in the heat so thick it rose from
the road in eddies. After a while, Sis became too numb to
catalog the many ways Hurricane Camille had destroyed the
Mississippi Gulf Coast.

As Jim's car moved slowly toward the Victorian house by the
sea, she tried not to think of what lay ahead. Camille was the
storm that refused to die. She'd already cut a swath through
Tennessee, Kentucky and Ohio.

And the storm wasn't finished yet. She was now rampag-
ing toward the Virginias. The only thing that lifted Sis's spirits was the sight of Sweet Mama's Café, still intact, not even a
single shingle missing, and of hardy coastal residents, already
plowing through the wreckage with hope in one hand and a
hammer in the other.

"Hallelujah," Beulah said, her head swiveling as the car
rolled down the street and she tried to keep the little café in
view.

"Amen," Sis said.

But even before she pulled up in front of her old address,
she had the gut-punched feeling that she was going to meet
a ghost. The house was a gigantic pile of pink rubble topped
by a splintered roof. She killed the engine and then sat frozen,
staring at the wreckage with the horror of someone who has
had the plug pulled on her entire history and was watching it

wash down the drain. Nearby, the garage had collapsed on top of itself like a balloon with all the air gone. If the mimosa tree and the rose hedge were still there, they were buried under an avalanche of boards and bricks and shingles.

"Sweet Mama's going to just die," Sis said.

"She ain't gonna die." Huge tears tracked down Beulah's face. "Ain't none of us gonna die. We'll get through this. That's all."

A quietness descended on them, the kind you get when you go to the funeral of a loved one and find yourself stripped of everything except raw pain.

Jim was the first to shake off the paralysis. He got out and headed straight to the fallen-down house, picking his way across the debris as if it were littered with mines. The thought of bones under the wreckage catapulted Sis from the car. She helped Beulah from the backseat, and they stood together, hands linked.

"Ain't gonna be nothing left worth saving," Beulah said.

"Maybe he'll find Sweet Mama's teapot."

Sis had heard of stranger things. Once she'd read how a hurricane had swept through, demolishing an entire house but depositing the sofa and the coffee table in the front yard. The owner had been drinking Coca-Cola when the order came to evacuate. The can was still sitting on the coffee table with not a drop spilled.

"Maybe so." Beulah shifted from one foot to the other as if she were carrying a burden too heavy to bear.

"I've found something," Jim yelled.

Beulah leaned forward as if she were being pushed by forces behind her. If Sis hadn't caught hold of her arm, she might have toppled.

"What you found?" Beulah called.

The distant hum of search choppers blended with the buzz of flies that were beginning to gather while the hot sun bore down with a weight that felt unbearable. Sis thought about trying to get through the rubble to see his discovery for herself, then discarded the idea as foolhardy.

"What is it?" Sis yelled.

He straightened up, holding on to a length of something shaped like a leg bone.

"Lord God, he's done found them bones!" Beulah pressed her hands over her face and began to moan.

"Beulah, are you all right?"

"Them bones is outta the ground and I ain't never gonna be all right again." Her wails got louder.

"Beulah, stop it." Sis caught hold of her shoulders. "Look, it's nothing but an old tire iron."

Beulah peeked through her fingers as the tire iron clanked to the ground. She shook off Sis's hands then walked a little distance away and picked up a tattered pillow that had once sat on the front porch swing.

"You needn't try to ignore me, Beulah. I'm right here and I'm not going anywhere until you tell me what you know about the bones."

"What bones?"

"The bones under the mimosa tree you and Sweet Mama chopped down in the storm." That jerked Beulah upright. "The bones you buried under a brand-new rose hedge while I was in school."

Beulah pursed her lips, considering, then turned toward Sis, as sturdy as a tugboat set to plow through rough seas.

"I guess you wanting to know who it was under them roses."

"Who was it, Beulah?"

"Peter Blake."

"My granddaddy?"

All these years Sis and her siblings had never even wondered why their grandfather left and never came back. Was it because Sweet Mama and Beulah made sure their life was full without him or was it because he'd never been more than a vague, shadowy figure, a picture on the wall of Sweet Mama's Café?

"What happened, Beulah?"

The story she told was of two scared young women who had passed a night in terror, fearful Peter Blake would take the life of one they both loved.

"Eustace would never hurt a flea," Beulah said. "He was the sweetest man who ever walked the face of this earth. And Lucy knew it."

She told of taking the boys out of the house before Peter Blake woke up, of being so fearful of what he would do that she and Sweet Mama had both spent as much time in the toilet being sick as they had outside his bedroom door, jumping at every little sound.

"I don't think I could have lived without Eustace, and Lucy knew it. Maybe she couldn't, either. He was the one who brought the stove wood inside and plowed the garden and patched the broken steps so we wouldn't fall and break our necks."

Sis was no stranger to desperate plans. She imagined how they must have felt during that long night and endless morning while they hatched their do-or-die plan to save Beulah's husband. Her grandmother and her dear friend Beulah had been forced to make a decision that would have bowed down a grown man twice their age.

Sis found it remarkable that they'd kept the secret for more than fifty years. She wondered if she'd ever have that kind of strength. If she could not only survive the past, but triumph and live a happy, productive life.

Still, there was one other question burning a hole through her.

"Why are you telling me this now?"

"Because you need to know it will be all right."

Suddenly, Sis felt both trapped and oddly comforted.

"Don't you think I know what happened to Larry Chastain?" Beulah added.

Of course she would. She and Sweet Mama were as close as sisters, and the cobbler would have already been cooking when Beulah left the house. That was the only timeline that made sense, for Sis had found Larry dying from oleander poisoning and trying to kill Sweet Mama after Beulah had sent her home from the hospital.

"How?" A dozen questions were wrapped up in one word, and Sis waited for Beulah's answer with the same mixture of terror and awe she'd felt as she watched out the window for Camille.

"I didn't know Lucy was planning it, if that's what you want to know. If I had I'd a tried to stop it. We ain't living in the twenties no more.

"Still, when I saw her in the kitchen with a pile of oleander laying on the counter, I knew what she was fixing to do. I sent Andy up to his room to color, and then I got what I needed out of my bedroom closet and doctored up that cobbler."

Doctored the cobbler? Sis racked her brain, trying to think what might have been in Beulah's bedroom closet. Either she was too weary or her mind simply refused to wrap around the truth.

Beulah took her hand and leaned in close. "I ain't never put out the welcome mat for rats."

"You put rat poisoning in the Amen cobbler!"

Beulah just nodded, and Sis looked over her shoulder in case somebody with acute hearing and a taste for gossip was passing by, in case the wind had lifted this dark telling and swept it into the hearing of the National Guard or the Coast Guard or any number of officials duty bound to report the truth.

"Did you think I was gonna let Lucy take care of that rat all by herself? Me and her has always stuck together, and I ain't about to let her down now."

If life were a movie, Sis would call theirs *The Saturday Night Avengers.*

She would tell her brother the story behind the bones later, in a quiet moment when it was just the two of them. As she watched Jim coming toward her, holding on to Sweet Mama's tea set, she felt herself becoming as indestructible as the sturdy, gray-haired woman standing at her side.

"Look what I found." Jim held the porcelain set aloft. "Not a scratch."

"Where did you find it?" Sis asked.

"Behind what used to be the garage. Two of the porch rockers are there, too."

"Ain't Lucy gonna be glad to see this." Beulah reached for the tea set. "Y'all load them rockers up. Me and Lucy's gonna have tea."

Sis didn't ask where she was going to get the tea. She and Jim just let the top down on the convertible, then piled the rocking chairs in and lashed them down with some rope her brother dragged out of the rubble.

Then they drove off to see if Camille had spared Emily's house, Jim behind the wheel with Beulah up front hanging on to the tea set while Sis sat squeezed in beside the rocking chairs. Traveling light. Starting over.

Thirty

Sᴡᴇᴇᴛ Mᴀᴍᴀ ᴀɴᴅ Bᴇᴜʟᴀʜ were sitting in rocking chairs on Emily's front porch having tea they'd steeped in Sweet Mama's teapot. She didn't know what day it was, or even what month. She thought it was September, but she couldn't prove it. She'd lost track of time long before Camille tore up the Gulf Coast.

Her Remembering Book was in the guest bedroom she and Beulah shared. Sis bunked in with Emily while Jim slept on the couch downstairs. It all felt just right to Sweet Mama, cozy and safe with her family in a sweet little house with a blue kitchen. She liked that little blue kitchen, but Sis didn't let her do anything in there except fix her sweet tea.

"You just rest, Sweet Mama," she'd say. "You deserve it. Leave the work to us."

Sweet Mama reckoned she *was* tired of cooking after all these years. Especially that Amen cobbler.

Sis and Jim had thought she'd be devastated to learn the storm had destroyed the pink Victorian house, but she didn't care a flitter about losing it. She'd never liked it in the first place. For one thing, it was too big to suit her and for another it was exactly like that heifer's house next door.

Hers was gone, too, Sis said, but she was now living in a HUD trailer parked on her lot.

Sweet Mama was giving her lot to her grandkids. Let them do what they wanted to with it. She didn't plan to live there anymore. She and Beulah liked Emily's neighborhood. Someday they might buy a little house here. She liked the idea of walking down the street to visit Opal Clemson, or popping by to see how Tom and James Wilson were doing. The roof had blown off Opal's house but she'd been in Hattiesburg at the time. Tom and James had lost nothing except their old cat, which had turned completely white that night, hunkered down in the attic scared to death while Tom and James lifted their mother up through the opening in a sling made from sheets.

Tom and James were in Emily's house now, along with Burt Larson, who had lost everything and was living with them now. They were all helping Sis and Jim rip the carpets out of Emily's first floor where the water had come in. They called this kind of thing *sidewalk parties* because a lot of the houses in the neighborhood had blown away, leaving nothing behind but the sidewalk. Some of the neighbors already had HUD trailers on their lots, but some were still in shelters, coming back every morning to clean their lots and get ready to build again.

Sweet Mama thought the whole notion was a good idea, neighbors pitching in to help each other. She even liked the idea that they called it a party. The human spirit will rise right back up, no matter what tries to stomp it down. The idea made her feel so good, she reached over and added another spoonful of sugar to her tea.

Andy's sweet power.

Her great-grandson came racing around the corner of the house, wagging that teddy bear he called Henry and trailed by the sorriest-looking dog Sweet Mama had ever seen, lanky legged and scraggly coated, its ribs sticking out like it hadn't had a decent meal in a month. And probably, it hadn't. There were lost and abandoned animals all over Biloxi, some whose owners had left them behind and never returned to claim them and some who had been blown so far away from home they'd never find their way back.

"Look what I found!" Andy plopped on the porch floor and the dog flopped down right beside him to lick his feet. "His name is Spot."

He didn't have a spot on him as far as Sweet Mama could see, unless you counted the mud spots. He didn't have on a collar, either.

"How do you know his name?" Beulah asked.

"He told me," Andy said with the confidence of the innocent who are certain they hear the voices of dogs and cats and angels.

"I think that's a good name," she added. "Nice and short. He'll learn it before you can say jackrabbit."

"He already knows it." Andy jumped up and raced across the yard, then clapped his hands and called, "Here, Spot." The dog trotted over and jumped up on Andy, his tail wagging so hard it looked like it would knock both of them over.

"See!" Andy beamed at them. "Can I keep him?"

"Keep what?" Emily said, coming through the door.

She still tired easily and sometimes she'd get a headache. But standing there, smiling pink cheeked, she didn't look like a woman who had been in the hospital. Sweet Mama didn't even try to remember when that was. Best not to think about things like time and the past. Just drink tea and think about the future. That was the ticket.

Sis was right behind her sister, a bandanna tied around her hair and her arms filled with wet carpet.

"My dog!" Andy hurried over and made introductions as if the dog and his mother both were movie stars.

"Well, my goodness, if you're not just the handsomest thing I've seen in a long time." Emily squatted beside the mutt and scratched behind his ears. "Let's see if we can't find some food in the kitchen to fatten you up."

"He can have mine," Beulah said. "When all this is over, I ain't ever gonna look at another can of potted meat."

It had been brought in by the ton. Every week Sis or Jim went to wherever they were giving out food rations and came back with a sack full of Spam and Vienna sausage. There were food trucks that made the rounds with hot meals, too, but they didn't come to your neighborhood every day. There were too many places to be, too many hungry people to feed.

It was a miracle Sis had found tea. She wanted Sweet Mama to ration it out because she didn't know when the Winn-Dixie would open again, but Sweet Mama said no. She was going to live life to its fullest, even if she could only do it for a little while. When the tea was gone, it was gone. She'd just drink water till she could find some more tea, that was all.

She refilled her glass while Sis toted the carpet to the Dumpster at the end of the street and Emily got food and water for the dog. The way they were carrying on over him— like he was already a member of the family—Sweet Mama might as well start calling him Spot. She'd even write it in her Remembering Book tonight, and if she forgot the name, she'd ask Beulah.

"Look a'yonder," Beulah said, nodding toward the end of the street. "Ain't that a sight?"

Sis was standing by the Dumpster talking to that nice man who'd come courting. Michael, that was his name. The funny thing Sweet Mama had discovered was that she didn't have much trouble remembering the names of good people. It was the bad ones she tended to forget. Maybe it was because she didn't try very hard with them. Maybe it was because they were best forgotten.

Like What's His Name Emily had married. Whatever had happened to him? Sweet Mama hadn't seen hide nor hair of him since she couldn't remember when.

Down at the end of the street, Sis was laughing, her head thrown back and the sun shining on her throat. She looked like a young woman. She really did. A woman who'd blossomed late and then found out she had a future to look forward to and a lot to laugh about.

Michael was laughing as well, a big boom that carried all the way up to the porch. He was handsome, too. But Sweet Mama couldn't make out why he looked so untidy.

"What's that he's got on, Beulah?"

"His National Guard uniform, Lucy. Remember? He's been helping clean up this mess we're all in."

"I'm not in a mess. I'm headed to Pikes Peak." Sis had said so. *Sweet Mama, as soon as Jim has helped us get the house and café straightened up a bit, he's going to take you and Beulah to Pikes Peak.*

Sweet Mama couldn't wait to go. She'd studied the pictures in her *National Geographic* magazines so much some of the color was wearing off.

"Did you see that, Lucy?"

"See what?"

"Sis and that beau of hers are out there in the street, holding hands."

"Good for them."

"That's what I say. It's about high time, too."

They were heading her way now, but they no longer had their hands linked. Sis snatched the bandanna off her head and wiped the smudges off her face. She looked nearly as young as Emily, coming up that sidewalk, smiling.

"Michael dropped by with some news." Sis reached over and drew Emily close. "Andy, do you mind running inside and telling your uncle Jim to come out here? And then I'd like you to go into the kitchen and have a little snack."

"Spot, too?"

"You can take the dog into the house," Emily said. "But just this one time. He has to have a bath and a good sprinkle with flea powder before he can come in again."

"'K." Andy marched off to his mission, his Superman cape flapping behind him.

That all sounded too serious to Sweet Mama. She'd had enough *serious* to last her a lifetime. Still, the look on Sis's face didn't match somebody bringing bad news.

When Jim got back to the porch, Michael started talking.

"We've found Larry Chastain's car," he said, which didn't sound like news to Sweet Mama. Cars had floated off everywhere. There was no telling where her Buick was by now.

"I wish you'd find my Buick," she said, and that polite young man told her, "I'll try."

That's what she was talking about. Michael Clemson was a good man, one worth remembering.

"It was in the Tchoutacabouffa River," he added. Sweet Mama noticed how pale Jim looked.

That boy needed to get out in the sun more. Ever since the hurricane, he'd been inside Emily's house and the café, working like there was no tomorrow. And maybe there wasn't. Sweet Mama figured all you could do was live your life from one minute to the next.

"Did you get it out?" Jim asked.

"Between the river and the storm, it was so badly wrecked it would have been a waste of man power to try. Divers went out, but nobody was inside so we just broke the windows and let it sink."

"What about Larry?" That was Emily, her eyes stretched as big as blue china plates.

"We never found a sign of him." Michael leaned toward her and took her hand. "I'm sorry. We don't have a body for you to identify, but your husband is now listed as a victim of Camille."

Emily covered her mouth with her hands, but it didn't look to Sweet Mama like she was crying. Sis and Jim just stood there, as expressionless as the wooden Indians Sweet Mama had seen in *National Geographic*.

"Sure 'nuff?" Beulah asked.

"Absolutely positive, Miss Beulah." He went up a notch in Sweet Mama's book just because he'd called Beulah *Miss*.

"Divers went down looking," he added. "They've been all over the rivers and the Sound. I wouldn't count on ever finding Larry Chastain."

"I wouldn't count on it, either," Beulah said, and then she gave Michael Clemson her widest smile. "Would you like a glass of sweet tea?"

"I don't mind if I do," he said, but he wasn't looking at Beulah. He was smiling at Sweet Mama's oldest granddaughter.

And then that nice, sweet boy in his National Guard uniform, who reminded Sweet Mama so much of her son Bill, reached for her granddaughter's hand and held on as if he'd discovered a map to his future. Sweet Mama thought about the perfect order of the world, how the things that are lost can sometimes be found and the people we cherish are there all along, just waiting to be noticed.

Epilogue

IT HAD BEEN THREE MONTHS since Camille tried to destroy the Mississippi Gulf Coast. Signs of her rampage were everywhere, but also signs of recovery. Ships were back in the harbor, gifts shops along Highway 90 opened their doors to hopeful displays of beach balls and souvenirs, and the banner across the front of Sweet Mama's Café said Grand Reopening.

Inside the café, Emily and Sis stood side by side in the kitchen, getting ready for the crowd. Emily was covered with her usual dusting of sugar and flour and she was singing "Take Me Out to the Ball Game," off-key, a not-so-subtle reminder that Michael Clemson would be coming to the open house this evening. And he wouldn't be coming for the pie.

Sis laughed as she tried to follow along with Sweet Mama's recipe for pigs in a blanket. She was glad Emily didn't point out that it was just link sausage stuffed into a roll. She was glad about a lot of things these days. Life after Camille was so different, she could barely remember the woman who had dreamed of going as far away from Biloxi as she could get. Now, you couldn't run her off with a herd of wild elephants.

"You're distracting me, Em."

"Good. Let's take a little break. I want to discuss pie."

"I'm the last person you want to discuss pie with. I can hardly stuff a pig in a blanket."

"Not the ingredients, Sis. The name."

The Amen cobbler was being retired from the menu. Sis had been adamant. Before they left, even Sweet Mama and Beulah had insisted that Emily take the famous cobbler off the menu.

"Everybody's getting tired of peaches and cherries," Beulah had said.

"Start your own tradition, Emily," Sweet Mama had added. "You and Sis are running the café now."

Emily poured two glasses of tea, then she and Sis went up front where Andy was sitting on the floor with one arm around Henry and the other around Spot. The shiny-coated dog with his pink tongue lolling out in a goofy dog smile hardly resembled the scruffy mutt Andy had rescued. They were watching replays of the stories that came out of the Camille disaster. Andy never tired of seeing the one about the dog who had been found in the public library buried under an avalanche of books, one of them titled *Man's Best Friend*.

Sis and Emily sat at a table underneath the photograph of Beulah and Sweet Mama when they'd first opened the café. Tacked beside it where the picture titled "The Jackass" had been removed was the postcard that came in yesterday's mail. "Pikes Peak or Bust." Underneath Sweet Mama had written, "I'm so high up I can see Heaven. But I'm not planning to go anytime soon. Have a grand open house! Home by Christmas!"

"I was thinking of calling the new menu item Lucy's pie," Emily said.

"I don't know, Em. I think Sweet Mama would want you to come up with a name that identifies you as the genius who created it."

They sipped their tea, each lost in her own thoughts until Andy called, "Mommy, look at this!"

There on the TV screen was a little red rocket, streaking across the sky.

"It's my rocket ship," he yelled.

In the foreground a reporter was saying, "Nobody seems to know where this little homemade rocket ship came from, nor where it was going. But everybody agrees on one thing: on that night of horror, the sight of this little red rocket streaking upward while everything else was being swept out into the Gulf was a symbol of hope."

The TV replayed the tape of Andy's rocket flying straight through the boiling clouds and out the other side where the light waited.

"I know where it was going." Andy jumped up and whirled around the room, a little boy's victory dance with his teddy bear and his dog. "It was going to the moon!"

"Yes, it was, Andy."

Emily got up to join her son and as they joined hands, Sis knew exactly what to call her sister's pie. *Andy's Moon Rocket Pie.* Named for a little boy who never lost hope that he was building a ship to take them all to the moon.

★ ★ ★ ★ ★

Acknowledgments

MANY PEOPLE PLAYED BIG roles in helping me bring *The Oleander Sisters* to life. My incredible agent, Stephanie Kip Rostan, provided unflagging support. Erika Imranyi and Michelle Meade, my wonderful editors at MIRA, guided me through the story with patience and a keen editorial eye.

Many thanks to MIRA publicist and all-around good guy, Emer Flounders, for making sure I get to meet the booksellers and fans who make writing a pure pleasure.

To Tara Parsons and the great team at MIRA, a big thank-you for making this book possible.

When I wrote myself into a corner, Debra Webb and Vicki Hinze, dear friends, fellow authors and plotters supreme, showed me the way out.

Big hugs to my family, who always surround me with love and support. I especially want to thank my granddaughter, Susan Elizabeth Griffith, for superb research and my grandson, David Joseph Webb, for clever bookplate design.

Though *The Oleander Sisters* is entirely a work of fiction, it does include historical events that occurred the summer of 1969. In order to portray those events accurately, I read *Hurricane Camille: Monster Storm of the Gulf Coast,* Philip D. Hearn, and *Women in Baseball: The Forgotten History,* Gai Ingham Berlage. For authenticity in portraying my six-year-old protagonist and Sweet Mama's Café, I consulted *Winnie-the-Pooh,* A. A. Milne and my mother's recipe books.

Thank you for reading. I hope you will love these characters and this story as much as you did *The Sweetest Hallelujah.* I promise to write more of the same!

THE OLEANDER SISTERS

ELAINE HUSSEY

Reader's Guide

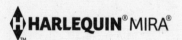

QUESTIONS FOR DISCUSSION

1. How far would you go to save someone you love? Discuss how this theme plays out in the lives of Sis, Jim, Sweet Mama and Beulah.

2. What do you think of Emily's decision to marry Larry Chastain? What does it say about Emily's character, about her role as a mother? Would you have made the same choice? Why or why not?

3. Discuss the role of family in the book. In what ways does familial love and responsibility drive the actions of the characters?

4. *The Oleander Sisters* features a cast of strong female characters: Sis, Sweet Mama, Beulah, Emily. Discuss each of their roles in the story and how they drive the narrative forward. Which of the characters do you relate to most and why? Do you have a favorite?

5. The novel is told in alternating perspectives from Sis, Emily and Sweet Mama. How does this affect how you read/understand the book? What are the advantages and disadvantages of multiperspective storytelling?

6. History plays a particularly important role in *The Oleander Sisters*. In what ways does the setting and

period (The Mississippi Gulf Coast in the summer of 1969) impact the story? How would the story have been different if it had been set in the present?

7. Discuss Andy's role in the story and how he influences the decisions of the other characters. Would Sis, Jim, Sweet Mama, Beulah and Emily have taken a different path if Andy had not been part of the story?

8. Discuss the role of Neil Armstrong's walk on the moon in this novel. Why do you think the author chooses to bracket the book with scenes related to the astronaut's famous moon landing? Do you think the moonwalk is an appropriate metaphor for the theme of hope?

9. Sis and Jim make a radical decision in this novel. Discuss how Hurricane Camille impacts that decision. Would the outcome have been different if Jim were not a veteran of the Vietnam war? If Sis hadn't considered herself the family's caretaker?

10. What do you think the future holds for each of the characters?

1. *The Oleander Sisters* is a heartfelt story about sisterhood, family and the lengths we go to protect the ones we love. What was your inspiration for the story and the characters?

This story was inspired by my two sisters and all the girlfriends who pick me up when I fall, cry when I'm sad, celebrate when I'm happy, encourage when I'm defeated and belly laugh with me just because it's good for the soul. I cannot imagine going through life without this strong, feisty, amazing sisterhood. *The Oleander Sisters* is my tribute to my own support system and the sisterhood of women throughout the world.

I never consciously base a character on a real person, though friends who read *The Oleander Sisters* in its beginning stages saw some of my outrageous Hussey relatives in Sweet Mama and Beulah. They cited some of my inner circle of friends as the basis for Sis, and some of them pointed out flashes of me in every character in the book. I won't deny it! Any story that is filtered through a writer's mind is bound to reveal glimpses of the author.

2. The novel is told from the perspectives of three unique and strong-willed women. Were any of them more difficult to write than the others? What is it like to tell a story from three very distinct points of view?

Telling a story from different perspectives allows me to give the reader a glimpse into the heart and soul of the novel—the characters. It also adds depth and complexity to the story.

Sweet Mama was the easiest point of view for me, primarily because she's a colorful woman with a checkered past, a true eccentric with a very strong voice. Emily's perspective was harder. It would have been easy to make her too sweet, too weak, a perfect target for abuse. The challenge was to give her enough grit so that she was more than a victim. Ultimately, I wanted to present Emily as a strong woman trying to live down her bad choices and doing the best she could under the circumstances.

Sis was a bit of a challenge, too. She was such an intrepid woman, she could have taken her baseball bat to Larry in the first few chapters and that would have been the end of the story. I had to step back from my admiration of her courage long enough to give her some vulnerability.

3. Larry's abusiveness toward Emily was quite unsettling, and it's easy to see why Sis and the family were so focused on protecting her. What was it like to write about characters going through such an intense, painful ordeal?

When I write, I feel every emotion of every character. I'm not simply telling about Emily: I *am* Emily. I *am* Jim. I *am* Sweet Mama and Beulah and Sis. That sort of transference is emotionally draining.

During the long winter months of writing *The Oleander Sisters*, I had to comfort myself with lots of cozy evenings by the fire with a cup of hot chocolate.

4. The Blake family's struggle takes place alongside two major historical events—Neil Armstrong's first steps on the moon and the devastating storm of Hurricane Camille. These events served both as metaphors and active players in the story. How did the historical setting shape the story as you wrote it?

I chose the summer of 1969 for *The Oleander Sisters* because those two events were perfect metaphors for my recurring theme of finding hope amidst heartbreak. Because I wanted hope to be the readers' takeaway, I used the moonwalk scenes to bookend the story. Of course, Andy's rocket ship grew out of Neil Armstrong's walk on the moon, as did the camping scene in Sweet Mama's backyard. Catching moonlight on the tongue symbolizes discovering hope and making it part of who you are.

Hurricane Camille was a perfect metaphor for Larry's abuse. It was also symbolic, not only of the great upheaval and internal struggles of the Blake family, but of an entire town forced to rise out of tragedy and seize hope. You'll see this metaphor played out in the small scenes that show Biloxi's citizens picking up their hammers to rebuild and having sidewalk parties whose only purpose is to help a neighbor.

5. What was your greatest challenge in writing *The Oleander Sisters*? Your greatest pleasure?

My greatest challenge was to tell the brutal truth—about the horrors of abuse, the tragedy of a Category 5 hurricane, the heartbreak of feeling helpless and drained of dreams—and still to write a novel that would leave the reader feeling uplifted and even triumphant.

As always, I enjoyed watching characters come alive and following them on their journey. Although I had the journey mapped out, I relished those moments when the characters surprised me and took off in a different direction. I loved it when they knocked my socks off with a word, a phrase or an entire scene that I didn't even know I was going to write.

But my greatest pleasure is bringing to the story to you, the reader!